HELLBOUND HEARTS

HELLBOUND HEARTS

Edited by Paul Kane and Marie O'Regan

Based on the novella *The Hellbound Heart*
by Clive Barker

Pocket Books

New York   London   Toronto   Sydney

Pocket Books
A Division of Simon & Schuster, Inc.
1230 Avenue of the Americas
New York, NY 10020

First Pocket Books trade paperback edition September 2009

POCKET and colophon are registered trademarks of Simon & Schuster, Inc.

For information about special discounts for bulk purchases, please contact Simon & Schuster Special Sales at 1-866-506-1949 or business@simonandschuster.com.

The Simon & Schuster Speakers Bureau can bring authors to your live event. For more information or to book an event contact the Simon & Schuster Speakers Bureau at 1-866-248-3049 or visit our website at www.simonspeakers.com.

Designed by Ruth Lee Mui

Manufactured in the United States of America

10 9 8 7 6 5 4 3 2 1

Library of Congress Cataloging-in-Publication Data is available.

ISBN 978-1-4391-4090-1
ISBN 978-1-4391-6475-4 (ebook)

To Clive Barker,
creator of this mythology—
and all those who followed.

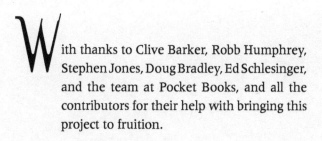

With thanks to Clive Barker, Robb Humphrey, Stephen Jones, Doug Bradley, Ed Schlesinger, and the team at Pocket Books, and all the contributors for their help with bringing this project to fruition.

Contents

Foreword
Clive Barker

The word "mythos" is used very liberally these days in regard to the characters and adventures of popular fiction. People speak of the Batman mythology, the Freddy Krueger mythology, and yes, the *Hellraiser* mythology. I have always been a little wary of this usage. It seems in some sense to be inappropriate, cheapening a word that I first encountered in reference to the deities of Olympus, or the gods and goddesses of Asgard. These mythologies are thousands of years old, and have survived many tellings and retellings, their underlying imagery often moved from one culture to another, yet still surviving at some fundamental level.

How then could the same word ever be applied with any seriousness to the products of a medium that is barely a century old? Does Pinhead's "mythos" really bear any comparison with the massive bodies of narrative that have collected around such legendary figures as Hercules and Jesus?

In one sense, of course not. Maybe a thousand years from now, some profoundly evolved version of a human being sitting at the console of a starship, exploring some distant star system, might chance upon an image of Pinhead and find that the creature means something to him. If so, then the word "mythos" may indeed be applicable.

Why would I even breathe such a possibility? On the face of it, a screenwriter/director such as myself referring to his own story as a mythology is immensely arrogant. But here, a more subtle distinction comes into play that may be worth a moment's study.

Even though I am the man who had the good fortune to bring this image to a popular medium and therefore facilitate its dissemination throughout much of the world, I am *not* the creator of this mythology. In fact, I think the real creators fall into three categories. First, there are all those nameless men and women who over the last many centuries created the fetishes of clay, rope, bone, and nails, which are in some part the inspiration for the character called Pinhead. These fetishes are, I was told, chiefly representations of anger, which seems oddly inappropriate given how chilly and dispassionate Pinhead is. But under all that cool reserve lies a massive potential for rage, as I think most audiences understand. So those fetishes and Pinhead have a good deal in common.

The second creators are of course the special-effects men who have, over the course of many movies, variously interpreted and reinterpreted the appearance of the character. There have been beautiful renditions of his appearance in comic books and on the skins of innumerable *Hellraiser* fans who have shown me the parts of their bodies where tattooists have left *their* interpretation.

Finally, there are the people who see these movies, read these comics, and wear these tattoos who in conversing with one another—and occasionally, at conventions, with me—further enrich the complexities of the idea. Their motives for doing so are occasionally erotic (there is a healthy appetite for the *Hellraiser* stories in the S&M community) or maybe metaphysical (one of the most complex articulations of the original *Hellraiser* story, *The Hellbound Heart*, came from a Russian Orthodox Priest).

In sum, perhaps it isn't so monstrously arrogant to speak of the mythos. I am not its maker. If it survives for another hundred years or is forgotten tomorrow, I have no say in the matter. *Hellraiser*—

its stories and images, its metaphysics and its sheer visceral energy—is the work of other hands and other minds. I am very happy and very lucky to have stepped into the river of the collective unconscious and to have found there a stone with the nails hammered into it.

Clive Barker
Los Angeles, 2009

Introduction: Raising Hell, Again

Stephen Jones

For many of us who worked on it, *Hellraiser* was a life-changing experience.

For Ashley Laurence, who made her movie debut as ingénue heroine Kirsty Cotton, it lead to a successful acting career that includes three *Hellraiser* sequels, two screen adaptations of H. P. Lovecraft stories, and a third entry in the *Warlock* series. She is also a very talented artist.

After portraying the coldly homicidal Julia Cotton, Clare Higgins has gone on to become one of Britain's most acclaimed stage actresses, winning numerous prestigious awards. Meanwhile, Oliver Parker, who portrayed one of the luckless moving men (a role he basically reprised in the sequel), is now better known as the director of such successful British movies as *An Ideal Husband* (1999), *The Importance of Being Earnest* (2002), *St. Trinian's* (2007), and a new version of *Dorian Gray* (2009).

Although originally conceived as a minor character with only a few minutes' screen time, Doug Bradley's Lead Cenobite became the character that most resonated with audiences—rechristened simply "Pinhead" for the sequels. The actor created one of the most eloquent and iconic cinematic monsters in popular culture and has become indelibly identified with the role.

For Doug and some of the other Cenobite actors, it has also led to a profitable side career attending conventions all over the world and signing stills of themselves buried under the time-consuming prosthetic makeup.

With *Hellraiser*, Bob Keen consolidated his skills as a special makeup effects designer, later expanding his talents into special effects and directing, while for producer Christopher Figg it was the start of a career that has led to such box-office hits as *Trainspotting* (1996) and *Dog Soldiers* (2002).

Of course, Clive Barker was already established as the author of the six groundbreaking *Books of Blood* collections and the novel *The Damnation Game* before taking on the mantle of both screenwriter and first-time director. He has subsequently enjoyed a successful career as a bestselling novelist, playwright, painter, and film producer—most notably of the Oscar-winning *Gods and Monsters* (1998).

And then there's me, listed way down at the end of the credits under "unit publicist" as "Steve Jones," *Hellraiser* was the first movie I ever worked on. John Carpenter had sown the seeds while I was interviewing him in Los Angeles, and upon my return to London, I contacted Clive—to whom I had been introduced a couple of years earlier by our mutual friend, horror writer Ramsey Campbell.

Clive liked the idea, and after meeting Chris Figg, I got the job. As a freelance film journalist I had visited the sets of a number of films and had often come away disappointed. So for a relatively low-budget film like *Hellraiser*, I decided to do something radically different.

I invited numerous journalists from all types of publications—but particularly the specialist genre periodicals—down on set to interview key personnel during filming. It helped immeasurably that the location was only two stops away on the London Underground from where I was living in North London at the time. (If only getting to work on a movie was always so easy!)

I also created extensive press kits during shooting so that the writers had all the background material they needed for their articles way ahead of time, and I produced T-shirts and button badges ("There Are No Limits") that we gave away to visitors and offered as competition prizes.

As a result, *Hellraiser* received unprecedented publicity for a film of its budget and expectations—while it was still in production. As planned, this extended coverage led to a heightened sense of expectancy long before the movie was released.

Even though my career as a writer and editor was starting to take off at this time, I also had a promising future as a producer and director of television documentaries and commercials. So I used my contacts to shoot an EPK (electronic press kit) featuring behind-the-scenes footage and interviews with the principle cast and crew. Again, this was almost unheard of at that time for a small film like *Hellraiser*. (And here's a piece of trivia for the fans: Many of the interviews on that EPK were conducted by a young journalist just starting out who wanted the experience. His name was Neil Gaiman.)

Anyway, when it finally opened in September 1987, *Hellraiser* was both a critical and commercial hit thanks to its literate script, strong performances, and stylish visuals. I also like to think that my innovative prepublicity campaign helped in some small way toward its success.

I never returned to my old occupation. Instead, I went on to work on a number of other low-budget horror movies on both sides of the Atlantic, including the next two *Hellraiser* films (or "the good sequels" as I like to think of them). Although I had very different experiences working on *Hellbound: Hellraiser II* (1988) at Pinewood Studios, just outside London, and *Hellraiser III: Hell on Earth* (1992) in High Point, North Carolina, by that time we had formed a tight little production unit that was committed to keeping Clive's creative vision intact.

Unfortunately, this was apparently not the case with many of the films that followed in the *Hellraiser* franchise. Increasingly it seemed that the Lemarchand Configuration Box and Doug Bradley's articulate harbinger of pain and pleasure were shoehorned into existing scripts that had little or nothing in common with Clive Barker's original themes or characters.

But even as the movie series became more and more diluted, so the *Hellraiser* brand profitably expanded into boxed DVD sets, collectable action figures, posters, T-shirts, comics, trading cards, and countless other spin-off merchandise. Despite being produced more than two decades ago—and with the prerequisite remake currently in development—*Hellraiser* continues to hold a fascination for film audiences and readers alike.

Which brings us to this current volume. Let us not forget that *Hellraiser* has always had literary origins. It was initially based on Clive's 1986 novella "The Hellbound Heart" (first published in George R. R. Martin's anthology *Night Visions 3*), and the new compilation that you hold in your hands is merely the next logical step in the story's fictional evolution.

Editors Paul Kane and Marie O'Regan have asked some of the best-known and most creative writers and artists in the horror genre—several of them already intimately connected with the series—to extrapolate upon Clive Barker's original concepts.

Over the past twenty years, numerous people have worked in the *Hellraiser* universe, perhaps not always successfully. However, this book probably represents the most impressive gathering of creative talent yet to add their own unique interpretations to one of the most powerful and enduring horror mythologies ever invented.

As a result, you will find a selection of stories that are guaranteed to shock, seduce, and surprise any *Hellraiser* fan. Prepare to be hooked by tales of puzzles both oblique and obvious, where hellish doorways lead to extreme gratification or endless torment as the unwary encounter some familiar Cenobites and entirely new demonic creations.

This anthology proves that after all this time, the images and ideas behind *Hellraiser* continue to be as vital and imaginative today as they were when Clive Barker first conceived them. Whatever your pleasure may be, the inventive contributors to this volume have such sights still to show you . . .

Stephen Jones
London, England
December 2008

HELLBOUND HEARTS

Prisoners of the Inferno
Peter Atkins

1

It's Mickey Rooney," Carducci said, as soon as Jack arrived at his table. "Mickey fucking Rooney. No shit."

The memorabilia dealer's head was twitching in urgent indication and Jack looked back up the length of the convention room in the direction of its spasms.

Flanked on both sides by good-looking young blondes—who, even sitting, had a good five inches on him—Mickey fucking Rooney was indeed seated at one of the autograph tables against the top wall. Jack was surprised that he hadn't noticed him when he came in, but then he tended to ignore the signing tables at these bimonthly events—usually manned only by second-string TV stars from the sixties and seventies—and head straight for the regular dealers' tables.

"What's he asking?" Jack said.

"About the same as the kid from *Rin Tin Tin*," Carducci said in a can-you-believe-it voice. "Twenty-five if you buy a picture, fifteen for a bring-your-own. You should get something."

Jack shrugged noncommittally. "Not my area," he said.

"Not my area," Carducci mimicked. "Get over yourself. He's fucking *golden age*, man! He banged Dorothy, for Christ's sake."

"No, he didn't," Jack said, having no real idea one way or the other.

"All right, Ava Gardner, then. Are you a collector or not?"

"Oh, I'm a collector all right," Jack said. "But apparently not as well informed a one as I'd thought."

"Yeah?" Carducci said, cocking an interested eyebrow.

Jack lifted his hand to show his friend the item he'd just bought. "How come I haven't heard of this?" he said.

Carducci was an old hand at the poker face but he actually twitched in surprise when he saw what Jack was showing him, and when he reached out to take the front-of-house still for a closer look, he held it almost reverently and was silent for a couple of seconds.

"Where the fuck did you find this?" he said eventually.

Jack had found it while flicking through the four-dollars-per box of eight by tens at some newbie's table. He hadn't expected to come across anything worthwhile and had hardly been paying attention until he'd felt his hands pause.

His practiced fingers, faster than his eye, had frozen in position like they'd just hit a seam of gold in a slate mine and Jack looked down to see what the fuss was about.

The still was sepia rather than simple black-and-white and—judging by the yellowing on the borders and the few tiny cracks here and there in the emulsion—obviously an original. And from at least the mid-nineteen-thirties. Maybe even precode. Jack lifted it out from among the various worthless dupes of anonymous westerns and forgotten melodramas to look at it more carefully.

The image displayed was of an actress—presumably the lead, though she wasn't anybody Jack recognized—who'd gotten herself into a bit of bother. She was in the process of being bound to an upright cruciform pillar in some kind of ceremonial chamber—a pretty fucking big one to judge by the hordes of out-of-focus extras in the far background—and was staring in left-of-frame shock at something unseen that was heading her way. Something that meant business, if the look of anticipatory horror on her face was anything to go by.

Her dress had been ripped away from her at both shoulder and thigh but it didn't have the artfully disarranged look you'd expect from a set dresser's tease. It looked much more urgent than that, looked like something or someone had torn at the cloth in a genuine frenzy to get to the flesh beneath. And the girl's open mouth and wide-eyed mix of expectancy and fear could have given even the great Fay Wray a run for her money.

The image's weirdly erotic charge was undeniable, of course, and was certainly part of what Jack liked about it. But it wasn't just that. It had that *thing*. That thing Jack loved, the sense that what he was being allowed to look at was something other than simply a photograph of a bunch of overpaid people playing dress-up. That was always the secret to the movies he loved. It didn't even have to be in the genre in which he pretended to specialize. It was as deliriously present for him in the art deco dreams of Fred and Ginger as it was when Lon senior strode down the opera steps in a skull mask and two-strip Technicolor. And this picture had it. In spades. A teasing glimpse from a forgotten world, a world that felt at once utterly real and yet utterly unreachable.

There was a title running across the border beneath the image. *Prisoners of the Inferno*, it said. Which rang no bells at all, other than the generic. Even then it sounded more like a title from the pulps of the same period than it did a movie. Jack wondered if it might have been a serial rather than a feature, though there was nothing in the rest of the minimal text to suggest that it was.

He took a carefully casual glance at the dealer and at what else was displayed on his table and the wall behind it. He could see in a second that the guy knew nothing. There was a *Topkapi* one-sheet that was way overpriced and a *City of the Dead* lobby card that was hilariously under. Some bandwagon jumper who was pricing his shit by voodoo and what other idiots told him.

Deserved what he got, then, didn't he, Jack thought and, surrounding his find on either side with two stills from *Gorgo* (neither featur-

ing the beast), he waved the three of them at the guy as if he was
considering doing him the favor of taking this crap off his hands.

"Three for ten?" he asked like it was no biggie, and the money
already in his hand like it was a no-brainer.

The dealer looked at the box, looked at Jack, and looked at the
cash. Didn't look at the stills. So there went his last chance to say
there'd been a mistake. Amateur.

"Okay," he said, prefacing it with a put-upon sigh and treating
Jack to a petulant grimace of the you're-killing-me-here variety.

Jack smiled politely, handed over the money, and walked away.
The dealer didn't even notice him putting the *Gorgo* pictures back in
the box.

Carducci repeated his question, with emphasis.

"Where the *fuck* did you find *this*?" he said.

"In the idiot's come-on box," Jack said, nodding back in the direction of the other guy's table.

Carducci stared across the room with a devastated look of missed
opportunity on his face, like it was the day before prom and he'd
just seen the prettiest girl in class say yes to the one guy who'd actually had the balls to ask her.

"Fuck," he said quietly and regretfully.

"So?" Jack said. "What do you know about it?" And Carducci
looked back at him.

"You *have* heard of it," he said. "Just not under that name. It was
recut and retitled *The Cabinet of Doctor Coppelius* and—"

"Oh, fuck you," Jack said, half disappointed and half relieved.
"You are *so* full of shit. *Coppelius* never existed. It's a ghost film. A
hoax."

He remembered the story well. Some buff with a website and
too much time on his hands—and, it had to be admitted, more than
passing skills at both Photoshop and bullshit—had started a little
viral frenzy nearly a decade ago. He'd been smart enough to bury it
in an otherwise-accurate filmography rather than write a big splashy
piece on the home page. You'd had to be interested enough to be

there in the first place (which, for any demographer, pegged you instantly as statistically likely to be an underachieving white male between twenty-five and fifty) and then choose to follow a couple of links. Even when you got there, there was no flashing sign or anything. It was just another item in a fairly exhaustive listing-with-credits of "Poverty Row Horrors Yet to be Released on Video." Among the perfectly legitimate and verifiable titles, the webmaster—what was his online name? Cap'n Cadaver? Something equally ludicrous, anyway—had inserted a quiet little entry for a film which nobody'd ever heard of but which the capsule critique made sound like a nasty little treasure:

The Cabinet of Doctor Coppelius US/UK 1932 71 minutes. Dominion Pictures. Alice Lavender, Catherine Hobson, Kurt Crandall, David Batchelor. Dir: Thomas Rheimer, Scr: Patrick Adams, Pr: Carl Bowman, Conrad Fisher. Less expressionist than the Caligari nod in the title might suggest, this low-budget programmer offers instead the kind of unblinking gaze at body-horror that wouldn't become common until after Franju's verité approach many years later. Crandall's mad doctor—hilariously obsessed with Flecker's noted line from Hassan, "For lust of knowing what should not be known," which he intones several times with an almost Barrymore level of hammy gravitas—teams with Batchelor's alcoholic toymaker to construct a "cabinet of transmutation" that transforms several cast members into life-sized dolls who wreak impressively vicious mayhem on several unsuspecting day players. Lavender, in her only movie, impresses as the plucky gal reporter swept into the lunacy.

Jack had let himself be drawn in to a couple of message board back-and-forths but the Cap'n—Colonel Carrion, was it? Corporal Carnal?—had stopped posting after several people had called him on his crap, and without a whipping boy to target, the activity on the boards had petered out.

"No," Carducci said to Jack, with the fervency of a true believer—and there'd certainly been some of them, including a handful of hipper-than-thous who claimed to have actually seen a print in revival houses in the seventies. "Not a ghost film. A lost film. I mean, *really* lost. Makes *London After Midnight* look like something that gets played every other day on TCM."

Jack took the picture back, pretending not to notice how reluctant Carducci's fingers were to let it go. "All right," he said. "Even if *that's* true, I never heard this *Prisoners of the Inferno* title mentioned in any of the forums. Why was it recut? Why was it retitled? How do you know it's the same movie?"

"Oh, it *isn't* the same movie," Carducci said. "They cut it a *lot*. The *Coppelius* version never killed anyone."

The website was still there—nothing ever really goes away on the net—but it was pretty damn dormant. The last update, according to the home page, was a long time ago and the last entry on the forum even older. Jack was more than half convinced that he was wasting his time when he posted a fairly long open inquiry on the thread about *Coppelius*. He mentioned the original title, even said he'd recently come into possession of an image from the film, but decided not to scan the picture and upload it. For all he knew, he had the last surviving artifact of a truly lost thing and he wasn't going to give it away to bootleggers, even if he doubted that anyone other than him was ever going to visit this site again.

He'd put the still in a Mylar sleeve and perched it in front of his Mr. Coffee so that he could keep looking at it while he nuked himself an excuse for dinner. His computer pinged at him and he wandered from the kitchenette to the main room. He had mail.

The subject heading was *Prisoners of the Inferno*.

He'd expected no response at all, certainly not this fast and certainly not by e-mail. He'd had to fill out a user profile to post on the site and the e-dress was a required field but, come on, who sends an e-mail instead of just posting on the thread?

The text wasn't as carefully worded as his own, and nowhere near as long-winded.

Very direct in fact. Just six words.

Do you want to see it?

2

Unlikely to be popcorn, then, Jack thought as he pressed the doorbell on the gone-to-shit bungalow in the middle of a tract at the ass end of Van Nuys.

The door was opened by a woman. She looked about sixty, and like she'd decided not to fight it; muumuu, carpet slippers, can of Molson. She looked at Jack for less than a second, then turned her head and shouted back into the house, "Walter!"

There was no reply. The woman walked away from the door without saying anything to Jack and he wasn't sure whether to step inside or not. After a moment, a heavyset man in an islands shirt appeared from a door toward the rear of the house. "JRosen101?" he called to Jack without bothering to come to the front door.

Jack nodded. "Jack," he clarified, stepping inside.

"Walter," the guy said. Thirty, maybe older. Hard to tell because the fat of his face kept it wrinkle free. "Come on." He sounded a little put out, as if Jack was late or something, keeping people waiting.

The room at the back was tiny but had been set up as a mini-theater with four easy chairs facing a small free-standing screen. Jack was surprised to see an honest-to-God movie projector behind the chairs—he'd expected to be watching a DVD-R at best—but it was too small for 16mm and too ancient for Super 8.

"Standard eight?" Jack asked, kind of delighted.

Walter shook his head as he gestured for Jack to take one of the chairs. "Nine point five," he said.

"You're kidding," Jack said. He'd *heard* of 9.5mm—a home format introduced in the early twenties by Pathé but essentially crushed by Kodak's 8mm just before World War II—but had never seen either films or hardware. Carducci claimed to have a 9.5 print of Hitchcock's *Blackmail* buried somewhere in his storage space, but then, Carducci claimed to have pretty much *everything* buried somewhere.

Another man came into the room. The Stan to Walter's Ollie, he was five-five and rail thin and sported a pair of black horn-rimmed glasses. Jack wondered if he'd already been in the house, or maybe had a key to the front door.

"Hey, Lenny," Walter said without enthusiasm and glancing at his watch. Jack waited for an introduction that didn't come.

"I'm Jack," he said as Lenny sat down.

"I know," Lenny said. "Did you bring it?"

Jack drew the Mylar-housed still from the computer bag he'd brought—it had been either that or a Trader Joe's tote, nobody had briefcases anymore—and Lenny took a cursory glance at it.

"Very nice," he said and then, half-turning to Walter, who was threading up an oversized reel into the projector, "The one Forry had? You think?"

"Probably," Walter said, dimming the lights from a remote.

"Stolen," Lenny said. "He was so *trusting*."

"Hey," Jack said. "I got this at—"

"No, no, no," Lenny said, interrupting him. "Nobody's accusing *you*. I mean, you *paid* for it, right?"

"Yes, I did," Jack said, refraining from saying how little it had cost him.

"Then it's yours," Lenny said in an annoyingly kind tone. Like Jack needed *his* fucking blessing.

Walter had sat down. "It's starting," he said, which was Walter for Stop talking.

The print was of the later cut, as Walter—he assumed it had been Walter—had told him when he'd replied to Jack's reply and e-mailed him the address. Interestingly, though, the main title card—the one that actually said *The Cabinet of Doctor Coppelius*—was in a font that didn't quite match the cards before and after it, which lent some credence to the idea that the film had once been called something else.

The dupe was a little washed-out—the blacks not really black and the actors' faces occasionally slipping into an unpleasant featurelessness against too bright backgrounds—but was otherwise in remarkably good shape.

The movie itself was worryingly slow paced, even for Jack—and he was a guy who could sit through the flattest Monogram six-reeler without checking his watch even once—and the acting was as alternately amateurish and histrionic as the website critique had suggested. Jack had begun to worry that, as was depressingly often the case, the mystery and intrigue surrounding a thing's loss was far more entertaining than the found artifact itself, but once he'd let himself relax into the film's willfully leisurely pacing, he realized he was starting to enjoy it.

The lead girl—Alice Lavender, the girl from his still—helped a lot. She was just adorable as the feisty little heroine trying to impress both her crusty editor and her policeman boyfriend by cracking the story surrounding the mysterious deaths. And the life-sized dolls produced from the toymaker's Cabinet and sent forth to murder and mutilate anybody dumb enough to piss off Doctor Coppelius were quite successfully creepy. Their skin, post-transmutation, had a pale inhuman smoothness and there was stitching—rather convincing stitching—on their faces and limbs. Their eyes were completely black—the blackness, unfortunately, put in with a traveling ink-out like they'd given Tom Tyler in one of the *Mummy* sequels—but the fact was that, when the actors stood still long enough for the blobs not to move, the effect was surprisingly powerful.

What was really fascinating—and torturously enticing—was how obvious it actually was that the movie had been cut and had had new scenes added, with both the cuts and the additions serving to dilute whatever power the original may have had. Some of the nastier doll-demon murders simply *stopped* midcarnage and jump-cut to the next scene, for example, and there was a higher than usual quota of those annoying bits where an Irving the Explainer figure went to quite ridiculous lengths to explain how what might have appeared to be supernatural was actually a combination of engineering wizardry and showmanship gone all evil-genius.

The most egregious and frustrating alteration came at the climax. The movie built to the capture of Alice's character by Coppelius and his toymaker and her insertion into the Cabinet. Thrillingly, unlike every other transformation, the camera followed her in. The Cabinet was bigger on the inside. Much bigger. So much so that it soon became clear that the inside of the Cabinet wasn't the inside of the Cabinet at all. The Cabinet was a portal to Hell and its unlucky entrants were quite literally prisoners of the inferno. This was where Jack's still had come from, this sequence in which the fetishized binding of the girl took on an overwhelming and shaming erotic power. And then, just as she was being dragged from the pillar toward the disturbingly elaborate doll-making machinery, another of those obvious cuts happened and the whole sequence was revealed as being merely the nightmare of the kidnapped girl *before* she was put into the Cabinet. And then, of course, the door burst open and her policeman boyfriend rescued her.

Jack *knew* that it hadn't been a dream in the original and that *Prisoners of the Inferno* must have culminated not only in the activation and operation of the machinery but in the reopening of the Cabinet and the disgorging of whatever doll-demon Alice had been turned into. He ached to see it.

It was starting to rain when they came out, and Jack found himself standing on the curb next to Lenny, both of them looking up at the sky with the vaguely hard-done-to expression common to non-native Angelenos whenever the weather wasn't perfect. As if Southern California had misled them, brought them here under false pretenses, strung them along like a lover who waits till after the wedding to mention that occasional little problem with bipolar disorder.

Lenny caught Jack's eye. "Did you like it?" he asked.

"Yeah," Jack said. "I did. Overall. How about you?"

"Not as good as the real thing," Lenny said, almost distractedly, as he pulled his jacket over his head like a makeshift hoodie and ran for his car.

3

Carducci had a small store in one of the commercial alleys off Hollywood Boulevard. Some nice stuff, but mainly repros and shit for the tourists. Kept the prime material for the conventions and the auctions.

"Oh, right," he said, when Jack swung by to ask him about Walter. "Fat guy, Hawaiian shirts? Lives with his mother in some piss-poor shack the top of Van Nuys?"

Jack deadpanned him. "Didn't you just describe every one of your customers?" he said. Couldn't help it.

"Oh, really?" Carducci said, looking Jack up and down blankly, like the sneer was implicit. "Who died and made you Johnny fucking Depp?"

Jack grinned, letting it go. "What about his friend Lenny?" he said. "Little guy? Horn-rims?"

"*He* was there?"

"Yeah. Like he had bragging rights. Thought he might have been, you know, the boyfriend or something."

"Stay the fuck away from *that* guy," Carducci said. "Seriously. Grade-A creep."

"What? Like a prick?"

"No. Like a fucking *creep*. As in creeps me out. For real. Him and his whole nasty little crowd. Used to hang around with Kenny Anger and LaVey. Seriously. They're not into this stuff for the same reasons we are. Got their own agenda. Not nice people."

Carducci's reads on people were usually pretty good, so when Jack got the phone call from Lenny a couple of days later, he wanted to be guarded and careful. But he couldn't be, not when he knew that Lenny—creep or not—could have only one reason for calling, that he was going to offer access to a print of the real thing, to *Prisoners of the Inferno*. He wondered if this was how newly hooked junkies felt when they got the first follow-up call from their dealer. Because that's what he was, Jack realized. Hooked. Hooked from the moment he'd stared at the still for the first time and felt that intoxicating rush of being allowed to gaze at the forbidden.

He had no doubt that it was going to cost him this time. Wasn't that how it always worked with junkies and their dealers? But he didn't care. He'd empty his fucking savings account if that's what they asked. He wanted to see more. He wanted to see, he wanted to know. *For lust of knowing what should not be known*, he thought, remembering Doctor Coppelius's knee-jerk little mantra.

But Lenny didn't mention money at all.

"You seemed . . . *intrigued*," he said, as if that were perhaps payment enough.

"Well, yeah," Jack said. Because he, you know, *was*. The fuck else was he going to say?

Lenny didn't reply. Like he was waiting for Jack to ask, and enjoying the wait.

"You said, *not as good as the real thing*," Jack said eventually, but still got nothing in return. "The other night." Just the sound of Lenny breathing. "In the rain." He didn't know why the fuck he mentioned the rain.

"I'm going to give you an address, Jack," Lenny finally said. "It's a private address, and I don't want you to write it down. Is that all right?"

Jack said that, yeah, that was all right and Lenny gave him the address and Jack repeated it and Lenny said he'd see him in half an hour and hung up.

It took only twenty minutes—no traffic for a change—and Jack circled the block a few times so as not to look too eager. It was a shitty apartment building on Franklin, one of those four boxes on top of four more with railed walkways running past all the front doors like the place had wanted to be a motel but had been too stoned to build a fucking lobby.

Jack rapped his knuckles on the third door of the upper level because the bell didn't work—*quelle surprise*—and Lenny opened it and ushered him inside. An old man sat in a La-Z-Boy with a blanket over his legs and smiled at Jack with a vague delight, like he couldn't ever remember anymore if he'd met someone previously but had learned to err on the side of presuming he had. *Really* old. Like he'd cracked a century or was about to.

"Hey there," said Jack, returning the smile. And that seemed to be it for the socializing because Lenny already had his fingers on the handle of the door to the apartment's only other room. "In here," he said, waiting till Jack was practically bumping into the door before gently pushing it open and stepping back to let Jack enter.

Lenny didn't follow him in. "We'll give you some privacy," he said and, even as he was closing the door, Jack saw him half turn toward the old man. "Shall I make you a pot of tea, David?" he said, just before the door clicked shut.

The room wasn't dark at all, though the light from the three grime-encrusted bulbs in the ceiling housing was a dull and bilious yellow. It had been intended as a bedroom, Jack assumed, but it now served another purpose and was untroubled by either furniture or people.

It wasn't empty, though.

There was no projector this time, because no projector was needed. Jack hadn't been brought here to see a film. Lenny hadn't been talking about a print, uncut or otherwise. When he'd said they had the real thing, he meant the real thing.

He meant the Cabinet.

It stood in the center of the room, looking surprisingly substantial for something that was supposed to have been built over seventy-five years ago for a low-budget movie. Good condition, too, with only some rust stains here and there on its patterned brass filigree to show the passage of time.

If Lenny locked the door to the room from the other side, Jack couldn't hear it. Not above the waltz-time minor-key melody that began to sound from somewhere inside the Cabinet, mechanical and painful, like it was escaping a music box built from razors and bone.

The Cabinet door creaked slowly open.

And Alice Lavender stepped out.

She was beautiful still, unchanged from what those audiences must have seen nearly eighty years ago. Unchanged by age, at least. But the Cabinet had done its work and her transmutation was long complete.

The doll girl, pale stitched face expressionless, black marble eyes glinting only with reflected light, came toward Jack with a mechanized grace, her head tick-tocking rhythmically from side to side and her slender limbs clicking audibly with each automaton step.

The fingers of her left hand ratcheted open one by one as she extended her hand to Jack.

Not in threat.

In dreadful invitation.

The transition from the initial darkness of the Cabinet's interior to the infernal light glowing endlessly from vast and distant furnaces was seamless. Jack was one place, and then he was another.

He couldn't tell when Alice had let go of his hand.

"Welcome," said the Doctor as he turned his own hands to show Jack his palms and the terrible implements that bloomed from their stigmata. "Time to play."

The Cold
Conrad Williams

December sleet, Shude Hill, Manchester. Six in the evening. Temperature dropping. Jesus wept. The things we do. The things we grow to be. No, Simmonds, I do not want another fucking coffee. Get on to Arley and find out when forensics are going to bring their tents and toothpicks over. And get that cordon sorted. We've had two scoops already from the *Evening News*, nosing around this offal. Do your fucking job.

Rachel Biddeford. Second this month. Obviously the same Joe. Dirty bastard. DNA not on our records. A newbie. Knows his way around a body, mind. Hospital worker? Medical student? Nylon ties around the wrists and ankles. Goes deep with his cutter. Deep vein. Cuts the jugular. Why does he do that? Why not the artery? Get it over with. But no. Slower death, see. He wants them conscious. He wants them to see him while he's masturbating.

Vein man. Vain man.

After death, a professional Y-cut. Postmortem spot-on. And what's he taking? Nothing. Organs intact. Sewn back up with neat little sutures. What is this clown? Ex-morgue? Did he watch too much police procedural on TV?

Talk to the residents. Talk to the vagrants. Talk to the brick wall. Nothing going on. Nobody knows. *No. Nothing. I wasn't. I didn't.* Victim killed elsewhere, then dumped, same as in Whalley Range, same as in Denton. No pattern to the locations. Faces laced with dried come. Pale as the time-whitened covers of the wank mags in the bookshops on Thomas Street. Girls from the university, no older than twenty. No obvious link so far, other than pretty, coltish. A blonde and two brunettes. An English student and two sciences. Merry fucking Christmas.

Forensics take pictures, take swabs. Midnight before the crime scene's secure and the body's on a trolley on its way to Path. Simmonds is pulling his coat on and I hoik him my way. Souness first, I tell him. I'm buying. I don't care how fucking tired you are, Simmonds. Sleep when you get to Hell. And believe me, son, that's where you're going. Anybody who makes tea as bad as you do . . .

Gravier fiddled with shreds of salad peeking from the lips of his bacon sandwich and put that morning's newspaper to one side. He had failed to progress beyond the first few lines of the article for fifteen minutes and could feel a headache assembling a nest at the back of his skull. When had a Souness ever really meant a swift half and then off? Why did boozing hold hands so tightly with officers on the Force?

The girl on the bicycle across the street would not stop thumbing at the bell on her handlebars and the sound was growing to irritate him. It carried through the traffic, permeating the glass and the hubbub in the café. His appetite having failed pretty much the moment he'd bought his breakfast, Gravier sat in the window seat staring through a halo of mist at the figure straddling her pale blue three-speed. With a frustrated grunt, Gravier gave up on his meal and barked his leg in his eagerness to be out of the door. The girl on the bicycle was gone, but the sound of the bell remained like a stain in the air. He walked across the road to where she had been, feeling vague and purposeless, and stood there for a while, fighting the urge to reach out and stay fingers that were no longer busy at their mischief. Something was itching at his mind, something about the murderer and his way with a needle and thread. Opening and closing bodies. Taking nothing away.

West Didsbury. South Manchester. February 1. Burton Road shops closed and dusty from the credit crunch. Browning Christmas trees dumped in back alleys. Buses advertising horror films dragging sullen, featureless occupants to and from the desk. Condensation in every window, every heart. Everyone's spunked money they don't have on presents nobody wanted. Pay it off just in time for Santa to come calling at the arse-end of this year, wagging his "I Want" list. Manchester winter. Everyone saddled with one sort of shit or another. Jenny Beaker most of all, at least today. And she's the only one not complaining. What the fuck is this, Simmonds? Café au porridge? I don't do froth, son. Take it back and get me a proper drink. I wanted a flask for Christmas. So I could whack a pint of honest UK tea inside it and flick the Vs at these wankhole coffee shops with their crappuccini and shatté and Ameriguano. What happened to the greasy spoon and the chipped mug of milk and two?

Jenny B. Twenty-one. Born in Swansea. Studying for a Creative Writing MA at MMU. You've found yourself a hell of a story here, babe. Talk to her student pals at the student house in Withington. Student faces slack as an old man's clothes rail. *I don't. I didn't.* Quiet as student mice. Kept herself to herself. Yeah, don't we all. Except him. Our friend the surgeon. Talk to the neighbors. Boo to a goose. Mrs. Vearncombe wouldn't be surprised. Mrs. Craven shudders to think. The only leads I have are the ones tying Jenny's wrist to the lamppost.

Jesus Christ, Simmonds. Milk again? I want my coffee black. Black as the eyes you'll be wearing if you don't pull your thumb out of your chute and do something right for a change.

He walked away and it wasn't Simmonds behaving like a queynt that got his feet moving. It wasn't the sight of Jenny Beaker gazing up at him with eyes that were large and wide, love-filled, almost. It was the paint on the wall by her body. Graffiti was everywhere these days, but not like this. It bothered him more than the gray, unresponsive flesh.

Thou art all ice. Thy kindness freezes.

What kind of spray-can fan came out with that stuff?

Later, at home, he discovered that the line was from Shakespeare. He snorted laughter as he closed his web browser and turned to the rank of bottles gleaming on the cabinet in his living room. He poured himself a glass of Scotch and sat by the window. Outside, he had a view of the main road that ran through Heaton Moor. Bars he didn't patronize, shops he didn't buy from. He didn't know why he was here. He'd prefer a small apartment in the center of town, but this was where his wife had wanted to be. Gemma had left him two years previously. Nothing to do with his drinking, or the hours he put in at the office. She'd met another guy, that was all. He didn't argue with her when she laid it all out before him. He reserved his bitterness for when the apartment was empty of her things. He tried to purge her merry ghost with elegiac songs by Interpol and Editors. He ate the food she didn't like, despite his not liking it either. One night he brought back one of the girls from the switchboard and fucked her standing up against the wall, a position his wife could not abide.

He downed the drink.

"Thou art all ice," he said, and his own voice made him jump.

Gravier had been in love once. And not with his wife. This was before he got married. It had been the breathlessness, the heart-stopping moment he'd heard about and scoffed at for so long. She was one of those glimpses-in-a-mirror women. A once seen, never forgotten type. The kind of girl you find rhapsodied over in the Personal columns of listings magazines. *You were by the bus stop, wearing coffee-colored eye shadow.* That kind of thing. He'd never swapped a word with her. No exchange of addresses or telephone numbers. Just a look. Less than that, really, but she had stayed in his thoughts with a kind of pain, like a piercing, like a branding. He'd been in his car. A winter afternoon. The sun little more than a trembling line, a careless scrape of orange crayon on a pale blue page. He'd seen a shadow fall across the hood. He'd been in a bad mood. Headache. It felt as though he was being gripped at the temples by some industrial tool. She had hurried by, raising a hand to move the black hair from her face. He caught a crystal peep of her eyes, the green of sour apples. Simple clothes. He'd opened the door without thinking, his heart fidgeting. He didn't know what he meant to say, but his mouth was open and something was coming. She was gone though. He ran around the corner of the street, but she had vanished into the concrete, it seemed. He'd been shocked by the force of his disappointment. The sudden grief of wanting something that you couldn't have. She flitted at the periphery of his dreams after that, maddeningly out of reach. He never was, and when he wakened he was always cold, as if she were a ghost reducing the temperature of the room.

He walked winter streets, angling into the sleet, wishing for the chill to climb up through his bones and seize his mind. It wasn't right, having her in his thoughts while the murders were piling up. She deserved a cleaner host, a better moment. Without any kind of pre-determination, Gravier found himself moving through the black slush of Shude Hill where the body of Rachel Biddeford had been dumped. All cleaned away now. All nice and tidy and back in its nasty little box. Just a yellow police sign, a piss into the wind: WE ARE APPEALING FOR WITNESSES. CAN YOU HELP US? MURDER. IN STRICTEST CONFIDENCE PLEASE PHONE. The forensics tents gone. The body gone. No trace. No angelic shape in the snow; nothing to say that a young, beautiful girl lay here. Gravier stood with his hands in his pockets, blowing steam at the cold, blue edges of the buildings. He didn't know what he was waiting for, but he felt something was about to happen. He had been blessed with some kind of itchy trigger, a sense of things about to arrive, whether they be clarity of thought, or something more concrete. It had served him well in the police and he always paused to answer its call when it came. Other people called it copper's instinct. Gravier wasn't so sure. He didn't want to dwell upon it for too long in case it went away. It was magic, of a sort.

Now he glanced around him. Sleet against the sodium-lit night like ash at the end of the world. Buses shifting through low gears, ploughing filthy slices of old snow onto pavements riddled with litter and grime. The muffled beat of a band playing the MEN arena. He used to love live music. He'd go to a couple of gigs a week in his twenties, if he could afford it. Gemma hated the sweat and the stink. The beer in plastic. She was a CD to his scratched vinyl. The glossy black windows of the Arndale Centre. The electric cables for the trams stretching out like exposed veins. Low-wattage bulbs burning in upper-floor flats. Secret homes. What went on? Who dared to know?

Over to the right, in an alley adjacent to a fish and chip shop, a line of industrial bins disgorged their contents onto paving stones that had cracked in the cold. On the wall above them was a faint silvery line, like the trail of a slug across a dewy lawn. More graffiti. He realized now why he had come here. He knew what he would find. A killer with a calling card. It was all the rage. He thought of Rachel Biddeford's torn body and thought of the pain she must have endured. The silent screams on these victims' faces seemed ingrained. They must have been so very violent to cause the corners of their mouths to split. No Hollywood shrieking here. No C-sharp in plum lipstick. No handsome A-list star to come to their rescue. They lay in the shit and the sleet, their eyes cramming up with snow until some drunk or graveyard-shifter stumbled over their solid bodies. And they remained frozen forevermore. In time, in the minds of the people they left behind. Iced hearts beyond thawing. Always associated with violence and loneliness and death.

"I'll warm you up, love," Gravier whispered. There were tears in his eyes and he couldn't even begin to kid himself that it was the cold bringing them on. He thumbed the lock on his mobile phone and called Simmonds.

"Hands off cocks, on socks," Gravier said, when Simmonds

eventually picked up. "I want you to take a ride out to the SoCs in Whalley Range and Denton. Check the walls for graffiti. Yes, Simmonds, graffiti. What do you think I fucking said? Tahiti? Look for silver paint. References to the cold or winter. Call me when you find it. I also want a list of all spray-paint manufacturers and suppliers in the Greater Manchester area. Automotive finishers, decorator centers, varnishing and coatings trades. The lot. And I want that about ten minutes before I called you. Check this out as well. *Three feet of ice does not result from one day of cold weather.* I found it at the Shude Hill scene. Very clever, isn't it. Well find out where it comes from. Oh, and Simmonds? Next time you don't pick up on the first ring, you'll be wearing your phone as a butt plug. Got it?"

He grew aware of something tickling the back of his scalp like fear. He turned to face the main road and saw a figure watching him from the tram stop platform. He was bathed in the acid white of floodlights, a tall, thin man in a long, gray coat and a dark, woolen hat. The man stared at Gravier, unabashed. His hands were deep in his coat pockets, writhing, as if he were wrestling to keep something from exposing itself. Gravier stepped toward him. "Could I have a minute with you, sir?" he called out.

The man did not move. The woolen hat was pulled down almost to the point where it blinded him. The closer Gravier got, the more he did not want to approach. It was as if he were being repulsed. When he was standing in front of the other man, whom he could now see was closer to six foot four, he noticed that the hat was not dark; it was a pale cement color, but it was covered with stains.

"Could I have a minute of your time, please?" Gravier asked again, having to give more spine to his voice than he was used to.

"You could. You could have more."

Christ. A smell hit him, of all the things that made him want to puke. Wet dogs, tooth decay, weeks' old piss in the doorways of dilapidated buildings. It was all he could do not to gag in front of the man, not that he'd notice. His eyes were shivering in their sockets.

"Are you all right?" Gravier asked.

"All right," the man replied. His voice was accentless. It was like water.

Gravier found himself struggling to even remember what he'd said. He glanced back at the bins and their overscore of painted wit. "We're currently investigating a murder, sir," he said, trying to summon some iron. "I wondered if you knew anything about what happened here, January twenty-seventh."

"Lonely man?"

"I'm sorry?"

"The lonely can take extreme measures to, ah, stop being lonely anymore."

"What have you got in your pockets?"

"My hands."

"Come on, mate. Empty them. It's too cold for this. You can smart-mouth me all you like down the station if that's what you'd prefer."

The man took his hands from his pockets and opened them, a conciliatory gesture. They were huge. The nails were like scimitars on his fingers, backlit: ten pearlescent crescents, packed with filth. Gravier felt dread shift inside him, like something concrete. This man was dangerous. "I have nothing in my pockets."

Gravier suddenly did not feel like frisking him for the truth. "What's your name?" he asked.

The man was sweating. It was maybe minus one or two degrees Celsius, yet here came tears of perspiration from the collar of his hat. *More worried than he's letting on*, Gravier thought. The man bore the expression of someone digging lightly for a recently forgotten item of information, and then: "Henry Johns."

"Henry?"

"Henry, yes."

"Do you have any ID on you, Mr. Johns?"

"I don't."

"Address?"

"I'm not from this place."

"Why are you in Manchester, then?"

"Business."

"What kind of business?"

"I represent a client in the entertainment industry."

"What, so you're an agent?"

"You could say that."

"And who is your client?"

Johns handed Gravier a card. Gravier took it. He couldn't remember where it might have come from; he was sure Johns's hands had been empty ever since he removed them from his pockets. The card was a translucent tablet with a claw-mark effect cut out of the top-right-hand corner. A name, in eggshell white, was just legible if you tilted the card away from the plane of vision. *Lady Ice.* No phone number. No address.

"Great card," Gravier said. "I bet she does a roaring trade."

"You'll find her when you need her the most. They all do."

Gravier was tired and cold. He wanted coffee. He gave Johns a card of his own. "Give me a call if you have anything interesting to say," he said. "A girl of nineteen was killed and then dumped here. Not good. Not good." He was turning to go, feeling bad about the whole thing, warning signs going off all over his head. *Nick him. Nick him now.*

"She's sweet," Johns said. "She could be yours, if you want her. She wants you."

Gravier stared at him. "What? What are you talking about?"

"Girl of your dreams, Detective Inspector."

Gravier ignored him and hurried away. He climbed into his car and turned up the heater, his hands shaking. The sweat drizzling out of the wool of Johns's cap was what had been staining it. Sort of dark. Sort of bloody. He closed his eyes to the impossibility of it and released the handbrake. He drove up Shude Hill, retracing the steps he had taken, until he was level with the tram platform. He saw Johns moving away down Balloon Street toward Victoria train station. Gravier watched him remove his woolen hat. He took it off tenderly. He peeled it away from the exposed lobes of his brain.

■　■　■

Back at the nick in time for breakfast. Sausage sandwich and a tangerine. Hot, sweet tea. You get it down you, somehow. A head full of black ice and white bone. Soaking, cold trouser cuffs. You should have arrested him. On suspicion of . . . anything you say . . . But too scared. Too old. It was in him, all of a sudden, this need to get out. You put the hours in, you became the job and happiness, fulfillment never came, and you ended up realizing it was because you had hated the job all along. What he'd seen, he hadn't seen. Put it down to a lack of blood sugar. Put it down to nervous exhaustion.

Gravier here. Ah, Simmonds. Nice of you to make the effort. Give us the griff, then. What's that you say? I found a Chinese proverb, did I? Well, well. He is an educated boy, isn't he? What about the others? Any luck? Yes? You found some? Excellent. We'll make a policeman of you yet. Well yes, you have to follow your hunch, don't you? As Quasimodo said while walking backward one day. E-mail them over, soon as you can. And, Simmonds? Thank you.

Whalley Range. Emma Tees. *A book must be an ice-axe to break the seas frozen inside our soul.* Denton. Gillian Jarvis. *The snow doesn't give a soft white damn whom it touches.* Simmonds had called him with the authors. Kafka he'd heard of. The beetle man, wasn't he? But E. E. Cummings? He didn't so much sound like a poet as a porn mag for mice.

Patterns in frost. The bodies so cold the blood had frozen to black plaques on their flesh. A confectionery crackle as they were peeled clear of pavements and roads. Gravier lay in bed, feeling the temperature drop. His skin felt old and papery, hanging from his body as if unattached. Get up too quickly and it might simply flutter away from his bones. He thought of the girl on her bike, bent over the handlebars, thumbing at the spring-loaded clapper of the bell. He tried to remember what it had been like to be young. The absence of responsibility, the irrelevance of effect. You didn't think ahead as a child. It was all seat-of-the-pants from one day to the next. He yearned for a little of that freedom now. He seemed to spend every waking minute inside his mind, the pulses of his thought processes pushing at the membranes that coated his brain. There was never any feeling of physical release. He was locked in; he was his own prison. And then he thought of the bars of a cell. He thought of ribs. A body opened and closed, like a police case, or a door to somewhere new. The killer had not taken a thing.

He stabbed his finger at the keys of his mobile phone.

"Simmonds. Get over to pathology. Get Mercer out of bed. Our friend, he might not be harvesting. But what if he's leaving stuff behind instead?"

Dead end. Sometimes the thoughts you believe might just blow your options wide open are the ones that close us down for good. Gravier accepted the pint from Simmonds and for a moment didn't know what he should do with it. Everything felt as though it should be kicked, punched, smashed; damaged in some way. It was not a good feeling. He was not having a good day. He swallowed half the pint in three savage mouthfuls. Nobody behind the bar or sitting at it would meet his eye. Danger radiated from him.

What's that, Simmonds? *Sir, if you'd just take it easy?* Don't you dare try the arm around the shoulder with me, Simmonds, or I'll punch you so hard you'll find you're suddenly rimming yourself off. Yes, I know the pathologist's report said there was no internal damage, nothing to write home about in any of the postmortems, but the pathologist isn't fucking Superman. Brian Mercer? Man's a sot. And half blind. If he wasn't wearing those Coke-bottle glasses of his, he'd take his scalpel to a turkey's twat and think it was a pensioner's mouth. Now fuck away off with you. Leave me alone.

Another night's torture for the brogues. Slapping through the wet, wondering why he never put on a thicker pair of socks, or invested in some of those Gore-Tex boots the younger generation clomp around in. Freezing wind wound itself around his neck and shoulders, reaching deep into his body. Some days he woke up with the core of his limbs giving him gyp, and could imagine his moldering bones turned damp with the cold. He used to walk through miles of rain when he was courting and never felt the needling of it. He was happy then. The only thing pressing down on his shoulders were the five-inch-thick firecheck doors he had to lug around the warehouse where he used to work summer holidays. Seventeen. Full of cum and muscle. Not a care. When did it all turn bad? When you got a job that held a mirror up to the world and showed it to be some foxed, blighted shithole, that's when.

How long till the next one? And there *would* be a next one. There always was, even if the killer was one of those twisted individuals desperate to be stopped. He sensed himself walking faster, as if an increase in speed might hurry a conclusion his way. His fingers worried at the stylized business card in his coat pocket. If he stroked the surface, he could just feel the raised pimples of the typeface outlining her name: Lady Ice. No address. No phone number.

Why was he moving in this direction?

Here was a part of town he didn't know so well. He remembered a few callouts here, many years ago. But not a place he lingered. Somewhere he couldn't give a name to now, no matter how hard he delved for one. He frowned and checked road names, but none impinged on his memory. He felt a weird slanting in perception, as if he'd had a dizzy spell and felt the world shift away for a second. He put out a hand to steady himself and burned his fingers on the frozen door knocker of a large building, which reminded Gravier of the neoclassical buildings in the town center—the libraries and banks—bought by brewery chains and transformed into spit-and-sawdust pubs selling alcopops and indigestible hunks of beef.

The door opened as he pushed to lever himself upright. He heard a female voice, strident, calling from farther along a dark hallway. "Get in. Shut out that unwanted."

He thought she meant the weather, but once the door was closed behind him, he felt sure she wanted the chill in, and him out. He couldn't understand why he'd even crossed the threshold, but there was something in her voice that brooked no argument. "Hello?" he called. "I'm a police officer. You should watch that door. I think the lock's faulty."

"Come in. Take off your coat. And wipe your feet. I don't want muddy prints all over my pile."

Gravier's heart was loud in the corridor. He took his hand off the latch and moved deeper into the house. Stairs vanished into a dark upper floor. A room to his left was a series of sagging browns: tired curtains, caved-in armchair, a rug, and a sleeping caramel cat. A kitchen containing a dining table covered with a protective plastic sheet. Dripping tap. A view through a back window of nothing but night's oily swirl of streetlamps and bad weather. He imagined himself closing the door on a filthy night like this and entering a kitchen filled with warm smells of good food and a woman who lit up to see him home.

A door under the stairs was open. He caught a whiff of patchouli oil and nubuck. Music was playing. Soft light curled against the bottom steps like smoke. Shadows swam languidly through it.

Gravier gritted his teeth and rapped on the door. "Could you come up here, madam? I need to have a word."

A light chuckle that might have come in response to his demand. He heard a loud crack. He'd heard noises like that in shooting ranges. Small arms fire. He had his hand on his phone when a face swung into the stairwell and smiled up at him. Her hair was a painfully white pagoda frozen into position with lacquer that he could see glinting even in this poor light.

"Come down," she said. Her voice had lost its edge. She laughed again and slipped back into the room.

Gravier descended. The smell of scented candles caught in his throat. He hesitated at the foot of the stairs when he saw the room and his first thought was, *Is there a crime being committed here?*

"Welcome to my dungeon," she said.

He couldn't focus on anything, because there was too much to take in. To settle on any detail for any amount of time was to invite insanity. His attention fluttered from the operating table to the dentist's chair to the cage and the things that writhed on and in them. There were glass shelves of glittering surgical instruments, wet from whatever task they had last been put to, ivory tables displaying monstrous dildoes sculpted from raw bone. Masks that weren't masks at all hung from cords and turned in the hot, still air, drying, curling like strips of jerky.

"You know me," she said. She ran a finger across his jawbone and it turned to a line of smoking powder. The pain didn't come at once. It was only when he raised his hand to his face that he felt a rind of necrotic tissue snap away, an icicle in his fingers. He screamed as the burn took hold and she was at the door, locking it, placing the key between her breasts. He tore his gaze away from her red lips, her black eyes. He tried not to look at the flesh that cracked and splintered between the shiny black curves of rubber, the vermiculate patterns of ice, like hoarfrost on a lawn at daybreak, or the leaves of ice that grow on the surface of a pond. Parts of her were studded with solid impact scars: white bruises. He heard the ding of the bell and turned, expecting to see the child on her bicycle, but there was only a woman on the operating table, her innards exposed, clamped back with pins like a dissected frog. Henry Johns was there, bent over as if in supplication, as if he was breathing in the aroma of her organs.

"Jesus Christ," Gravier managed. "She's still alive. You bastards."

The woman was arching against her bonds; blood squelched beneath the suck of her back.

The dominatrix hobbled to a bookshelf, her form cracking and squealing against itself. She hefted a volume in her hands and began to turn pages. She turned the book so that he could see a picture of the woman from his dreams, a sliver of a face from long ago. Despite the horror rising around him, he felt the familiar pang of a missed connection, of a chance gone by.

"Who is she?" he asked.

"Her name is Rebecca Tavistock. She is your soul mate. We all have one. The lucky ones find each other by a combination of detective work and good fortune."

Gravier could hear the sound of the bell again, but everything was slowed down, deeper, more resonant. Now the tinkle of that bicycle toy was the great, monotonous din of a cathedral angelus.

He felt each toll in the gaps between his vertebrae. The vibrations were so forceful that scraps of plaster were pulling away from the walls, showing the bones of the house beneath. Henry Johns's exposed brain shook like a jelly against the collar of what remained of his skull. His feverish eyes were like those of a speed reader, sucking in as much detail as time allowed.

"Rebecca," Gravier breathed.

The pages shifted under the dominatrix's fingers. The photographs moved of their own volition. "Are you finished?" she asked Johns. She turned to Gravier. "You'll have to excuse the Diploë. He has quite execrable table manners."

Gravier watched the girl beneath Johns die. He saw something of her drift up from the center of her body and vanish like inhaled smoke into Johns's mouth and nostrils. Then she was still.

"We've been looking for you since you were born. Hard to latch onto the cold, the ones who recognize the vacuum at their hearts but do precious little about it. The warm are easy. But now that we have you, we can get you two lost souls together. How romantic is that?"

"She . . . she's here?" Gravier turned to the empty corners of the room, but that delicate woman he'd seen just once before was absent. The thin, pale tilt of her chin as she turned to regard him. The achingly lovely green of her eyes.

"Will you go to her, gladly?" the dominatrix asked him. Her mouth was open and she was showing her teeth. They were tablets of ice. He felt he might melt her away with the heat of his sudden need.

The sound of the bell raged through the walls, through the floor. It seemed to come at him from all angles, and it married precisely the beat of his heart. When he turned his head again, it was to view the ragdoll of something long dead come jerking through a gap in the floorboards. Its mouth was opened, a cracked, decayed ring of black teeth and unspoken secrets. The Diploë closed his eyes and flaunted the wet, black shreds that dangled from his fingernails. The dominatrix was panting, her hands a restless knot at the molten center of herself. There was a sense of sinking, of leaving what he knew for something almost too large to comprehend.

For the first time in his life, as he folded beneath her arthritic grip and her jaws found a way into the softest part of him, Gravier understood what it meant to give yourself to the person you had been intended for, even if you had been born a couple of hundred years too late.

The Confessor's Tale
Sarah Pinborough

A wolf stole Arkady Melanov's tongue when he was ten weeks old. It crept into the village from the surrounding forest and followed the sound of his cries as if they were the scent of a fresh kill. Eventually, its pricked ears reached the Melanovs' tiny one-level dwelling at the back of the bakery where the boy's father worked. The wooden door had been left an inch or two open to allow any passing breeze to alleviate the stifling trapped heat of the ovens, and the beast simply padded into the house. The source of the noise found, it tore Arkady's tongue free from his screaming mouth before disappearing out into the summer night, leaving only a bloody trail of silence. When Arkady's mother ran into the bedroom and found her mutilated baby, she couldn't bear the weight of her own guilt at leaving him to cry. She stood by the crib and hacked at her wrists with the pin from her hair until she bled to death.

That was how the story went.

There was, as always, another, quieter story whispered in the narrow alleys and smoky cook rooms of the village. It poured from mouth to ear, accompanied by nods of knowledge and raised eyebrows. The gestures spoke of Arkady's mother, the dark Ekaterina, discovered over her baby's cradle, her rosebud lips full of blood and meat and her eyes equally red with the madness of too many sleepless nights brought on by her infant son's incessant rages against the world. The Boyar's men took her to the castle and, after he and his entourage had had their fill of her, with one last glance back at daylight she was buried alive in the flower garden, as was the fate of those unfortunates who broke the law in the region of Kashkent.

That was how the other story went.

By the time he was five, Arkady had heard the second version of events several times through the cracked walls of shops and houses; the words carried easily on the fresh, hot summer winds. They didn't affect him. He found he didn't care much at all which story was true; the outcome remained the same. He would never scream again, nor gurgle with laughter, nor utter a single word. Arkady had learned his lesson young.

When he was seven, Arkady's father died. This came as no surprise to anyone, not even the young boy. Whereas Mikhail Melanov had once been a strong and handsome man, he had aged and weakened since his son lost his tongue and those two stories were born. He was often plagued by coughs and chills, until eventually his broad chest crumpled into itself, a hollow space where only a broken heart lived. Arkady would watch his father's arms tremble as he lifted the heavy trays of hot bread, often nearly dropping them before the next bout of racking coughs would hit him, the boy doing what he could to help and fetching his father water from the jug in their small home at the back of the bakery. Mikhail Melanov would take it and nod in awkward thanks to his silent son, and the young boy would pretend not to see the distaste in his father's eyes.

When the long winter of that year came, the temperatures fell far below zero as they did each cycle, but this time the breath of the cold blew hard, and in the face of the ice and the winds, Mikhail Melanov's lungs decided enough was enough and breathed their last. It was not without a sense of relief. Arkady dutifully held his father's hand as he passed, and then stared long and hard at the cooling body and wondered where the man inside had gone. With no outlet, the question stayed trapped inside the isolated boy.

It was natural that the widow Samolienko and her son Sasha, who had stepped in to help when it was clear that Melanov was reaching the end, should take over the running of the bakery, and most of the village were pleased with the transition. The bread no longer had a coating of germs, and the babushka and her son worked hard to make sure enough loaves were baked each day for no one to go hungry. Young Arkady had a knack for kneading the dough and she kept him on, providing a small bed for him in the room where the wolf or his mother had stolen his tongue. Being neither sentimental nor unkind, she treated the boy with relative indifference. Having only ever lived with his father, who had never hidden well his un-ease with his son, this seemed perfectly normal to the young boy.

A few days after the widow Samolienko took up residence, she called Arkady away from his work. Arkady saw his father's few clothes and possessions had been piled up in the middle of the dusty floor. The babushka's weathered eyes appraised him.

"I need to make space for my own and my son's clothes."

Arkady nodded. He wasn't quite sure what the widow wanted with him. Her hands stretched out and nestled in their floury palms sat an oblong box.

"I found this hidden at the bottom of the cupboard. I think it belonged to your mother." She shrugged. "It has her name scratched on the lid anyway."

His eyes fell to the box.

"I think it is some kind of game. Perhaps a puzzle of sorts." She shook it, and Arkady heard the pieces rattle inside. "Anyway, it seems poorly made and can have no value, so it is yours if you want it."

Somewhere behind the hardness in her charcoal eyes, Arkady saw a hint of pity for the orphaned boy with no tongue. He took the box and gave her a rare smile. She nodded, satisfied, and sent him back to his work.

■   ■   ■

Arkady waited until the widow and her son were sleeping before he lit the tiny candle by his bed and pulled the rectangular box out from under his pillow. His breath formed a crystal haze in the night, even the heat from the cooling ovens not enough to keep the arctic winter at bay. He ran his fingers over the rough surface, feeling the strange shape of his long-ago disappeared mother's name under them. He swallowed hard, his heart beating with an unfamiliar anticipation.

There were ten oblong pieces in all—carved and worked into uneven two-inch tiles—and he carefully took each one out of the box and placed it on the bed next to the one before it, creating a line, before picking the first up again and examining it more thoroughly. He swallowed, his throat dry. Its pale surface was smooth and cool and he knew with a certainty he couldn't place that it and the others were formed from the bones of dead things. Each piece had a distinct pattern carved into it in fine lines, the grooves stained with black ink. Arkady frowned, his eyes flitting from tile to tile as his numb hands rearranged them, finding each one that linked with the next. When he was done he sat back, vaguely disappointed. He'd expected more from seeing the finished arrangement. Being quietly shunned by the other children of the village whose mothers' superstitious natures saw too many bad omens in the one thus far defining moment in his short life, Arkady had little experience of puzzles or games, but he thought they should take longer to complete.

He looked at the linked network of delicate lines laid out before him. It felt unfinished. There was more to it; there *had* to be. His eyes recorded the curves and straights of the design. Even dull and dead as the tiles were, he felt some satisfaction in watching them. Had his mother felt this way? Outside, in the heart of the forest, a wolf howled. The desolate sound danced sadly with the icy blasts that wrapped around the village, seeking any form of company. Having known no different, Arkady couldn't share the creature's sense of isolation, but its interruption did break his moment of reverie.

The box and its contents were carefully replaced under his thin pillow, and where the shape should have disturbed his sleep, he found it brought him a quiet comfort.

Arkady heard his first confession two months later. The widow Samolienko had shooed him out of the house in order to greet the family of Elana Vidic. The last thing she needed while encouraging a good match for her son was the strange little orphan boy. Arkady didn't mind. He was as happy as he knew how to be when in his own company.

Winter still had the landscape in its grip; white knuckles peering through the gray skin of the fields. But the wind had moved on to pastures new, and wrapped in Sasha's overcoat and scarf, Arkady wandered down to the riverbank, where he thought he might skim some stones over its frozen surface to pass half an hour or so.

He picked a spot that was usually quiet, even in the hot summer months. It was too close to the dense forest and slightly too far from the village to be deemed safe for children to play at. Arkady felt at home there on the edge of things and whenever he had some time of his own, which wasn't often, as the widow was a firm believer that the Devil made work for idle hands, it was where he found his feet taking him.

On this occasion, he had been beaten to it. Ivan Minsk sat on the snow-covered bank, his knees tucked under his handsome chin as he stared at the frosted mirror of the muddy water. If it hadn't been for the stream of breath lingering in front of his mouth, Arkady might have thought the older boy was dead, he was so still. It was only when Ivan turned his head to see who had joined him that Arkady noticed Ivan's hands. They were covered in blood, a stain of guilt on the blanket of white that surrounded them both. He raised his wide eyes to find Ivan's cold blue gaze on him. The boy's perfect face twisted into a smile.

"You're Arkady Melanov? The boy without the tongue?"

Arkady nodded. He didn't look at Ivan's hands.

"You can't talk?"

Arkady shrugged.

"Can you write?"

Arkady shook his head. His father had had a basic grasp of a few words and, as much as writing would have been a useful tool for Arkady, there was no one except the church who had sufficient knowledge to teach him. And as the widow Samolienko would say, if there was no one able to read his words, then what would be the point of him writing any?

Ivan's smile stretched. "Do you know what I've done?" He looked down at his own hands, turning them this way and that, watching the pale sunlight sparkle on their crimson coating. He didn't wait for an answer. "I've killed a pig. One of Korkova's. Fat bastard probably hasn't even noticed it's missing yet. I took it into the forest and carved it up while it was still alive."

He looked at Arkady, expecting a reaction. Arkady felt nothing. He knew that to steal a pig was a terrible crime, and in winter, when all food was valued, then it would be even more so, but there were things in Ivan's eyes that he couldn't understand.

"I could feel its fear and pain. It was beautiful." Ivan seemed lost in the moment and Arkady shuffled from foot to foot, wishing that the other boy would just go and he could bounce the small collection of stones in his pocket across the river.

"And there was so much blood." The boy raised his hands to smell them. "I think maybe, next time, I might try it with a person. I think that would be better, don't you?"

He looked at Arkady and smiled. Arkady, of course, said nothing. After a few silent moments, he left Ivan to his reverie and found a different place to throw his stones, but his mind couldn't quite leave the perfectly handsome boy with blood on his hands who was sitting not so very far along the curve of the river.

Ivan Minsk was found dead the next morning. It seemed he'd been skating on the river down by the forest and the thick ice's surface had given way in a freak accident. The women of the village wailed and sobbed and the men's faces were grim at the loss of such a strong and handsome boy. The widow brewed hot tea in the large samovar she kept for special occasions, and with a plate of freshly baked sweet cakes between them, the babushkas gathered in the home behind the bakery to shake their heads and gossip under the guise of bemoaning the cruelty of the world.

Arkady took refuge in his room and wondered if he was the only one to notice the lack of ice skates on the blue and frozen body that was pulled through the grieving village. Probably. His fingers sought out the comfort of the tiles inside the box, and when the level of noise was such from the other room that he was sure he wouldn't be disturbed, he tipped them out onto the bed and proceeded to make the now familiar pattern.

As he turned over the first tile, his eyes widened. It had changed. Where the delicate carving had been inked in black, the pattern now was filled with red. Arkady stared, before carefully placing it next to the others, their surfaces still dull and dead. His heart raced with rare excitement. He had been right; the puzzle hadn't been complete. He thought of Ivan and his stained hands and looked back at the crimson color that ran like blood through the veins of the tile. There were nine more tiles to go. And then . . . what?

That night, he found it hard to sleep.

Arkady never sought out the confessions. Having no method of communication beyond gesture, he grew into a natural pragmatist. As often as he wishfully turned the tiles over in his hands, he also knew that fate would roll her dice as and when she was ready. That part of the puzzle was not in his control. For the main, in the years that followed, Arkady got on with the business of growing up and working hard for the widow, for Sasha, and for Sasha's new wife, Elena.

But the confessions found him all the same; eight more over the next six years. In a side street while trying to make a shortcut on his deliveries for the widow, a sobbing fat man told him that his wife had not died of a fever the winter before as was believed, but that when it seemed that she might recover, he pressed a pillow over her face, not being able to bear the thought of more years chained to her natural misery. He'd seen her ghost though, every day since. Arkady nodded and passed the man by.

A drunk told him how he liked to creep into his small daughter's bedroom when she slept and slide his hand under her nightdress. One of the most respected wives of the village told him how she craved the rough skin of workmen on her body and paid them to service her and thus make up for her husband's impotence.

Each stranger that found him in those isolated moments poured out the dark sins of their soul. They were eager to be free of their guilt without having to truly face justice; that much was clear in their hungry faces. Arkady could see the burdens lift from their shoulders as his ears took their words. When he left, they were always smiling, just as Ivan had been down by the river. Arkady didn't begrudge them their happiness. By the third time, he knew what the next day's outcome would be. A heart attack, an unfortunate fall, a sudden pox.

He would listen for the slow toll of the church bell before pulling the box of tiles out from their safekeeping in his bed. With each death, a fresh piece would come to life, its veins of pattern turning bloodred. Arkady felt nothing for their deaths, but there was a quiet excitement that his soul couldn't deny each time his trembling hands revealed the changes in the puzzle. When it was complete, then so would he be. By the time he was fourteen, there was only one dark tile left. As the first crisp leaves of snow fell outside his window that winter, for the first time in his life he felt a glimmer of warm hope. The completed pattern would free him from this half existence. He was sure of it.

When the summer came, it was obvious it was time for a change in the living arrangements at the bakery. Sasha and Elena's lively five-year-old twins were getting too big to sleep in the same room as their parents, and the baker's wife's belly was already growing a new sibling for the family. The house at the back of the shop was too crowded and the widow took it upon herself to rectify the situation.

"I have arranged a new position for you, Arkady." She smiled as she spoke. She had grown fond of the boy in her own way over the years; he was a good worker and had never caused her any trouble. This change would be good for him. It would bring him some security. The boy looked up at her blankly.

"You are to work for the Boyar. You will go and live within the castle walls as a manservant." She paused. "I think a young man like you will do well there."

Arkady knew what she meant. The Boyar could be considered a fair ruler as far as taxes and tithes were concerned, but stories that leaked from the high walls that surrounded his castle and the dwellings and merchants within told of excessive debauchery and pleasures taken in the most deadly of sins by their landlord and his knights and clergy. Those who were caught spreading the stories were often hung on crosses outside the castle walls, their beaten bodies soft for the buzzards that would circle and peck hungrily, tearing strips of flesh from the still living victims.

To speak ill of the Boyar was a crime, and although there were great rewards to be had in the trust of the Boyar's employment, the risks concerning accusations of malicious gossip were high. It was, after all, an easy way to remove a rival. With no tongue, it was a crime that Arkady could never commit. The old babushka, who had lived long enough to understand the ways of men, knew that with both his pliable nature and his silence, Arkady could not fail to impress the Boyar, and perhaps one day he would see fit to reward the old woman and her family for this gift. It was not that much to hope for.

The Boyar's men came the next day and Arkady left, the puzzle tucked carefully into his jacket pocket. He didn't look back at the village, the horse beneath him carrying him confidently the few miles uphill to the high castle walls. It was only when the gates closed heavily behind him that he thought of the whispered stories of his mother's demise within these very grounds and at his new employer's hands. Arkady found himself still empty of any feelings. His mother was not even the memory of a scent, and as he had several times before, he found himself wondering whether the wolf that took his tongue had somehow taken his heart, or perhaps some small part of his soul, with it.

The more he watched those in the world around him play out their small stories, the less he felt a part of it. On those nine occasions when people had shared with him the darkest secrets of their sins, he simply found himself puzzled by the range of emotion presented to him; their passion, their lust, their greed, and the heavy weight of their guilt. He'd felt nothing but mild curiosity. It was only when he placed bone against tiled bone and watched the puzzle coming together that he felt anything at all.

Arkady settled into life within the castle, and the summer months passed easily. The Boyar had grown fat and gout-ridden as he crept into his middle age, but if anything, as his body degenerated, its desires increased as if, by feeding them, he could somehow delay his inevitable demise. There were plenty among his retinue who were more than happy to encourage his pleasures in order to satisfy their own. Screams echoed up from the dungeons where new tortures were devised to be carried out on local thieves and petty criminals.

Lithe young women, and sometimes older ones, roamed naked between the castle's bedrooms, herded in from the surrounding towns and villages and drugged with alcohol and herbal liquors brewed by the Boyar's apothecaries. If they were lucky, their moans of pleasure did not turn to howls of pain. For the others, once they had fallen still and silent with relief, their deaths ensuring their ordeals were truly over, Arkady was always there with his bucket and hard wooden scrubbing brush to clear the floors of warm blood and then fill the baths with sweet-smelling water for the knights and their leader to bathe in.

The Boyar learned to appreciate his silent manservant, and Arkady quickly became invaluable to him. Arkady cleaned up after his excesses without a raised eyebrow or even the slightest dilation of pupil at some of the sights that he found in front of him. The Boyar always watched carefully for any such reaction in all his men, and he found that even among those who shared his delights, there would occasionally be a small tremor or a flinch of shock at some physical experimentation the Boyar had tried. He was so used to this that Arkady's indifference was like a soothing balm. He did not have to wonder what Arkady might be thinking, because he had a curious feeling that Arkady did not spend any time at all thinking about the Boyar's unusual habits, and coupled with the boy's inability to speak, this made him completely reliable.

Arkady was soon moved to the small bedroom annexed to the Boyar's by a discreetly hidden door in the rich wood-paneled walls. It was a vast improvement on his tiny room at the back of the bakery, but the luxuriously sewn silk bed coverings and the roaring fire in the grate failed to impress Arkady. The fire was not that different from the warmth of the bread ovens, and a bed was simply a bed. That was the truth of it. Sometimes, as he pulled the puzzle box free from beneath his soft pillow and emptied the pieces out, seeking distraction from the sounds in the room next door, he wondered if maybe he saw the truth of too many things. The Boyar himself was one such example.

Did the old man even know that his depravities had slowly become more extreme since Arkady had been in his employ? Probably not. But Arkady, despite his youth, could see it clearly and also the way the fat lord would look at him when he came in to clean up. He would feel those piggy eyes bore into him, seeking out some kind of reaction. It was simple. The Boyar wanted to shock Arkady. Despite enjoying the freedom from guilt the boy's indifference gave him, his need to feel powerful made him want Arkady to be affected by his deeds. And that was the truth of it.

It was only in the delicately carved tiles that the truth evaded him. They remained simply a wonder; a vague promise of hope, of change, of some kind of new life.

He was absorbed in them on the evening that the Boyar burst into his small room, his robes covered with blood, the glint of relieved madness fading from him as the monster left and the man returned.

"Arkady, I fear that you may need assistance . . ." He paused, his eyes snagging on the box and its contents as Arkady tried to hide them away.

"Give that to me." The Boyar held out his bloody hand and Arkady found himself passing over his treasured box.

The Boyar stared at it, and then frowned before sitting slowly down on the edge of Arkady's bed. "Ekaterina." His finger did as Arkady's childish ones had so many years before, and traced out the shape of the word. "The beautiful Ekaterina."

He looked up, as if seeing Arkady for the first time. "I remember her. She was different from the rest." One hand waved dismissively toward the door of his bedchamber and the bloody remains of whoever had been unlucky enough to find themselves called in for company that night. "She was . . . special."

He opened the box, tipping its contents onto the bedclothes, turning each tile over in his fat hands and almost absently placing it next to the one before. "Was she your mother, Arkady?" He didn't look up. "Of course she was. I should have known. A boy with no tongue from the villages. It had to be you." He shook his head, a soft smile stretching his bloated, too-red cheeks. "Why I did not think about it, I do not know. Too easily distracted, I suppose."

The Boyar let out a long sigh and looked toward the small window. Despite its being covered with heavy drapes, he seemed to stare out to the stars beyond, the puzzle pieces forgotten.

"Your mother distracted me . . ." He started softly. "She was exquisite. They had washed the blood from her mouth when she was brought to me, but I could smell it on her."

Somewhere in the distance, Arkady heard the low peal of a church bell ringing out. The lamp against the wall flickered as if a gust of wind had caught it unawares and threatened its existence. For a moment his entire being stilled. Unlike the Boyar, Arkady had not forgotten the puzzle. This was it. The final confession. Something pounded in his chest and he realized that at last, his heart was alive.

"She enjoyed the pain," the Boyar continued, as if he couldn't hear the terrible chimes that were calling to them both. "Almost as much as I enjoyed hurting her." He frowned. "She had no limits. Until her, my tastes had been base, *ordinary*, but she forced me to new levels."

Arkady wasn't listening. Something was happening with the puzzle and it echoed deep in the core of him. The final tile had shivered into crimson, and with shaking hands, he formed them into their pattern, his heartbeat and the bell and the Boyar's confession rolling into one hum of excitement in his head.

It was complete. The puzzle was finished. The red lines burst into life, glowing as if made from some insane phosphorus. Arkady rose to his feet, and as the wall in front of them cracked and dissolved, the Boyar finally stopped speaking, his mouth dropping open in awe and wonder. Arkady did not look at him. He was no longer important. The pieces clicked, twisting sideways, each a tiny box of its own, and hooks flew out from each one, embedding in Arkady's soft skin. They dug into his flesh, warm blood trickling as they pulled and tore at him, tearing him exquisitely, releasing his true self so long trapped inside. It felt wonderful.

Arkady stared at the doorway that had been the wall, aware that beside him the Boyar had started to scream and jibber and shake. His fear felt good. Hooks found his mouth, and as they ripped it wider over his teeth and jaw, he watched the two figures emerge. Behind them, the darkness hummed with pain and confusion and he felt it tingle in his every cell.

"Have you found your tongue, Arkady, the Confessor?" The being was scarred on every inch of its damaged flesh, its strange clothing sewn through its skin, never to be removed. When it spoke, a scent of vanilla and putridness hung in the air. Arkady sucked it in, relishing it. His eyes widened as thick, black tongues erupted from his torn mouth as if tasting the creature's breath, rippling as they did so like the snakes of the Medusa's hair. More hooks embedded in the back of Arkady's skull, leaving his mouth wide open forever, home for the swirling mass of meat that filled it.

The Confessor. He rolled the words round in his mutilated mouth, letting all his tongues taste them. It felt right. It felt good.

"You are Cenobite. One of us."

If Arkady's jaw had not been stretched apart beyond limits, his torn bottom lip pulled over it, it would have dropped at the beauty of the second speaker. Its voice was a soft whisper, and every inch of it appeared tattooed, jeweled pins driven into its skin and skull at regular intersections on the network of grids.

"We have been waiting for you."

Arkady's hellbound heart split with joy, and stepping forward, he happily left his humanity behind. He was going home.

The Boyar had crumpled to the ground, and the fat man's head shook as he cried and sobbed and begged for mercy.

The door in the wall was closing, and reaching down with his own bloody hand, Arkady pulled the lord forward, the weighty frame as light as a feather. The gloom embraced him and he thought he saw a flash of Ivan's smile somewhere in the shadows of the endless night. No matter. He would hear the Boyar's confession first, and if it didn't come easily, then he would force it. He had all of eternity to introduce the man to the possibilities of pain and pleasure.

And he would enjoy it.

Hellbound Hollywood

Mick Garris

So it had come to this.

I stood in the relentless suburban London gloom, a Hitchcockian black umbrella protecting me from the gritty drizzle that had already overtaken my socks within my shoes. The location van would meet me in an hour or so, but I had always preferred to arrive on my own beforehand, so that I could scope out the place before the others dove in.

London was once my town. Back in the early nineties, when the British film industry had struggled under virtual collapse, as the world turned a cold shoulder to all that the Brits had to offer on the big screen, as cinemas contracted and toppled across the United Kingdom, I, new and brash and filled with an artistic reach unbound by practicality or even social graces, had crafted a little something called *Double Deception*.

I thought you might remember it: BAFTAs, Golden Globes, even a couple Oscar nomination certificates sit proudly on my mantel in silent honor to my genius. But then, so does a collection of wedding scrapbooks, three of them, tucked away in a lockbox of memories better forgotten.

It's funny how long ago 1992 seems now.

The parties, the laughs, the free ride, the international festivals, the awards, the open checkbooks represented what was surely the best time of my life. Unlike the world that Charles Dickens had so well chronicled, *that* was the best of times, and this was surely the worst. My brilliance had been fêted from coast to coast; the film I had written and directed had become not only a cause célèbre for a downtrodden, downright moribund production industry but its shot in the arm, a reanimation of its corpse.

And here I stood, staring at the weathered face of No. 55 Lodovico Street, a grimy stone edifice in an even grimier neighborhood, on a location scout for—I shudder to even type the words—a horror film. And not just any horror film, mind you, but an *independent* horror film. No vast, cozy studio where any set you could conceive of would be constructed by a talented coterie of skilled artisans; rather, everything was to be shot on location, where walls won't wild, Pinocchio-nosed neighbors gather for a peek inside the windows, and tree trimmers set their chain saws on high until they are paid off into silence. The budget is paltry and the story impoverished. How far the mighty have fallen.

No. 55 Lodovico Street was an address of some infamy: back in the 1980s, it is said that it was some sort of wicked black hole, an Old Dark House that feasted on the blood and flesh of the innocent in order to feed the wicked souls of the guilty ghosts within it . . . or some bullshit like that. It's a tale no doubt concocted by parents to keep their towheaded little monsters on the straight and narrow, a sort of *Candyman* urban legend, with all the British trappings of sexual repression and its revolution of whips, chains, and submission.

Had I retained any of the libido I had used up in the two-decade party that was my life after *Double Deception*, I might have given a shit. But I hadn't, so I didn't.

The hate-bearing, leaden clouds darkened in portent, and tears of coal battered my umbrella with less mercy than before. I knew it was futile to try the door before the location manager arrived with the key members of the film crew, but I reached out and touched the tarnished old doorknob anyway. It turned in my hand, and with an ominous groan, the heavy old door, weighted down with dozens of layers of surely lead-based paint, crept open.

As I stepped into the dusty, musty hallway of the long-deserted old house, motes danced in the shaft of gray light, drifting apart in a curtain, as if to welcome me inside. When the door closed behind me, seemingly of its own accord, the silence became absolute. When what was surely my own imagination whispered my name, its lips brushing against the edge of my ear, the tiny hairs at the base of my neck tingled. The old stories stirred my imagination, which had, of late, been impoverished. Though my blood was chilled, I took that as a good sign, a greeting.

The bottom floor of the three-level row house was practically devoid of furniture . . . only fitting, since it hadn't been occupied in some twenty years. It seemed a pity that local superstition had kept such prime real estate—well, prime for this neighborhood, anyway—from being put to use, especially in these eccentric financial times. An overstuffed sofa sat under the great window, covered in a gray and dusty sheet. The carpeting had been torn asunder, leaving warped wood flooring fully exposed. The draperies were decayed and torn, letting what light there was into the gloom. I pushed the button for the lights, but the room stayed dark.

The room was actually rather large and the ceilings were high. This bade well for the camera and lighting package we would need to shoot here. Actually, this wouldn't be a bad room to shoot in at all. The great windows offered access to good daylight exposure, and sliding wood doors opened up to reveal a sizable dining room. Though it was bereft of furniture, there was a set of long steel chains in the middle of the floor. The heavy steel was crusted with a dark brown rust. And each chain ended in a gleaming, dangerous-looking hook. And under the pile of chain, stained with coffee or rust or tea or something, a St. Valentine's card. I kicked the heavy metal aside and knelt to open and read the message within. In a palsied, struggled script, written as if by a rightie using his left hand, were the words *With All of my Love, All that you Dream.*

I wanted to vomit.

Sentimentality and I were at war. I had no use for the mealy, squishy world of emotion and feeling. I had bared my soul to the world, which first took me to suckle at its breast . . . but then it turned that intimacy against me, tore open my heart, and poured salt deep into the wounds. No, I would never again reveal myself so fully, neither to an audience of a million nor to an audience of one. I had known love, found that it was desire wrapped in deceit, and had given it up for Lent. And Lent was ongoing. Since I no longer needed or desired sex, love was obviously out of the question.

I let the valentine drop to the floor and stood at the base of the stairwell at No. 55 Lodovico Street. As I stood looking up into its heart, I could feel, if not actually hear, its pulse beating in rhythm with my own. Clouds gathered in the darkness at the top of the stairs, threatening a rain that promised a more powerful storm than the one that battered the windows outside.

With a wide lens—perhaps a 14mm, or maybe even a 10— looking up this impressive if weathered stairway, I might be able to capture its growing sense of dread. Especially if I placed the camera right on the floor as it looked up to the next storey, and crept it forward ever so slowly. Yes, this actually might not be such a bad place to shoot, after all. We could spill some blood here . . .

"What have you dreamed?" asked the whisper in my ear.

It woke me. I had no idea how I'd arrived on the third floor, or why I was asleep on its bare, dusty wood-planked floor. I sat up, drenched in a bath of sleep-sweat, my own scent assaulting and insulting my nose. The door was shut, and the windows painted over with a solid coat of black, yet still there was enough illumination to see through the shadows.

Through the murk, all I could see were bare walls and total emptiness. The silence, save for the pounding sea within my head, was complete, and I was shrouded in a loneliness of which I had heretofore believed myself incapable. Solitary and tiny in this vast open space, I could feel the dampness that seemed to breathe from the walls. The air was thick, sultry, close. And it *rippled* around me.

My skin prickled into gooseflesh and I slowly stood, feeling someone's—something's—presence rise with me. It was then that I saw I was not alone.

Standing across the room, a figure, shrouded in darkness, faced me: still, ominous, threatening. My heart pounded violently within my rib cage, and fear—an illogical, entirely unmotivated fear—dropped over me like a blanket. I took a step back . . . and so did the figure. I stood still, and so did this mocking, vile stalker, never turning from me, its eyes hidden in the dark.

"What do you want?" I demanded. But it wouldn't answer.

I took a bold step toward it, and it did the same.

The perspiration that covered my body suddenly dried . . . but the walls in the suffocatingly warm room broke out into a sweat of their own, a rising damp of mounting temperature.

Two steps closer to each other, the figure remained silent.

"Who are you?" I asked, trying not to let my voice break.

When it offered no reply, I took yet another step forward, and the thing in the shadows aped me again. As the light, a warm, amber glow that seemed to somehow emanate directly from the walls and floor, bloomed into mere duskiness, I saw more clearly.

Standing across the bare room stood a soul even more naked: my own. One wall was fully occupied by a mirror, cracked like a road map, big patches of its silvered backing having flaked away. I had struck fear into my own heart. I walked to the mirror and was startled by the depth of pale fright reflected on my own visage as it stared back at me in relief. I was two of my own Marx Brothers, no, even more ridiculous, Lucy and Harpo playing peekaboo. If only I could laugh.

My pulse hadn't even the time to return to normal when I turned back toward the door and saw that the room that I had entered, the room that was reflected before me in the fractured mirrored wall, was not nearly so empty as I had assumed.

Now, filling the room that surrounded me, were implements that seemed concocted during the Crusades, oversized tools crafted of dark wood and heavy metal by the blackest of imaginations, obviously constructed to coerce, to inflict pain, to torture. But these were beautiful in their viciousness: structures of oversized chains, hooks, wooden racks, gleaming metal blades, some kind of revolving apparatus that I knew without asking was intended for peeling flesh.

Was this apartment or abattoir?

The dense, fetid air took on a familiar rusty tang that filled my nose and mouth: the iron-rich scent of blood.

And then, again, that voice in my ear:

"What have you dreamed?"

I spun 'round, but this time, I was not alone with my reflection. Rather, a being of indeterminate sex stood before me, shaded by the appalling tools of torture. It stepped out of the darkness to reveal itself to me, and it was a horror I shall not soon forget. It was dressed only in tight chains that were wrapped in haphazard fashion around its formless body. Rusted padlocks, surely not intended to ensure chastity, as this creature seemed to be made of sex, dangled from the chains. And on closer inspection, I saw that some of them were locked through folds of its horrid gray flesh, not just through the steel links. Its arms were wrapped in barbed wire, digging into its anemic tissue without drawing blood, despite the depth of its chew.

The chains kept its voluptuous, pendulous breasts from hitting the floor, and crisscrossed its leering, dangling phallus in a relentless metallic strangle.

I was repelled, but unable to look away, fascinated.

It's what a filmmaker does, isn't it? It is my job not to look away, to find fascination in the hideous as well as the everyday. It's my vocation as well as my avocation to look, and especially not to look askance. I leave it to the great unwashed to look away. In contrast to my mind, my eyes know no fear.

At least that is what I thought until I saw its face . . .

Taking another step closer, it stood fully revealed before me, daring me to stare at it without tumbling into madness. And I came close to losing the dare, as well as my breakfast.

Its head had sparse patches of hair in various tufts that welled out of corrupted, dying flesh. There were scars and stitches wrapped around the face, and the eyes, my God, the eyes, one sea green and the other some kind of muddy shit brown, seemed to roam loosely in mismatched sockets, the lower eyelids open and an angry, wet red. Even the eyeballs had raw, primitive rows of stitches around the retina.

But worst of all was what passed for its mouth. It occupied most of its face, a long, vertical slash that roughly bisected its visage. If there had been a nose, it was long gone, replaced by this gaping hole that resembled nothing more than, okay, I'll say it, a huge, loose vagina. Its vertical lips were wet, hungry, horrid. And there was a row of teeth on either side, barely concealed by the labia majora: worn, round nubs, they looked like nothing more than miniature human heads trapped in a forever scream.

I ran from this beastly creature, needing the door more than I needed my breath. But there was no exit now; the door was hopelessly locked, no matter how madly I beat against it.

I turned to see that this creature, this beast made of sex and violence, was laughing at me. Its hideous, thumblike nipples curdled into excited prominence, leaking a milk of thrill; its horrific, rotted penis began to rise in a repulsive, desiring salute.

And, damn me forever, I could not look away.

I was backed against the door as this bastardization of human life approached me with what could only be described as an amused vertical smile.

"What have you dreamed?" it asked me again.

The question, now posed for a third time, unlocked memories of dreams, erotic and ferocious: the dreams that had erupted without my control in my sleep, dreams that drenched me in guilt and sweat and repulsion and desire. My mind, wherever it was hiding, was answering this thing's question without my control, and the dreams, no, the nightmares, the transgressions of the flesh that I had so carefully locked away from my conscious mind, were set free by this question.

"I don't dream!" I answered, but knew this living corruption could tell I was lying. It could see the bodies, the implements, the flesh, the blood, the fluids that soaked my sleep. Again it laughed.

"You can have all that you dream and more," it told me, but I wanted no part of it.

"I don't dream!" I repeated. "I dream awake! It's what I do, put dreams on the screen for others."

The machines that littered the room stood high around us like a city of sadism, a testament to torture, the antithesis of love. It made sense that a creature like this would be here.

"It is why you are here," the monster said to me. "Because you possess . . . *imagination*."

It had been a long time since I had been accused of *that*.

"Surely you have needs," this beast, neither man nor woman but assembled from both, prompted me.

Yes. I need a studio film, a return to prominence, more gleaming statuettes to fill out the mantel, a home back on Rodeo Drive in Beverly Hills, the place where I was honored and catered to and respected and desired. Where ridiculous sums of money were exchanged for the value of my distinctive services, where my vision stood out among the others, where my style was adopted—no, coopted—by talentless music video directors who masturbated with their RED digital cameras and spattered their issue all over the Internet as they pretended to tell stories without words.

I still had tales to tell, I wanted to say to this bastardization of human sexuality, and new ways to tell them. This . . . this—ugh!— *horror movie* was my last hope to return me to creative solvency. If the tale of Lemarchand's Configuration could be told with enough sex and blood and rock 'n' roll to reignite interest in a fallow market for tales of cinematic terror, then I might too rise from the dead like one of George Romero's folk heroes.

But this creature stood before me, waiting for an answer, its rheumy eyes glinting in the waning light, its vaginal face lifted proudly—or tauntingly—as its slavering lips smacked lightly but wetly in the breeze of its rotted, piscatorial breath.

"Nothing you could help me with," I finally answered. God

knows why I bothered. Well, if there was a God, he knew. Of course, if there existed demons so monstrous as this foul beast that stood before me, the concept of a Supreme Being no longer seemed so far out of the question.

It's difficult to tell if the thing smiled, since its orifice was vertical, but it seemed that that was the expression it took on. Its glistening, moist lips widened somewhat, revealing the nubby little tooth heads. It took a step closer to me, its horrific but stunted erection leading the way. Its penis had two mushroom-shaped heads, and both of them were pointing at me. I didn't know where to look. When it spoke again, I looked into its face. It drooled when it spoke, a thick, aromatic liquor that ran down its chin and dripped onto its tethered, swollen breasts.

"I can offer you much."

"No," I countered. "You can't offer me what I want."

"Surely you know the voluptuousness of desire."

At one time I had. Now I couldn't afford it. I just shook my head, wondering how I'd stepped into this dusky, seething cauldron of evil.

"Surely you desire the touch of flesh against your own, the penetration of one body part into another, the exchange of hot, percolating bodily fluids, the explosion of wet conclusion, only to start it all over again. Surely you recall its power."

I stood my ground. I was repelled not only by the creature but also by what it offered.

"No. I have had all the bodily contact I need. My desire has atrophied along with my creative reach. My needs are more earthbound than that. I need box office more than I need box."

"Thanatos sings your name," the creature told me. Its voice was clogged, choked, gargly. "All your power is derived from your lust; all desire is ignited by arousal. Give in to your physical need and your more . . . grounded desires shall be fulfilled as well."

Well, that didn't make a whit of sense to me, and I told this creature so, wondering why I bothered. It drew even closer to me, reached out long fingers that were more like talons, grabbed me forcefully by the shoulders, and pulled my face to its own. Its damp stench was overwhelming as it planted a greedy, moist kiss along the length of my face, leaving my head shellacked in its ooze. I should have been repulsed, but instead, I felt nature's heat coursing through my body. I had barely shaken hands with arousal in the last couple of years, but here it was, like an old girlfriend back for an eager one-night toss, and my body responded in kind. I tried to fight off the raising of my manhood's flag, but the *cranial minora* had a mind of its own. The otherworldly being devoured me with its hungry patchwork eyes, then it slid its mouth-pussy around my head, sucking on it as if on the head of a six-foot penis.

I couldn't breathe . . . but I ejaculated furiously almost immediately after my head was swallowed in hot, wet darkness.

I woke to the call of the first assistant director, an able old Irishman who'd been working the boards since the Roger Moore Bond days. I was lying on the floor of the empty third-floor room, which was now free of the torture devices, the smell of seafood, and old Cunt Face. Terry Deakins stood over me, assuming another drug casualty by way of Hollywood, doing his best to keep from judgmentally clucking his tongue. Luckily, my sticky wet crotch was hidden by my coat, though the ooze covering my face must certainly have given him pause. The scent, though diminished, was still unpleasant at the very least.

"James," he said to me, "are you all right?"

Well, if I were all right, surely I would not be a puddle on the floor, my face covered in pussy jam, unconscious under my spurts of ecstasy. I looked up to see the rest of the key crew members on the location-reconnaissance mission fanned behind him, eyes wide in near horror. Most of them were young or old, not much in the in-between. If they were the top of the game, they wouldn't be working on this piece of shit, no matter how revered the fable. And this one wasn't.

The windows were no longer covered in black paint, and the room itself was no longer suffocating in sultry heat. It was cold enough to see breath. Only the huge, decaying dancer's mirror remained, reflecting our little group innocuously.

I stammered as I stood: "I came in early and must have gotten locked in. Guess I panicked when I tried to get out and the door wouldn't give. It was so oppressively hot in here. I suppose I passed out."

The gathered minions looked at one another. Surely they were watching the further decline of Hollywood's crash and burn, the toppling of another British genius who'd abandoned the mother country until being forced to return to her arms, tail between his legs, to direct a scary movie. There was no pity in their gaze. Perhaps only I minded that the audience for this grotesque piffle was in its teens, years, if not lifetimes, away from their first sexual encounter, their spotted faces agape at the spurting blood that was the closest they'd get to an explosion of bodily fluid that did not rely on their own right fists.

It was a man's world here; only the script supervisor, a comely young woman named Iris something-or-other, provided some balance of estrogen to our little army. She reached out to help me to my feet, and I could see at least a trace of pity in her eyes. I could also see the tiny bleat of a pulse in a soft blue vein barely revealed when she brushed the golden cascade of her hair from her eyes.

I zipped the coat tight over my telltale wet spot before my little, what—experience? Dream? Fantasy?—was revealed, but I was not embarrassed. Instead, I could not keep my eyes and mind off of the increasingly alluring Iris, whose charms kept blooming, reigniting memories of heat and arousal. When she looked briefly at me and found that my eyes were already locked on her, she blushed sweetly and looked away.

I wanted her in a way I hadn't wanted in a long, long time.

Her scent pulled me like a magnet, and it was fortunate that I was draped in a long overcoat that cloaked my carnal desire for her. I could tell with a single intake of breath that she was on her menses. Far from repelling me, it made my own blood boil. I stayed close to her like a nervous puppy as we continued the reconnaissance, making notes on lighting, camera angles, scene placement, and the like, my filmmaker's sense jumping into its autopilot mode. But this brief creative explosion was overshadowed by the pounding of Iris's heart when I stood close to her. I wanted our pulses to beat in a passionate, accelerated union.

Not soon enough, the location scout was over, and I held back as the crew headed down the stairs and out the door. I gently placed my hand on Iris's elbow. "Can I give you a ride home?" I asked her.

She blushed, and the scarlet flush that filled her cheeks made my heart—and parts even more private—dance. She smiled sweetly and looked at the floor, like a scene from an old movie, anachronistic but charming, and then said, "I'd like that."

The rest of the crew climbed their way into the van, giving us the knowing eye as I kept Iris behind with me. Surely they giggled and made ribald conjectures about us all the way back to Bray.

"Wait," I told her as she started toward my Jaguar. "I want to show you something."

She looked at me trustingly but questioningly. I put my finger to my lips, conspiratorially, then closed the door, shutting out the world.

I took her hand and led her up the stairs.

"What is it?" she asked.

"Something amazing," I replied, my body tingling with an erotic thrill that filled me with giddy eagerness unknown since my first phallic insertion.

At the top of the stairs, I paused for a moment before I reached out and opened the door to the uppermost chamber. A wedge of waning sunlight led the way, and I stepped her inside. The room, now bereft of all but the huge mirror, was heating up again.

"It's hot in here," she said, tiny beads gathering in the fine, virtually invisible fuzz above her glossy upper lip. I wanted to lick it off.

"I noticed that, too. Here, look."

Through the shadows, I led her to the mirror. The room began to fill with its own glow, feeding on the heat of her menstruation. I could feel the room itself swell with excited anticipation.

I stood her in front of the mirror. "Look how beautiful you are." And she did. Her face, now sanguine with heat and thrill, was delectable. I eased up behind her and kissed the nape of her neck. Perspiration was emerging everywhere, sheening her body in a glitter of wetness. She closed her eyes and turned her head to me for the kiss, and I did not disappoint her. I nursed on her lips, eased my exploratory tongue into her receptive, sucking mouth, and held her face against my own, my hands holding on to the back of her head.

When finally we pulled apart, we were both breathing hard.

I took the top button of her blouse and opened it, starting it for her. "Let me see you," I told her.

She was hesitant. "It's . . . it's my time of the month."

"Do you think that matters a whit to me?" She had no idea it only made me hungrier. "Please."

I stepped away from her as she slowly unbuttoned her blouse, revealing sweet, barely adolescent breasts that did not require the assistance of a brassiere. She was shy about them, but I pulled her hands away as she tried to cover them. "No. They're lovely. Now the rest."

"Only if you do." I smiled and kissed her again, this time more perfunctorily. And then I, too, proceeded to disrobe before her and the mirror. She stared into my eyes and at my gradually revealed body so intently that she did not seem to notice what the mirror now reflected behind her: the hungry, gleaming Stonehenge of torture that surrounded us.

It was so unlike real life, like a cheesy romantic movie, the two of us standing there naked, having kissed only twice. But there we were, sweating, dying for each other, filled with an unquenchable thirst that went out of control in this mad room, this dungeon, this abattoir. I folded my arms around her and, as her eyes closed in ecstasy, backed her away from the mirror and into the center of the torture devices. I saw a tiny rivulet of blood trickle down her bare thigh, and felt the room rear up in hunger.

And then, as she grew slick with welcome, I eagerly entered her.

The heat inside her body was almost unbearably joyous and thrilling . . . for a moment. But as soon as I was fully inside, her vagina closed its mouth and clamped tightly shut, locking me in as tightly as if with teeth.

It hurt.

And then, blessed unconsciousness . . . *again.*

And *again* I woke in this cursed manse, this time suspended above the wooden floor by chains that ended in hooks that had been ripped all the way through my wrists and ankles. Iris, still naked and sweating and rosy of complexion, was likewise crucified. Both of our bodies were drenched in a hot, slick overcoat of our own blood, and the pain was excruciating. Excruciating enough that we were locked together at our nexus by my uncontrollable throbbing erection.

But we were not alone, nor were we in the dark.

Bright lights artfully illuminated us to best effect, as the familiar thrum of a 35mm film camera rolled. I looked up to see that Cunt Face had been joined by two other members of her ilk: stitched, malformed, reformed monstrosities that had once been human but now were merely humanoid—hungry, slavering beasts bound in thick, heavy chains and dense black, bloodstained leather. One watched through the eye of its penis-head, its collar pulled back like a foreskin. The other was a patchwork of fur and flesh, stapled together in seemingly random fashion.

It became immediately apparent to me, and surely to Iris, that we were there to serve a purpose, to feed a need, both literally and figuratively. Made of flesh and blood, living, breathing, bleeding puppets of meat and mind, we were conjoined and displayed for the amusement and edification of the underworld. Our life and death would be eternal, captured in a magic box that would love us as we loved one another: sloppily, hungrily, with a beginning, a middle, and an end. It was a different kind of love story; boy meets girl, boy penetrates girl, boy and girl are mounted and displayed and dismantled to entertain us. A meet-cute without the cute.

Technicolor blood dripped onto the hungry wooden floor below, as the familiar stuttering mechanical sound of film passing through the gate commenced.

And then the machinery came alive: blades began to whirr and move in with an insatiable appetite. Iris and I both screamed in agony, fear, and mutual orgasm as blades began to spin and strip us of our meat. It began to revolve and peel a long strip of our flesh, and we took on the appearance of a barber pole. The cameras rolled, and I lost my grip on consciousness, unable to call out "Cut!"

Mechanisms

Christopher Golden & Mike Mignola

Illustrations by Mike Mignola

O n that particular October morning—a lovely fall day, a Wednesday—the autumn light fell across the rooftops of Oxford with a hint of gold sufficient to transform the view from mundane to wondrous. Colin Radford, a young man of serious scholarship, found himself so taken by the panorama visible from the classroom window that he had difficulty following the threads of Professor Sidgwick's lecture on Suetonius. This was especially troubling when Colin considered that the biographies that comprised the Roman historian's *De Vita Caesarum* had been amongst the most compelling reading that the young man had encountered in his time at Oxford, second only to the comedic plays of Aristophanes.

Colin Radford adored university—all the thinking, the constant discourse over questions of philosophy, scholarship, and theology. At times he felt as though he had been waiting all his life to escape dreary Norwich, with its forbidding cathedral and the chill wind that swept across the Channel all the way from the Russian steppes. He had found in Oxford a truer home, where men put their minds to work upon the mechanisms of intellect. There were kindred spirits here, competitive though they might be.

So for Colin to allow his mind to wander required a vista of unparalleled beauty. And yet on certain mornings, Oxford glistened in such a way as to have earned the lyrical nickname that romantics had bestowed upon it.

The City of Dreaming Spires, they called it.

Had he known on that morning that he would never see it again, Colin would have been filled with such grief as to make him weep. And yet there was so much more grief to come.

A mods student named Chisholm hurried into the room the moment the lecture concluded, earning a disapproving glare from Professor Sidgwick, even as he handed a folded sheet of cream parchment to the bespectacled old man. Colin watched Sidgwick dismiss the lad with a sniff and then glance at the note, which could only have come from the headmaster's office. Somehow, even before it happened, he knew what would come next. Sidgwick lifted his gaze, glanced around the room, and they locked eyes.

"Mr. Radford, come here, if you please."

Colin felt a strange heat prickle his face. He did not fear Sidgwick the way he knew some others did, though if he thought the professor had caught him drifting during the lecture, he might have done well to be afraid of his wrath. Yet the look on the old man's face, the way he stroked his pointed beard, and the almost militaristic manner in which he held that crisp letter still half raised in his right hand, made the young scholar cringe.

"Yes, sir," Colin said, and as the other students departed, he made for the lectern.

Sidgwick looked at him over the tops of his spectacles. "You're from Norwich, lad? I'd never have thought it."

The significance of this—whether it contained compliment or insult—escaped Colin, so he did not reply.

"Instructions from the headmaster," Sidgwick said, proffering the note in his right hand, fingers bent as if in a claw, half crushing the parchment. "You're to return home at once. You've a train leaving in less than two hours, so you'd best be on your way."

Poison twisted in Colin's gut. Expelled? How could it be? He'd done nothing.

"But, sir—" he began.

Sidgwick must have read the reaction in his face, for the old man instantly waved a hand in the air as though to erase such thoughts.

"It's not expulsion, boy. You've been summoned."

Reluctantly—as if by not doing so he might avert his fate—Colin took the note.

"But why?" he asked as he unfolded it and began to read.

Sidgwick did not wait for him to discover it on his own. "It appears," the professor said, "that your father has disappeared."

The Radford ancestral home rested on a hill in the city of Norwich, on the eastern coast of England. The seventeenth-century manse neither perched nor loomed upon its hill, and though there were many trees on the sprawling grounds, neither could it rightly be said to nestle there. Even to say the old house "stood" on that slope, with its distant view of the blue-gray waters of the English Channel, would have been a kindness. No, Colin had always thought of the house as resting there. After more than two hundred years providing hearth and shelter for the Radford family, its halls echoing with the shouts and laughter of Radford children.

Now, as the carriage that had awaited him at the train station climbed the long drive up to the front door, Colin stared at the house and considered another interpretation for his insistence upon the lazy imagery that accompanied the house's personification in his mind. Absent his father's inhabitance, the house seemed a body without its soul, a still husk of a thing, awaiting burial. Whether his own arrival might breathe some new life into the stones and beams of the place he quite doubted, as he had no intention of remaining forever, or even for very long, once his father's whereabouts had been ascertained.

For all the golden, autumnal beauty he had cherished in Ox-

ford, here in Norwich there was only gray. The sky, the stones, the prematurely bare trees, the pallor of its citizens, and the wind-chopped water of the Channel, all gray.

The carriage came to a halt, and it was not until he had climbed down and retrieved his single case that he realized he had taken for granted the comfort afforded him by the familiar clip-clop of horses' hooves on the road and the rattle of the conveyance itself. Without it, here on the hill, the only sound remaining was the wind, which, when it gusted through the hollows and eaves of the old house, moaned with the grief of a forlorn spirit or a heartbroken widow.

Fortunately, Colin Radford did not believe in ghosts. Prior to university, he had lived all of his life in this house and he knew it as a lonely place, but not haunted.

Still, he hesitated as the carriage driver snapped his reins and the carriage began to roll away. The sound that had been a comfort receded; soon not even its promise would remain and the wind would rule. Better to be inside. The timbers and stones still moaned, but sorrowful as they were—gray sounds in a gray house in a gray city—they were familiar sounds.

As he started toward the door, it swung inward. Colin looked up, expecting Filgate or one of the other servants, but the silhouette that greeted him—stepping forward, bent and defeated—belonged to the nearest thing the estate did have to a ghost: his grandmother, Abigail.

"Took your time about it, didn't you?" she said.

Trouble on the rails had delayed his arrival in London until after the last train had left for Norwich for the day, so he had been forced to spend the night in the capital and board the rescheduled train this morning. But the old woman's disapproving tone and baleful gaze discouraged any explanation. Let her think what she wished.

"I came as quickly as possible," he said, carrying his case into the foyer, where he set it down as Grandmother Abigail closed the door.

They faced each other in the elaborate foyer, surrounded by the odd religious icons that had been his father's passion and then peculiarity over the years.

"I suppose it's too much to hope that he's turned up," Colin said.

Grandmother Abigail shook her head, her lips quivering slightly, a tiny yet startling concession to her fear for her son.

"Not a trace, Collie. Not a trace," the old woman said, and then the familiar, hard mask he knew so well returned. "Word has spread throughout the city for people to be on the lookout for him, but there's been no word. The grounds have been searched and every room in the house, from attic to cellar, but the only thing down there is Edgar's mechanism."

Colin frowned. "Mechanism?"

His grandmother fluttered her hand in a way that revealed a new delicacy in her, one that he had never seen before, brought on now by fear or advancing age or some combination of the two.

"A strange contraption of metal and wood, with no purpose I ever saw or he ever shared," she said, her disdain obvious despite her concern for her son.

"I never imagined Father as much of an inventor," Colin said, mystified.

"He began building it last year, not long after an argument he had with that ugly Irish spiritualist."

Colin shivered. Finnegan had been a charlatan, no doubt, but his father had always seemed somehow to enjoy the man's company. The birdlike man with his small eyes and misshapen nose had always tried to get Colin to call him "Uncle Charlie," but as a boy he had only managed it once or twice, and as a young man, Colin had wanted nothing to do with him.

But he'd been away at university for more than a year, home only for brief visits in the summer and at Christmas, and had never thought to inquire about Finnegan. He had not even been aware that his father and the ugly Irishman had had a falling-out.

Perhaps Sir Edgar Radford had finally realized that, no matter what he claimed or what sort of show he put on, Finnegan's mediumship was a sham. The Irishman had been trying to help Sir Edgar contact his dead wife for more than a decade.

"Do you want to see it?" Grandmother Abigail asked.

Colin frowned. "See what?"

"Why, your father's mechanism. The very thing we were just discussing."

"I'd think my time better spent in joining the search, wouldn't you?"

Grandmother Abigail dropped her eyes, as though worried what he might see in them. "Perhaps."

"And yet?" Colin prodded.

The old woman lifted her gaze. "The infernal thing troubles me, that's all. In the past few weeks, your father spent so much of his time down there, and he grew increasingly irritated at any intrusion. Fervent in his efforts and . . . hostile, yes, toward anyone who might question them. But you see, I had no desire to linger in the cellar. The thing makes me uneasy, even if it doesn't . . ."

Dread climbed his spine on skittery spider legs. "Doesn't what?"

Again she glanced downward. "It doesn't work, of course."

"What is it you're keeping from me, Grandmother?"

With that, she shook her head and waved him toward the stairs. "Go on. Put your things away. Martha has seen to your room, and I'll have a meal prepared for you. I imagine you'll wish to speak to Thomas Church, who is organizing the search."

Grandmother Abigail turned away, bent with age, and began to retreat along the corridor that led to the kitchens. "Perhaps it's better you keep away from the thing after all."

Befuddled, Colin watched her go. The old woman had never treated him with the kind of warmth many associated with the role of grandmother, nor did she exhibit the witchlike sort of behavior often portrayed in stories. Neither kindly matron nor wizened crone, Abigail Radford kept mostly to herself and had a fondness for coffee over tea and biscuits rather than scones. When not knitting or strolling the grounds on watch for "pests," she had forever seemed to lurk just over young Colin's shoulder, ready to tut-tut at any seemingly imminent infraction. If he attempted to slip into the kitchen for an early taste of dinner or to snatch a cooling scone from a baking sheet, she would be there. If he jumped on his father's bed, slid on the banister, or tried to climb up onto the roof of the house, Grandmother Abigail seemed ever present, and able to dissuade him with a clucking of her tongue and the knitting of her brow.

A gray, joyless woman. And yet he knew she believed her efforts were all to keep him safe, and that in her way she loved him, a vital bit of knowledge for a boy who had grown to manhood without the benefit of a mother.

As a child, he had been told that his mother had gone off with the fairies and that one day she might return. A million fantasies had been born of this lie, and he had often imagined himself wandering into the woods in pursuit of his beautiful mother, joining her in the kingdom of the fairies, living with sprites and brownies and other creatures of magic and mischief. By the age of eight, he had begun to realize that this was mere fancy, but it was not until he turned twelve that his father told him of his mother's drowning.

Now, with his father having also "vanished," he could not help but remember the lies about his mother's death. Had Edgar Radford also gone off with the fairies? Had the old man wandered off in the grip of some dementia, been killed by brigands, or suffered some fatal misadventure?

Colin meant to find him, no matter the answer. The idea that his father's behavior had altered so radically over the past year with Colin completely un-aware of the changes unnerved him. He would join in the search. If necessary, he would begin it again and conduct it himself.

Yet even as he made this silent vow, climbing the stairs and striding down the corridor toward his childhood bed-room, he realized just how impossible a task he had set for himself. Norwich was no tiny hamlet, but a city, with thousands of dark nooks and shadowed corners, not to mention the woods and hills, and the ocean that had claimed Colin's mother. And if Sir Edgar had left Norwich somehow . . . well, he would be found only if he wished to be found, or if some unfortunate happened upon his corpse.

The quiet emptiness of the house—despite the presence of his grandmother and the servants—closed around him, suffocating, as he stepped into the bedroom. A fire had been laid in the fireplace, and logs crackled and popped, low flames dancing. The room had been decorated in shades of blue and rich cream and it ought to have been filled with the warmth—if not of the fire, then at least of memory.

Yet it was cold.

■　■　■

He did take a look that afternoon at what his grandmother had called "Edgar's mechanism," once he had searched his father's study and found no note or journal or other document that might indicate the man's state of mind prior to his vanishing.

Sir Edgar had left behind only the mechanism.

Though its intended use confounded him, Colin did not find himself unsettled by the machine the way the old woman seemed to be. Concerned, yes, even troubled—its seeming lack of purpose made him worry for the state of his father's mind—but nothing more than that. If anything, the madness inherent in the contraption's design made him hopeful that his father remained alive somewhere, that as Colin suspected, dementia had crept into his father's life and he had subsequently wandered off somewhere, forgotten the way home, and would eventually be found and returned to his family.

Dementia seemed horrid, but Colin told himself he would prefer that to learning of his father's death. Sir Edgar might be experiencing a certain amount of mental slippage, but at least Colin would be able to see him again, to provide him some comfort as he faded from the world. The man deserved that. For all of his eccentricities, Sir Edgar had been a proud, loving, and patient father.

Colin had left him behind without a single reservation, presuming that he would always be there, that there would forever be a home to which he might return, and the strange wisdom of Sir Edgar Radford to draw upon.

The air in the cellar was close and damp, warm even though the October days were chilly in Norwich and the nights even more so. Filgate had seen to it that there were lamps burning in the cellar before Colin descended, but as he examined the machine, he wished he had arranged for more light, or less. A single lamp would have done the job almost as well. With several, the light shifted and shadows played tricks upon his eyes, so that he had to use the lamp in his hand to take a closer look at the various gauges and turns and vents to ascertain their true shape and attempt to determine their purpose.

No matter how much light he shed upon the mechanism, however, he could not divine its use. During its construction, the cellar had been separated into three distinct spaces—one a wine cellar, one for cold storage, and one built around the base of a chimney, so that goods could be stored there in winter without freezing. Subsequent additions to the house had included expansions of the cellar, and it was in one of those that Sir Edgar had built his mechanism.

To Colin, it looked like discarded pieces of other machines, a tangle of pipes and flues, enormous cogs and gears, wooden joists and shelves and pulleys. Colin pulled levers and turned cranks, but his experiments with the thing yielded no result save for a clattering here and a grinding there. The machine, whatever its ambition, did not work. It did not run.

What puzzled him most were the thick iron pipes—perhaps four inches in diameter—that led off from the apparatus and directly into

the stone walls in half a dozen places. They seemed intended to carry water or steam, but the mechanism worked not at all and so Colin could not determine which.

After half an hour wasted in the gloom, he doused the lights and ascended the stairs, to find Thomas Church awaiting him in the parlor. The ruddy-faced man had the paunch and thinning white hair of a friar, but his strong, scarred hands spoke of his youth as a mason, before circumstances conspired to raise him to a life in the magistrate. As a child, Colin had always found himself impressed by the air of authority Church carried with him, in spite of his meager beginnings as a tradesman.

He spoke with authority as he told of the search effort's utter failure.

"We've peered into every hole in Norwich and combed the hills and fields," Church said grimly, running his fingers through his shaggy beard. "If Sir Edgar isn't hiding, or being hid, he'll turn up at some point. The lads I've got out looking aren't ready to give up quite yet, but in a couple of days I'll have to call it off. They've got lives to return to, y'see. Jobs and families."

"I understand, Mr. Church," Colin said. "And I hope you'll pass along my gratitude to each of them."

It was obvious Church wanted to say more, that he felt gravely dissatisfied with his own performance, but Colin could think of no words he might have spoken that would have provided solace and so he offered none. He watched Church withdraw and then depart, allowing himself no outward expression of the despair that had begun to gnaw at his heart.

That night, in the darkness of his bedroom, he felt sure he heard the walls whisper his dead mother's name.

At first he thought it might be the moan of the October wind through the gap he had left in his window. He had surfaced from a deeper sleep into a state of disorientation, that drowsy, floating limbo that always waited on either side of wakefulness. Now his thoughts began to clear and he listened more carefully, ascribing any sound to the wind, the creak of old houses, or the rustle of curtains.

And then, now fully awake, he heard it clearly. "Deirdre?"

Not a cry or a shout or even a moan as he had first believed, but a calling, as if the name were spoken by a blind man, lost and wandering, reaching out for the touch of the familiar. Colin did not recognize the voice, but it had a parched, weakened quality that might have masked its true timbre.

He sat up in bed to listen and, sure enough, the voice came again, calling his dead mother's name. "Deirdre?"

"Father?" Colin said, his own voice equally thin and reedy in the dark. Though the voice did not sound precisely like his father's, who else would be calling for long-dead Deirdre Radford in the middle of the night?

Colin sat and listened closely, but long minutes ticked past without any further occurrence. Over time, however, he slowly became aware of another sound, a low thrum or vibration, so minimal as to be almost unnoticeable. Had he not been listening so keenly, he never would have heard it, and the sound would have remained part of the shush of the world's quiet noise; the voice of a distant river, the wind on the grass, the soft breath of a slumbering lover.

Alighting from his bed, he went to the fireplace, at first believing it to be the source of the thrum. It did seem louder there, but when he bent to listen more closely, he realized the tone did not emanate from within.

As he cocked his head, trying to ascertain its origin, he placed his hand upon the mantel, then pulled it abruptly away as though he'd been burned. Thoughtfully, he put his hand once more upon the wooden mantel and felt the vibration there. With a glance around the room, wondering if the thrum was more pronounced in some corners than in others, he traced his hand along the mantel and then pressed his palm against the wall beside the fireplace.

That contact was rewarded with a shift in tone. The vibration became louder and turned, for just a moment, into a grinding noise, followed quickly by the clank of metal, like gears turning over, and then a sigh as though of steam, before it finally diminished once more to its original volume and tenor.

Somewhere in the midst of that noise, he might have heard the voice again, calling for Deirdre, but he could not be sure.

Barely aware that he was holding his breath, Colin pressed an ear to the wall. Beneath the continuous thrum he could hear a soft clicking, as of cogs turning. Abruptly he pulled away from the wall, fetched his robe, and slipped it on. Tracing his fingers along the wall to be sure the thrum did not subside or diminish, he went out into the corridor.

Colin kept his hand on the wall and then on the banister as he descended the stairs, but he already knew his destination. Only one new mechanism had been installed in the house during his time at university, and he had no doubt that his father's mysterious invention must be the source of these unfamiliar sounds.

No one else stirred as he made his way through the foyer and then along the hall to the cellar door. He thought that one or more of the servants might also be roused by the noise, though perhaps they had all grown accustomed to it over time. His grandmother had not been awakened, but she was an old woman and he presumed her hearing had deteriorated with age.

Constantly alert to any change in the sound, afraid with each creak of a floorboard beneath his feet that it might cease, Colin fumbled to light the lamp that hung by the cellar door. Its soft glow cast strange shadows as he lifted it down from its hook, so that he turned quickly, thinking that Filgate or Grandmother Abigail had heard him wandering the house and come to investigate, secretly sure in the back of his mind that his father had appeared from some hiding place to explain all.

But Colin was alone there, in front of the cellar door. And suddenly it seemed to him a dreadful idea to be up by himself in the middle of the night, about to descend into the cold and the dark and the queer depth of his father's obsession. As a boy, he had always feared the cellar, and somehow in the burgeoning confidence of his time at university, he had forgotten that fear.

Now it returned.

But that mechanical hum still vibrated in the air, and when he touched the cellar door, he felt it far more strongly than before.

"There'll be no jumping at shadows," he promised himself, and so doing, he opened the door and started down.

The cellar looked much as it had earlier. Colin took the time to light several of the lamps that Filgate had arranged for him, though it now occurred to him that some of them had likely been put in place by his father, when Sir Edgar had been working on the contraption.

Whatever he had been expecting upon his descent, however, his imagination proved far more active than the mechanism itself. The sound had gained in volume with every step as he approached the room wherein the thing had been constructed, but when he stepped inside, he had to stop and stare in surprise. No levers moved. No steam escaped the valves. Cogs did not turn. The machine was absolutely still.

Holding a single lamp in his hand, he maneuvered around the mechanism just as he had earlier in the day, his robe catching on a hinge and tearing slightly. Colin swore and continued his examination. He reached out to touch one of the bars of the mechanism with a hesitation akin to that felt when petting a stranger's dog, but only the dullest vibration could be felt in the machine itself, less so than in the wood of the cellar door.

Yet there could be no denying that the sound had grown louder as he entered this room. Colin began to walk the perimeter of the room to see if there were places where the volume rose or fell, and when he stepped over one of the pipes that jutted from the mechanism into the wall, he paused and looked back at the metal cylinder where it entered the stone foundation.

Crouching, he grasped the pipe. His whole arm trembled with the vibration traveling through it, and he pulled away. Glancing back at the machine, he saw that nothing had changed. It remained still as ever. But here, where the pipe entered the wall, its extremities thrummed with the workings of some other machine or some unknown engine to which this one was attached, off beyond the cellar wall.

Colin rose, staring at the wall. He turned in a circle, trying to figure where the pipes might lead. One by one he walked to each of the seven pipes extending from his father's mechanism, checking

to be sure, and he found that each of them vibrated just as urgently as the first. As he checked, he fancied he could hear more subtle noises now, his ears adjusting to the thrum. There were clicks and whirs, hisses and clanks. Machines.

But two of the pipes led into a wall that separated this room from another cellar chamber, and when he checked, he confirmed that they did not exit on the other side of that wall. One led into a wall that bordered nothing but stone, and must have run far under the remainder of the house, although how his father had managed to install it without excavating down through the floor of the parlor, Colin could not imagine.

This chamber sat at the southeast corner of the house, and of the remaining four pipes, two each had been pushed through holes in the south and the east walls, respectively. Colin wondered about those pipes. The two that led into the adjoining room did not emerge in that room, but what of these, which could run under the grounds outside?

He knew of only one way to find out.

With one last look at Sir Edgar's mechanism, Colin doused the lamps and retreated up the stairs. He did not bother returning to his room. Rather, he fixed a pot of tea and nibbled on a leftover apple tart in the kitchen as he waited for the sun to rise, so that he could pay a visit to Mr. Church.

"There's nothing wrong with my hearing," Grandmother Abigail insisted.

The old woman frowned at him, arms sternly crossed. When Colin had returned from town with Mr. Church and half a dozen of his workers, Grandmother Abigail had demanded to know what he thought he was doing, ordering them to dig holes in the grounds around the house.

Reluctantly, he had told her the story of his experience the previous night, including his amazement that the sounds he heard in the walls did not rouse any of the house's other residents from their beds. He had long suspected Filgate of relying heavily upon brandy to carry him off to sleep, which would explain the man's sound slumber, but his suggestion that perhaps age had diminished his grandmother's hearing brought this angry protest.

"I intended no offense," Colin said, his tone as apologetic as he could muster. "I simply cannot imagine how you managed to sleep through the noise. Granted, it wasn't especially loud, but so consistent that the irritation alone would be enough to drive one mad if it persisted long enough."

Grandmother Abigail's expression faltered, and she shrank slightly. It lasted only a moment, but long enough for Colin to realize that her pique had been a mask behind which she hid some other, more subtle, response to his inquiries.

"What is it you aren't telling me?" he asked.

She shook her head and looked away, gazing out the window at two of the workers, who even now plunged shovels into soft brown earth, piling rich soil high beside the waist-deep hole they'd dug.

"I don't know what you mean," his grandmother said.

"You did hear it," Colin guessed. "You know precisely what I'm talking about."

Her jaw seemed set, as though she might never utter another word as long as she lived. She took a deep breath and released it before turning to him.

"I heard nothing of the kind," she said. "But your father heard . . . something."

Colin straightened up. "Tell me everything."

"He said almost exactly the same thing, about the sound being enough to drive one mad, given time enough. He heard . . . vibrations, yes, but he said whatever those machines were that he heard, they had a rhythm."

Colin nodded. Though it had not occurred to him in those precise terms, he understood what his father had meant. "Was that when he began to build his own mechanism?"

Grandmother Abigail seemed pale in the sunlight shining through the window. "He thought if he could match his own machine to the rhythm, find a way to get the two in harmony, he could make his mechanism function on its own, without his—"

She'd cut herself off.

Colin stared at her. "Without his what?"

She shook her head, willing to go no further.

"Without his what?" he shouted. "Grandmother, please, there must be some connection to this mechanism and his disappearance. If there is, the only way I will be able to discover it is if I understand what he was thinking while he built it."

Grandmother Abigail regarded him coolly, as if she had separated herself from him somehow.

"He managed to make it work in some rudimentary way by placing himself within the machine. Those shelves are seats, the levers and valves meant to be operated by hand."

"But Father left no designs—"

The old woman narrowed her eyes as if daring him to challenge her. "I burned them."

"Why would you do that?"

Her mouth quivered a bit, and then she lowered her gaze. "I was afraid for you, Collie. Your father thought . . . he . . ." She steadied herself, raised her eyes, and looked at him with the clearest warning he had ever seen. "You know that ever since your mother's death, your father has been obsessed with the idea that the connection they had could not be severed, that there must be some way for him to speak to her, even beyond death. Beyond life."

Colin nodded. "All of those séances with Finnegan—"

Grandmother Abigail's expression turned to stone. "He educated himself, talked to spiritualists and scholars alike. If he heard even a whisper of some method he had not yet attempted, he experimented with it. Finnegan indulged him all along, let poor Edgar think his wish might one day be granted, and lined his own pockets with your father's money. But when your father began to talk of the sounds he heard in the walls, and when he began to build that mechanism in the cellar, Finnegan urged him to stop. No, *more* than stop. Finnegan wanted him to break it into pieces, threatened to have nothing more to do with Edgar if he refused."

Fingers of dread crept up Colin's spine. "What happened?"

"Your father had Filgate throw Finnegan out of the house and told him never to return," Grandmother Abigail said. "He kept working, building, testing that infernal machine, and less than three weeks later, Edgar vanished."

Colin turned and stared out at the hall that led to the cellar door.

"Whatever you hear in the walls, lad, you mustn't listen," the old woman said.

"And if that means we never find him?" Colin asked.

Grandmother Abigail lifted her chin, trembling slightly. "Better that than risk losing you along with him."

Colin thought on that for several long minutes, alternately looking out the window at the diggers and back into the house in the direction of the cellar. When, at length, he finally met his grandmother's gaze, she must have seen his decision in his eyes, for her shoulders slumped with sadness and surrender.

The old woman turned from him without another word and left the room, as if he had already disappeared.

Church's men dug all around the foundation of the house at the rear corner where Sir Edgar's mechanism filled the cellar room, but they found nothing. The pipes that penetrated the walls in that chamber did not emerge on the other side. Church had no explanation, nor had Colin expected one. The pipes must simply have stopped several inches into the wall.

Colin did not believe that, of course. He had jostled one of the pipes enough to know that it did not end after a few inches. And then there was the matter of the nocturnal thrum, the vibration, of the machine. Where did that come from? Colin supposed that his grandmother might be right, that he might have imagined it just as his father had done, but if that was so, then where *was* his father?

An answer to that question had begun to coalesce in the back of Colin's mind once Grandmother Abigail had told him of his father's falling-out with Finnegan, but he tried not to dwell upon it, for it seemed impossible. Felt impossible.

All that day, as Church's excavations revealed more and more of nothing and Grandmother Abigail's words resonated deeper and deeper in his mind, Colin felt a growing anxiety. With the onset of evening, emotional tremors passed through him, a queer combination of unease and anticipation. There could be no doubt what his next course of action must be, and over the dinner table he saw in his grandmother's eyes that she knew it as well. They barely spoke during the meal, and when it had concluded she excused herself, claiming a headache, and retired for the night.

Soon enough, Colin found himself alone in the parlor with a glass of brandy and a crackling fire, all of the servants having withdrawn.

He did not even pretend to retire for the night. Instead, he waited there in the parlor, listening for the hum and staring at a shelf of his father's old books without even the smallest temptation to pluck one down to read. He sipped brandy and felt himself grow heavy with the influence of the alcohol and the warmth of the fire, but as drowsy as he became, he would not allow himself to doze.

He felt his father nearby, as if, were he to close his eyes and reach out, he might grasp Sir Edgar's hand or tug his sleeve. The feeling chilled and warmed him in equal measure, and it occurred to him that this must be how his father had felt for so many years about his late mother. He had always talked of feeling her nearness, of his confidence that her spirit lingered, awaiting him, attempting to contact him, if only he could find the means to receive that communication.

Enough brandy, and the walls Colin had built inside his mind to prevent him thinking about his more outlandish theories regarding his father's disappearance began to break down. A little more, and he stopped denying to himself the certainty that had formed in the back of his mind. Somehow, in attempting to contact his mother, his father had succeeded in breaking down a wall, tearing away the curtain between what Colin knew as tangible reality and some other existence. Whether his father was alive or dead, he did not know, but he felt sure that in matching the rhythm of the vibration in the walls, he had slipped out of the world.

Yet he felt just as certain that his father was still in the house— still down there in the cellar—and if he could match that same

rhythm, as his father had done, it might be possible to draw the curtain back one more time and let Sir Edgar return.

A loud, sobering voice spoke up at the back of his mind, warning him that he might share his father's fate, but he took another sip of brandy and pushed the thought away. If his father had stepped onto another plane of existence, joining him there was far from the worst thing Colin could imagine. And *not* attempting to save his father was inconceivable.

Sometime after midnight, his vigilance was rewarded with a whisper.

"Deirdre," said the walls. But now he felt sure the voice belonged to his father.

The thrum began moments later, and Colin set aside his brandy snifter, rose from his chair, and walked from the parlor, swaying only slightly.

■　■　■

Intuition guided him—at least that was what he told himself at first. From the moment he hoisted himself up onto the wooden shelf that functioned as a seat, and settled his arms onto the two smaller shelves that were angled downward toward the levers, he felt in tune with the machine. The support behind his arms gave him leverage, the seat taking his weight left his legs mostly free. Some of what had seemed to be levers were actually pedals.

But it wasn't enough simply to work those levers and pedals. One valve protruded from a metal arm that, when swung in front of his face, behaved more like the mouthpiece of a trumpet. When he breathed into it, the valve seemed to draw greedily from the air in his lungs until he found the perfect rhythm of inhale and exhale.

His breath powered the machine, as did his arms and legs. He listened so carefully to the rhythm in the walls, the clank and grind, the thrum and vibration, and worked his body—his own mechanism—to match it. Somehow, he knew, he had to find a way to meld himself to his father's machine, to turn the two mechanisms into one, acting in concert, and then extend that unification to the other machines beyond the walls, wherever they were, and to the mechanism that was his father. He could feel Sir Edgar there with him, breathing with him, moving with him, as if the man's body had been scattered into tiny particles that filled the air of the chamber.

The brandy had numbed him at first, blurred his thoughts, but soon it seemed to help crystallize them instead. Inhale. Exhale. Left hand, right foot, left foot, right hand, both feet, twist of the neck, inhale, exhale, inhale-exhale, as though playing a tune, a one-man orchestra, his body, the mechanism, a symphony.

Hours passed. His body did not require rest, did not crave food or even water. The machine was enough, feeding him, breathing through him. His limbs began to move of their own accord, instructed not by his own conscious thoughts but by the necessity of the machine.

"Deirdre," a voice whispered, so close it might have been breathing in his ear.

The rhythm, perfectly matched.

Elated, he opened his eyes, unaware that he had ever closed them, and saw that the curtain had at last been drawn aside. There were no walls any longer, only the machine, only mechanisms as far as his eyes could see in every direction.

Close by, perhaps twenty feet away, Sir Edgar Radford moved in unison with the machine, in perpetual motion. Arms and legs, inhale-exhale. Pulling his mouth away to whisper and then darting forward again to place his lips on the valve. Pipes passed into his flesh and out the other side. Some seemed made of bone. Cables of sinew ran around pulleys, moving his limbs like the strings of a marionette.

The man's eyes gazed into the awful distance where cogs turned and pulleys rattled and levers rose and fell, and he never blinked.

"Father?" Colin said, his voice a new part of the rhythm between inhale and exhale.

His father did not seem to hear. He only stared deeper into the machine, far off across the joined mechanisms of this place behind the curtain.

"Deirdre?" Sir Edgar whispered.

Then Colin heard it, from far off. A reply. "Edgar?"

He watched as his father bent to his labors, working the mechanism feverishly, that one whisper of his name enough to drive him on with the promise that he had almost succeeded in his goal, that if he could draw back one more curtain, he might be with her at last.

"Deirdre?" Sir Edgar said again.

But this time, the voice that replied did not speak his father's name.

"Colin?" it said, so close he could feel her there, just out of reach.

He tried to scream but the valve stole his breath, requiring it to maintain the rhythm of the machine.

Inhale.

Exhale.

Every Wrong Turn
Tim Lebbon

He knew the way to Hell, because he had a map.

"There," he said, even though there was no one to hear, "just there." And he sat slowly in the long, lush grass, dropping his rucksack, water bottle, and hat. He was sweating, even though the air was cool and the leaden sky promised snow. The only item he refused to let leave his grip was the clear plastic wrapper containing the map. He had laughed, once, just after leaving the main road and starting down into the valley, because he'd imagined himself as one of those Sunday-afternoon orienteers he and Michelle had so often watched from the pub window. Come rain or shine they had always appeared, and come rain or shine he and his wife had taken their usual seats by the bar, watching, mocking. After that first burst of laughter two days before, he had mocked no more. He realized now part of what drove them: the need to know the way. And he knew the danger in maps.

Where routes and roads had once led here there was now forest, and streams, and places where the sense of wildness would put off many casual travelers. It was an easy place in which to get lost, and several times he had seen evidence of people having come this way, only to turn back again: abandoned walking gear, discarded food wrappers, and once an old tent that had been home to moss and flies. He wondered what thoughts would intrude to wanderers coming this far without knowing for sure what they sought. He thought perhaps they would return home with the urge to kill, or to hurt even more.

But he had gone farther, and found his way.

The old house seemed to be in good condition, considering it had been abandoned for so long. The map placed it farther along the valley floor. Perhaps it moved sometimes, when no one was looking; or maybe the mapmaker was insane. He stared down from the lower slopes of the valley side at the place where he was going, and tried to take stock. The walls were alive with ivy and other parasitic growths. The grounds were overgrown, yet order was still discernable here and there; walls stood upright, rose arches protruded above barren paths, and trees were set at precise spacings across the extensive gardens. Between trees and rose gardens, beyond a pond gone to scum, he could just make out the elaborate entrance to the maze.

Labyrinth, he thought, because it was so much *more* than a maze. The hedges beyond the stone entrance were confused from this distance by overgrowth, and he was worried that time had stolen the route away. But then he looked at the map again and knew that was not the case. The map said "maze" but promised so much more, and such promises were rarely wasted on lies.

Carrying only the map, he started down the hillside on his final approach to the place where life would change. Already he had come farther than most, and he felt a scratch of pride at that. He smiled—a sad, vacant expression like a corpse opening its mouth. Pride would be taken from him soon. He was where he needed to be, and solving the labyrinth would punish him for every wrong turn he had made in his life.

"Take me," he whispered, hoping that Hell would reach forward and snatch him away. It knew his intentions and perceived his mind, didn't it? It knew that he belonged? But it could never be that easy.

As he climbed the dilapidated wall marking the boundary of the garden, he prepared himself for what he would soon face.

The house itself held no interest for him. It was said that an old man had once lived here, a one-eyed veteran of the Great War who had returned with something he'd found on the battlefields of Ypres and gone about constructing the labyrinth that bound the house to the valley forever. It was common knowledge that he had disappeared many years ago, but the truth of his disappearance was more precious. According to the map, and the jumbled and confused notes inscribed in its borders by some of those who had used it, the old man was still here.

So he walked into the garden, and it had gone wild. Rosebushes with stems four inches through ran rampant. Grasses grew long and swayed in the slight breeze. Brambles had invaded from beyond, smothering less hardy plants, and here and there he saw the vain attempts of those drowned plants to peer through; weak flowers, insipid leaves. That they were not yet dead meant, perhaps, the brambles were still embarking upon their gradual invasion. Close to the garden pond, a spread of Japanese knotweed had one part of the garden all to itself. He could still make out evidence of cultivation and some form of order, but now it was only slight. Easier to perceive it from a distance; this close in, he saw only the wildness.

It had the air of a fairy-tale garden, but he knew there was no princess trapped at its center.

He stopped to pick some fruit. They looked like strawberries, though easily twice the size of any he had ever seen, and the color was a deep, rich bruise purple. When he touched a fruit, though, it was warm. He left it alone.

The map clasped in his hand, he pushed his way along a path that was no longer there. The house loomed to his left, dark and gloomy with the sun falling behind it. There were open windows there, and doorways shorn of their doors, and he thought he saw the glitter of smashed glass. He was not close enough to hear the whisper of windblown ivy, but he could still make out the subtle movements even in the darkness, as if the house's skin were flexing as it prepared for night.

"This way," he said, challenging the garden to tell him otherwise. From a distance the route had seemed clear, but down in the garden the fear persisted that he was going in the wrong direction. He had seen the stone entrance to the labyrinth, but if he could not find it, would it remain open for him forever? Panic settled over him like a dusting of pollen, and he started to push faster through the exotic undergrowth.

One moment there was a wall of foliage before him, alive with the movement of flies and insects; the next, a spread of unkempt lawn, and then the stone gate. He gasped and paused, glancing back the way he had come, expecting to see nothing but lawn behind him as well. But the wall of undergrowth stood behind him, and there was no evidence at all of where he had just emerged. It was as if he had been standing here forever.

"There it is," he whispered to the air, expecting and receiving no answer. "That's the way." He walked forward slowly, reached out to touch the stone surround . . . and then stopped. *Is this my last chance?* he thought. He looked back up at the hillside, trying to make out the place from which he had so recently observed this gateway. But he could see nothing. He tried to blink away darkness, but the hillside had shunned sunlight and welcomed the shadows. "I deserve this," he said, and a flush of such intense self-hatred washed across him that he could have finished it there and then.

But if he did that, there would be no *more*.

So he passed through the stone gateway into the labyrinth, a smile on his face.

He had spent a long time looking for this place. He'd explored labyrinths far and wide trying to find the right one, and researched those of antiquity: the Cretan labyrinth, created by Daedalus to imprison the Minotaur; the labyrinth of Clusium, ordered by King Lars Porsena of Etruria for his tomb. And more modern constructs had featured in his research as well, from those built in the grounds of great manor houses, to the less obvious labyrinths contained and hidden within inner-city housing plans. Each had fascinated him; none had been what he sought.

And then the map. He had been searching for a long time, but in the end it had found him. And that is what convinced him of its worth.

Heart beating, skin sheened with sweat even though the sun was going down and the already cool air was colder still, he followed the path away from the stone gate. Minutes or hours passed, and not for an instant did he know what to expect. So he walked on, fascinated by the walls of the labyrinth, because they seemed to be maintained.

Given time and neglect, this place would have filled in with untempered growth. But the routes he took were free of intrusion. *There must be a gardener*, he thought, and he listened for the sound of shears.

Around the next corner he saw the first of his great sins.

He gasped and went to his knees. *I always knew it would be this*, he thought, but the reality of being faced with such a moment from his past was almost too much. His blood ran cool, and yet, as if to mirror the great sin, the blood in his crotch flushed hot. He closed his eyes in shame, but opened them again in lust.

So then, and as now, lust overcomes the shame.

She is far too drunk to even stand, and he has one arm slung around her back, hand beneath her armpit to prop her up. She is laughing and giggling, crying and muttering, and he is half dragging, half carrying her uphill toward the park. People pass them on the way home from the pubs, most of them too drunk to even notice.

He does not have that excuse. A few drinks, yes, but he is far from drunk, and far from not knowing right from wrong. Yet every now and then her loose left arm stiffens a little, her hand stealing across to the front of his trousers as she utters something between a purr and a belch.

"I'm taking you home," he says, and that is not the truth at all. The park gates are closed, but the railings have been bent aside by a generation of drunken teens. He feeds her through and follows, picking her up and guiding her toward the bandstand.

She slips from his grasp, loose and weak, and vomits as she falls onto her side. She has passed out completely now, and he looks around, trying to judge whether it is safe enough here, or if he should pull her into the shadows.

He watched himself, knowing what was to come next. His erection had subsided, because the memory was too harsh to bear, and though he tried to close his eyes, he could not, and he saw himself turning the unconscious girl over and tugging at her clothing.

To his left lay another route into the labyrinth, and he went that way before he had to see any more.

"I'm sorry," he whispered. "I'm sorry, Michelle. So sorry." He had married her four years later, and she had always remembered their first lovemaking to be in her own bed weeks after that dark incident in the park. Over time he had somehow driven it deep down in his mind, giving it the hue of some minor indiscretion rather than what it actually was. And sometimes during their marriage, Michelle liked to role-play, and she asked him to treat her rough. To his shame, the memory made that much easier.

He started running, as if to outrun the recollections. He glanced back, but already his younger self was lost to a curve in the path, still grunting back there in that park from many years before. If only he could go back and change things . . . but this was not about going back. This had always been about going forward. His greatest wish was that he could do so without reliving the reasons why.

Still running, he came to another junction. *Always keep left,* he thought. *Or is it right?* But he was sure that such rules would not apply in here.

He paused and looked up at the dusky sky. A few stars were out already, and he wondered whether any of them would be in constellations he knew. That chilled him, and for a moment he almost turned back. *What have I done?* he wondered. He still clasped the map in his hand, and though he willed his hand to open, he would not let it go. Bringing it closer to his face, he tried to see whether anything on it had changed. But it was growing too dark to see.

What he wanted, craved, was here, he knew it. What he *deserved*. Such things he had done in life, and in death—or whatever death became in a place like this—he would experience so much more. Much of it was the suggestion of punishment, but beyond that, hidden deep like the memories of that secluded park's rape, was the need for him to feel what this place offered. His loathing of mediocrity had often been his target of blame for the things he had done, and now here he sought the means to go beyond the mediocre spread of sensations he had experienced through his life. He sought more, and there were such stories . . .

He turned right, and soon the path led down a set of stone steps, treads worn through time and use. The paving underfoot changed from simple lawn to an elaborate jigsaw of stone pieces. The hedges continued higher than before, so that even if he jumped he could not touch their heads. Roses and brambles, flowers and fruits hung heavy. Some of the roses were scented to match their appearance; fleshy, secretive. He found himself aroused, so he ran again in case more memories came back to him.

The path opened into a small square, surrounded on all sides by the high hedges. There were two other exits from the courtyard, and before one of them he saw a man he had killed fifteen years before.

He froze, gasping in a breath that would not come. *Of course not, no breath, no air, because this is when it happens, this is when they come for me, when they're reminding me of one of my greatest sins.*

But a breath came then, and with it the memory began to play out.

Marcus is twenty-five, and he thinks he knows pain. His body is a shrine to agony. Piercings have given way to more intrusive adaptations: a tin can inserted into his abdomen; three thick nails driven just so that they pierce but do not break his skull; tattooed skin flayed from his legs, stretched and hung around a framework of matchsticks and knitting needles. Marcus cries often, and sometimes his tears are dark as blood.

But he knows the truth. He knows that Marcus is a fake, and that the bloody tears are simply dye injected into his tear ducts each morning along with the heroin that goes into his eyes.

"I'm going further," Marcus says.

"You're pathetic," he says, laughing.

Marcus looks sad, offended, dye-streaked eyes wide as a whipped dog's.

"Look at you," he says. Such a command is easy, because Marcus has his room lined with mirrors, both walls and ceiling. His dedication is such an indulgence. "You think pain is the way, and then you dull yourself with that shit you inject every day. You strut through town, thinking that stares are the badge to being different. But you're still just like them."

"No . . ." Marcus begins.

"Yes! Still average, still just another fucking number on a computer somewhere, because this . . ." He takes hold of the delicate rack around Marcus's right leg. "This is only skin deep." And he pulls.

Marcus screams. He sounds like a pig being slaughtered.

"Shut up," he says. He grabs at the tin can in Marcus's stomach, twisting, driving it deeper than the wound allows.

Marcus screams some more, a snotty, gargling sound.

"That's better," he says, because he can feel something happening. He sees himself in the mirrors, echoed endless times as he performs endless tortures, and the surroundings begin to feel unreal. Mirrors steam and flex, making Marcus's reflection extraordinary at last, and he grabs a mug from a table and rests it against one of the nail heads in the pathetic fucker's skull.

The scream halts, and silence screams even more.

Marcus is looking at him now. Pleading. Crying tears of real blood, shaking his head, denying everything he has ever wanted.

"Pussy," he says.

Turning away, he gasped as he ran to the exit from the courtyard not blocked by this memory from his past. The final events in that mirrored room he had no wish to see again. From behind he heard the dull thud of china against metal, and then metal through bone.

"He made me angry!" he shouted. "He was a . . . *charlatan!*" But if the labyrinth heard, and even understood, it offered no judgment. So he ran faster, trying to outpace the screams that he knew were coming. He turned corners, skipped through junctions without a thought, desperate to put as many walls and turns as possible between him and the echo of his time in that mirrored room.

When Marcus's screams came, they were just as he remembered them.

All he could do was run.

And all at once, the labyrinth changed. Hedges vanished, to be replaced by sheer fences made of curved, intertwined twigs. The ground was overlaid with thicker branches, and here and there soil protruded through, wet and coiled. He could still see the sky if he looked up, but it was hazy now, and drifting skeins of mist gave the impression of uneasy movement.

"Where is the end?" he whispered. His voice carried hardly at all, and there was no echo. "Where is the middle?" He was slowly solving this labyrinth, he was sure, because those bad memories were marking the way to damnation. He did not deny their truths, but neither did he have any wish to live through them again. The memories were bad enough when he slept, or when his mind wandered . . . being shown them, hearing, smelling, that was all too much. Though he still clasped the paper map in its clear wrapper, he now followed the map of his mind.

The stick fences rattled as he passed by, his movement setting them shivering. He slowed to a fast walk, and at every junction he let instinct guide him on. Left, right, straight ahead, but he never once turned back. That would be too much like admitting fear, and that was one thing he could never do. He had never been afraid.

At the next junction, he sees his daughter Jenny sitting in her bedroom, playing with a collection of farm animals and dinosaurs as if they can live together. In her mind they can . . . she is a sweet young girl, innocent, beautiful, and given the right chances she could grow into someone wonderful. But the door opens, and he enters, readying to take those chances away.

"No," he said in the labyrinth, but his feet would not move him away.

"Daddy!" she says. Her eyes go wide—she has not seen him for some time—as he enters the room. Michelle is downstairs crying, because she knows what is to come. Her hopes that he had come back to stay were just that: hopes. He is far too selfish. This is all too . . . *normal* for him.

"Jenny," he says, "got something to tell you." Her little face drops, because she's not so innocent after all. In her world of cows and sheep and T. rex, good things can happen because she wishes them so. In this harsher, more grown-up world, reality bites.

He does not care. His eyes are far away, his attention directed somewhere distant and much darker than here. As he tells her he is going away forever, and that she will never see him again, and that her mother will raise her and tell her what happened when the time comes, he does not once look at the crying little girl.

"She won't have to tell me!" Jenny says, sweeping her hand through the rank of plastic animals. "I know it all myself. You don't love me, that's it, and you're just what she says . . . a cow . . . a cow-wood!"

He shows the first sign of emotion then when he looks at her.

And in the labyrinth, he backed away at last, but the great twig fences had closed in around him. There was only one way to go, and he ran, leaving the terrible memory of the next few moments behind. He knew that fleeing would mean he heard nothing, because there had been nothing to hear. Jenny had not screamed when he hit her then, but she had spent the rest of her life screaming. A shattered prospect. The ruin of a girl.

He ran on, surprised at the moisture on his cheeks. He glanced up but it was not yet snowing. The sky was dark now, and peering between clouds, long-dead stars observed his fate.

"Come and take me now!" he shouted. "I *know* what I've done!

I don't need reminding! They told me you were hungry, so come and feast." He had discovered the map in a junk shop in Tintern. Overshadowed by the ancient remains of the ruined abbey, More Things had opened its doors to him as he walked by, and inside, an old man had been running a razor blade gently across his right eyeball. He'd smiled and said, "All the better to see you with."

And then the map had been in his hands, and as he'd turned to leave, the old man had laughed behind him, and several voices had emerged at once from the shell of a dead grandfather clock. Its hands must not have moved for many years, because they were dusted into place. That frozen time had spoken of tortures and delights that he could barely imagine; voices intermingled, a woman, man, and child, and others, all speaking the same words and combining to make the same steady, ecstatic voice. Spilled out onto the street, the shop's facade now changed to a boarded-up ice cream parlor, he had sat and cried until he realized he still held the map.

"They told me you were *hungry!*" he shouted again. The memory of those voices had always haunted him, because they had been ghosts.

But his exhortations brought no success. He went on, passing through more sections of the labyrinth, trusting instinct to guide him deeper. True night came, and in the darkness he was shown times in his past when the worst of him came to the fore. Each was an illustration of why he was here, he knew, and why he would find the center. But he found their replays . . . *repellent*. He had no wish to see the time he had beaten Michelle around the face with a knotted rope. He had no desire to hear his own gargled cries as he let three strange women tie him and pour containers of stinging wood ants across his naked body. The nightclub dancer he had assaulted . . . the weak man called Duke who had let him inject him with a drug cocktail of his own making . . . the tattoo artist, drunk and scared, trying to tattoo the exposed bone in his sliced thigh—all things he had no need or means to deny, but events he felt compelled to turn away from. Hadn't living them been enough? They were guiding him in, after all, and the faster he reached the center, the faster this last part of the beginning of his life would be over.

So he ran quicker, and every time he turned a corner and saw a fresh tableau laid out before him, he turned away, avoiding the route that memory marked.

Eventually, just as dawn came and sunlight began bathing the labyrinth afresh, he reached the center.

But this was not the center he sought.

The thing standing in the middle was connected to everything. He knew it was one of them, but at the same time he felt a terrible, creeping dread. *Something's wrong!* he thought.

"Yes," the creature said, "something is."

"Who are you?" He had fallen to his knees at the edge of the clearing, the map still clasped in his right hand.

"The Gardener. I . . . tend." And even as it spoke, the thing *was* tending. Its arms were raised, rose branches and other plants stretching from the tips of its fingers to the surrounding hedges. It flexed those fingers, and the hedges blossomed. Its head was a knotted sculpture of wood, skin harsh and leathery, and one eye was covered with the remains of a black eyepatch. Its feet were rooted to the ground.

"I've found you," the man said, because it was what he thought he was supposed to say. Even as the words left his mouth, he knew he was wrong. He had found this thing, this Gardener, but what he had been searching for was still very far away.

The Gardener was naked, skin slashed and shredded where the shoots of new things nosed out from inside. He noticed that nuggets of dried flesh clung to the many long stems stretching across the clearing, and on their thorns the blood was fresher.

The realization hit him then: This thing was not simply at the center of the labyrinth; it *was* the labyrinth.

"You have indeed," the Gardener said.

"But . . . but . . . won't you show me?"

The Gardener laughed. It was a horrible sound, because it came from a throat that still thought itself human.

"Show me . . ." he said again, pleading this time. "I found my way through the labyrinth, looking for you, just like the map said."

"Did the map say to follow your desires?"

"Yes. Yes!"

"Then why did you avoid them?"

"I . . ." the man began, but he looked away from the Gardener then, glancing past at where other routes opened up in the clearing's edges. *Through there*, he thought. *Maybe through there. All I have to do is get past, a final test.*

"You saw every moment that should have given you to them, and you closed your eyes to them all."

He ran. Denying the truth of what the Gardener said, denying the fact that he hated the things he had done, and did not adore them as he had first thought, and yet craving still that ultimate sensation and experience, because there was really nothing of him left. Not after so long, after so much. This was his whole reason, and he had come so far.

"I belong here!" he shouted.

He made it halfway across the clearing before rose stems whipped around him, holding him fast. Inch-long thorns penetrated his throat, chest, scrotum, neck, eyes. He cried out, laughing because he thought this was it.

The Gardener stroked one gentle tendril down his cheek. He became aroused. And then it plucked the map from his hand and whispered into his face, "Until you learn to relish the pain of every bad thing you have ever done, you belong . . . nowhere."

Pain ended.

Noise began.

He shouted in surprise, because he was trapped. He saw where he was, but he had no control. He was all inside, the shout silent and agonizing, and loaded with such a sense of loss and failure that he was sure he must go mad. But he was also sure, as understanding dawned, that madness would be far too easy.

And it would never be allowed.

"Gonna get me another drink?" Michelle slurred into his mouth. Lights flashed, music blared. She was young and pretty, this first time he had met her. But she'd already had far too much.

The Collector
Kelley Armstrong

The wooden puzzle box floated on my computer screen, a 3-D model perfectly rendered, the liquid display bubbling under my fingertips as I traced the series of twists and turns that would unlock its mysteries. There, and there and . . . yes, *there*. I smiled.

I couldn't resist mousing over to it and clicking, just in case it proved interactive. It wasn't, of course. Simply an amazing piece of art, the splash screen gateway to the website of a small publisher of puzzle books.

I clicked the *enter here* entreaty, feeling a frisson of grief as that perfect puzzle evaporated, replaced by a perfectly boring website. Now I imagined the solution to another challenge—how, as a web designer, I could make this site so much better. From the looks of it, though, my services would be more than they could afford, so I directed my gaze to the upper right-hand corner, where, as I'd been told, there was a second entreaty—this one to try an online puzzle and win a prize.

So I clicked and read, checking it out so carefully you'd think they were asking me to donate a kidney, not enter a free contest. But you can't be too careful on the web. Ninety-nine percent of freebies are bullshit. Fortunately, most of those are obvious—badly worded and misspelled missives that never quite explain how a Nigerian prince got the e-mail address of Mrs. Joe Smith in Nowhere, Idaho.

There is, however, that other 1 percent—legitimate giveaways for promotional exposure—and this seemed to be one of them. Solve a puzzle; win a prize; progress to the next level for a bigger prize. The entry-level contest would win you a downloadable sixteen-page puzzle book. A reasonable reward for a reasonably simple puzzle, one I solved absently, as most of my brain was still occupied reading the page's fine print.

I entered the solution for the anagram and was redirected to a page with my prize available for immediate download. I scanned the file for viruses, of course, but it was clean. And that was it. They didn't even request an e-mail address to be signed up for "exciting promotional offers." The page simply gave me a code that would allow me to progress to the next level . . . after a twenty-four-hour waiting period.

I jotted down the code, bookmarked the site, and flipped back to my work.

Over the next week, I proceeded through four more levels, solving a Sudoku, a tangram, a Tower of Hanoi, and a Takegaki, and winning a sample book, a three-volume collection, a limited-edition omnibus, and a brass-plated n-puzzle with the company logo on the tile's squares. I needed to provide a mailing address for those, which was fine. I gave my name—common enough—and a post office box. I wouldn't be rushing to collect them, though. My reward came in knowing I'd already gotten further than anyone in the puzzle enthusiast e-mail loop that had first announced the contest.

By day eight, I was sitting at my computer, one eye on the clock, waiting for my next twenty-four-hour hiatus to be up.

My cell phone chirped. When I saw the number, I smiled and picked up.

"Hey, there. Conference end early?"

Daniel sighed. "I wish. I just called to say hi, see whether you'd be free for dinner Friday when I get in."

"You aren't tired of eating out yet?"

"As long as they don't serve conference luncheon rubber chicken, I'm good."

A message box popped up on my screen, telling me it was time, and I missed what he said next. I um-hmm'd appropriately, but my mind was already on the next puzzle. It was a variation on the classic zebra puzzle, otherwise known as Einstein's Riddle. Now this was something worth solving.

"And then I rode a camel through Pittsburgh . . ."

"What?"

"Ah, you *are* listening. Working?"

"Caught me."

"On a puzzle?"

I swore, and apologized. He only laughed, then let me go after we set a date for Friday. Even as I hung up, I was pulling over a sheet of paper and drawing my grid for the puzzle.

I solved it, of course. I shouldn't say that so nonchalantly. It was hard. Damn hard. Logic puzzles aren't my forte. By the time I figured it out, I'd passed my twenty-four-hour waiting limit. Even when I submitted the answer, I wasn't certain I had it right, and the site didn't tell me, just said the answer needed to be manually processed and asked for my e-mail address, with a promise to provide a response within twelve hours. I gave them my throwaway Hotmail one.

Dramatically, at the top of the eleventh hour, the e-mail arrived. My prize? An invitation to try for the grand prize: five thousand dollars. The catch? I had to go to the publisher's office and solve the same wooden puzzle that was rotating on their splash page.

Now, as a small business owner, I could see the point in this. If you're going to give away real money, you want to get your promotional mileage out of it. Have the prospective winner come down, solve the puzzle, and film the big event for your website. Travel could be a problem for some respondents, but according to the address given, it was just over an hour away. Asking me to drive there was perfectly reasonable for a five-grand payoff.

And yet . . .

I didn't buy my house until I could afford a 50 percent down payment. I'd been dating Daniel for four years, yet had dodged the marriage question, waiting to be sure we'd make it to five. I vetted every client before accepting them. I checked the weather forecast before going out. I had never jaywalked in my life.

I don't take chances. Not even when it comes to my beloved puzzles.

So I researched the puzzle publisher. I verified that the address given was correct, as was the phone number. Then I called using a blocked number.

A woman answered the phone. Elderly, by the creaks and warbles in her voice. Her son owned the business and she was his office assistant. She explained the deal exactly as outlined in the e-mail—come to the office, solve the wooden puzzle, win the prize. Of course, if I won, I had to agree to allow my name and photo to be displayed on their site, et cetera, et cetera.

I was given an appointment time. There was street parking, but the municipality towed after an hour and was usually waiting to jump, so she advised me to park a block away at a strip mall.

After the call, I reloaded the company's splash page and started mentally working through the puzzle again.

The office was what I expected—a few rooms in a small building. As I'd been warned, there was a tiny lot for the building's other tenants—a nightclub and an after-hours clinic—but it had been split in half, one side for each business, with signs warning that anyone else would be towed, which seemed highly unfair to the publishing company, given that it was open when the others weren't.

With everything else closed, the building was quiet, my footsteps echoing through the hall, the silence ominous in that horror movie "walking down a dark alley" kind of way that made me check over my shoulder every few steps.

When I reached the publisher's office, though, I relaxed. The cheery yellow walls and comfy furniture helped, but it was the rest of the decor that put me at ease. Puzzles. The room was filled with them, from wooden ones on the coffee table to visual ones on the wall to special pieces on pedestals.

As the publisher's mother put my coat away, I walked over to a very old Moku-Zougan Japanese puzzle box and brushed my fingertips over the worn finish, shivering.

"You're a collector, Mrs. Collins?" I asked as she returned.

"My son is. Call me Nell."

Nell wasn't as old as I would have guessed over the phone. Maybe sixty, but careworn, her face lined, hair white, a slight stoop in her shoulders.

She looked around absently, as if for a moment forgetting what she was there for, then said, "Let me get the puzzle."

She bustled off. I heard her speaking in the inner office, her voice too low to make out the words. She returned with the puzzle box, held at arm's length like an offering.

"My son's getting the video camera for us. He's so much better at that sort of thing."

I balled my hands to keep myself from snatching the puzzle box from her. It was even more exquisite than it had looked on the screen, each piece worn smooth from countless hands trying to unlock its mysteries.

"It's not easy, I'm afraid," she said as she handed it to me.

I smiled. "If it was, you wouldn't be giving away such a prize. Have there been others?"

"A few. But they haven't . . ." She trailed off.

"Haven't solved it."

"Yes. I'm sorry. I shouldn't be discouraging you."

I flashed her a bigger smile. "Oh, I'm not discouraged. The worthiest puzzle is the one no one else can solve." I turned a piece, pulse leaping as it snapped into place. I started to turn another, then stopped. "Should I wait?"

"No, no, that's fine. He'll come when you're closer to the end. It may take a while."

I looked at her. She was leaning forward, eyes fixed on the puzzle, glittering as I turned the second piece. Then the third.

"Do you do puzzles yourself?" I asked.

She shook her head, gaze never wavering from the box as I continued to click the pieces into place.

"You're very good," she said.

I said nothing, only kept turning, kept hearing that satisfying click.

"No one's ever gotten that far." She breathed in an awestruck whisper.

"It's almost done. You might want to get your son."

"He's busy. If you solve it, we can always restage it."

I set the puzzle box down. It clacked against the glass tabletop and she jumped at the sound.

"But . . ." she began. "You were almost—"

"I trust you have a standard release form drawn up?" I said.

"Release form?"

"Giving you permission to use my name and image for promotional purposes. As well as guaranteeing me my prize, should I solve the puzzle."

Her eyes narrowed, eyeing me as if I were an unreasonable child.

"I suppose I could get one," she said, turning away.

"Good. And I'd like to meet your son."

She froze, shoulders stiffening.

"Do you even have a son, Mrs. Collins?" I asked.

She pivoted slowly, not answering. I hefted my purse and headed for the door.

"Stop," she said.

I turned to see a gun trained on me.

"Ah," I said. "That's how it is, then."

"I would like you to complete the puzzle, Ms. Lane. In fact, I insist on it."

I walked over and picked up the puzzle box. I turned it over in my hands, the wood so velvety smooth, so inviting, that it took all my willpower not to start turning the final pieces.

"A Lemarchand's Configuration, I presume?"

She blinked. "You know it?"

I lifted it to eye level, peering into its dark cracks. "It's a legendary collection of pieces. Every enthusiast has heard the story."

"Well, I'm not an *enthusiast*." She twisted the word like an insult. "My son is. The puzzle is his."

I glanced toward the inner office and heard sounds within—an oddly wet, squelching noise, as if someone was pacing in sodden slippers.

"My son," she said. "He solved it two years ago, and *they* came."

"The Cenobites."

"Yes. The things they did to him . . ." She shuddered. "But he escaped. He came back and I found him. He was in pain, so much pain, and the only way to ease it was to feed him."

"Not with steak and eggs, I presume."

She looked at me sharply and lifted the gun, as if to remind me this was a serious situation and perhaps I should be a little less blasé about the whole thing.

I went on. "So you lure people here with your contests and feed them to your darling boy. And no one wonders where they've gone? I find that hard to believe."

"Do you? Puzzle enthusiasts are a solitary lot, as you might know, Sarah Lane, age thirty-four, self-employed, never married, no children, no siblings, mother deceased, father in Brazil."

"You've done your research. Let me guess: after you kill me, you'll take my keys and move my car from that distant lot, so when someone does look for me . . ."

"You were never here."

It was a far from foolproof plan, but from the burning glow in her eyes, I could tell she was beyond caring. However, mad though she might be, outside of bad movies, I suspect villains don't stand around explaining the situation to their victims. Which begged the question . . .

I turned the puzzle over in my hands. "You *do* want me to solve this. That's why you run the contests, looking for someone who can do it. But why would you want the box opened if you've seen what happens?"

"I want to summon them. Those Cenobites. To take him back." She met my gaze. "There is a limit to maternal obligation."

"If I succeed, you'll be free of your son, and if I fail, he'll be fed."

"Precisely. So"—she waved the gun at the puzzle—"if you please."

I completed another twist and again heard the satisfying click of success. As I started the next, she leaned in, gun lowering, gaze fixed once more on the wooden box. The piece clicked into place. I pulled my hand back, reaching to the other side to complete the final turn, and grabbed her wrist, shoving the gun up.

She didn't relinquish the weapon. Put up a good fight for her age, actually. But I was younger, faster, stronger, and when the gun fired, it wasn't my head it was pointing at.

As I knelt beside her body, an unearthly wail battered my eardrums. I looked up to see a figure in the doorway of the inner office. He looked as if he'd been ripped apart and haphazardly sewn back together, every joint from his jaw to his fingers gaping, held together with thick black thread, shredded flesh hanging, bones poking through.

When I didn't run away screaming, he hesitated, confused. Then he charged. I lifted the gun and put a bullet through his gut. He fell back with a howl.

"Hurts, I know. I can't kill you, but sometimes, that's worse, isn't it? Not being able to die."

With a roar, he charged again. I fired again. He screamed again.

"I have a few questions to ask—"

"I'm not telling you anything," he said, his garbled voice wheezing through the gap in his severed neck.

"Is that a challenge?" I smiled. "Excellent. Let's begin, then."

■　　■　　■

He eventually answered all my questions. Then I let him feed off the blood of his mother and left, locking the door behind me. I took the puzzle box, of course. At home, I put it on a shelf with the others.

As collections went, this one was pitiably small, and had taken me more time and effort to accumulate than I cared to calculate. But it would, one day, be worth it. What I collected was not simply the puzzles, but their stories—the stories of those who opened them, and the mistakes they had made.

Normally, I was there to witness the story unfolding. As Nell Collins said, the boxes were not easy to open, and there were far more collectors who knew the story than those who could unlock the configurations. So they went looking for someone who could. They found me, and I opened all but the last twist. That final one I left for them. They conquered the puzzle . . . then it conquered them, while I hid and watched, and collected their story.

Someday, when I had enough stories, I would solve the greatest puzzle of all—how to use the box properly and win the glories foretold. And then, I would make that final turn myself.

The doorbell rang.

I took one last look at the new puzzle box, running my fingers over the wood. An exquisite piece, and an equally rare story to go with it. An excellent addition to my collection. Then I closed the secret closet. Locked it. Double-locked it. Put the mirror back in place over the door. I am a careful woman.

Daniel was at the door to take me to dinner. As we were leaving, my BlackBerry pinged, telling me I had a message. He gave me a look.

"Yes, I'll turn it off," I said.

As I did, I checked the message. It was from a collector who'd heard of my reputation and hoped I could help with a puzzle box he'd just acquired. I would, of course. And it would probably turn out to be a mere imitation. Most were. But I never turned down any possibility, however slight, to add another story to my collection.

Bulimia

Richard Christian Matheson

I stare.

Oval water; a tomb.

Fingernails press soft locks that guard throat.

Stomach kneads; surrenders.

I rise to white sink. Rinse acrid taste. Kneel on floor, again.

Lean over, see my reflection. My mouth stretches. I feel the shapes slide out; a struggling gush. I shut eyes.

Hear them; distant, tiny survivors on ugly sea. Diseased murmurs.

I look into undigested broth.

See them. Paddling, furiously. Staring up at me. Malformed; hideous. I flush them. Get closer as they're swallowed into plumbing. Drowning voices hiss, shriek. Swirl into bowl.

The water is clear.

I feel them stirring inside. Impurities. Angry poisons. I can never be perfect with them in me. It is my fault.

I look at my watch.

Minutes. He's waiting. Drinking coffee. Happy.

My stomach twists. Vicious things gnaw, hold tighter. I shove raw fingers between lips. Force more out. They fight me. Hate me.

Suddenly howl up my throat, lunge from me, into vile water. Ghastly legs splashing. Struggling. Resentful noises bubble. They leer up with despising mouths, swallowing water, unable to breathe.

I'm still not empty.

I bury three fingers into throat; raw, burned reflex. Some refuse spasms; grip harder. Others can't. They shriek through my cracked lips, infuriated; evicted. Spiderlike faces spit up at me as they drop into the septic bowl; thrash in bile, dark nails scratching toilet's side. They cling to one another, choke toxic water, know they are dying. One reaches to escape. I quickly flush them. Listen to them drown.

I force more out; teeth bared over toilet, dress damp.

They plunge from my mouth. Writhing anemones. Some with thorns that scrape my throat. Others covered with countless, repulsive mouths from which more slither. Cruel ones stare, unafraid. Use the dead as rafts, crablike pincers reaching at me, tongues clicking. Others jet from my guts like sticky, black string, nesting on the water; infected islands.

I press harder. Chaotic, colorless ones emerge like blown glass. They try to hide, curl passively; eyes pleading. *Always the last.* The ones I've had forever; since I was little and puzzles crept. When everything went bad. When I couldn't protect myself. Flee mazes of hurt.

They hope I'll reprieve them. They float; confused, bloodred shells shining. The strong ones try to hurt me with their sadisms. The weak ones are scared of them. Traumatized shards. In time, they will all get me.

I hate them. My loathing zoo. I flush them. Watch them suffer.

I am ugly; broken. I deserve this.

I am finally empty. I rinse mouth. Brush teeth. Reapply lipstick. Use a drop of breath freshener. I walk back into the restaurant. Men watch me. Women. They whisper. He hugs me. Tells me he missed me. Tells me I look beautiful. He loves me. I take a bite of dessert he offers. He looks into my worthless eyes. I smile for him.

In the red, dark of me, I feel them stir.

I am filling.

Orfeo the Damned

Nancy Holder

Seriously, the man said that's all you have to do. You twist and turn the little panels and you're gone," Danai told Lindsay.

They lounged like opium smokers on the big beige-tone bed Lindsay shared with Jake in their large and very beige apartment. Danai had made himself a nest of monochromatic pillows, the Grand Odalisque of the Upper East Side, and he shimmied and shook, unfolding his sinewy arms and legs, pantomiming being opened. "Away from Jake. And all *this*."

Danai, a slender man with a close black buzz cut, flopped onto his side and waved his right arm like a sorcerer revealing his best trick. He was gaunt, Gypsy dark in a boatneck spandex top splotched with dark blue and crimson as if he'd been shot and his blood ran in rainbows. The multiple zippers of his baggy black parachute pants striated his quads like ligaments or scars.

He extended his gnarled, bare foot toward the ceiling and held out the box in his open palm à la abracadabra toward Lindsay, her one true serpent in the garden. Danai loved her so much. He pitied her. He understood how terribly unhappy she was. Or thought he did. She wasn't that unhappy. She wasn't.

"It takes you someplace," he whispered. "It's like drugs, or hypnosis. It's virtual reality at its best. Or so he promised."

"He" being some street vendor. She was shaking. Her therapist had told her to stay away from Danai, but here he was, and she could feel herself beginning to melt down.

"Then why don't *you* twist and turn the little panels?" she asked him, trying to sound snarky, hearing the anxiety building in her voice. Danai wouldn't understand; he never would. He was everything she had run away from.

All her life.

"I tried," he confessed, crossing his eyes, mugging stupidity. "I couldn't get it to work. Besides, you were always better at twisting and turning." He smirked, and then he sighed. "And you need an alternate reality worse than I do."

"I don't." Her stomach clenched. "I'm very happy here. With Jake. This is me." With the help of antidepressants and anti-anxiety meds. Evened out. Safe.

"Well, anyway, I got mixed up. I thought it was your birthday, so here's your present."

He held it out to her. In her sedately lit, inoffensive bedroom, it shone like a black-hearted Rubik's Cube limned in damascene. Symbols and scrollwork glittered like molten promises. Danai had made promises—never to leave her, and to bust her out if she ever gave the word. But she had made her choice. The right choice.

Then *why* was Dr. Everson increasing her dosage? Why couldn't she sleep? Or clean the house or make dinner?

She touched the box. There was a spark—static electricity—and Danai raised a beautifully plucked brow in surprise. Languidly, he lay back on his elbow, leaving the object in Lindsay's grasp. Then he sank to the mattress and clasped his hands across his tight, flat stomach.

"See? It loves you best."

"Pretty," she said, but it wasn't. It was frightening. Shocking, in a way she couldn't describe—or could no longer describe. She had lost all the passionate words, the ones Danai wrapped himself in, layer upon layer, until even the most prosaic events in his life sparkled like Excalibur. Jake said Danai was a drama queen. Danai said Jake was a pompous ass. Dr. Everson told her to stay away from Danai and listen to the pompous ass. After all, he was the one she was married to.

She used to be like Danai. A dancer, a Broadway gypsy, looking for signs in Chinese fortune cookies and tea leaves that it would be worth it. Buffeted by the winds of artistic yearnings. When she danced, she was fully alive. But between gigs, there was cutting, and a couple of suicide attempts. Jake didn't know about those. No one knew. She hadn't even told Dr. Everson all of it. Maybe he was increasing her meds in retaliation.

"You don't really believe it would work, though," she said, moving her gaze from it to him with extreme difficulty. It was mesmerizing. Maybe she should press on that panel. Or tap *that* panel . . .

. . . No.

"Of course I don't." He raised his chin. "But if you twist it, I'll know you're ready to start packing. You can move in with me again. We'll have fun."

Into his rat-infested walk-up hall of dreams. Danai didn't view anything in his life as a failure, but as myriad possibilities yet to be realized. He snuggled his toes beneath her right thigh. "The man I bought it from said I would know the right person to give it to. As soon as I handed him a twenty, I saw your face in my mind."

No, no, don't think of me. I can't handle it.

The front door opened. Jake was home. She sagged with relief. She wanted to start crying and she didn't even know why.

"Hello?" he called.

"Fun's over." Danai slid off the bed like a snake and got to his feet. He adjusted his top as if to regain his modesty and shook his head as he helped her up. "This is so pathetic. This is not how you were supposed to grow up."

"I'm fine," she said briskly.

"You're pudgy," he said, shuddering. "And you're wearing pastels."

The two filed out of the bedroom. "Hi, Jake," she sang out. Did he hear the tremor in her voice?

There he stood, a little rounder, more wrinkled. Tireder. The quintessential man in the gray flannel suit. He was almost thirty-eight. She was twenty-six, three years older than Danai. And she felt . . . disappointed. She had been waiting to see him all day, trying to last long enough, but now that he was here, she didn't feel the relief she had been hoping for.

Jake bent slightly so Lindsay could kiss his cheek and peered at her. She smiled harder. He sighed.

"Hello, Dan," he said.

"Hello, *Jacob*," Danai said, and if Jake heard the mocking in his voice, he ignored it.

"So . . ." Jake said, looking from her to Danai and back again. Lindsay felt a rush of intense guilt, as if Dr. Everson were standing next to Jake and both of them now saw how clearly she did not want to get well.

"I'm afraid I talked her into something crazy," Danai went on. Jake pulled his chin in, bracing himself.

"We made borscht," she said in a rush.

Jake considered. "Borscht's not so crazy."

She was flattened. Jake was right. Borscht was not crazy. But all afternoon, as she and Danai chopped beets and cabbage, her heart had fluttered. It felt like something new. Like an adventure. But it was just beet soup.

She felt her being gravitating toward Jake, seeing herself as someone Jake could be seen with. Solid, steady, understated. Danai's apartment bulged with tacky junk. He wasn't dreaming; he was fooling himself. Jake was her answer. Not that Danai was even an alternative prospect as a lover. He was gay.

Her eyes welled. Something inside her made her return to the bedroom and pluck up the box. It had built up another static charge and it zapped her, hard.

"What's that?" Jake asked.

She lifted it up, showing him. "It's a puzzle box. Danai gave it to me."

A frown flickered over Danai's features, and she felt a rush of shame for sharing any part of their afternoon with Jake. *He's my husband*, she wanted to remind Danai. But then he would probably tell her that traditional heterosexual marriage was on the way out—and good thing, too, because it ruined people.

"Oh," Jake said, not interested.

She put it back in the bedroom.

At dinner they ate the borscht and Jake asked if there was something else to eat, something more substantial, like a brisket. Lindsay felt that strange, horrible pull she often experienced when in the presence of two strong personalities: Danai's wacky, magical artiness; Jake's linear, stolid serenity. Jake believed in hard work and good habits, and they had the financial security to show for it.

Danai had once begged them to take Desdemona, a floppy-eared puppy he had impulsively purchased at a pet store. Because of his unpredictable schedule, the poor thing was cooped up for hours. Desdemona scratched the door of his walk-up and he needed money to get that fixed, too, before his landlord saw her. Then she started having seizures. Lindsay wanted to take her; Jake said no way. There was something wrong with her and she would be expensive to take care of. Then Desdemona was gone. Lindsay didn't know what had happened to her, but there was a part of her that always wondered and fretted about her. She would have taken Desdemona on. Jake had stood between them.

I could have insisted. I'm not his slave, she thought, not for the first time. He was just . . . firmer in his answers.

Lindsay knew how many strikes she had against her: her alcoholic parents were dead; her father when she was nine, her mother just before she turned sixteen. She had lived with an aunt and an uncle who didn't want her. She had moved out when she was eighteen and got raped. It had gotten worse, for a long time.

"Jake is exactly what you need," Dr. Everson had informed her. Over and over. But she was miserable. Lonely.

"You've got this list," Jake told her once. "It's a hundred miles long. And it's all the things that have to be okay before *you're* okay. You are incapable of being happy."

He had apologized. Even Dr. Everson said it was a mean thing to say, unlike Jake himself, who was patient and uncomplaining. As she should be. But their life was so vanilla, so boring.

It's a cage, she thought, as she served the borscht. Danai was barefoot. Jake was disapproving. She was trying very hard not to cry.

Dinner was strained. Danai seemed to enjoy the tension. Jake was quiet; Lindsay wondered if something had happened at work or if he was just really angry at her for letting Danai come over. She wasn't supposed to.

The meal was over quickly, since all there was, was purple soup. Chairs pushed back, the three went to the door, where Danai defiantly kissed her forehead. It was raining and he had no coat, no umbrella. He refused to borrow anything.

"You'll catch pneumonia," Lindsay argued.

Danai flung his hands over his head, two lightning rods. "It would be worth it."

When the door shut behind him, Jake snorted and tsk-tsked. "Lindsay," he began.

"I'm sorry," she said, but she wasn't sure she was. She didn't know what she was feeling. "It's just . . . he . . ."

"He didn't have any money, did he?" Jake said flatly. "He was hungry."

"No, he's doing great. He's in a show." She was lying to him.

He studied her. And then she smiled faintly. "That's great. But you agreed not to invite him over. He upsets you."

He touched her cheek. She laid her hand over his but she couldn't actually feel his skin on hers. Then he headed for his home office, which they had actually planned to be a nursery. *That* hadn't happened, either, and Dr. Everson said maybe that was really why she felt so teetery all the time.

After he shut the door, she burst into tears. She ran into their bedroom and flopped into Danai's nest. Damn him to hell and back again. Damn them both. Why did Danai have to make her admit how lonely and *nothing* she was? He *was* a snake and she *was* going to stop seeing him. And as for his stupid box—

She grabbed it up. It was warm to her touch. Startled, she gazed down at the etched sides, at the metallic runes and sigils, which seemed to be *moving*.

Lindsay thought she saw a little section that extended from the top of the box, like a lever. Her palm seemed to melt around the sharp corners; she hissed, sensing a cut being made; feeling pain, but at a distance. *Feeling*.

I don't feel anymore, she thought. *Not really*. Sex? She faked all of it, timing her gasps and her writhing so that Jake would be pleased and finish sooner. Sex was beige, like her bedspread.

She ran her fingers along the top, the side, of the cube. A droplet of blood ran into a channel, and she saw the steps she must take to open it. Saw how she had closed the box of her life around herself:

If I hadn't moved in with Jake, I would dream of dying from pneumonia. But I did move in. And so . . . who wants to die of anything? That's so crazy. Danai can talk like that because his mind won't fixate on it like mine. Mine is scrambled.

Danai's free to be as silly and irresponsible as he wants. Oh, how I wish . . .

She jerked, seeing that she had pressed a circle on one of the sides. The top of the box rose up, star-shaped, and began to rotate counterclockwise.

A bell tolled, low and deep, and the room filled with light. No, the light slanted, glowing stripes of blue light, cyanotic. The stripes became rectangles—doors, widows. Her hands shook as she whirled in a circle.

Am I really seeing this?

"Jake," she whispered, wrapping her hands around the puzzle

box; the bell tolling as if from deep inside her rib cage, *Bring out your dead*.

The blue-white color stretched and bloomed. Shapes began to form—human figures, outlined with purplish black auras. She heard the clanking of chain and snap-crack of a whip.

Then a man stepped out of the icy blue light. His skin was dead white and his eyes were two wounds; his eyelids and lips were wrenched back by hooks. He wore a black robe, like some kind of monk, as the light swirled around him like mist.

She had gone crazy, really and finally. Psychotic break. Dr. Everson had threatened her with it. Jake had fretted about it. Danai told her to embrace it, learn from it, and move back out of it. He hadn't understood. He had never understood.

The man focused on her, moving toward her. He didn't smile, just kept coming. She backed away, her calves grazing her solid bed frame.

"You're not here," she whispered.

"Oh, but I am. What is your pleasure?" he asked her. His voice was icy hot, like frost and lava. His mutilated eyes were red-and-black circles. What had happened to his lips? And there were chains in his skull, inside the bones . . .

Two more figures materialized in the blue. One was a bald woman in a stiff black gown with a wide, belled skirt, the bodice cupping her breasts. The ends of needles gleamed on either side of her swollen nipples. Black leather fabric crisscrossed her torso, revealing flesh sliced open with myriad cuts from beneath her sharp chin to her sex, which was shaved. Hooks pierced her stark flesh and folded it back in intricate folds, like origami, the underside a scintillating crimson.

The third was a creature that was nothing but an open sideways mouth on stiltlike legs, chittering and gibbering through clacking fangs. It was six feet tall and as it skittered toward her, mucus dribbled over the rows of sharp white teeth. Mucus and blood.

Lindsay trembled as the coppery odor of blood slid over her face. She was swaying, reeling. Unbelievably, the blare of the TV permeated the room. Jake had turned on the football game. Jake was close by.

"What is your pleasure?" said the man again. His voice was a caress across her cheek . . . and then a slap.

And then a kiss.

She jerked and backed away.

"This isn't happening. This isn't real."

"You summoned us," said the man. He raised a hand and pointed to the box gripped in her hand. Blood was running down her forearm and dripping off her elbow. "We came. Now you belong to us."

Then a fourth figure appeared in the room, a man wearing a half mask of black leather that appeared to be sewn to his face. The black leather mask molded features hard and leonine, with sensual, pierced lips curved in a smile. His black hair was pulled so hard into a ponytail that oozing cracks had formed along his scalp line. His nipples were pierced. Large multifaceted stones, like rubies, dangled from them. Ornate scars ran beneath his navel to his penis, which had been sliced open; two silver spheres dangled from the bifurcated head; and when he walked toward Lindsay, they chimed in unison—the tolling bell she had heard. Was *still* hearing.

"I didn't summon you," she croaked. Her lips were numb; she wasn't sure how she could manage to speak.

"We're here. You'll be coming," said the first man, with the jeweled head.

The naked man in the mask laughed and came toward her. He was erect. His smile was hellish.

"You'll be coming," he echoed, and she fell into his voice, low and seductive and like nothing she had ever heard in her life. It held her up as something slid along the curves of her body and she *felt*—

"No, there's been a mistake. Jake!" she cried, as the crowd on his TV burst into cheers and applause.

"No mistake," said the man in the mask. "Let us begin."

A hook shot across the room and ripped out the darkest, bluest vein in the back of her hand. Another caught her cheek, and yanked.

■   ■   ■

"I'm sorry," the police detective told Jake. Her name was Maile Baker.

"Thank you," Jake murmured in as neutral a voice as possible. He stood in the detective's windowless, airless office, reeling. *Cold case*. His Lindsay.

Detective Baker indicated the plain cardboard box on her desk. "These are her things. You're free to take them. You must know how frustrated we are," she said. "It's been a year."

Almost to the day. His chest was tight. "Yes, thank you."

He took the subway home, the box in his lap. When he got home, he examined each object: some postcards and letters, her laptop computer . . . and the puzzle box, which Dan had given her the night of her disappearance. About a month later, Dan had disappeared, too . . . into insanity. He had always had a fragile hold on reality, that one. Which was why Dr. Everson and Jake had ordered Lindsay to steer clear of him.

"She's in the box," Danai had gibbered. To him, to the police. "Open the box, Jake in the Box, open the box."

No one could get the box open, and the police investigated other leads. Now she was a cold case.

Thunder rolled across the ceiling. Jake sat in his bedroom, once *their* bedroom, and held the box up to the artificial light from a lamp beside the bed. The box felt warm in his hand. And—

"Ouch," he said, as a static charge shot through him.

And . . . *there*. He saw how to open the box as clearly as if someone was standing beside him and pointing to the indentation in the center panel of wood. His lips parted. How had no one noticed it before?

He touched the panel, and the box *zzz*'ed with electricity. A soft blue glow emanated from it.

He pushed on the panel, and it rose straight up.

A tolling bell rang inside his hollow chest, inside his hollow heart.

■ ■ ■

He was the Ravisher, and he was Lindsay's Cenobite. He had penetrated her and taken her and tortured her and skinned her; he had
raped her and violated her and the pain was unbearable. He slid a
knife under each cell of her body and pulled it back, hooking it in
place; he pierced her labia and her urethra and he sounded her with
lightning bolts and knives, talons, teeth, fingernails, and the screams
of his other victims. He tormented her and dissected her.

Every second of every hour for centuries of time.

Hell had other clocks; the Engineer had made all of them, and
they ticked too slowly to endure; clanged the alarm too fast for
human hearts to catch up. The Ravisher brought Lindsay to life each
time she died in sheer agony, *from* sheer agony; she was spread-
eagled so tightly and so often that her body would explode into
pieces by sheer force of habit.

The pain . . .

The pain . . .

"You're not there yet," he would hiss at her, and strike her, and
slice her. She thought she would become numb to it; she moaned
and writhed, trying to fake the worst she could imagine, so he would
stop; because while he tore her apart, he fucked her apart. He had
sex with every wound, incision, and fragment. He pushed and he
came, all over her and often. All she felt was agony. Endless.

She panted, moaned; then, after more centuries of new and inventive torments, she fell silent.

"Yes," he whispered into her soul.

More centuries.

And more.

Then:

She stood in the center of a labyrinth. The cold gray walls
spread outward, like her arms and legs, pinioned to the torture bed
of the Ravisher. She saw the road she had traveled, Jake and Danai's
road that she had *not* traveled, and the roads of other possibilities.
Spurred into heightened self-awareness by her pain, she crawled

down the passages, then staggered, then walked. Blood gushed down the corridors and striated the walls; she knew she was inside her own body, and then inside her own mind, pushing hard to be born.

Inside her own soul, tearing it apart herself. With his help. Her tormentor, her beloved. To let her out.

To let *her* out.

"Yes," she whispered to the Ravisher, floating, rising to her heaven. He was her angel; he had pushed her through to the side of pleasure. Endorphins of the body and the soul, to the essential core of death. "I know who I am now. You did this for me."

"It was you who did it," he told her, as they flew through black skies together, on the wings of delight. "Your pain spoke to you. Without pain, there is no growing.

"And I have given you more pain than anyone can imagine."

Turn it this way and that way and this way, said the voice in Jake's mind. Lightning flashed and thunder rumbled, and he listened to the voice as the room turned blue; as tears streamed down his face and *someone* moved the cube in his hands while the panels opened.

The bell tolled.

"I will come for you," he whispered, half mad.

"I know who I am now," Lindsay told the Ravisher, as he stretched her and racked her. As he forced her and brutalized her. "I know exactly who I am."

"That is good," he said, smiling broadly, as she fainted again.

When she woke, she expected to see his masked face above her. Instead she saw Jake's. A little rounder, a little older, and his eyes huge with horror.

"Oh my God, Lindsay," he whispered, reaching out to her, drawing back his hands. His face was white, and tears were streaming down his cheeks. "My darling, my poor darling."

She stared at him, then down at herself. Large leather straps held her in place as she was spread-eagled on two wooden beams over a fiery pit. White-hot irons pierced her sex, and she smelled her own cooking flesh.

"I'll get you out of here. Can you help me? Is there a key?" He looked at her restraints. Then he turned and vomited.

"How . . . ?" she asked. And then she knew. He had worked the puzzle box.

"It took me a long time to believe," he said, wiping his mouth. "I'm so sorry it took me so long. But I'm here now. We'll go—" Then he broke down sobbing. "Oh, God, this is *Hell*."

"Yes," she said.

Then the Ravisher stepped from the shadows, along with his three original companions: the leader, with the hooked eyelids; the tattooed Cenobite with the jeweled pins; and the woman in the ball gown. They gazed at Jake.

"You summoned us," said the Ravisher.

"No." Jake shook his head as he backed away from the Ravisher, then bravely moved between the quarter and the fiery pit to wrap himself around Lindsay, as tightly as he dared. "I snuck in," he whispered to her.

"What is your pleasure?" asked the tattooed Cenobite with his glittering jeweled pins.

"Let her go," Jake said.

"That will not happen," the Ravisher informed him. He extended his hand; it became a talon, and he walked toward Lindsay and Jake. Jake released Lindsay and stepped away. The Ravisher ripped Lindsay's left nipple into two equal halves. She threw back her head and screamed.

She screamed. It was she who screamed.

"You summoned us and you must stay with us," said the woman in the ball gown. "And we will tear your soul—"

Her soul. It was hers.

The Ravisher sliced open her right nipple, then impaled himself upon her, as Jake cursed and shouted.

"Let her go!"

The Ravisher maimed her, tortured her, *her*, and when she knew herself as she did her own pain, hers, he stopped. He lifted up her bleeding head so that she could see her husband, who was kneeling on the floor between two more Cenobites dressed in black leather and intricate arabesques of scars and bleeding wounds. Each of them held a long piece of chain that ended in a hook. Each was bending down and grabbing one of Jake's wrists. Jake was naked; his body gave off steam, or mist.

"You came here of your own free will," the Ravisher told Jake. "It's your turn."

"Wait," Jake begged. Then, "Wait." His speech was halting. "If it's my turn . . . then hers is over."

"No," Lindsay whispered, and the Ravisher laid a possessive hand over hers. Then the Ravisher unfastened her restraints and picked her up in his arms. Bits and pieces of Lindsay's flesh remained stuck to the cogs and blades of their bed. And to his cheek and his teeth.

He carried her toward Jake, and stopped. Droplets of her blood sprinkled Jake's bowed head, like a blessing.

"What exactly are you saying?" the Ravisher urged in a low, coaxing voice.

There was a long moment of silence. Lindsay heard Jake weeping. And praying. She looked down at him, remembering how afraid she had been of everything. She slid her gaze to the Ravisher, who smiled, reading her expression.

Then she wobbled. What *had* the Ravisher done to her?

For a moment she felt the old panic. Then it was gone, and bloody tears washed down her face. He had awakened her and given her the gift of life. *Her* life. Her real life.

"I'll take her place," Jake said. "Only, let her go. I'll stay with you. I swear it."

"He wishes to be tortured in Hell for all eternity, for your sake," the woman in the gown announced.

"I-I love you," Jake whimpered, as the Cenobite with the hooked eyelids laid a cat-o'-nine-tails across his shredded back. He grunted, and slumped.

"He means it," said the tattooed, jewel-pinned Cenobite.

Hooks flew out of nowhere. Lindsay knew those hooks, remembered her screams, and her pleas for mercy. Jake would utter them, would suffer, and suffer more, and then . . .

"He will never make it to the other side, where you are," the Ravisher murmured in her ear. "He will remain in torment, endlessly. That would cause you . . . agony, would it not?" His finger became a razor, and sliced down the side of her face. The cut was deep, unkind.

"Yes," she breathed.

One hook sliced through Jake's forearm. He screamed. The sound bounced off the cold walls of Hell; off the skulls, piled up, of other victims. Playmates. Off the layers of viscera, shimmering and exquisite.

"Oh, no, no," Jake gasped. "Oh, God, stop."

"He will never understand," the Ravisher said. His voice spoke of eagerness, cruelty, impatience. A sonnet, a paean to Lindsay's achievement.

A second hook caught Jake in the groin, piercing his sex. This time his head fell back and he groaned low in his gut.

"For some, we are angels," said the Cenobite with the jewels. "For others . . ."

Another hook. Lindsay held up her hand.

"No," she ordered. *Ordered.*

The Ravisher stared at her in disbelief. The others did as well.

Jake gasped, perhaps at the reprieve.

The Ravisher dropped her to the floor, glided up to Jake, and grabbed his hair. "You came to make a bargain?" he asked. "You would change places with her?" He gazed hard at Jake. "You would become my property?"

Before Jake could answer, the Ravisher turned to Lindsay. "You would agree to this?"

"Let him go," she said. "I'll stay."

"Lindsay," Jake whispered.

"*I will stay.*" She took a breath. "I *want* to stay."

"You don't," Jake gasped, as the Ravisher held her attention with his dark, hellish eyes. "You don't know what you're saying."

The room fell silent again. Lindsay heard the tolling bell. Heard, far away, the screams of someone else.

Then the Ravisher threw back his head and laughed. The other Cenobites joined him, and their howls crackled and reverberated against the bones of Lindsay's skull, each of which had been crushed and reshaped a dozen times, a hundred.

The Ravisher rushed like a whirlwind and caught Jake under the chin as if he were hooking a fish. Jake gurgled blood.

"Is this what you want *forever*?"

"I'll stay!" Lindsay begged.

The other Cenobites laughed harder. The Ravisher pressed his nose against Jake's. "That's what she *wants*," he hissed. "She wants to stay. Think of what little you have felt of the gifts we give. I have been infinitely generous with her. Infinitely." He swiveled his head toward her. "And you want it."

"Yes." She wouldn't look at Jake. He would never understand.

"He's relieved," the Ravisher told her, grabbing Jake's head and craning it backward so hard Lindsay braced herself to hear the bones break. "He wants to play the white knight, but he doesn't really have the balls."

"I want to stay," she said. "It's what I want."

The Ravisher turned away from Jake and returned to Lindsay. He yanked her up to a standing position. "Who are you, either of you, to dictate to *us*? We don't make bargains."

"Let me stay, please," Lindsay babbled. "*Please*."

He kissed her, like a human lover, and then he dropped her to the floor. "No," he said. "You'll go back with him. You'll live with him. You'll fuck him. And if you leave him, or try to end your life . . ." He smiled down on her with demonic glee. "Then we'll come for him. But only for him."

"*No*," she wailed. It was too cruel. "I'll lose myself again."

"Lindsay, what the hell are you saying?" Jake screamed, but the Cenobite in the gown slammed her fist against his chin.

"You'll leave now. You will never see us again," the Ravisher commanded.

Down the corridors, naked, both of them. Jake led the way, holding Lindsay's hand, as she brokenly, openly wept. She could feel the Ravisher watching her. The other Cenobites were with him, their bon voyage party.

"You're in shock," Jake said. "We'll be home soon. We'll be safe."

She tried to take comfort in the knowledge that the Ravisher was still torturing her, that, thanks to him, she would be miserable for the rest of her life. But already she could feel her unsureness, her lack of certainty, of *self*, creeping back over her like a shroud. Death by a thousand denials. Depression was a veil that he had lifted. But now, knowing what she did, losing paradise . . .

"Lindsay, it's going to be okay," Jake said.

"Don't look at me," she begged him.

"I'll take you home," he promised. "It's going to be all right."

She could feel the caving-in. The death. The burial. He would never know. He would assume he had saved her, never realizing that he had smothered her to death.

Was that true? Was that correct? Or had all that pain driven her insane?

She considered, searched, sobbed at a sharp stab of pain deep in her soul. There. That was she. She was misery. She would have to hide herself carefully. Guard herself jealously, or she would lose herself, and the Ravisher, forever. Her life would not be Hell, just a pale imitation. And if Jake knew, she would lose even that.

"Don't look at me," she whispered to her husband, as he led her out of the land of the dead. "Ever."

Our Lord of Quarters
Simon Clark

Constantinople, AD 1401

The monk greeted the Emperor's entourage at the steps of the palace, just as the siege engines recommenced their bombardment of the city. His eyes flashed with fear; his right hand clenched around the Cross of the Orthodox Church. Approaching the Emperor's Chamberlain, he bowed, trembling.

"S-sire," the monk stammered. "I beg to convey the Emperor to the Church of Holy Wisdom." Terror gripped him. "It's the Demon, sire . . . the Demon has been prepared."

The Chamberlain motioned the monk to lead on. Ahead, the vast dome of the church cut a smooth, dark mound from a star-filled night. The terrified monk moved quickly, head bowed, as he muttered prayers of self-protection.

Following at the tail of the procession, the Slave. This teenage boy from rural Mistra tingled with excitement. Often he'd been beaten for staring. Yet tonight he could not escape being beguiled by this exotic sight. The Imperial bodyguard flanked His Imperial Majesty, Manuel II. A tall, gray-bearded figure, clad in the gorgeous purple of kings, he glided with serene grace across the square to

St. Sophia. This, the greatest cathedral in the world, lay embedded in the pulsating heart of the fabulous city of Constantinople.

Metropolitan life enchanted the Slave. From the life of a tanner's boy in a Greek backwater to this splendor! His mother fluttered with pride that her son had been dispatched to the capital. Before he'd left, she urged him to do well. If he impressed his masters, he might become a freedman. Once he attained wealth, he could restore the social standing of his once noble lineage. "But a greater purpose may fall upon you," his mother had told him. "If your Emperor's life is in danger, then you must sacrifice your own to preserve his. He protects Mistra from barbarians. Save him, and you save your brothers and sisters, too."

At that moment, his senses overflowed. Beautiful palaces, the elegant homes, the great square that spawned alleyways lined with taverns, warehouses, shops, brothels, workshops. Tonight the streets were deserted of people, yet aromas still thronged the place: mouthwatering scents from the bakeries, spiced lamb roasting in ovens, sandalwood incense from shrines, the rich perfumes of the courtiers. It swamped the Slave's mind.

To prevent the city's charisma from making him giddy, he focused on the Emperor's fool. *Infuriating little beggar!* The Clown made the Slave angry. Not because of his vulgar jokes but because he was disrespectful to royalty and commoner alike. He cavorted in a comical cut-down version of the Emperor's own robes. As he pranced, he brandished a stick. Attached to the end, an inflated pig's bladder and a fistful of keys that tinkled like bells. "What a beautiful night!" trilled the Clown. "What a gorgeous night for love." He cupped a hand to his ear. "Hark! A delicious night for a siege." In the distance, the thump of rocks being hurled into the city by Ottoman catapults the size of beached ships. "Ah! And what a ravishing night to meet the Demon!" With his jester's bladder-wand, he struck the monk on the buttocks. The weight of the keys hurt the man, which only compounded his misery. Nervous laughter sprang from the lips of the courtiers. The Clown sang out, "Our friend with the tonsure fears the Demon. What! Aren't Christ's prayers powerful enough for you! Don't you believe our saints can protect you from the Devil locked up in that poor little hut?" He pointed at the sacred edifice with its soaring buttresses and mighty dome.

The Slave gritted his teeth. *The Clown is making mischief again by implying that the monk isn't pious. He wants the man to be whipped.*

"You don't fear the Demon, do you ladies?" The fool singled out a Duchess in extravagant gold silks. "Oooh, I can just see you ogling the Demon. Yes—ogling! You'll caress the naked Devil with your glances. Heart pounding in your breast, you will gasp, 'Oh! Handsome Demon, sir. Will you make me your bride? Hop on board this stately galleon of female flesh. Sail me in umpity-bumpity waters to your heart's delight!' "

The courtiers sniggered. This only angered the Slave. *Why don't they cut out the imbecile's tongue? He's not amusing; he's a sadist.*

A rock hurled from a siege engine crashed into a house nearby. Dust, pale as a ghost, rose above the rooftops.

"What a lovely night for bombardment!" The Clown shrieked with laughter. "What a beautiful night for death!"

One of the catapults dumped its missile into the square. With a slap hard enough to make the pavement tremble, a headless corpse found the earth again. Unperturbed, the Emperor regarded the cadaver: evidently, from the uniform, a captured Byzantine soldier. The courtiers were less stoic. They fluttered their hands, whimpered, backed away from the bleeding ruin.

"Fear ye not!" piped the Clown. "Dead men don't bite. Especially those without a head." He rapped the cadaver with his bladder-stick.

The moment he did so, the chest of the decapitated corpse heaved. It seemed as if it had returned to life, and was eager to draw air into its shattered torso.

"Witchcraft," cried one of the ladies.

Even the Clown sheltered behind the dignified stature of the Emperor. Guards drew their swords, ready to battle the enchanted corpse. As horrified courtiers watched the writhing of the bloody husk, pellets of fur sped from its neck.

"Rats!" squealed the Clown. "The naughty, naughty Ottomans

have stitched rats inside the fellow. Then they . . ." He mimed carrying a body to the catapult, lying it in the scoop, kissing it fondly, then pulling a lever to fling it into the heart of the city.

The Slave knew that Ottoman forces, who now besieged Constantinople, intended the rats to spread disease through its population, so weakening their resolve to hold out. Those scurrying rats unmanned the monk. Screaming in terror, he fled toward the church.

Several courtiers followed in blind panic. That sacred colossus would, they prayed, offer divine protection.

"Ah ha!" The Clown applauded their flight. "They're eager to see the Demon." Then he fixed the Slave with a cruel eye. "Or have they forgotten that he's in there? The diabolus. The evil one. The captive Satan." He winked. "As you, too, had forgotten. Isn't that so, my little Greek goat?"

It wasn't the Slave's place to answer. Instead, he obediently followed the entourage that remained with His Imperial Majesty. The beautifully clad advisers, the secretaries, the bald eunuchs, and the bodyguard that bristled with weaponry.

"Here goes, little goat!" The Clown linked arms with the Slave. "Let us lead our Emperor, so he might gaze upon the Demon!" Then he called out to the entourage. "Follow me! Remember! Don't spit in church. No cursing. No nostril picking. And absolutely no farting!"

Silence. The cavernous interior of the church lay engulfed in quietude. With total silence came utter stillness. Even smoke from the incense burners appeared to hang motionless within the immense void of the dome: pale ghosts, neither rising nor falling. The myriad pillars that supported the structure were still as cedars in an enchanted forest.

The courtiers froze at first sight of the Demon. Every single man and woman locked their gaze on that figure. Nobody, it seemed, dare draw breath in its presence. The Slave's heart pounded. He strived to absorb every detail of the creature that sat on a wooden chest in the center of the floor.

A man strode from the gloom. His proud military bearing and the arrogant thrust of his jaw proclaimed his exalted rank.

In a deep voice he boomed, "Don't be afraid of the beast. He's uglier than sin itself. But I myself have bound him with straps made from elephant hide. Even Hercules couldn't break those. Besides, here in this fortress of God, he will be powerless." He bowed smartly. "Emperor. I am your devoted servant, General Spirodon, commander of your eastern legions. It was I who captured the Demon. I humbly offer the creature to His Majesty." There was nothing humble about this cocksure soldier. "May it bring you amusement."

"The Emperor is most pleased." The Chamberlain eyed the Demon with unease. "Perhaps you would describe its capture for the court's edification."

"I would be delighted, sire." The General clearly relished the art of self-glory. "I led my men to scout for Ottoman forces. Whereupon in Edessa, close to the source of the Euphrates, I encountered the town elders. They begged me to save them from a demon that had been discovered beneath a pagan shrine. My men were so frightened by the unnatural darkness within the tomb that I ordered them to stand back. Thereupon, I entered alone."

Eyes shining, his voice growing louder, the General declaimed his heroic deeds. Meanwhile, priests lit oil lamps that encircled the *thing* sitting on the box. The lamps' glow clearly revealed the Demon in its most awful detail. The seated figure captured the young Slave's attention. Endlessly, his eyes roved over a body that mingled beauty with repellent monstrosity.

The Demon appeared to have the dimensions of a mortal man. He sat on the chest of reddish wood as a mortal rests upon a bench. His eyes were closed. He did not move. Yet how could he move? Surely he must be dead. Such a ruinous body could not possibly be alive. In the lamplight, the Slave feasted on the minutiae of its blasphemous anatomy. Perhaps three-quarters of the Demon's body consisted of dried flesh that adhered like dry mud to a stick. Part of the rib cage lay exposed. Beneath it could be glimpsed a fist-sized brown lump that was the heart. Along one forearm, which rested on its lap, the bone had been entirely denuded of muscle. Yet that limb terminated in a perfectly formed hand. Fingers curled in slightly. Nails, a healthy pink. Short yellow hair framed a blighted face. That countenance resembled those found on the ancient mummies of Egypt. Fissures ran down its cheek. One shoulder was white bone, the other was clad in the firm flesh of an athlete. Likewise, the legs were mainly decaying sticks of shin and thigh. Yet the right leg beneath the knee was clothed in flesh. The foot appeared entirely mortal.

What struck the Slave most forcefully were the curious additions to the body. Those elephant hide restraints around the wrists were readily explicable. It was the more esoteric accessories that made the Slave tremble. For, running from the heart, which showed behind the ribs, flowed a slender chain. An extraordinary chain, no thicker than a rat's tail. Its delicate links were of a bloodred metal; they shimmered with an inner radiance. The chain connected the heart to an iron loop in the timber chest. A tether of sorts? Even more striking, the sight of what had been embedded in its flesh—the good flesh, that is.

There, in the lamplight, gleamed dozens of metal disks. The Slave recognized them as coins. Gold, silver, bronze. Some perfect disks, some misshapen in the manner of archaic currency. Many bore the heads of known kings; others, from distant outlands, had been impressed with mysterious hieroglyphs. By what process he didn't know but the coins had been neatly embedded. And in rows, so that one slightly overlapped the other until it appeared the metal disks resembled the scales of a fish.

The General rested his foot on the box as he grandly pointed out features of the Demon. "Behold armor fashioned from coins. See the chain embedded in the heart?"

Emboldened, the Clown approached. "General, who captured the Demon—yet who missed seeing the Ottoman army march over our borders? Sir, don't your guts go all watery in the Demon's presence? Has fear purged your colon? Brave, noble, sir. Aren't you bedeviled by nightmares?"

The General had no intention of answering, but the Emperor nodded. "Tell him."

"As you desire, Your Highness." The General had no idea that the Emperor doted on the Clown. "As you might have noticed, the Demon's eyes are closed. It is quite blind. Nor since its capture has the creature moved even a finger. The Demon is intimidated by my presence." He pointed at its mouth. "It dare not even speak."

"Until now . . ." The Demon's head darted. Jaws snapped. *"There was nobody worth talking to."*

It spat an object at the Emperor's feet. The Slave saw it was a bloody finger. The General stumbled backward, blood pumping out over his fist.

The Demon's eyelids slid back to reveal plump, white eyeballs. In each, the iris was formed from a gold coin. When he rose from the box, the elephant hide restraints around his wrists pulled tight, but they didn't trouble him. He merely looked Emperor Manuel in the eye. "You are the ruler of this empire?"

Unflinching, the Emperor met the Demon's gaze. "I am. What's more, I have no terror of you."

"I'm delighted to hear it." The grotesque face tightened in a smile. "Seeing as your grunt did such a poor job of introducing me . . . I am the Lord of Quarters." The smile became pure menace. "It is time we opened negotiations."

"Why should I negotiate with you? I have everything. You have nothing."

"You tell him!" The Clown brandished his jester's stick. The keys jingled loudly, until their echoes in the dome above became a peal of bells. "Ha! The Lord of Quarters? He's nothing more than a pigeon carcass. All bone and bad pennies."

"Shush, little fool." The Demon bared his teeth—coins set edgewise into crimson gums. "Or I'll tell the Emperor what secret doors those keys on your rod open."

This statement worried the Clown. Mouth clamped shut, he sheltered behind his master's purple robes.

Still mantled in quiet dignity, the Emperor spoke. "I have seen many a novelty brought to the city. A twin-headed lion, a counting ape, a Persian girl who could float in the air. Nothing interested me. So what do you bring that will?"

"What you *need*, of course. What you *wish* for with all your heart."

"I am Emperor. I have *everything*."

"You preside over an empire in decay. It is a withered, little thing in comparison with the Byzantium of two centuries ago. The city is crumbling. Its palaces are propped up with timbers to stop them toppling into the gutter. Sir, *this* is what you need." The Lord of Quarters ran his fingers over bright, gleaming coins that sheaved his flesh. "Money. And money is power. I speak the truth, don't I?" He flashed the gold coins in his eyes. "The treasury is empty. Your knights ride warhorses that are so old they're not fit to pull garbage carts. Army wages go unpaid. Meager platoons fight with broken swords. Your warriors don't even have the thread to darn their socks. Am I not right?"

Instead of replying, the Emperor turned his head slightly as the thud of a rock from an Ottoman catapult echoed inside the church.

The Lord of Quarters took pleasure in that symphony of destruction. "Constantinople is under siege. Its city walls are rotten. Children could kick holes in its gates. They won't keep out the invader for long."

"I am promised money."

"But when will it arrive? Those foreign kings, who once offered you finance, keep it locked away. Instead, they'll make deals with the Sultan when he is ruler of this noble slum." The Lord of Quarters's softly spoken words painted images inside the minds of everyone present. He described the imperial treasury. That apart from dust, ankle-deep in every vault, all that it contained were empty boxes. He restated the Emperor's poverty. That he lacked the money even to police a fish market, never mind vanquish the Sultan's army. Or confound the enemy ships that blockaded the port. Soon Byzantium—poor, impoverished, ill-nourished Byzantium—would die. Constantinople, its capital, would be overrun. The once revered imperial dynasty would end.

Then the Demon spoke of riches that lie in the treasure houses of neighboring realms. How vaults overflowed with coins. Foreign kings complained that the coins cluttering up their palaces were a nuisance. Accountants overseas were at their wits' end to find storage for their mountain of cash. Blast those infernal coins! Fling them into the river. Use them to repairs holes in the roads. Coins, coins, coins! Bury them. Shovel them into wells. Anything to be rid of them. The whole world outside Constantinople was awash with money. In this city, however, it would be easier for the Emperor to pull stars out of the sky than gather even a handful of change.

With his picture of the Emperor's destitution so adroitly accomplished, the Lord of Quarters hissed. "Listen. I can invest in your empire. Albeit in a way that will escape your comprehension for now. However, once your borders are secure, trade will be restored, tax revenues will flow once more. That means you will have enough good, hard cash to restore this decaying city to the glorious capital it once was. You will recapture past splendor. After all, the real power in your world is not an army; it is not a crowned regal head; it is not your God—it is money. The bulging purse is the supreme ruler of all." The crunch of another catapult missile echoed through the building.

The Emperor's shoulders sagged. He knew all would be lost if he didn't act on the Demon's offer. "If I agree, what do you require in return?"

"I am the Lord of Quarters." Gloating oozed through the voice. "Therefore: I want a quarter of everything." He licked those cracked lips. "A quarter of your empire. A quarter of your people. The appetites of my Cenobite masters are insatiable." Dreamily, he added the following, luxuriating in the reward he, himself, would earn. "The Cenobites will be grateful for these gifts I will offer them. They will elevate me to their exalted status. And I will be free to roam the centuries again."

"What will happen to that quarter of the population you demand?"

"Ah, a detail that shouldn't concern you. Your empire will be restored to the glittering jewel it once was. For you, that's the matter of supreme importance."

"Will the Cenobites harm my people?"

"You, sir, are hardly the one to be squeamish. Your life is a litany of execution; mass blinding of prisoners. You've even castrated your own nephew."

"Where is the money?"

"Lift the lid." The Lord of Quarters stood aside from the wooden chest as far as the leather restraints would allow. The coins in his flesh chinked as he did so. As did the bloodred chain that trickled delicate links from his heart.

The Emperor raised the lid. Hanging on to the hem of his cloak, the Clown.

"Old chicken carcass is tricking you," sang the Clown. "There's no gold, only paper to wipe your arse!"

The Demon shot the Clown a fierce glare. "That is my contract."

"The print is awful small." The Clown pantomimed reading the indenture's rash of minuscule lettering. "Clause, subclause, penalty clause, warranties, codicils, exclusion notices, terms of payment, terms of forfeit. A contract is a riddle dressed as a puzzle . . ." Crossing his eyes, he scratched his head. "Or is it a puzzle clad as a riddle?"

The Emperor sighed. "I need time to study it."

"Of course." The Demon smiled. "Your jester speaks the truth. You must read the contract and unravel the complexity of its language. Then, when you have the document all figured out—if you have the wit to do so—sign it."

The Emperor frowned. "How will you deliver the money?"

"There's no gold involved."

"What?"

"Sign. And the invaders will go."

"How will they be compelled?"

"My Cenobite masters have their ways," chuckled the Demon.

"Read the contract, then sign! Once I have delivered the document, bearing your signature, to them they will grant me the power to help you."

The Clown opened his mouth to add a vulgar comment.

"Sign in the fool's blood." The Demon toyed with the heart-chain. "Oh . . . by the by, you will have a special coin struck to commemorate the breaking of the siege. When you do, add this chain to the coin's alloy. Let us agree that it will symbolically seal our deal."

Understandably aghast at being used as an inkpot, the Clown scrambled under the Emperor's cloak to hide. The Lord of Quarters enjoyed his fear. "Skewer the infuriating little piglet. Dip your pen in his vein. Sign the contract. Then pull the chain from my heart."

The Slave had been watching events closely. It had been disturbingly easy to picture the Demon becoming lord of a quarter of the Byzantine Empire. True, the Slave knew nothing of these Cenobites, but it wasn't difficult to imagine the Demon's masters. Surely the Cenobites would be as malevolent as this creature with its scalelike adornment of coins. Yet they needed the Emperor's signature on the contract before they could act. Until then, they wielded no power over him or his people. Then, in his mind's eye, he saw the heart-chain being dropped into a pot of molten bronze that would become newly minted coins. The bronze solidus would quickly be in circulation. Virtually everyone would carry such a coin. In exchange for goods and services, it would transit through bakery, tavern, brothel, church, and tax office alike. And in that coin would be a trace of the Demon's heart-chain. It would spread through the Empire, just as plague spreads through a population. The Slave recalled the corpses filled with live rats that were catapulted into the city. Wasn't there a similarity? The rats were tiny, yet the disease they spread wreaked huge damage. Might not the Lord of Quarters be infecting the monetary system of Christendom in much the same way as the Ottomans attempted to infect the populace?

Guards bellowed curses as they endeavored to drag the Clown from the Emperor's purple robes. The Clown begged his master to save him. Meanwhile, the Emperor wiped away a tear. He was sorry to do this, so very sorry, but sacrifices must be made in order to restore Constantinople to its former glory.

When the Emperor had second thoughts regarding his beloved Clown, the Demon spoke confidentially. "You know those keys? The ones on the fool's staff? Well, they open the doors to your concubines' rooms. Need I say more?" The Lord of Quarters chuckled. The heart-chain quivered to the quick rhythm of his amusement.

Clearly, it would be calamitous if the Demon's chain came to be smelted with the alloy for the coin. Just what kind of disaster, the Slave didn't know, but it would be grave. Instinct told him that, for sure. Just as instinct told him this procurer for the Cenobites had been waiting entombed for centuries. There he'd bided his time for such an opportunity as this. Yet what could the youth do? The Emperor wouldn't listen to advice offered by a slave.

The guards had the Clown by the ankles. They tugged. However, for the sheer love of life, he hung on to the imperial robe. The courtiers clamored, either overcome by the turn of events or shouting advice to the guards.

Now!

The Slave darted forward. He gripped the heart-chain in both hands.

"Not you!" the Demon howled. "It's not supposed to be you!"

The Chamberlain shouted, "Stop him!"

The Slave heaved at the chain. He saw the heart pulled forward through the ribs. It peaked into a cone, such as when a thorn is drawn from skin. Another heave—the heart-chain plopped out with a squirt of dark ichors.

The guards would have easily caught the Slave. However, the Clown's frantic struggles resulted in a maelstrom of people trying to part jester from Emperor. Men stumbled over one another; feet caught in cloaks; soldiers tripped.

So the Slave ran free. In his hands, the heart-chain. The bodyguard pursued him. There was one, however, who moved faster. The Demon had snapped the leather restraints.

"Give it back!" The hurricane force of his shout extinguished the

oil lamps. Yet in the gloom of the church, his demonic form glowed bright as a hell-given flame.

The Slave fled. Never before had he run so fast. His path took him across the deserted square outside St. Sophia. Above him, stars shone hard on the woes of humanity. He leapt over the headless corpse that had spawned rats. Then he ducked into an alleyway. Here, sheets billowed: death shrouds in the darkness. They were ready if once-mighty Constantinople should fall. Though who would bury its dead, let alone grieve?

Boulders from siege engines rendered houses to dust. But worse, far worse than the thunder of rocks tumbling from the sky . . . *the Demon wants me*. The Devil ran through those death shrouds. One flapped around his face, white cotton pulling tight, then the Lord of Quarters's visage burned its impression into the fabric, leaving a permanent shadow.

The Slave raced on through the labyrinth toward the city's fortress walls. Their alternating lines of cream and red masonry resembled layers of fat and bloody meat piled high on a butcher's slab. Atop the wall, the city's defenders at last deployed their creaking, worn-out, dilapidated engines of war. With a *whip-crack* the catapults hurled missiles at the Sultan's warships, where they were tightly packed in the narrow straits of the Hellespont.

"My chain! Give it back!" The Demon ran so fast he blundered against buildings. Then the coins embedded in his skin would spew torrents of sparks. At that instant, the Slave could have believed he was being pursued by a fiery comet.

Panting, the young man scrambled up the steps to the battlements. Starlight revealed the enemy fleet; soon they'd land troops where defenses were at their weakest. The heart-chain clinked in his fingers. At times it was cold; other times it was hot as entrails plucked from a pig's belly. Just its touch conjured images of the Lord of Quarters coercing many a king or pharaoh of a doomed realm into signing his pernicious contract. And perhaps his achievements would eventually earn him promotion to the rank of Cenobite.

Ahead, on top of the ramparts, Byzantine soldiers loaded throw-

ing pouches with amphorae containing volatile oils. These they ignited before launch. The Slave watched the weapon, known as
Greek Fire, arc through the sky; a blazing trail that fell onto ships;
inferno upon inferno blossomed; they introduced to the invaders a
searing portion of Hell on Earth. Screams of agony shimmered over
the face of the water.

When the Slave reached one such catapult, ready for launch, he
stopped dead. There he waited for the Lord of Quarters. The Devil
roared down at him, a snarling, spitting cauldron of rage. When he
clashed his jaws together, blue sparks jetted from his lips. The soldiers that manned the catapult fled in terror.

"I'll take back the chain. Then I will destroy you."

"Go on, do it!" The Slave gripped that rat's tail of a chain. "Lord
of Quarters? You won't capture even a thousandth of my soul."

"Oh, a believer?" The creature grinned. "How cute. How naive."

"Give up, Demon. You've lost."

"Oh?"

"See the invasion fleet? It's burning. The Ottoman attack has
failed. The Emperor won't sign your contract."

"True. But will that save your bonny hide from my attentions?"
The Demon advanced. "Do tell me how?"

"It won't. I accept this is my final hour."

"Good boy. Clever boy. Now give me the chain."

The Slave didn't flinch. "You'll have to take it back."

"Oh, you want to play, do you?" The gold coins in the monster's
eyes flashed. "Why not? You do realize, though, this empire is moribund. Its currency is worthless. Smell the decay. Even the palace
timbers are rotting."

"Constantinople isn't dead yet."

"Soon though, very soon. So why martyr yourself for a city that
isn't worth dying for?"

"If, by thwarting you, I've given my family a few more decades,
then I'm content. My sacrifice will have been worthwhile."

"Ah, noble, altruistic fool. And I thought the Clown was the one
with the jingling stick. Not the man standing right—no!"

The Slave thrust the heart-chain through his own lips into his mouth. He didn't stop there with its metal resting on his tongue. Steeling himself, he forced the chain into his throat with his middle finger. He felt each sharp link scrape down through his gullet. Through his chest. Into his abdomen. There it glided through the snug configuration of pathways that was his gut. One second the links burned hotly, the next they were cold as a corpse inside of him.

The Demon tut-tutted. "As if that will save you." The creature flew at the Slave. But didn't attack. Instead, his body became elongated—as slender as that of an eel. It dived headfirst into his mouth.

Gagging at the force of that powerful shape driving through his gullet in pursuit of the chain, the Slave stumbled backward, a plan crystallizing in his mind. When his body slammed into the catapult, he clambered into the throwing pouch that would normally hurl the Greek Fire. He gasped with pain. The Demon's body coins rasped the delicate linings of his intestines. Cries spurted from his lips as his gut distended. Inside him, a sensation of most horrendous pressure as the Lord of Quarters swam downward, as a pearl diver plunges down through the ocean in search of treasure.

The Slave flung himself half out of the pouch so he could punch the lever of the catapult.

A moment later, the boy was no longer of this Earth. The huge timber arm of the weapon flung him out across the Hellespont. That throw's brutal fury snapped his spinal cord. All pain left him as the Lord of Quarters clawed and chewed and raged through his inner workings. Soon the heart-chain would be in the Devil's hands. Not that it mattered anymore.

The Slave realized that the Demon's power was limited by the rules of this infernal game: rules that he and his Cenobite overlords must obey. And those rules dictated that the Demon must persuade the Emperor to sign the contract of his own free will. No doubt the monster could fly back to the church in moments; however, by then the Emperor would have gleaned that the Sultan's battle fleet was ablaze. Consequently, nothing would persuade him to sign away a quarter of his empire in the full knowledge that Constantinople had halted the invasion. The Demon would be compelled to travel the world in search of another victim.

Calm now. Detached from the sufferings of this world, the young man glided with dreamlike serenity through the night sky. Below him, burning ships. Above him, eternal constellations; the radiant adornment of Heaven. He knew this flight would soon end with lethal finality. And he knew the monster inside of him could not die. Moreover, Byzantium would linger for only a few more years. That didn't trouble him. He'd given his own brothers and sisters a chance of survival. With his life, he'd bought them time. Furthermore, his sacrifice had frustrated the Demon's plan to contaminate Byzantium's currency with the heart-chain. That's what mattered. Unlike his body, his contentment was indestructible; his death, merely the bridge between worlds.

Receding, the lights of Constantinople grew dim. Its churches and towers drowned in shadow. He knew the time had come to gaze on Byzantium no more. The boy closed his eyes and was gone.

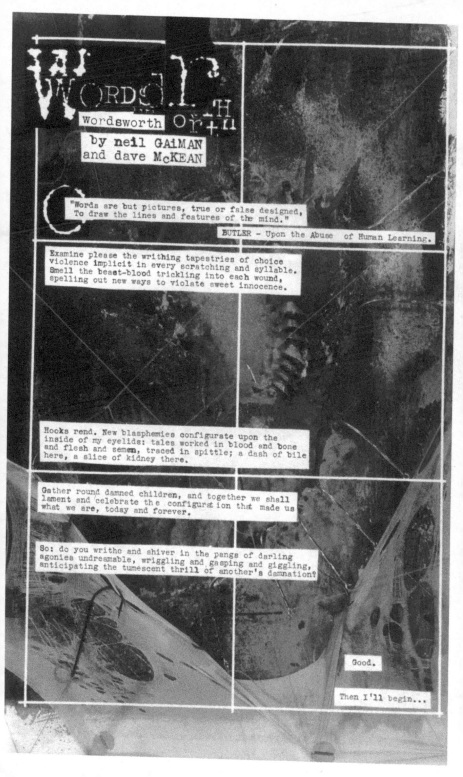

WORDSWORTH

wordsworth

**by neil GAiMAN
and dave McKEAN**

"Words are but pictures, true or false designed,
To draw the lines and features of the mind."

BUTLER – Upon the Abuse of Human Learning.

Examine please the writhing tapestries of choice
violence implicit in every scratching and syllable.
Smell the beast-blood trickling into each wound,
spelling out new ways to violate sweet innocence.

Hooks rend. New blasphemies configure upon the
inside of my eyelids: tales worked in blood and bone
and flesh and semen, traced in spittle; a dash of bile
here, a slice of kidney there.

Gather round damned children, and together we shall
lament and celebrate the configuration that made us
what we are, today and forever.

So: do you writhe and shiver in the pangs of darling
agonies undreamable, wriggling and gasping and giggling,
anticipating the tumescent thrill of another's damnation?

Good.

Then I'll begin...

His name is Wordsworth.

The final clue, 12 down:

12: You imply no blazing fronds grow in the abyss?

Inferno.

He writes it down and sighs dustily.

Then, crossword completed (6 minutes, 12 seconds), Daily Telegraph abandoned, Wordsworth stares out of the carriage window at a parade of allotments, at the ugly backs of houses.

Unsatisfying.

Wordsworth gazes at the paper in dismay. No true crossword here. He scans the first clue, expects nothing of substance.

Wordsworth ponders. An anagram, perhaps? He combines permutations of 'you', and 'U', with both 'Rabbit' and 'hare', and, as an afterthought, 'lapin'.

1: What you did to the rabbit. (7)

2: Miss Watson'

It isn't coming.

But deep inside his dry soul something flutters. He **knows** he knows the answer...

He just doesn't know what it is.

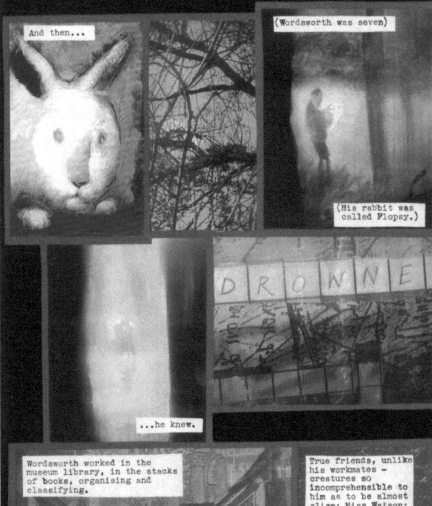

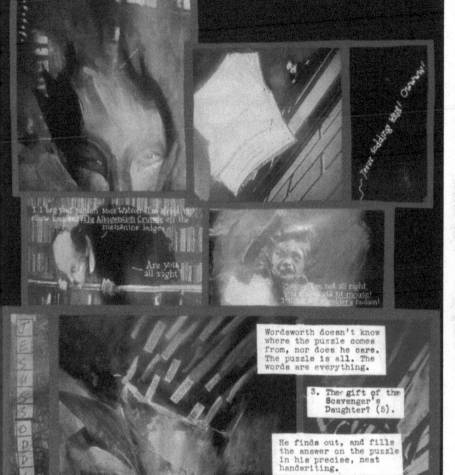

From that province he takes away a scarred back and expertly pierced genitalia; and, more importantly, he fills another **nin**e squares on the puzzle.

Wordsworth attends a meal, at which noble and affluent coprophiliacs dine for twelve courses on forty kinds of human shit.

He's there for the last word on the menu: it turns out to be coffee. Someone has a sense of humour...

The delights of reluctant perversion chill him, although each new experience has a specific end in view.

Words.

For a word he cuts a dog apart and casts its entrails upon his kitchen floor, seeking sense in the loops and whorls of its intestines.

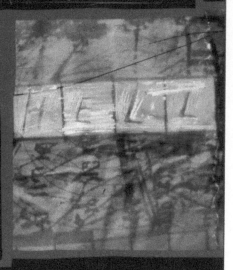

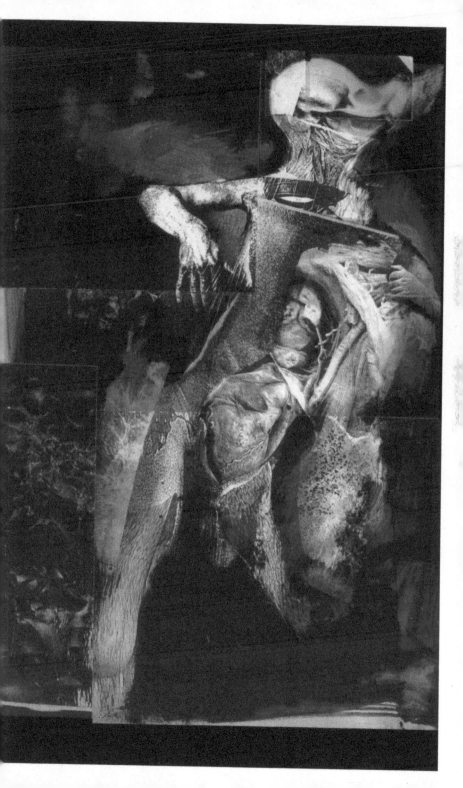

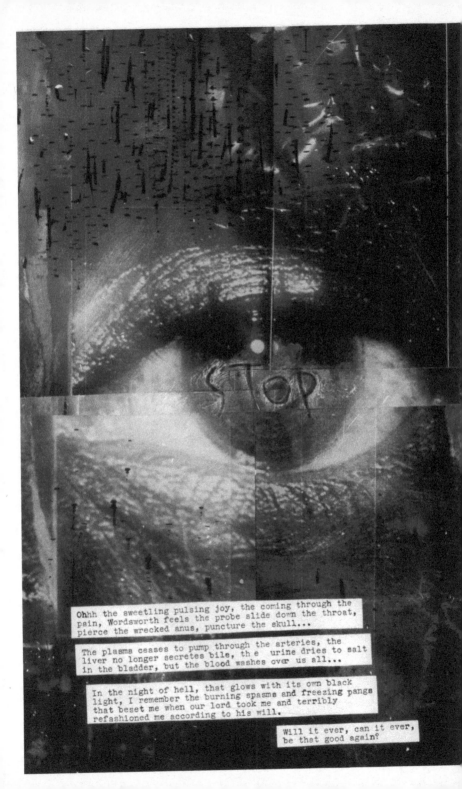

Ohhh the sweetling pulsing joy, the coming through the pain, Wordsworth feels the probe slide down the throat, pierce the wrecked anus, puncture the skull...

The plasma ceases to pump through the arteries, the liver no longer secretes bile, the urine dries to salt in the bladder, but the blood washes over us all...

In the night of hell, that glows with its own black light, I remember the burning spasms and freezing pangs that beset me when our lord took me and terribly refashioned me according to his will.

Will it ever, can it ever, be that good again?

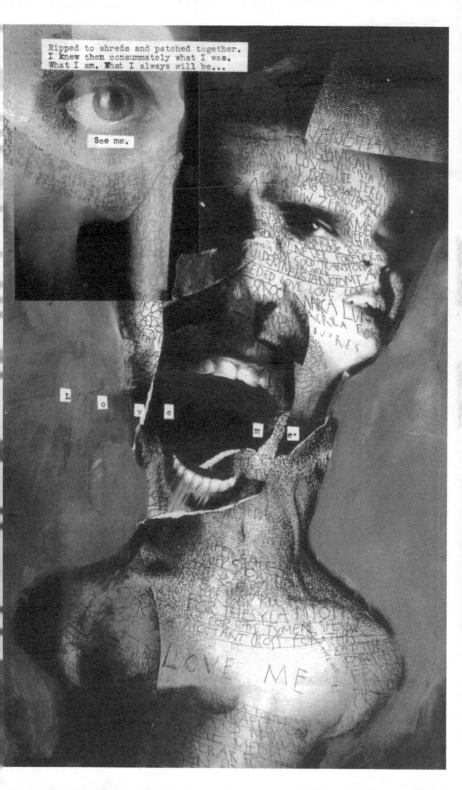

Look at my words.

(Examine the writhing tapestries of choice delight implicit in each scratching and each syllable.)

I guard th e words.

I keep them tenderly, express them with my tangled flesh and tattered tongue.

Words that form stOries, or tales, or patterns.

Words that can but hint at the delights of damnation, of the ultimate pleasures that wait for them all on the beyondside of pain.

I'll show you another.

Stg with me, my shattered children. Stay and listen and stare and learn. Was that tale good?

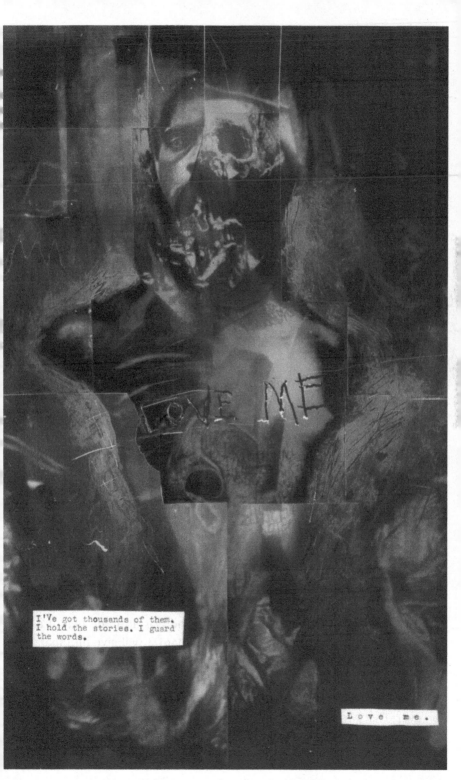

I'Ve got thousands of them.
I hold the stories. I guard
the words.

Love   me.

A Little Piece of Hell
Steve Niles

I know bad people when I see them, and Gordon Fuller was a world-class, evil scumbag, son of a bitch. He also happened to be my best friend.

Funny how things work out.

What that makes me, I do not know.

Since meeting him back in 1996, I'd personally witnessed him beat the shit out of several individuals, and at least one woman (Debbie . . . Donna . . . ? Can't remember anymore). Granted she stabbed him about two inches from his dick, but that doesn't make up for the beating he gave her in return.

I've seen Gordon steal people's money and drugs, usually from right under their noses (with drugs, that was *especially* the case). I've seen him con his way in and out of some of the most fucked-up situations and lie like it was an Olympic event.

Gordon was a prick. No doubt. But he was also one hell of a stand-up guy when the shit came down hard. I will give him that. And seeing as I had a knack for getting in some tight spots, he proved to be a decent friend.

I almost feel sorry that I personally led him to Hell, but whatever. That's where he was headed anyway.

■   ■   ■

It was the middle of March and Los Angeles was having a strange spell of mixed weather days. One second it would rain, the next the sun would come out. The nights were cold, and the constant wind made it all raw, uncomfortable.

I was living in an apartment off Franklin. A scuzzy, roach-infested little dump, but it was cheap and times were tough, so it suited me fine. Not like I ever threw dinner parties or anything.

The last time I scored was six weeks prior and only because I'd walked into a bar that looked like it had been hit by an alcohol bomb. It was closing time and mating standards had dropped for the remaining bar hags, so one of them came home with me.

Julie was her name, I think. She was about as homely as I am, and I remember she sounded like a rattle when she walked. I later found out it was because she carried Tic Tacs in her purse, but I'll always remember her as the Rattle Girl. The last woman who'd even touched me.

Julie was the first person I'd ever heard speak about that stupid box, as well. She talked a lot but all I was thinking about was getting in her pants. Somewhere between foreplay and whatever passed for actual penetration, she told me about a friend, some shitbag named Andy Getz, who recently found a strange little box in an alley. Sold it to a pawnshop for a couple bucks, only to discover later that the pawnshop had turned around and sold it for, get this, ten thousand dollars.

That got my attention.

Ten grand for a fucking box?

I told Gordon about it later on and amazingly he knew Andy. He said Andy used to be the go-between for a guy he bought weed from. Gordon's hunch was that the box was full of drugs or something—that it was the contents that made it valuable, not the box itself.

We decided to check it out. It had all the elements of interest for Gordon: easy money and the chance to screw someone over.

■   ■   ■

We found Andy Getz at a dive bar in Hollywood, just past the cleaned-up touristy section. It wasn't even noon and he was already drunk.

I slid up next to him on the right and Gordon flanked him on the left.

Gordon spoke first.

"Andy," Gordon said in a mildly threatening manner. "This is my buddy, Ed."

Andy looked at me with glazed eyes.

I nodded. "We hear you had some kind of box that you sold."

Andy's shoulders slumped like he was revisiting his biggest regret. "Aw, man," he whined. "Everybody in town know about that shit?"

Gordon said, "Some bitch named Julie told Ed here about it."

Andy looked at Gordon and then back to me. "Yeah, I fucked her, too."

I rolled my tongue in my mouth and tried to remember if I'd used a condom.

Gordon ordered a round of beers to make the situation friendlier. After a few, Andy spoke freely about the box and the deal he lost out on.

"It was about so big," he said, indicating what seemed to be a drunken, palm-sized square. "And it had these grooves with metal and shit. I tried to open the fucking thing but all that happened was a little static spark."

I looked at Gordon. "Spark?" I asked. "That's fucking weird."

Andy drunkenly nodded, swinging his head side to side depending on which one of us was talking. "And I'll tell you something. That box freaked me out. Honest. It was weird. Stupid little box and it gave me the creeps."

He was getting sloppy. It was time to get the key info. Gordon took the ball and ran. "So what pawnshop was it again?"

Andy thumbed back over his shoulder and almost fell off the stool. "Iz that place over by, what the hell's it called, the Scientist Building?"

"Scientology?" I corrected.

"Yeah, thaz it. The shop in the strip mall across the street."

Gordon and I exchanged another glance. The pawnshop was called *Dexter's*. It was four blocks from my apartment in a strip mall behind some trendy restaurants. We thanked drunken Andy, slapped him on the back, and slipped out of the darkness of the dive bar into the blinding light of day.

We headed over to *Dexter's Pawn Shop*. Neither of us had a car, so we had to take the bus, of all things, from Hollywood a few dozen blocks north back to my neck of the woods. I got off the bus behind Gordon, and as he stepped off onto the sidewalk I noticed the angular bulge under his shirt.

I grabbed him by the shoulder as the bus pulled away. "You carrying a piece, man?"

"Yeah," Gordon said like it was the dumbest question in the world. "Of course I am."

"Why?"

Gordon rubbed his chin mockingly. "Let me see," he said. "To shoot someone in the fucking face if they mess with me. How's that sound?"

I didn't reply. I just shook my head and walked toward the strip mall where *Dexter's Pawn Shop* sat between a Korean barbecue and a dry cleaner's that had gone out of business. We approached the shop. Gordon grabbed the door, but despite the OPEN sign hanging crooked in the window, it didn't budge.

Inside I could see a mountain of a man with a beard, perched behind the counter, on a stool that looked like it grew from his ass. I waved and the man mountain reached under the counter and released the door lock.

I entered first with Gordon trailing. The dude at the counter kept his hand underneath it. I assumed that's where he kept his gun.

"How can I help you, gentlemen?" he said, removing his hand, evidently deciding we were safe.

"Are you Dexter?" I asked.

"No," he said. "Dexter died years ago. I'm Jerry. Anything in particular you're looking for?"

Gordon stepped up. "Name's Gordon. This is Ed. We're looking for some information."

Jerry eyeballed us hard. "You guys cops?"

Gordon laughed out loud and I just smiled. "Good Lord, no," Gordon said. "We're anything but cops."

"What kind of information you looking for?" Jerry asked, and I noticed his hand inching under the counter again.

"We're looking for somebody who bought something from you," Gordon said.

Jerry shook his head. "That's not being very specific. Besides, we don't give out that kind of information."

My heart almost stopped as I saw Gordon reach for something behind him and relaxed when he came back with his wallet and not the gun. He pulled out a twenty and laid it on the counter.

"Somebody bought a small box for a lot of dough."

Jerry took the twenty, then wrote a name on a scrap of paper and slid it back.

"Thanks, Jerry," Gordon said and abruptly turned and went for the exit.

I nodded at the man mountain named Jerry. He nodded back, and I saw the corner of his mouth curl slightly, and his eyes narrow like he knew something we didn't. A chill snaked down my spine and I almost ran into Gordon as he waited for the smirking man mountain to buzz the door.

The name on the paper scrap was Thomas Harden. Anybody who lived in Los Angeles or watched a movie knew who he was. I sure did. He was a producer known for spending very little money on movies and making millions back.

He specialized in horror movies, the films that teens flocked to on weekends. Harden knew how to snag the kids. He put in lots of violence, graphic and horrible torture and mutilation, and added just enough sex and nudity to keep the censors at bay.

Even Gordon thought Harden was a sick fuck. That's saying a lot.

In one film I saw, there was a scene where a nude girl was skinned alive on camera. It lasted ten minutes without cutting away, and just the sounds of the girl's shrieks would have been enough to turn my stomach. That was the last time I watched a Harden-produced movie.

And this was the guy who had spent ten thousand dollars on a stupid little box.

Gordon and I took buses all the way to the base of the Hollywood Hills, where the bus lines stopped on Ventura Boulevard.

From there we walked it because Gordon didn't want to take a cab. I went along with it, in active denial of what was really happening. We actually didn't take a cab because we didn't want any record of where we went or what we were doing.

Strange the way crimes start sometimes, no? Most people think it's all planning, premeditation. The scary thing is, it can be unspoken right up to the point of break-in or murder, just a silent agreement between two nasty bastards like me and Gordon.

As we approached the gates of Thomas Harden's mansion perched in the hills we both knew, without so much as speaking a word of it, we were going to break in and get that box, one way or another.

Something about the very idea of the mystery box had, and I know this sounds odd, possessed us both. Maybe it was the ten grand Harden had paid. Maybe it was the loss in that loser Andy's eyes or the dangerous smirk on the man mountain's lips, the look on his face; but something beyond simple greed drove us up those long, winding roads.

We stopped just short of the paved driveway and the black iron gates flanked by security cameras. The house was tucked inside high walls and thick foliage planted to deter unwanted fans and intruders.

I flinched and backed away when I saw the cameras, but Gordon squinted and raised his hands.

"They're not on," he said. "Look."

I looked up. He was right. The red indicator lights below the lenses were off, and the cameras hung at a sort of dead level. Even if they were on, they would only catch our feet at best.

Curious, I gave the gate a push, and to both our surprise, it creaked open. Nothing was on or locked. As I pushed the gate open wider, I got the sense that the whole place was shut down. Something wasn't right.

Even Gordon felt it, and that prick never felt anything. He pointed ahead, up the shoehorn driveway. The arc peaked at a huge, modern/Spanish-style mansion. It was the oddest house I'd ever fucking seen—instead of sections, it just looked like stacked stucco squares with way too many windows offset at different levels.

"Is that his house?" I asked.

Gordon took the gun, some kind of semi-automatic, from his waistband as he walked ahead. "Sure looks like it. Come on. Let's make this a quick in-and-out."

We walked fast and steady up the driveway to the front door, which we found open a sliver.

Gordon looked at me. I shrugged.

"We're just getting the box and then splitting, right?" I asked. I felt a quiver in my voice.

And Gordon heard it.

He grinned at me and lowered his head. "Let's see what there is to see."

The tone in his voice screamed trouble, and if I'd had a lick of sense I would have turned around right then, but I didn't. Instead I followed Gordon as he pushed open the front door of the odd mansion, and the smell of sulfur and urine hit us both like an unexpected wave.

"Fucking hell," I said, throwing my hand over my nose and mouth. "Stinks!"

Gordon pulled up his T-shirt, used it to buffer the stench, and pushed on down a long narrow hall covered with framed movie posters. All horror. All produced by Harden. Besides the posters, everything was white.

The walls were white. The carpet was white. The closed door in between the last set of posters was so white, that if not for the silver handle, I might not have noticed a door at all.

Until we reached the end of the hall and the carpet started fading to red; sopping-wet, bloody red.

The spacious living room was a huge white square, not furnished, nothing on the walls . . . until recently, it seemed. The walls were splattered with blood that still ran and dripped. Chunks of matter, skin and organs ripped to tiny shreds still pried loose from the walls and slapped to the soaked carpet.

I'd never seen so much blood in my life, not even in one of Harden's films.

In the center of the room was a perfect clean spot, like a white crater on a planet of blood. There sat the box we'd come for. It sat on a pad of paper.

I looked at Gordon. "We should get out of here."

Gordon looked nauseous. He was staring at the ceiling, where larger pieces of shredded flesh were coming loose like wet tiles and falling to the sopping carpet with an audible slap. That was the first time I ever saw Gordon afraid . . . and it wouldn't be the last.

Despite all this, Gordon was still greedier than smart or frightened. He shook his head and stepped onto the soaked carpet. The sound was loud and wet as he let his foot sink into the gory slush.

Just watching him walk, hearing the squish of his steps and the sounds of dripping from ceiling to floor, made my stomach lurch and twist. What the hell had happened in here? It looked like a bomb had exploded and the box was ground zero.

I stood at the edge of the hall, where, even as I waited, blood seeped and spread wider, closing in on me. I watched Gordon take careful steps across the bloody carpet until he reached the clean area, where he immediately picked up the box.

I watched as Gordon tried to find a way to open it, but he had no luck.

"What's on the pad of paper?" I asked, yelling above the rising din of raining gore.

Gordon paused and bent down. "Looks like someone was trying to figure out how to open it."

"Probably Harden?"

Gordon gestured around the blood-covered walls. "This is probably Harden, too."

Gordon tried to pass off his comment as a joke, but even I could see he was nervous.

He turned and gestured for me to follow him, but I shook my head. "I'm staying right here," I said, "and I think we should get the fuck out of here."

"Are you kidding me? You fucking pussy?" Gordon mocked. "Look at this joint. I'll bet my last dime that there's drugs and money, if not both, stashed here somewhere."

"Okay," I snapped back. "Then what are you doing?"

Gordon started to kneel, placing the gun down beside the ornate box. "I'm going to open this thing and see what's inside."

A shiver ran down my spine as I watched Gordon kneel before the box. I looked around to see what else I could find, but there was blood blocking my path to the stairs across the living room, and to the door leading to what looked like a balcony, and another door to a tiled room I guessed was the kitchen.

Maybe Gordon hadn't thought of it, but stepping in that blood meant leaving tracks, and leaving tracks meant leading the cops right back to us. They'd tie us to this entire mess, not just a burglary. Maybe Gordon wasn't thinking, but for once I was. I'd done a stint in the penitentiary when I was a kid—I had no intention of going through that hell again.

While Gordon studied the notepad, I looked back down the hall to the door we'd passed by. Maybe that was another way into other areas of the house?

"I'm going to look around," I said. "Yell if you need me . . . and hurry."

Gordon only half glanced up at me. He was enthralled with the box that I had already lost interest in. Seeing its modest size, I had serious doubts it held any great value.

The door between posters for *Slaughter Me Saturday* and *Feel the Pain* was locked, but that didn't stop me from opening it. I used a plastic card to shimmy the bolt and popped it right open. On the other side were some stairs leading down.

I tried the lights, but they weren't working, which explained why all the security was down—no power.

I took out my lighter and walked down the steps that led to a small basement room. I laughed out loud when I saw it was a personal torture chamber, with a leather harness swing and a table with straps and handles shaped like a large X. It was Harden's own sex dungeon.

The walls were lined with whips and straps and various other toys you could find at any sex shop in West Hollywood, but farther along the wall, the toys turned from kinky to downright bizarre. There were whips with metal balls on them, and others with spikes. There was what looked like a vest and panties made of razor wire and a mask made entirely of barbed wire. All of the weaponlike toys looked like they had dried blood on them.

On the farthest wall there was a medieval shield with two crossed swords behind it. It looked like something from a B-movie version of *Camelot,* and as I stepped closer I could see it hung awkwardly from the wall.

There was something behind it.

I put out the lighter and waited a moment for my eyes to adjust, then lifted the surprisingly light shield off the wall. Behind it was a wall safe, and the reason the shield had hung awkwardly was because it had been left open.

Hoping for stacks of cash, I pulled it open to find instead stacks of pornography; graphic shit, violent, not what I would have called sexy at all. There were pictures of women tied up and being fucked, and others of men bound and having their balls tortured. Not my cup of tea at all.

Then, behind the stacks, I saw the drugs. There were bags of white powder and bottles of pills. Not cash, but just as good. I took the bags and bottles one by one and filled my pockets to capacity. I was taking one last look inside when I heard Gordon scream upstairs and felt the entire house rumble.

Thinking it was an earthquake I ran for the stairs, but by the time I reached the top, the rumbling had stopped, and when I peered toward the bloody living room, I saw that Gordon was no longer alone.

Four figures stood around Gordon, who held the box, now oddly reconfigured, in one shaking hand; his gun in the other.

My pockets loaded with thousands of dollars in drugs, I almost ran, thinking the leather-clad figures were police. As I looked closer, though, I saw they were anything but cops.

I wasn't even sure they were human.

One stood in front of Gordon, one behind, and the last two flanked him. All wore what looked like black leather, but no two looked the same. The lead figure, facing Gordon, appeared to have the leather sewn into his skin up the sides of his arms and torso.

Exposed areas of deathly blue-white flesh were covered with gashes that were held open by wires. The leader's head was a maze of slashes and slices and wires that held them open, forming an intricate maze of designs, cutting into the figure's face.

If these figures were male or female, I could not tell. Except for the leader facing Gordon, their chests and crotch regions were so severely mutilated that I simply could not even begin to guess.

But the leader, he was male, or had been at one time. I glanced down in horror, feeling my breath cut off and mouth go dry. What I'd first thought was a vagina was instead the figure's penis, cut down the middle in at least six slices, pulled and pinned around his belly and legs like a seeping bloody flower of flesh.

I took a step forward, trying to see what was happening, and the pills in my pockets rattled so loud that all of the figures—even Gordon—turned and looked at me.

Gordon cried out. "Ed, help me, man!"

The leader tilted his head and stared at me with large, black eyes. "Would the witness care to change places with his accomplice?" he said, his voice sexless, both high-pitched and low, like two voices speaking simultaneously.

It seemed to know who I was, or what I was to Gordon at least, but I sensed some doubt in the inhuman tones. My presence was unexpected, that much was clear.

The leader, with the head and face of gashes and wire-maze mesh, looked at me and the expression was like nothing I had seen before. It was almost a smile, but a smile of pain; pleasure and pain intertwined, love and hate crushed together in a vise.

I couldn't help myself. I smiled back at the inhuman creature as if we knew each other's game.

"No," I said, "I won't."

The leader nodded.

I'd played my hand and it was understood.

Gordon looked at me with disbelief and raised the gun, "You fucking bastard!"

He fired the weapon, but the leader with the flowered penis and understanding, loving eyes raised his hand and blocked the muzzle, taking the bullet through his own palm.

As the shot tore through his hand, the leader bent his head back and opened his mouth in pure ecstasy, an orgasm of pain.

What happened next was a blur. I watched as weapons appeared in the hands of the humanoid figures surrounding Gordon; an array of blades and razors and hooks. They hacked into Gordon all at once, tearing away his flesh as easily as his clothing. The figure behind him slashed down his spine, sending him reeling in agony.

The screams brought odd titters of laughter from the deathly, mutilated shapes, like children giggling at something naughty.

Gordon wailed as he was taken apart layer by layer. Flesh gave way to muscle. Muscle gave way to bone, and while he still stood, they hacked into his organs before they could fall to the floor.

Only the leader paused in the slaughter, to pick up the puzzle box Gordon had dropped. He held it in his hands as he faced me, and I watched as it reconfigured into a box shape right in the palms of his hands.

Then he looked at me one last time. "Are you sure you would not like to play?"

I shook my head and backed away, and the leader began cackling. Behind him his brethren demolished the last of Gordon, even though his head, lanced on a hook but still intact, managed to scream in pain.

I turned and ran, feeling the house rumble and the electricity suddenly coming back on. I didn't yet fully realize what had happened and just scrambled for the door, but as I reached it, I turned back and saw the leader standing alone with the box.

Gordon was gone. Only his blood remained.

The leader had stopped laughing, but the smile of pain lingered.

I didn't get it until the lights flickered on and the alarm system that had been silenced came back to life with a slowly winding screech.

I looked one last time at the leader, who seemed to be fading into the light, and the smile was gone. Instead he looked at me with a sort of pity, like I was the fool who had played a game I didn't understand and thought I'd won.

I didn't even try running. I walked out of Harden's mansion with my hands raised in the air as police cars screamed through the gates and up the horseshoe driveway.

Behind me was unimaginable carnage, a safe with my prints all over it, and I had a pocketful of stolen drugs.

The leader was a clever one. I had to give him that. Even with a searing anger welling inside, knowing I'd been fooled, knowing I'd played his game despite imagining I'd played by my rules, I had to give the mutilated man his credit.

I'd be blamed for all the crimes, and the death of Gordon—

second biggest scumbag in the world, and the only person I had personally sent to Hell, condemning myself as well.

I thought about what had happened as the cops surrounded me, pointing guns and yelling the things cops yell. I had never touched the box, and I certainly wasn't the one who'd opened it, but I now understood.

I thought I was so smart, and I had played right into the leader's hands. It wasn't just the handling of the box that allowed them access to my life; it was my interaction with him. I had entered their world, with their rules, before I even knew what was happening.

I'd played his game, thinking I wasn't, and I lost regardless.

Now I knew why the leader laughed as he had. I'd thought it was a communion of souls facing off, but the leader had simply played me as Gordon had the box, and both of us had lost our souls—one in Hell and the other on Earth.

Well played.

The Dark Materials Project
Sarah Langan

A lot of thoughts crossed Absalom's mind when he discovered that his pregnant wife had left him. As he confronted his Mr. Coffee machine, bewildered by its myriad buttons, he wondered: Was it his halitosis? Was she a spy for ExxonMobil? He'd known her less than a year, and back then she'd had a man (or woman) on the side, so was the child even his? He looked at the refrigerator, where the kid's sonogram was taped like an edible fetus, then around the empty kitchen. His wife was nowhere in sight.

He found her note on the passenger seat of their blue Saab. A tribute to the obvious:

> *I'm sorry. It's getting too dangerous.*
> *All My Love,*
> *Mireille*

On the radio, some NPR dipshit reported on Stanford University's renegade black hole. The EPA had evacuated the entire campus and would soon do the same with all of Southern California. It was spreading too fast to contain. A nuke was the only way to hasten its collapse, but so far nobody wanted to suggest it.

As warmth poured through the vents that cold winter morning, he blew on his hands to get his fingers moving again, then set Mireille's note ablaze with the car's cigarette lighter. It didn't crackle as it burned. Instead, it singed. His parents, his little brother, his college professors, his contemporaries, even his protégés—they'd all betrayed him. Stolen his work, lost faith, mocked his ambitions, taken jobs in other countries just to get away from him. Why had he expected that Mireille would be any different, just because he'd paid for her?

He looked up at their old colonial as he pulled from the driveway, and imagined that she was trapped inside the master bedroom while a voracious fire burned. Would she scream? Or would she maintain an infuriatingly stiff upper lip as the flames licked her cheeks? He hoped to find out.

The Servitus Labs were a three-block radius of sprawl surrounded by barbwire and armed guards. Six years ago, its CEO recruited Absalom to manage the Dark Materials Project, and every day since then, the saboteurs had gotten bolder. Eco-terrorists, anti-eugenicists, university competition, random crazies who needed a cause—they all flocked to Winchester, Massachusetts, sandwich boards and spray paint in hands like they'd discovered the new Roswell. They wanted either to halt the project or to have a piece of it. Sometimes both, so long as it gave them a few seconds of fame.

Winchester was prettier than most suburbs, full of colonial mansions, kids' parks, and independently owned boutiques selling high-priced crap like antique Underwood typewriters that didn't type and sterling silver jewelry crafted by hippies with rich parents. The town was far enough away from Boston to keep the operation secure, but close enough to lure the top scientists. You could raise a family here, which, until recently, had been part of his plan.

At the first checkpoint, he rolled down the window so the infrared laser could scan his retina. Upon recognition, the gate lifted, and George and Juan waved him through with the butts of their semi-automatics. He'd always gotten the impression that neither of them liked him. But that was fine. They were rent-a-cops, and he was on track for a second Nobel Prize.

"It's a mess," Dan Stephens announced as the second Absalom walked through the third security door. A missing wife, and no morning coffee. He had to agree: it was a mess.

"The chimps. The dogs. Even the fucking rabbits," Dan said. He was a lanky guy who wore cheap Men's Wearhouse suits to work every day, even though he could afford better. A geek, like everybody else here.

"More mania?" Absalom asked. They were standing in the hallway. Ionized, filtered air hissed through the vents. It smelled sweet.

"Two of the chimps bashed their heads against their cages last night. They killed themselves." Dan pinched the skin between his eyes and took a couple of gasping breaths. "Animals don't commit suicide. They were scared of something!" Dan's eyes got misty. He was unmarried, and called the chimps his babies.

This entire Winchester Complex, which Absalom managed, was devoted to the discovery and study of Shadow DNA; dark matter. Blue eyes, wide smile, agility of synapses: all were determined by run-of-the mill chromosomes. Humans have twenty-three pairs; chimps, twenty-four; fruit flies, four; E. coli, one. Shadow DNA were more sophisticated. Personality, sense of humor, moral compass, human soul—these variables existed outside the parameters of the double helix. There was a reason that, until now, no geneticist had accurately predicted their expression, even after the entire human genome was decoded: they were determined by Shadow DNA.

A decade ago, Absalom was the only scientist in the world who'd anticipated that the dark matter attending all mass also existed in the human genome. What he hadn't guessed, and the reason it had taken so long to find the stuff, was that only mammals possessed it. The rest—bacteria, fruit flies, lizards, even sharks—none were complex enough to warrant the extra genetic material.

Shadow DNA's commercial potential was huge. Parents could special order the best and brightest children. Medicines could be targeted against mutated Shadow genes, so that humorless duds suddenly became prom kings. In another generation, this society could clone itself, and no one would ever have to die.

In college, while every other wannabe MD had gotten laid by promising his money-hungry girlfriend a white picket fence, Absalom had sat in his dorm room, gazing at a poster of the double helix while jerking off, convinced that something so perfect proved God. He'd worked his whole life. Forty-two years old, and his back was crooked from leaning over a desk eighteen hours a day, seven days a week. But now he headed the most important project in history, and raked in millions. He'd been able to buy a Porsche, a summer house on the Cape, present Mireille with a fucking ruby tiara and tell her she was his queen the night they got hitched. Five years ago, *Time* magazine had called him the smartest man in the world.

"I'm worried. I'm not sure we should keep doing this," Dan the geek announced. "Something's not right." Above them the fluorescent lights blinked, and the vents hissed.

"I hired you to do this. It's your job," Absalom answered.

Dan was the head animal behaviorist. As Shadow DNA codes were cracked, it was his job to juxtapose them against discrete animal behaviors. So far, he'd discovered that those animals with thin dark matter base clouds were hostile, while those animals with thicker bases tended toward more rational thought.

Last month, Absalom's team had finally cracked the chimp code. It made an elegant picture: a double helix surrounded by a spinning cloud of nucleic acid strands thin as cobwebs. On the computer screen, it looked a little like a sandstorm. Not long after Dan began mapping the cloud, and tacking it against these animals' souls, the chimps had begun to act strangely. Cannibalism. Self-mutilation. Devouring their own offspring when not fed on time.

"You're almost done, aren't you?" Absalom asked.

Dan wiped his eyes. Tears of indignant rage. "It's hurting them. It'll hurt us, too. You need to shut the project down."

Absalom took a breath, stared at Dan, hard. Mireille, holding that fat stomach, had voiced the same concern. Anecdotal evidence.

Random coincidence. Bad press. Just as easily, it was Stanford's black hole making the animals nervous, or the radiation from that spill in Alaska.

He'd put his heart into this project. Sacrificed his wife for it. Fired his closest friend, who'd leaked the animal mania results to the press. He'd given up his health. His eyes were 40/40, and he got so dizzy from all the numbers spinning in his head that when he was alone, he talked to himself. He wasn't about to stop now, when he was so close. If this thing worked out like he hoped, in another couple of years, he'd have a new body. A new life. A whole new Mireille, if he wanted.

"Pack your desk," Absalom said.

Dan gasped, and began to wail. The sight was ridiculous. "Don't be a pussy," Absalom spat, then headed for his lab, his stride fast and furious.

Coffee was waiting for him at the lab. Black with three sugars, just how he liked it. His desk was perched a few steps above the thirty-man workstation like a throne. Below, the world's top statisticians and geneticists typed madly, calloused fingers click-clacking. Their faces glowed green from the reflected lights of their computer screens.

He sighed. Sipped his coffee. At least here, he was happy. He belonged. In truth, he never should have married Mireille. He wasn't the marrying kind. He'd never been home for dinner, or taken her out for a night on the town. No honeymoon. Then again, that's no reason to leave in the middle of the night, and steal the Porsche and jewelry. At eight months along, she must have greased herself with Crisco to fit behind that wheel.

Clack-clack, typing away. The sound was like music. On the large console, percent complete figures ran for each individual sequence. Everybody except Phil was ahead of schedule.

Absalom's heart warmed. He picked up the phone and dialed. A mistake, surely. The rash behavior of women. He'd give her another chance. She worked one building away, in public relations. They'd met last year, when he'd discovered the first evidence of Shadow

DNA in the brown rat. She'd composed the press release, and coached his staff on how to handle reporters. As soon as the story broke, Winchester was swarmed with media. Stanford, MIT, and every nickel-and-dime pharmaceutical corporation in the country tried to reproduce his team's findings. None of them succeeded, and so long as the federal order to reveal their methods remained pending in court, they never would. Stanford had screwed up the most egregiously by toying with dark matter electrons. A black hole swallowed their entire astrophysics lab, and now everybody was pointing fingers. Absalom's photo had been on the cover of the *New York Times* with the caption "Hero or Traitor?" Through it all, Mireille had been his rock.

Then again, last week her ex-boyfriend had visited from Boston. His junk-heap Plymouth had been parked in the driveway like it belonged there.

After the third ring, Mireille's voice mail picked up. "This is Mireille Vitols. I no longer work at Servitus. Please direct your call to reception."

So she'd given notice. She'd planned this. He clenched his fist and imagined her skin peeling from her bones. Even last night, a hot dinner had been waiting for him in the oven, his suits dry-cleaned and filed in his closet like charts. The sneak.

He hung up the phone just as Phil from the cubicle in the back row stood. "This is suspicious," Phil said. Phil was convinced that everything was suspicious; he had a severe case of paranoid schizophrenia. A lot of the crazies were good at math.

Absalom looked at the bottom of his empty cup. "Somebody get me more," he called, then descended the steps like a king and entered the lab. The series on Phil's screen wouldn't stop running, even though there were only 250 million base pairs to quantify— they'd isolated the distinct genes that coded for suppressed memories. But the screen registered 511 million base pairs. It was at 302 million and counting. Adenosine-Thymine, Guyanine-Cytosine: AAAAGGGCCCAAAGT. Like souls possessed, the screen was a series of letters and statistics, running fast as blurs.

"It's not looping back from the beginning, is it? What's it sequencing?" Absalom asked. As he watched, the screen blinked. He thought of Mireille, and the first time he'd reached across her desk and touched her. The kid couldn't be his. The ex-boyfriend, the kid at the 7-Eleven, the guy at the car wash. Any of them. All of them. He'd seen how they looked at her. He should have fucked her up the ass like he'd always wanted. He should have kicked her in the gut the second she'd shown him that pink stick.

"I think we found it," Phil said.

Absalom took a deep breath. Human Shadow DNA. *Yeah, maybe.*

"Run a diagnostic," Absalom said.

Just then the lights flickered. He looked around. Suddenly, every interface in the thirty-person lab looked like Phil's. Sequences fast as runaway trains. Dizzying. Overwhelming. In his mind, Mireille. Then, just as quickly, all the screens went dead.

Corinna brought him his coffee, then called maintenance. The twenty-person squad ran their diagnostics. Four hours later, the computers were still dark. A virus, the techs agreed. They found an e-mail opened by Absalom's most recent hire. Its sender was on the "do not trust" list: ExxonMobil. Absalom fired him on the spot. To his credit, unlike Dan, he didn't cry.

At five o'clock, Absalom sent everybody home. At eight, the techs left to see if they could trace the root of the virus to the server in the basement, while Absalom worked off his personal computer, which wasn't connected to the network. Around nine that night, the screens blinked back on. All ran the same code, then blinked off again. He snatched what he could from their memories, then plotted the data on his personal computer.

The series was more than halfway to completion: 392 million. The plot made a picture that spun and grew: a double helix with small fishing-line filaments that dangled from its phosphate sugars. He zeroed in on the filaments and saw that the letters were all wrong. Full of U's—RNA, not DNA. And another letter, unknown nucleotide Z.

His heart caught in his chest, like love at first sight. What *was* this?

Then his screen blinked, and he remembered the Peeping Tom that had scared the crap out of him growing up. The guy was arrested for exposing himself in a movie theater, but before that he used to troll the neighborhood, peeking through windows. He waved at Absalom now, like he'd waved at him through his childhood window thirty years ago as Absalom had prepared for bed, naked and climbing into plaid pajama pants. He smiled, only his skin was scored with fishhooks. The lights flickered. His face appeared on every screen. The laptop crashed. Everything went dark.

Absalom took a jagged breath. What the hell? And then he understood, sneaky Exxon bastards, the virus was airborne.

Back at the house, a message was waiting on the wall screen television. She looked great. Her blonde hair was thicker and wavier than ever, and her cheeks bright as new apples. In the image, she held her engorged stomach, and he imagined that it was dead in her womb.

"It's me. I thought I should let you know I'm okay," she said. "I just think this is best. I'll call again soon, when I figure out what to do next." The overhead lightbulb popped and went out. He remembered the double helix, its flagella swimming.

He turned on the lamp, and for an instant, he really did see her on fire, the child inside her boiling. She didn't act like he'd expected. She screamed, while beside her, the Peeping Tom rubbed himself raw.

Then the image righted itself. "I know you're taking this badly, but please remember that I love you. It's just, how can you argue with someone who's never wrong?" she asked as she signed off.

"Considerate," he said to the screen, then smashed the damn thing into rubber and silicone bits. He didn't sleep that night. Instead he researched. For inspiration, he took the fetus down from the fridge and taped it to his chest.

On his drive to work the next morning, the dipshit on NPR was still talking about the black hole. The whole of Southern California had been evacuated, except for the Hispanics, because there weren't enough buses. Dipshit's special guest, a mathematician from MIT, babbled about how playing God opens doors that ought to stay closed. "Honestly, the numbers don't add up," he said. "I know this is going to sound strange, but I don't think this has to do with traditional dark matter. I'm starting to think it's some kind of symbiotic life-form attached to human DNA that Servitus discovered. And not a peaceful life-form, either."

Absalom rolled his eyes. Sure, yeah. Academia screwed up so badly they were going to have to drop an H-bomb, but somehow it was all corporate America's fault. Funny thing MIT hadn't announced these suspicions a month ago, when the Fed had been doling out grants.

"Dark matter, Shadow genes—they're all connected," the expert said. "And I guess I'm a Johnny-come-lately, but I think we should have left them alone. I'd advocate that the federal government shut it down. Servitus, the universities, everything. At least until we know more."

Absalom autodialed the radio station at the red light between State and Servitus streets. A yellow school bus in front of him opened its doors and picked up a pile of well-adjusted brats. On the other line, an intern with a high-pitched voice asked, "What's the nature of your call?"

He was about explain that he worked at Servitus, and nobody here had decimated the state of California. Instead he said, "My wife left me. I think she was a corporate spy. Got my codes and sent a virus through the system. Or maybe she was a Jesus freak. The kid's not even mine. I've been betrayed too many times in my life. I deserve respect. This time I'll get her back. This time I'm going to kill her."

The intern cleared his throat. The school bus moved on. Absalom turned right and entered the complex, where protesters burned the effigy of a fetus. "Save the future!" they chanted.

"Have you ever had sex?" Absalom asked. He winced as he said it.

"Uhhh," the intern said.

"Yeah. I thought so, you snot-nose fuck. Why am I talking to you?" He hung up.

At the office, the virus had spread. Not even the coffee machine worked. He spooned grounds into warm water, then swirled them in his mouth. They got the computers back online, but not much had changed. Numbers ran. More tails off helixes, more unexplained codes. "I think God called me last night," Phil said. "It was very suspicious."

Corinna showed up with weeping sores across her skin. "I did it to myself," she said with puzzlement. "Why do you think I went and wasted perfectly good cigarettes?"

Behind them, Absalom saw the Peeping Tom light his wife on fire. Did his staff see, too? The multitailed helix swam across the room. It had lost its beauty, and now seemed like a rough beast.

Maintenance couldn't get the system operational. Absalom sent everybody home. Plotted the new data to his personal computer. There were 412 million base pairs and counting. This time, the tails surrounding the helix coalesced into an oval like the outline of a face.

He jabbed his index finger against the screen. "Well, fuck you, too," he said, then picked up the phone to call Mireille just as the lights flickered, and the line went dead. All the power went out.

Back at the house, he continued his research. Fetus taped to his chest, he boiled the ingredients over a stove.

There was another message from Mireille. She was holding her stomach like it hurt. Behind her was a Sears photo print of flowers, and brown wallpaper. Some cheap hotel, he guessed. "My mom lived in LA," she said. She was frowning, like it was his fault they'd finally set off the nuke. He was reminded of Miss Teschmacher from that *Superman* movie, who'd also been a dingbat.

On the drive to the lab the next day, downtown Winchester was in flames. Down low they were blue, then orange, then red. Like the core of the earth was leaking. The NPR dipshit was interviewing a psychic. "Yes, that's right, the traditional definition of Hell is chaos. A place where logic doesn't reign. Ask yourself, why is the nature of man so impossible to determine? Why is the universe an unlockable mystery? Dark matter. Shadow DNA. The invisible hands that guide us. We tried to harness that potential, and in doing so, offended God."

"So you're saying we've somehow opened a door to Hell?" Dipshit asked.

"Look around you. Wouldn't you agree?"

"I don't believe in Hell."

"Finally. The man says something smart," Absalom piped in.

"That's fine," the psychic answered. "Hell persists without your belief. We humans have a darker side, and we've unleashed it with Shadow DNA. We are our own rough beasts of Bethlehem, born at last."

Next to him in the passenger seat, Absalom's Peeping Tom waved. The fetus wailed. His college mentor, who'd stolen his research and published it under his own name, hitchhiked by the side of the road, a cleaver wedged deeply into his skull. He'd perfected the art; a perfect thumbs-up.

This time, no intern answered the line at the station. Just Dipshit. "What is it, caller?"

"I'm the head scientist at Servitus. We haven't cracked the code yet for human DNA. Sorry to break it to you." He thought about the tails. Spindly filaments like those from jellyfish. Perhaps they stung.

"Well, do you have a response to that?" Dipshit asked the psychic.

"I don't think you have any idea what you're doing, or what you've done," the psychic said.

Absalom shook his head, disgusted. So did his mentor. At least on this, they'd found common ground. "It is the purview of all great men to build or destroy at their discretion. Evolution happens in leaps, not increments, and the commoners like you have nothing to do with it."

"You're a monster," the psychic answered.

"Trenchant," Absalom answered. "You should carry a sandwich board and protest at my office like the rest of the crazies." Then he hung up.

Security was missing at the complex. George and Juan had abandoned their posts. Along the halls, chimps and dogs roamed. Most were bloodied from battle, dragging themselves by their paws. Dan had probably set them loose, like an imbecile.

In the lab, green-lit screens blazed, all running the same permutations. There were 446 million base pairs out of 511, and counting. What would happen when the sequence finished and the puzzle was solved? He diagrammed the data to a picture again. The helix was buried underneath an oval face and taloned arms shaped like hooks. It reached out through the computer and sliced him.

He thought he was dreaming when Mireille showed up and bandaged the wound, then wept into the crook of his neck. "It's ending, I think. And it's your fault. So why are you the only person I want to be with?" she asked.

Yes, he'd been certain he was dreaming. That's why he bound and gagged her. Dragged her to the trunk and shoved her inside, even though, with that belly, he'd had to press down hard to get her to fit. Drove home in the dark. Pulled her out, pinched her nose, made her drink the vitamin C and caffeine brew he'd stewed.

Peeping Tom watched. He was missing an eye now, and his mouth was sewn shut. The room seemed to blink. Slants of light played chiaroscuro across the walls. The smell was fetid. Mireille surprised him: she screamed.

He helped her to the couch. Spread her legs while she moaned. The sonogram was taped to his chest underneath his suit, and his sweat broke it in two. Her labor took seven hours. The child was large and she bled. She didn't curse him like he'd expected. Instead she cried and clung to the dead thing as she, too, took her last breath and expired.

■　　■　　■

He didn't wash the blood from his hands the next morning before leaving for work. Dipshit wasn't on NPR, either. Just dead air. The laser eye-reader didn't work, and none of the guards were around, so he crashed the gate.

In the lab, the numbers were gaining: 508 million. In another hour or so, the sequence would be done. Dark matter, of course. So, yes, this was Shadow DNA. The end of the world, too. He took some consolation in the fact that at least he'd been the author of this thing, and not its victim.

He plotted the data to a picture. It was a human body. Grotesque and sneering. The tails were tight skin that ended in hooks. Something dripped onto his desk. He realized his nose was bleeding.

Back home. Drove there fast. Found her corpse. The baby's too. Not much later, a hole opened in the sky, and he knew the sequence had finished.

His Peeping Tom grinned like a bogeyman, and he remembered now that his father had blamed him for that visit thirty years ago. *You and your books. Of course he came to this house, looking.*

The baby crawled at his knees, dragging its placenta.

"He was yours," Mireille told him.

If she weren't dead, he wouldn't have believed.

Out the window, the Peeping Tom watched, only he wore Absalom's face. The child squawked.

"Be honest, you never loved me," he told her.

She was pulling her hair out, strand by strand. The pressure was too great for her thin skin, so much of her scalp came with it. "I used to," she said.

It was only by her admission that she no longer cared for him that he believed she'd ever loved him, and he understood the depth of his loss. Long filaments grew from his smooth face and body. They ended in hooks. A tear rolled down his cheek as the Peeping Tom relieved himself of his futile burden and the black hole enveloped the western sky.

Demon's Design
Nicholas Vince

You're scaring me. I don't like being scared,"
I said. "And can we please stop running?"

"We don't have time."

I stopped. "Justin, I'm not going further till you tell me what the
hell is going on."

He turned and looked at me, slowed as he saw I wasn't following. He half smiled: "Hell is indeed going on, or will be unless we
stop it."

We were standing near the middle of a bridge over the Thames,
with St. Paul's Cathedral at our backs. Our breaths frosted in the
light of the full moon as he walked to me, his back to the power
station converted into an art gallery. This was about eleven o'clock.

"Listen," I said. "I know your father's not the 'manly hug for
his only son' type, but what you said . . . I mean, you're not really
telling me he intends to kill dozens of people at midnight. You are
joking, aren't you?"

He looked at me.

"Okay," I said. "You *are* telling me he's going to kill dozens of
people and we've only got an hour to save them." I paused. Smiled.
"Why not twenty-four?"

"What?" He looked exasperated with me.

"Well, that Jack guy gets twenty-four hours, and even Dale and Flash Gordon got fourteen hours to save the world." We'd watched that movie the previous weekend, both loving the camp OTT performances. We'd only been seeing each other for a couple of months and it was our first source of private jokes.

"Well, if you'd had your bloody phone on, we'd have more time. I've been calling since six o'clock this evening, trying to find you . . ."

He raised, then dropped, his hands in frustration and started to walk on. He didn't want to say, "Where were you?" It would have been too possessive of him. We weren't at that stage; not yet.

I ran a few steps, put my hands on his black duffel coat and turned him. I kissed him on the lips and then rested my forehead on his.

"Okay. Okay. My bad. I let it run out of juice. Look, I'm just having trouble processing this thing with your dad. I mean, why aren't we going to the police with this?"

He pulled away and we started walking hurriedly toward the gallery. "I don't think they'd believe me."

"Okay. So tell them some convincing lie."

"No, I mean, they wouldn't even begin to listen to me." He looked slightly guilty.

"Uh-huh . . . and the reason for that?" I folded my arms and looked at my feet.

"It was before I met you. Last year. I was using back then and . . . I reported that one of his pieces on display at a prominent gallery of modern art was the remains of a real person—pickled."

"I see . . . all right, no, I don't see. Why did you tell the police that?"

"He'd pissed me off."

He pushed his shoulder-length blond hair from off his forehead and started rubbing the back of his neck.

"How, Justin?"

"Does it really matter now? If we're going to stop him—"

"I'd never heard of this . . . I mean, you've never told me much about him, and the more I know about you and your father, the mighty modern artist Caruthian Sanders, the more . . . the more . . . well . . . just tell me. Please."

He slumped slightly and rested against the railing of the bridge, his hands in his pockets against the cold.

"I'd gone to him for help. I hadn't been home for months—I just turned up on his doorstep a few weeks after Mum died. I suddenly realized all the safety had gone from me. There was just empty darkness. My mouth always tasted of ashes."

He looked across at the gallery building and started walking toward it. I followed.

"Mum could always lift my spirits," he continued. "I never knew how she did it—but whenever the depression really hit, half an hour talking to her on the phone and I had some perspective. I mean, we didn't need to discuss what was bothering me. We'd just talk. She'd tell me about my cousins and the old people she helped. Just stuff, but I'd know, I'd really know, it would be all right."

"So what's this got to do with the police?" I asked.

"I told my father how I was feeling—it was like the Buddhist hell of the crimson lotus."

"What's that?"

"Despair. True despair. Imagine you pull your head so far forward—fold into yourself with such ferocity—the ribs of your back split from your spine and open your back like a gory flower. That is the cold hell of the bloodred lotus."

"Yeuch. What did he say?"

"Something about me being a 'Mummy's boy.' "

He paused as we turned onto the ramp at the end of the bridge, leading to the embankment outside the gallery. Then he stopped.

"A month later he asked me to the opening of his new show. It was the usual canapés, champagne, white walls, celebrities, chatter,

chatter, and then the unveiling of his . . . you've guessed it, his *Hell of the Crimson Lotus*. You can't quite see it, but I know it's got my face. He even dedicated it to me."

He was choking back water in his eyes. I hugged him.

"You should have seen their faces. Everyone looking at me with embarrassed pity. I ran to the nearest police station and told them about the installation being a human cadaver.

"Father came down a couple of hours later and 'explained' how the drugs had affected my mind and promised he'd get me professional help. In the car home he didn't speak and when we got to his place, he showed me my room, said the one word: 'Sorry.' Then he left me. Next day he made a lot of phone calls, got me help, and I've been clean ever since."

We started walking away from the bridge, my arm still around his shoulders, toward the entrance to what had been the power station's turbine hall.

"And why do you think he's about to kill all these people?"

"I found this in his studio this morning."

He unfolded a piece of paper and passed it to me. He'd copied it by hand from the original. I read:

Hell has its dominions. Nor Man's Desire or Demon's Design, may extend its bounds. Apart from the prescribed portals and summonings in the hearts of humankind. Philip Lemarchand.

I looked up from the paper at him.

Before I could speak, he said, "There were some drawings with it, disturbing drawings. I did some research on Mr. Lemarchand. He was a French toymaker in the late seventeen hundreds. It's all a bit confused. Some stories say he sold his soul to the Devil, others that he was tricked into using his skills as a mechanical toymaker to create puzzles: the portals he refers to here. Wherever these puzzles turn up, then there's always flesh for the flies to feed on."

"You didn't just Google this, did you?"

He scowled at me. "I used my reader's card for the British Library. There were more recent stories. A couple of brothers in North London, in the 1980's. One of them apparently got hold of a Lemarchand toy. Both brothers and the wife of one were killed or disappeared. Don't you see? What if I was right? What if *The Hell of the Crimson Lotus* was really a person?"

"In other words," I said, "what if he's really insane and—"

"Ah, Justin, I'm so glad you could make it. And I see you've brought a friend with you."

Caruthian Sanders was standing a couple of feet away. My mouth opened and closed a couple of times, like a hooked fish. I dropped my arm from around Justin. I could see in Caruthian's face he'd heard me.

He was a tall man in his late thirties, dressed in a smart suit, and he'd shaved all his hair, apart from a mustache and goatee—which he'd dyed blond.

In a world of chaos, where beliefs—only slightly understood by the majority of the public—encouraged young men to murder by suicide and a tattered world economy, his works of symmetrical forms satisfied a public craving for certainty and stability.

He didn't look insane, just rather concerned for his son. I wasn't sure if that was the way he usually regarded Justin or a reaction to seeing us together.

He walked past us down the ramp to the turbine hall, calling back over his shoulder. "Come on, the both of you. I expect you're dying to see my greatest masterwork."

We entered the hall, and beyond the bridge, halfway down the hall, I could see the installation. It was a cube, around sixty feet high. Made of metal girders and stairways, you could see through the framework in some parts into the interior. Scattered around the surface were panels in bronze.

It wasn't much warmer inside the hall than outside, and our breath still frosted. There were a few men in overalls, working on the installation, plus waiters and catering staff. They were all men and wore the same shaved head, mustache and goatee—also dyed blond.

There was no sign of the other guests yet. If Caruthian was planning mass murder, then he didn't seem worried about witnesses.

The installation was so magnificent, I naturally walked straight to it, leaving Justin with his father. The things attracting my attention were the bronze panels. I realized these were more than just the abstract swirls and curves I'd taken them for from a distance. Each showed carved figures, and I worked out that if you solved them correctly, there were stories here. Not nice stories. Mostly, people died—some pulled apart by hooks on lengths of chain. Many pictures included what looked like escapees from the most extreme S&M club I could imagine. In other panels there were objects, some of them small boxes around four inches square, and these toys changed, transformed.

I admired the scale of this thing and how much work Caruthian must have put into it. His passion for this piece must have been extraordinary. I realized he was driven by desires far deeper than I'd imagined.

One panel stopped me dead. It clearly showed Justin and me on the bridge, talking, walking, and kissing. I looked for the next picture in the sequence. Here we were shown meeting Caruthian, next standing in front of the installation. I scanned the walls for another picture, the next in the sequence, but found none.

I became aware of my heart in my chest. It felt trapped, tight.

I started working out how we might escape this place—without simply screaming and running. Turning to speak to Justin, I saw he was walking with his father to the entrance to the installation. I hurried to catch them up.

All right, I hesitated for nearly a minute, trying to catch my breath—just wanting to run. Then I had to practically drag my legs, muttering to myself, "This is stupid, this is stupid . . ."

Caruthian spotted me approaching and they waited for me to reach them.

"Justin's just been telling me about his researches today. It's good to know he's taken such an interest in my work," said Caruthian. He stepped inside the installation, assuming we'd follow.

Without looking at me, Justin also walked in. I was finding it really hard to breathe normally, but I followed.

"I call it *The Alignment of Regrets*," said Caruthian, leading the way down one corridor after another and climbing or descending stairs. It was labyrinthine and the carvings continued here. The corridors led to small rooms and in some there were life-sized statues. Some were cast in metal, others were made from plaster. He'd used every material I could think of, including what looked like animal remains coated in plastic. They had a simple theme: the manipulation of flesh. Each character was pierced and twisted and standing proud. Where a face could be discerned, the expressions were serene and in some cases smiling seductively. I touched or stroked most as we passed. Caruthian saw me doing this, but didn't indicate I shouldn't. Rather he seemed pleased. Absurdly, I still felt guilty. Memories of school trips to galleries and museums and the teachers' brays of "Don't touch, don't touch."

As we walked, listening to Caruthian describing the inspiration for some of the statues, I looked for anything in the construction of the installation that could be considered dangerous. There was nothing, no sharp edges. There were no pumps or moving pieces of any kind. Nothing there to harm anyone—that I could see. I began to relax.

We turned a corner and Justin groaned. "How could you? Jeeesus! After last time!" He slowly sank to his knees.

I didn't understand what had upset him. His father was standing in front of more statues. He looked confused.

"But I haven't used your name, have I? No one will know." He turned to me. "You speak to him. I . . . I give up." He stalked from the room.

I sat beside Justin and put my arm around him.

"I'm guessing this is another piece where you can see your pain put on display."

He turned his head to me. "No, not really. But it's the longest-standing argument between us. I asked him once, 'Which is stronger? The man who beats another man to the ground or the other, who holds out his hand to the fallen and supports him to his feet. Which shows more courage?' "

I could see his father's answer. Either side of a small neon sign saying STRENGTH? there were two tableaux. To the left a masculine, virile, and handsome man, stripped to a loincloth and priapic beneath it, was spearing another man through the chest who lay on the ground. To the right was the figure of a third man, standing with arms outstretched, supporting a man on each shoulder. These two men, also with arms outstretched, were each supporting two more men. This went up three levels, so the lowest supported fourteen companions. The expression on that man's face was terrible strain and despair. He was dressed as a clown.

Justin continued, "He told me that being strong enough to beat your enemies was the only strength that really mattered."

"What about the strength to fight evil?" I asked. "I don't mean with violence. Having the strength to do what is right, facing down the bully, fighting your own negativity and overcoming your own fears and phobias. Beating the demons within. I think that's what strength is, that's what takes courage."

The light changed suddenly. The bulb, in the middle of the room, hung without a shade, swayed slightly. My heart started racing again as I realized what Caruthian's departure meant. So far, I hadn't been afraid of this box while he'd been with us. Now though, if this was a trap, then Justin and I were caught. My heart pounded again and I realized I had no idea how to get out.

I pulled Justin to his feet. "Come on," I said. "I want out of here."

He moved slowly as we left the room and I was forced to drag him.

"Shit, shit, shit!" I said. This wasn't going to be easy. Caruthian had built in mirrors and trompe l'oeil corridors, and I banged my nose twice on these. Where I did recognize a statue and thought I remembered the next in the series, another was in its place. I tried to calm myself, recited mantras in my head. What had I said to Justin a few minutes before? Something about overcoming your inner demons. Yeah, right. It was my fear, always my fear: denying me dreams and lovers, hobbling my mind.

I dragged Justin behind me. He shouted: "You're hurting my arm!"

"Well, stop loitering and help me find the way out!"

"Oh," he said. "It's this way. Why didn't you just ask?"

He pushed in front, took my hand, and walked off, with me stumbling behind him.

He was right. As I followed him, we passed statues that I recognized and in the order I remembered them.

"How do you know this?" I asked.

"You know, sometimes you simply have to ask me for help. Just because you're older, doesn't mean you're always right."

Ouch.

"I told you, I spent the whole of today doing research. This is one of Lemarchand's designs."

We emerged from the entrance and were greeted with a round of applause. Caruthian's voice came over loudspeakers: "Ladies and gentlemen, thank you for that warm reception for these first two explorers in the further reaches of experience. Now, honored guests, you all have your tickets and maps, yes? Good. Simply follow your personal routes and you'll find treasures for you in the room you've been allocated. Remember, the tickets are numbered and you should enter in that order. And you may not end up with the partner you arrived with tonight." There were titters of naughty expectation at that. I wondered just what they were expecting once they were inside the installation. Was this the prelude to some unique orgy?

"Justin, please bring your friend to join me here."

We looked up and saw Caruthian standing alone on the bridge above us.

"We might as well," said Justin.

We left the hundred or so guests politely allowing one another to walk into the narrow entrance to the installation, as they'd been asked. They were a strange bunch. A mixture of ages and nationalities, many of them dressed soberly in evening attire. Others were fetishists wearing leather and chains or simply dressed erotically. All wore masks. They nodded amicably to one another.

"What are they going to find?" Justin asked Caruthian.

"That depends. Their destinations are based on my intimate interviews with their friends, other artists, and enemies. I've learned there are those who apparently hated, but relentlessly desired, others. There are some in there whose pursuit of forbidden delights, separated by marriage or childhood, have nearly ruined them. But tonight I've promised them anonymity and a taste of hidden desires fulfilled."

As he talked we began to hear voices from the installation, cries of delighted surprise. After the last guest had entered, a man in overalls closed the door.

"You know, Justin, I realize you've never really understood why I used your stories and our fights for my work. I have to create from what I know of my life, and you're part of that. An important part. I've always loved you, you must know that."

"How, Father? How am I supposed to know? You've never encouraged me, never praised me."

"That was your mother's way. I want you to be strong enough to take the pleasures life has to offer. To experience all its wonders and those beyond this world."

I've long believed that human communication is mostly based on fear and misunderstanding. They lapsed into silence.

"Time to play, I think," said Caruthian. He looked up and signaled to someone in a gantry at the top of the hall. A walkway was lowered, allowing him to cross from the bridge to the center of the installation, where there was a large blank disk of the bronze panels.

Before stepping onto the walkway, he kicked off his shoes and loosened his tie. Crossing the walkway, he removed his clothes, so he was naked when his feet touched the installation. The walkway returned to the gantry.

Caruthian walked around the perimeter of the disk. As he did so, sparks of light snapped at his feet and for a moment he paused.

It had obviously hurt and briefly I thought he would stop, but he walked on.

The installation juddered. Inside it, the groans, sighs, and screams of pleasure ceased. There was a sense of expectation like you get in the queue for a roller coaster. Now sections of the box began to shift and rise. I wondered how Caruthian was meeting health and safety rules here. I didn't remember seeing seat belts inside.

As one section rose, we heard screaming; screaming and calls for help, mercy and of despair. One of the men in overalls ran to the entrance door to open it, but that section was suddenly traveling toward the ceiling.

Hidden smoke machines came into action and Caruthian had obviously arranged for lights to be buried in the wall, as shafts of blue fell from them and became the only illumination in the hall.

A section rose and swung past us. Through the tang of the smoke, I smelled excrement and blood and saw a young woman, standing at the entrance to a room, which now moved over a fifty-foot drop. She looked at me and then stretched out an arm. She was yards away from us, ridiculously out of reach, but I raised my arms to her. The next moment, the floor beneath her swung down and she dropped. I closed my eyes and put my hands over my ears. Even then I could hear a church bell tolling.

I started to act sensibly. I ran.

No, no. I mean I ran for help, reaching into my pocket for my mobile phone to call . . . but my phone was out of power and . . . and I just ran. I left Justin throwing up on the bridge and I ran from the things coming through the walls.

I was scared and I don't like being scared.

The newspapers were bewildered. Justin's talk of *The Alignment of Regrets* and the work of an obscure French toymaker didn't add up. They concentrated more on the insane artist and his son, and speculated on an unnatural physical relationship between them. They crushed Justin, blaming him for not alerting the world earlier to his father's plans. After all, he'd been living with him for months; surely he'd known.

Ah, well, Justin's subsequent suicide couldn't be helped. The police denied all connection with Lemarchand, and rightly so. They hadn't found any plans or diagrams by Lemarchand in Caruthian's studio or flat.

I'd made sure I kept the paper Justin gave me on the bridge. While he was calling me that final evening, I was removing the evidence of my dealings with Caruthian.

Part of my price for the plans had been his silence about my enjoyment of his son—a dalliance necessary to ensure Justin knew nothing of his father's wanton desires for that night.

I still have Lemarchand's designs. One day, I may show them to you.

If you have the desire.

Only the Blind Survive
Yvonne Navarro

Wikvaya found the sand painting a morning's walk from the wash.

The sun hung high in the sky, strong and hot, and the Almighty had made it a good growing season so far. The villagers' prayers and offerings had not gone unheard by Rain Cloud, and the seasonal rains had been regular and steady, occasionally overly generous and swelling the wash so that the water rose and the wind sang through the entrance and across its liquid surface. Because of this, the People had named this place Aponovi, *the wind that blows across the gap*. But all of that could change so quickly. And it *would*, if Wikvaya did not get back in time to warn the other spirit warriors.

He stared at the sand painting, unable to resist watching it shimmy and shift. The unseen hand wielding the colors was expert, the lines precise and myriad. Never in his twenty-two summers had he seen such complexity and beauty. The combination of textures and the odd, dark hues were mesmerizing, pulling him closer because he couldn't wait to see where the lines would go next. Was there a sound? Was it whispering to him, enticing him to reach down and try adding a line or two of his own to the pattern, something to bring it closer to completion? Another step—

Something screeched over his head and Wikvaya jerked, looking up. The wind had risen and an eagle, perhaps the largest one he'd ever seen, perched on the swaying branch of the old and battered acacia tree that overhung the ground where the sand painting was taking shape. The eagle's golden eyes seared into his and Wikvaya realized he was shivering, so cold that he felt like he'd been standing for hours in the snow. He was supposed to be running back to Oraibi, his village, to warn them of the sand painting. What had he been doing? How long had he been standing here? With horror Wikvaya realized the sun had sunk halfway to the horizon. It was the painting on the ground, of course; it had robbed him of precious time as surely as if it had formed hands and held him in place. Even now its surface squirmed and re-formed, beckoning, but Wikvaya forced himself to turn away. He would not let himself be bewitched again.

"Thank you, Kwahu," he murmured to the eagle. It merely watched him with unblinking eyes. Its silent disapproval weighed on his shoulders like boulders, but Wikvaya did not know how to make amends for his foolishness. All he could do was turn his back on the sand painting and begin the long run back to Oraibi.

His strength and youth carried him well, and even though he'd run the entire way, fear made Wikvaya arrive at the village with energy to spare. His brothers were waiting in the family pueblo, and Wikvaya could see the irritation in their expressions. He was supposed to have been here hours ago to help weave his future bride's wedding clothes.

"Where have you been?" Cheveyo, his eldest brother, was sitting next to their father and the youngest boy, Hania. It was clear that they'd been working on Cha'kwaina's wedding clothes for quite some time. He and Cha'kwaina were to be married in five days, and tradition dictated that the males of his family would all help weave her attire. Wikvaya should have been here earlier in the day to do his part, but things would be altered a great deal from the plans that had already been set. A lot of people would be unhappy, most of all his bride-to-be, but that could not be helped. "Cha'kwaina will be here at sunrise to grind corn," her father told him. "Your mother is looking forward to her help and to making sure she will be a good wife for you."

His thoughts spun and for a moment Wikvaya said nothing. Was he absolutely sure about what he had seen? It all seemed so far away now, and there was a part of his mind, a small, insidious voice, that insisted the sand painting had been nothing but his imagination, the result of too much time spent beneath the high desert sun and too little water. There was so much to do in the coming days—

No . . . it *had* been true. Nothing else could explain the hours he had lost or the painful redness on his shoulders where the sun's rays had scorched his unmoving skin. "I bring news," Wikvaya said hoarsely. "I have seen the gate of evil."

The other men stopped their weaving and looked at him, their eyes wide. Honaw, his father, set aside his work, then stood. His movements were slow and ponderous, much like those of his aged namesake, the bear. "Tell us."

"It is as the stories have always foretold." Wikvaya chose his words carefully. "An image in the sand that forms by itself, created by something unseen."

"Perhaps it was the wind," Cheveyo said. "You were gone for most of the day. The sun can play tricks on a man."

"It can," Wikvaya agreed. "But it was the image—a sand painting—that spirited away the hours. It . . . *called* to me, and I wanted to help complete it." At his father's look of alarm, Wikvaya added hastily, "But I did not touch it."

"Are you certain?"

Wikvaya turned to stare at Hania. "What do you mean?"

"You admit that the sand painting stole many hours from you. What did you do during that time? Do you recall?"

"I . . ." Wikvaya could not finish. Instead, he looked at his hands, but the flesh seemed unchanged and told him nothing.

"As I thought." Hania settled back, Cha'kwaina's wedding

clothes forgotten. "We must ready ourselves for battle. According to the dark prophecy, we must be strong and stop the gate to the Underworld before it can open."

"In case we are too late, the village must be rendered sightless," Wikvaya added. "Legend says that any beast that comes through cannot harm those who cannot see it. Those who see it, fear it, and the creature's power comes from fear. So—"

"—only the spirit warriors may have vision," Cheveyo completed.

"Yes," Honaw said. "Only the four of us."

Cha'kwaina had just finished gathering her things for her three-day stay at the home of Wikvaya's family when she heard shouting outside. Grandmother Chochmingwu, ancient and becoming hard of hearing at fifty-seven summers, was bent over her grindstone, and the old woman looked up only when Cha'kwaina touched her on the shoulder. "Something is happening outside," she said in a near shout. "Everyone's running around." Reluctantly the elderly matriarch pushed herself to her feet and followed Cha'kwaina to the doorway, leaning heavily on a twisted mesquite cane. Not for the first time, Cha'kwaina was silently amazed that one so old and frail could be so revered in the village, so powerful. Chochmingwu's daughter—Cha'kwaina's mother—had died birthing her second child, a son, so someday Grandmother Chochmingwu's position as village matriarch would pass to her granddaughter. As it always did, the prospect brought a roll of anxiety deep into Cha'kwaina's belly. How would she deal with such huge responsibility? How would she lead?

Their adobe was a full level up from the common area, and while Cha'kwaina scurried easily down the ladder, her grandmother waited by the doorway, watching the activity; while her hearing was slipping away, there was little wrong with her eyesight and nothing at all amiss with her perception. Even though she went down to find out what the excitement was all about, Cha'kwaina found herself glancing upward to check her grandmother's reactions.

"What's going on?" Cha'kwaina called out as girls she knew ran past. Everyone seemed to be abandoning their chores and heading back to their adobes. "What's happening?"

But no one took the time to stop and answer. Finally, Cha'kwaina spotted Wikvaya and his brothers at the far end of the plaza. They were huddled together with their father like a bunch of old men trading stories about a bygone hunt. Shouldn't they be working on her wedding attire? In five days she and Wikvaya would be married and he would join her grandmother's household, turning his attention and energy during the day to supporting her family's cornfields. If the great spirits looked on them with favor, the nights would work to ensure that they had babies of their own in the coming years.

Tired of trying to figure it out, Cha'kwaina strode to the men and touched her groom on the shoulder. He spun in surprise, his eyes unaccountably wild, and she almost back-stepped. "Wikvaya," she said. "What is all the excitement about? No one will say."

Instead of answering, he took her by the elbow and started guiding her back the way she'd come. "You must go home," he said urgently. "You and your family must stay inside, and you must cover your eyes with fabric or skins—"

"What!"

"The whole village must do this," Wikvaya continued. "Haven't you noticed? People have already started, and there's no time to waste. No one can remove the eye bindings until the spirit warriors tell the elders that it's safe."

Cha'kwaina pulled against Wikvaya's hand, slowing him. "Spirit warriors? What has happened that we need those?"

"The warnings that my grandfather's grandfather gave us have come true," Wikvaya told her. His solemn face was covered in fine desert dust, there were worry bags beneath his eyes, and his mouth was drawn into a hard grimace. He looked as though ten summers had passed since she'd seen him just yesterday. "I have found one of the gateways of which he spoke. The town must be rendered sightless until the opening is destroyed."

"What?" Cha'kwaina repeated in confusion. "That makes no sense, not in real life. Those are just big stories told by old men breathing smoke fire down in the kivas. If there really is a gateway, and *if* something comes through, blinding ourselves is the worst thing to do—we won't be able to see it, to run or fight."

Wikvaya shook his head. "No, the tales are *true*. The ancestors testify that this has happened before, many times since the First People. If the gateway is not closed, a terrible creature will come through and destroy the world with fire just as Sóyuknang destroyed Tokpela, the First World. But this time, there will be no place for the People to hide, and we will all perish."

Cha'kwaina stared at him. "But who among us can defeat a creature with that kind of power?"

"As has been written, the four spirit warriors," Wikvaya told her. "The legends command that if a person cannot see it, the creature cannot see the person. It cannot harm what it can't see. Only the spirit warriors may remain sighted in order to battle and kill it."

Cha'kwaina took a step back. "The spirit warriors—you mean you? Your brothers and father? You can't be serious."

He scowled at her. "What makes you so doubtful? These are the ways of the People. We have always known this."

"The ways of the *Old* People," she said firmly. "I am nineteen summers and have never seen any gateway. It is a story invented by the elders to frighten children into behaving, just like the kachinas, when they come in costume, dance, and then hit the boys with sticks. The People have always been safe in the past, and they always will be."

"Safety is not something to be taken for granted," Wikvaya argued. "It is something to be watched over, and sometimes you must fight to keep it."

"Times have changed, and it is silly to let ourselves be frightened by ancient, irrational myths. There is nothing here that threatens us," Cha'kwaina snapped. Her face darkened as a thought slipped into her mind. "Perhaps you have reconsidered our marriage and this is nothing but a means by which to ensure that the wedding does not take place."

Wikvaya's mouth fell open. "I have done no such thing. No one would be so reckless as to do something so involved just for that. Our wedding will take place after the gateway is closed."

"But—"

"And so it shall be," a gravelly voice interrupted her. Cha'kwaina spun and saw her grandmother standing behind her. She had no idea how the old woman had climbed down the ladder. "Come. We return to our home now. We darken our eyes as instructed, and we do not come out until the spirit warriors say it is safe."

Cha'kwaina started to say something but Grandmother Chochmingwu held up a weathered hand. "This is not a request," she said. "You *will* do as you are told."

And because she could do nothing else, Cha'kwaina bowed her head and sullenly followed her grandmother back to their adobe.

"We are too late."

Wikvaya stared at the ground while the others crowded around, their expressions as horrified as his own. The sand painting was still there, but it had divided in and upon itself into dozens of pieces, all different shapes and sizes; the result was something huge, a visual cacophony shot through with streaks the color of dead deer's blood. Wikvaya realized that it hurt to look at it—it felt as though his eyes were being pierced by the spray from a hundred boiling pots. When they slapped at their eyes, he knew that his father and brothers felt the same. Hot tears streamed down his cheeks, but Wikvaya would not look away, would not allow himself the comfort of diversion. When the torment quickly passed, he couldn't help but wonder if what they'd felt had been real or ancient memory, an instinctive response built upon the experience of those who had come before. For, as the legend decreed, if they could see, so could whatever beast had passed through the gateway from the dark world beyond it.

"There." Honaw pointed. "Just beneath the edge of the rock. The beast leaves us a trail."

"Or bait," Cheveyo said. "Knowing that we will follow—"

"—because we must," Wikvaya finished. To his father, he asked, "What do you see?"

"The shadow of rotting blood," his father said in a low voice. "Of death and evil, and the agony that will come if this creature is not driven back to its origins or killed."

Something snapped in the dry summer grasses behind him and Wikvaya whirled, his spear ready. But there was nothing . . . he thought. No, he hadn't imagined it. His brothers were standing in a crouch to either side of their father, bows drawn, their faces ashen with tension.

"We must hurry," Hania said. "If the beast should reach Oraibi . . ."

"They will be safe," Cheveyo said. "They have been blinded. They have been warned."

Wikvaya nodded and fell in step behind his father as the old hunter followed the traces left by the unspeakable creature, thin trails of sand that carried traces of black and red. Everything it had touched was desiccated, all moisture and life sucked away until nothing remained but twigs and powdery dust that might have once been leaves or small desert creatures. The generous rain this season had spotted the earth with bushes and tufts of bright green grasses, creosote and weeds; the acacia and mesquite trees were thick with leaves, while the cacti were plump with moisture and fragrant blooms over which bees and other insects challenged one another for the best position. But cutting through it all was the path that he and the others followed, a trail that reeked of decay and seemed to widen as it went along.

What this demon could do to the People was unspeakable, but Cheveyo was right—everyone *had* been warned. The plaza had been nearly empty by the time they had left, with only a few latecomers rushing to put their most necessary items where they could be found without eyesight.

All Wikvaya could do was head back to Oraibi and hope with all his spirit that those who waited could be patient and strong.

Cha'kwaina sat with her back against the wall and listened to the wind slipping past the windows on its way through the rest of the pueblo. It had intensified and was spinning dirt and pebbles against the walls, occasionally pushing grit through the small openings and into the room where she and Grandmother Chochmingwu waited. The gusts made a noise that shifted between a thin wail and a moan, and the air felt heavier and uncomfortably hotter than normal, more oppressive with each thud of her heartbeat. She wished the wind would stop and that things would just go back to normal, that they would be rid of this nonsensical tale of legends and monsters and gateways to a dark spirit world that no one had ever seen.

The old woman was calm and silent and Cha'kwaina was too angry to make conversation. How long would they have to wait like this, with scraps of woven fabric knotted around their heads? It was a waste of time—she should be at her future mother-in-law's right now, preparing to show the woman how well she could grind corn and perform a wife's duties for Wikvaya. And what was he doing, her future husband? Out playing warrior with his father and brothers, perhaps painted to look like kachinas or striped like the Koshares, the black- and white-striped clowns that represented little more than gluttony and crudities. As angry as she was about the postponement of her wedding, Cha'kwaina knew that involving the entire pueblo in nothing more than an effort to procrastinate was unlikely, but was the whole village *really* in on this? Grandmother Chochmingwu had ordered her back to the adobe and they had moved so quickly that Cha'kwaina had been able to speak with no one.

Perhaps something else entirely was going on, something other than the ridiculous tale of gateways and demons that Wikvaya had related. It could be nothing more dire than a desert windstorm, and her fiancé was using it as a joke, some sort of premarital prank to elevate himself in the eyes of his brothers and his friends. If that were true, how would she and Grandmother Chochmingwu know, sitting here as they were, blindfolded and separated from those who inhabited the rest of the village?

Moving very carefully so that her grandmother would not hear, Cha'kwaina reached behind her head and untied the knot that held her blindfold in place.

■ ■ ■

Although it was a more difficult trek, they circled around and came down the ridge behind the pueblo, pushing themselves to travel faster than they normally would have dared. The path was there, but it was strewn with loose rocks and periodically angled to the point of being dangerous, well-camouflaged so that rival tribes could not find it. It took longer but would give them a double advantage: they could approach the village from a different direction than the one the beast had taken, and they would have a rare and unobstructed view of the entire pueblo at once. Standing there next to the men of his family, Wikvaya realized that sometimes the thing you work so hard to attain is also that which you're the least prepared to face.

Without the cover of the desert—the shrubs, tumbleweeds, and twig-choked branches of the acacia and mesquite trees—to conceal it, the track of the creature was impossible to miss. Its trail came out of the last stand of mesquite trees as a scrambled brown line at the western edge of the village; the closer it came to the dwellings, the more it drew in on itself as it twined from door to door, clearly searching for victims. It looked like the sandy dirt had become a living entity crisscrossed with horrid, sunken veins, pathways that wove among the adobes and around the three plazas and kivas, circling the central well a half-dozen times before moving on to the next doorway. The discoloration crawled up and around the pueblo windows, twisting inside and coming out again like a crazed spider trying to find a target in the ever-so-silent village.

Until its course eased into the doorway of a certain second-level adobe . . .

And disappeared inside.

It was standing by the doorway.

The blindfold fell away and Cha'kwaina gasped before she could stop herself. Despite the wailing of the wind, the creature heard; it spun and focused on her, then grinned terribly as it shuffled forward. She backed away, struggling against the thick scream that tried to bubble out of her throat, knowing that Grandmother Chochmingwu, so frail and old, would still rip off her own blindfold and come to her aid. How foolish she had been not to listen to Wikvaya, to think that the old ways were dead and useless. All those warnings that she should have heeded . . . but she couldn't think of those now, they would do her no good. Instinctively she knew that covering her eyes would no longer help—she had already seen and her mind would now fill in that which her eyes could not perceive. Perhaps she could angle around and get outside, where she would have room to flee—

But each way that she stepped, the beast moved likewise, and swiftly; each time she turned, it did, too. It was playing with her, a bobcat toying with a desert mouse before devouring it. It was a terrible thought, compounded by the way the monster looked at her through hungry eyes filled with dark, shifting sand above a mouth that had cactus needles for teeth, needles that were as long as her thumb and purple like the plentiful prickly pear spines at the height of summer. As it tracked her, a tongue, black and forked, flicked out of its mouth and tasted the air like a rattlesnake before probing the edges of its own lips until the sharp spines opened its flesh and left it bleeding and twitching. Would it eat her, tearing at her skin like the coyote ravaged the stricken rabbit? Or was there some other nightmarish fate that awaited her in the dark underworld she had claimed did not exist?

The beast reached for her. Its spiked hands were the color of cacti, green and shriveled with drought and disease. Cha'kwaina could sense its urgency, its craving for the moisture within her body, could feel everything that was inside her—water, blood, the very essence of life—being pulled toward it. It was impossible for her to look away, and she realized that she had been played, *steered*. Now she was trapped in the corner, with Grandmother Chochmingwu sitting quietly against the opposite wall and oblivious to the danger only a room's width away.

The beast glided across the floor and sank the ends of its fingers into her shoulders. The sensation was agony, like pushing skin-first into the wreckage of a dead cholla. Cha'kwaina tried to pull away as her mouth opened involuntarily, but she locked her throat against the wail that wanted to come out. Pain erupted everywhere it touched her, and red sparks, like the embers from an out-of-control fire, swirled across her vision. But she would *not* make a sound, she would *not*—

Just to make sure of that, the creature closed its cactus-spine-covered mouth over her lips.

Nothing that Wikvaya had ever imagined could have been as terrifying as coming through the doorway and seeing the monstrosity latched on to Cha'kwaina. He catapulted into the adobe and screamed, slashing at the monster holding his bride-to-be at the same time his father leaped over to Grandmother Chochmingwu and held her blindfold in place. "Return to the darkness!" Wikvaya bellowed, thrusting his spear into its back again and again. "Let her go!"

"Cha'kwaina!" Grandmother Chochmingwu grabbed at her face but Hania stopped her before she could pull the fabric aside.

"Be still, old woman," Hania commanded as he slapped her hands away. "Let the spirit warriors do as they must." She sank back to the floor, but her hands fluttered at the ground around her, unable to stop their search for her granddaughter.

Wikvaya's brothers rushed forward as the beast finally released Cha'kwaina and turned to face them. The young woman dropped without a sound, her eyes open but unfocused, her mouth seeping blood from a hundred punctures. The barbed ends of cactus spines protruded from the bottom half of her face, and more speckled her bare shoulders from the creature's grip.

The monster itself seemed barely fazed by Wikvaya's attack. It was a hulking abomination, the opposite of everything good that the Sun Spirit or Grandmother Spider had ever created. Its form was a collection of desiccated pads of prickly pear; they shifted as it moved, not sliding but *dragging*, stabbing itself a thousand times over with every motion. Below a half-crushed, misshapen nose, its wide, grinning mouth was an unspeakable pit of sharpness, and the sight of Cha'kwaina's blood rimming it like war paint made Wikvaya want to vomit. Its eyes were fluctuating pits of dirty sand, light and dark streaks that moved constantly and tried to mesmerize him—

Wikvaya didn't wait for it to charge. He hurtled forward and rammed his spear into the monstrosity's chest. Instead of going down, the creature *laughed* at him—or at least that's what he thought the twisted noise that came out of its throat might be. It clutched at the haft of the spear with its spine-studded fingers, trying to pull it out. Wikvaya held on with both hands, grinding his teeth at the beast's unexpected strength. His weapon began to push back at him, sliding out of the deep crevice the spear's blade had opened just below the monster's neck. He wasn't sure he could hold it, he was losing ground—

Then Cheveyo was there, hacking with his obsidian knife. The cactus-skinned beast stumbled at the ferocity of Cheveyo's blows but recovered instantly, releasing the shaft of the spear as it swiped at this new attacker. Cheveyo ducked and stabbed again, then screamed as the monster swung backward and its spine-tipped limb opened the skin of his face from his cheek to his neck. Blood sheeted from the wounds and soaked his chest as he staggered backward, and the sight and smell of it seemed to renew the evil thing's strength. Wikvaya's spear still protruded from its chest, but it did nothing to slow the beast as it lunged after Cheveyo, drawn to his lifeblood. Wikvaya hauled backward on the spear but it was like trying to hold back a crazed bear; he couldn't let go, but his feet slid uselessly on the dirt-covered floor as he was pulled behind it. With one hand slapped against his mangled face, Cheveyo made it back up to his knees and scrambled after the knife he had dropped. Wikvaya's face twisted in repulsion as he realized the fiend was following the trail of his brother's blood, sucking it right off the ground and into its blighted skin like some kind of abominable parasite.

"Hania!" Wikvaya shouted. "We must stop it—"

Hania's arrow shot past Wikvaya's shoulder and buried itself in the mass of pads at the beast's shoulder. It roared in anger and tried to turn, nearly jerking Wikvaya off his feet. But Wikvaya refused to release it, and this time he pushed as it pulled, driving the weapon deeper, searching for something, *anything*, vulnerable. A mixture of sand and rancid oil abruptly oozed from the chest puncture, as if inside the beast were earth that had soaked up the fat of a bloated deer carcass. Still it paid no heed to Wikvaya as he desperately tried to force it to the side and angle it away from Hania while he readied his second arrow.

All of them were shouting at once but there was too much confusion for any one of them to be heard. Honaw gave up and shoved the struggling old woman toward Cha'kwaina, swinging his own spear forward and jabbing at the creature. His spearhead found its mark again and again but it had no effect. Cheveyo's hand brushed his knife and he snatched it up, scuttled forward like a scorpion, and hacked furiously at the back of the beast's legs.

For a moment, all the air seemed to disappear from the world and time slowed. Hania stood his ground and calmly pulled back on his bowstring, even though all four of them knew the youngest brother could not fire and still escape to safety. The monster swayed beneath Cheveyo's slashes and kicked backward, embedding a hundred spines and shredding the flesh of Cheveyo's arms just as Hania let go of his bowstring. Then Hania's arrow pierced the shrunken, discolored spot between the hellish beast's eyes, and the screams of all four spirit warriors mixed together as it fell onto him, enfolding the youngest warrior inside its murderous grasp.

And to the end, the horrible creature never let go of its prickly, terrible smile.

"Everything is ready for the ceremony tomorrow," Cha'kwaina said. She glanced sideways at Wikvaya, who nodded slowly and watched as she drank deeply from an earthen pitcher of water. Did he think of his brothers—one dead and one hideously maimed forever— when he looked at her? Did he blame her? Perhaps. Even now she was sure he wanted to say something, then decided against it. "What is it?" she prompted.

"You're so parched," was all he said.

"I worked a long time in the sun today," she told him. "Grinding corn and making the piki bread."

Wikvaya nodded again but said nothing more and she dismissed him by turning back to her chores. There were many tasks ahead and her groom didn't seem to know what to do next, a drawback of people who had relied on outdated traditions for far too long. Much of the matrimonial steps remained, but Cha'kwaina had changed the order to suit herself, disregarding Grandmother Chochmingwu's instructions and, to a substantial extent, shocking the others in the pueblo.

No matter; Grandmother Chochmingwu was old and would not live much longer. When she died, Cha'kwaina herself would be the matriarch of the entire village, the one who made all the important decisions regarding ceremonies and traditions, things like the endless grinding of corn and the way her soon-to-be groom walked the desert every morning searching for ancient gateways painted in sand on the ground.

After a few minutes, she heard Wikvaya sigh, then finally leave. Cha'kwaina stayed where she was, her strong hands deftly working to crush the corn beneath the grindstone as Grandmother Chochmingwu's sharp gaze shifted toward her from time to time. When the old woman was finally gone—and that would definitely be *very* soon—Cha'kwaina would see to it that the old ways became the dead ways. Then the new ways could move right in. For now she faced away from her grandmother and kept her head lowered, as if nothing in the world mattered more than the task at hand.

Smiling mindlessly, Cha'kwaina made sure to blink away the dark swirls of sand that gathered in the corners of her eyes.

Mother's Ruin
Mark Morris

Heaving his bulk from the stool, Elliott peered over the counter to discern the source of the approaching rhythmic squeak. At first he saw nothing, and then the library door bumped open, dragging a wheelchair behind it. The occupant was wizened, twisted, bald, and childlike, black spectacles that more closely resembled aviator goggles transforming its face into a simian skull. The creature propelling the chair was almost as grotesque. Dressed in a blue nurse's uniform, the woman's mottled, grayish skin seemed to hang in wattles from her face. Elliott had to make an effort not to stare at her sagging eyes and slack, rubbery lips. It was as though the flesh she was draped in was designed for considerably larger bones.

His nose twitched at the odor that accompanied the couple. It was a hospital smell—chemicals, sickness, and something else; something raw, animal. As the woman brought the chair to a halt at the counter, Elliott stepped back, feeling faintly nauseous.

"Can I help you?" he mumbled.

The woman regarded him with an odd and unsettling expression. An expression somewhere between sadness and fury, which she communicated almost solely through her eyes. She stared at him for so long that Elliott began to feel uncomfortable. He was about to repeat his question when she awkwardly, stiffly, folded her body in two, reaching for something in the well beneath the seat of the wheelchair. She straightened with a supermarket carrier bag in her hand, the white plastic stretched and shiny with the weight inside. Elliott took another involuntary step back as she swung the bag toward him. For an instant he was certain there was something wet and soft in the bag—a lump of raw meat, perhaps even a dead animal. Then, in a strangely muffled voice, the woman said, "We're paying no fines. We've got no money," and the bag thumped on the counter with a solid weightiness that could only be caused by books.

Elliott glanced again at the creature in the wheelchair. He thought it was a man, but he couldn't be sure. The creature was chattering to itself, or perhaps cackling softly, its tiny gnarled fists pressed to its puckered mouth, its head nodding in spasmodic jerks. Slick drool looped in glittering strings from its twisted fingers and formed gleaming runnels like slug trails on the bib of its stained black smock. Elliott shook his head disdainfully, causing his several chins to wobble, and plucked at the neck of the bag.

A dank odor, barely preferable to the operating-theater stench of the couple, rose to meet him as he craned forward. Bracing himself, he lifted out the topmost book, pinching it between thumb and forefinger. The pages were wrinkled and bloated with mildew, the transparent dust jacket so brittle that it broke off in dry fish-scale flakes beneath the pressure of Elliott's plump fingers.

He squinted to read the title—*Doorways to Hidden Realms: A Treatise on Summoning Magicks* by Guillaume Barsac. The volume was unfamiliar to him, as were the others—*Configurations to the Endless Kingdom* by Johan Goodrich and *Beyond the Veil of Night: A Warning to the Unwary* by Millicent May Dublin. Each of the volumes was equally aged and repellent to the touch. Elliott placed them side by side on the desk before him and reluctantly pried open the first.

Something scurried from beneath the cover, causing him to snatch his hand back. But it was only the desiccated corpse of some long-dead insect, animated by the cold draught ghosting through the old building. Irritated by his own nervousness, Elliott examined the card detailing the book's borrowing history. The most recent date was March 30, 1969.

He blinked in disbelief, and then opened the second book, and the third. The inner pages of *Beyond the Veil of Night: A Warning to the Unwary* were seething with blue-black mildew, rendering much of its contents illegible. Elliott could still ascertain, however, that the return dates on all three books were identical.

"You do realize these items were due for return almost forty years ago?" he muttered.

The woman glared at him. Her slack mouth quivered.

"We're paying no fines. We've got no money," she repeated.

Elliott sighed. He felt greasy, itchy sweat gathering in the folds of his fleshy body. He could make an issue out of this—call in his supervisor, threaten the couple with consequences—but what would be the point? In truth, he just wanted these people gone. They disquieted him in a way he found hard to rationalize. He felt there was something fundamentally *wrong* with them, that they brought with them a hint of . . . what? Danger? Foreboding? It sounded absurd, but he couldn't deny the unaccountable sense of dread in his belly. With a supreme effort, he forced his doughy features into a smile.

"Let's forget it, shall we?" he said. "Let's say no more about it."

The woman stared at him, and now there was a hint of longing in her eyes, or perhaps regret.

Elliott's smile became fixed. He felt a bulb of sweat swell and burst on his forehead.

"It'll be our secret," he said desperately. "Is there anything else I can help you with before you go?"

The little man gibbered. The woman's face sagged like melting wax. In her odd, mushy voice, she said, "We've done our duty. It's up to you now."

"That's right," said Elliott, nodding in encouragement. "It's up to me now."

The woman hovered a moment longer, and then to Elliott's horror, her hand wavered upward, as though to caress his sweating face. Then she hissed, as if in sudden pain, and snatched her hand away. Abruptly she gripped the handles of the wheelchair and propelled her charge out of there, the wheels squeaking, squeaking; leaving Elliott with an image of her gray, loose-fleshed hand, tipped with bruise-blackened fingernails, stretching toward him.

He remained motionless until the squeak of the wheels was no longer audible, and then he released a juddering sigh. With the tip of one stubby forefinger he flipped each of the books closed, wondering what to do with them. Strictly speaking, they were still the property of the library, but after four decades, they would almost certainly have been replaced or declared permanently lost. If Elliott wished, he *could* add them to the catalog, but they were in such a state of decay that he really couldn't see the point.

Better, then, just to recycle them, get them gone, like the couple who had brought them here. What had prompted them to return the books after half a lifetime's absence Elliott couldn't even *begin* to fathom. People were a mystery to him—their motivations, their emotional connections, their petty drives and desires. He had never understood the rules of interaction, the urge to pursue friendships, to exchange information for pleasurable purposes, to seek out laughter. The company of others did nothing but confuse him, annoy him, disgust and discomfort him. As far as he was concerned, there were only two things that made human existence worthwhile, only two experiences that elevated life above the numbing mire of the everyday:

Sex and pain.

Pain and sex.

The exquisite agony.

The unendurable rapture.

Closing his eyes, he let out another long, bubbling sigh. As an antidote to the grotesque couple, he began to think of Chloë, of what he liked her to do to him, and he felt his stubby cock stirring in its humid nest of fat. Leaning forward, he mashed his growing erection against the inner surface of the counter.

"Everything all right, Mr. James?"

Elliott only just managed to stop himself crying out in shock as his eyes snapped open. His supervisor, Miss Sheridan, was standing on the other side of the counter, copper hair shining glossily, a tantalizing V of lightly freckled chest displayed beneath her throat. She was slim and young and smart, and in the fetid warmth of Elliott's room at night, he imagined her trampling on his naked body in her high heels, piercing his skin with her razor-sharp stilettos.

His tumescence throbbed. Though his lower body was out of sight, he felt certain she could sense it, and that her indulgent smile was nothing but mocking.

"Just got a . . . bit of a headache," he mumbled.

"It's these fluorescents," she said, nodding at the strip lights. "They get me the same way. Take a break, Elliott. Have a cup of tea and a paracetamol. I'll get Ann to cover."

"I will," he muttered, but by the time he had thought to add, "thanks," she had swept away on a swirling wake of sweetly scented air.

The prospect of Ann's arrival was enough to goad Elliott into action. Ann was a nosey, gossipy old bullfrog who lived alone and had worked at the library since the dawn of time. Elliott knew that if she spied the returned books, she would ask him a million questions about them. To avoid being drawn into conversation, he snatched up all three books, grimacing at the blackly furred mildew which foamed from between the covers like the filling of an overstuffed sandwich, and carried them over to the big recycling bin.

Lifting the lid, he saw that the bin was half full of shredded documents and yesterday's newspapers. He leaned over, scooped out a hollow, and dropped the books into it. It was only when he had rearranged the tangle of paper to conceal the books that he noticed a small card, shiny and rectangular, had slipped from between the covers of one of them and landed on the carpet. Stooping with a grunt, Elliott picked up the card and flipped it over. When he saw what was printed on it, he paused, blinking with surprise.

"My word, *there's* a sight for sore eyes," a voice trilled behind him.

At first Elliott thought that Ann was referring to the image on the card, and then he realized that her words were a comment on his mountainous backside. He straightened with an even louder grunt than before, stuffing the card into his pocket. Ann was standing where Miss Sheridan had stood minutes earlier, eyes like currants behind her red-framed spectacles, froggy lips stretched into a grin that to Elliott looked nothing but spiteful.

"Trying the old head-between-the-knees tactic, eh?" she said. "Any success?"

He was saved from having to reply by the appearance of a mother and her two bleating children, who wanted to exchange not books but video games. As Ann turned her grin on them, Elliott sloped away.

The image on the card stayed with him for the rest of the day, and the first thing Elliott did when he arrived home was to punch in the number of the only person he ever willingly spoke to.

Instead of the bright greeting he was expecting, however, a clogged and weary voice said, "Hullo?"

Elliott switched off the phone without a word; he had clearly gotten the wrong number. He tried again, pressing the tips of his bulbous fingers more carefully against the upraised digits on the display panel of the cordless. His breath was thick, a little raspy, as he waited for a response.

After four rings the same voice said, "Hullo?"

Elliott gritted his teeth in frustration. "I want to speak to Chloë," he muttered.

"Speaking."

Elliott was taken aback. This wasn't Chloë. The Chloë he knew was cheerful and always accommodating. She had the ability to put even Elliott at ease—as long as they didn't talk for *too* long. He paused, wondering whether he should just put the phone down and try again.

"Who is this?" asked the clogged voice.

"It's Elliott."

"Oh, Elliott," said the voice, and all at once he realized that this *was* Chloë, after all. There was something about the way she seductively emphasized the l's in his name. "How are you?"

"I need to see you," Elliott said.

There was a gravelly rumble, which it took him a moment to realize was a chuckle. The rumble splintered into a series of hacking coughs.

"Sorry, Elliott," she said eventually. "I'm ill. Gastric flu. I'm not seeing anyone this week."

"But I *need* you," Elliott said. "I need you *now*."

"Down, boy," she rasped. "Save it till next week. It'll be all the sweeter then."

"But it's my birthday," Elliott wheedled. "I'm forty."

"Today?"

"Tomorrow."

"Aww," she cooed. "Happy birthday. When I see you next week, I'll bring you a cake."

"I can't wait till next week," he said stubbornly.

This time there was a hint of steel in her croaky voice. " 'Fraid you're gunner have to, *lover boy*."

Elliott squeezed the receiver so hard that it creaked against his ear. He could smell the rankness of his own sweat trickling between his flabby man-breasts.

"I'll pay you extra," he blurted. "Double."

Her sigh was like the sea dragging back over sharp stones. "Money's not the issue," she said. "I've told you, Elliott, I'm *ill*."

"I don't care," he said.

"But *I* do," she retorted. "To put it bluntly, Elliott, I've got it coming out of both ends. It's not a pretty sight."

"I don't care," he repeated sulkily.

"Oh, fuck off, Elliott," she snapped, and put the phone down.

He rang her back twice, but she didn't pick up. The third time she didn't even have the answering machine on.

"Bitch!" he snarled and threw the cordless across the room. He sat and simmered, breathing hoarsely through his nose like a bull.

He wondered whether Chloë was *really* ill, or whether she was just making it up as an excuse not to see him. She didn't like coming here, he knew that. She thought his flat was squalid and dirty; she thought that it smelled bad. She was forever urging him to "brighten the place up a bit," forever bringing along scented candles or throwing open windows for "a bit of fresh air." Sometimes she even brought clean sheets for the bed, claiming that she didn't want his to get messed up. "It's all part of the service," she would tell him cheerfully.

Elliott stayed where he was until the light had almost completely drained from the featureless sky outside the window, and shadows had settled and thickened around him. He wondered, as he sometimes did, whether his life would have turned out differently if he had not been abandoned by his parents. He had only survived beyond his first few weeks because an elderly neighbor, concerned by his increasingly weakening cries in the flat below hers, had called in the authorities. The police had broken down the door to find Elliott alone in a stinking cot, so severely malnourished that he had been given less than a 50 percent chance of survival. His parents had disappeared, leaving behind their clothes and belongings, their passports, their money, their credit cards. Foul play had been suspected at first, but no sign of his parents, or any indication that they had been involved in anything unlawful, had ever come to light. Elliott had spent his childhood drifting from care home to care home, and from foster parent to foster parent, never settling anywhere, never making friends. He had been a problem child, sullen and withdrawn, given to bouts of rage and depression. As a teenager he had become, for a time, uncontrollable. His counselor had told him that his contempt and mistrust was directed not at society *per se*, but at his absent parents, and that if he could only accept that the majority of people wanted to help him, he would soon learn to form friendships, enjoy life, put the past behind him.

Elliott had hated having to talk about his feelings, to explain and analyze his actions. To avoid doing so, he had pretended to listen, to take on board his counselor's words. He had been intelligent enough to realize that the more compliant he appeared, the more he would be passed over, ignored, left to his own devices.

And so he had started to do as he was told, and in time he had dropped off the radar, become invisible. His contempt for society and his dissatisfaction with life he kept to himself. Eventually he managed to all but detach himself from people, quickly narrowing his reason for existing down to his twin pleasures. He found his job in the library purely as a means to procure the funds to finance his specific desires. His life became as simple and as basic as he could make it. He ate, he slept, he went to work, and whenever he could, he indulged himself. The greater part of his life was a silent howl of misery, or at best a nothingness, a wasteland. But the fleeting moments of ecstasy, of delectable torment, kept him going, prevented him from putting an end to it all.

Darkness had clotted the room, blotting out the shape of the world, by the time Elliott stirred. With a groan, he leaned back on his sagging sofa and stuffed his fat fingers into his trousers pocket. He pried out the card that had fallen from the book and padded over to his desk. He turned on the dusty lamp beside the computer and stared once again at the image printed on the card's laminated surface.

Was it a piece of artwork or a photograph? It *looked* like a photograph, but perhaps it was computer enhanced, or a special effect? Elliott found himself hoping it was real. He shuddered in delight as he gazed at the needles sticking out of the girl's pink tongue like porcupine spines. The erect penis which rose up in front of her face was scored with hundreds of tiny scratches, slick with blood. The girl's green eyes were wide with adoration or longing, gazing up at the unseen face above her. Behind her head was a black background, printed on which was a website address in small white letters: www.scar-tissue.co.uk. Elliott licked his lips. His heart throbbed like a fresh wound. Forty tomorrow. He reached down between his legs with a meaty fist and squeezed until it hurt. But hurting himself gave him nothing. He needed someone else to do it. Someone naked. Female. He looked at the girl's tongue again. The needles.

Sex and pain. He jabbed at the start button of his computer. The blue light came on. The throaty whirr of the fans matching the throaty rasp of his breath. In and out. His heart racing. Blood engorging his cock. Flowing beneath the thin, rubbery coating of stretched skin. Seeking release.

Fingers trembling. Skin oozing. He could smell himself, hot and musty. Blood beneath the skin. The couple in the library. The smell of chemicals. Like . . .

Like laboratory rats, splayed out for dissection. Preserving fluid. Hiding something underneath. The rank rawness of dead meat left for too long in the hot sun. Spoiling. Going rotten.

The squeak of wheels behind him.

Elliott swiveled as quickly as his bulk would allow. Beyond the lamp the room was black, packed with shadows. Was there something there? Something silent? Watching him? He grabbed the lamp with a sweat-greased palm, tilted it. Items of mismatched furniture sprang forward, bleached with light. But there was no one. No living presence. He had been mistaken. Imagination, that was all.

When he turned back the screen was steel gray. The words www.scar-tissue.co.uk pulsed red in the center. Beneath this, in capitals, the word ENTER. Elliott couldn't remember typing in the website address, but that didn't matter. His trembling fingers squeaked on the plastic mouse. The cursor edged warily toward the inviting word.

Double-click. Done.

The doors parted and a world of wonders opened up to him. Naked flesh, sliced and scratched and bruised. Faces contorted in orgasmic pain. Blood and leather, metal and sweat. Stark light and pitch-black darkness. An escalating series of images, each more extreme than the last.

Elliott wanted to linger over each one, but was simultaneously eager to move on to the next, and the next. His finger clicked feverishly on the mouse. Sweat dripped from his chin onto the keypad as he craned forward over his vast stomach. He licked his lips, the sound preternaturally loud in the fusty room, like the sound of wet things moving stealthily in the darkness. His erection ached. He ground his fist against it.

The last shot showed a man chained to a wall, spread-eagled, head thrown back, scarred and bloody. Imprinted over the top of this was an address. Before Elliott had even finished reading it, the picture began to corrode, like rusting metal, spots of gray leaking through the image, then joining up, forming larger patches. In a panic, Elliott reached for the blue plastic beaker full of pens to the right of his keyboard. Knocked it over, pens scattering everywhere. He scooped one up, a green CD marker, wrenched off the lid. He tried to write on the back of his hand, but it was too sweaty; the ink spread out along the tiny creases in his skin, like green blood rising from a wound. "Fuck," he muttered, "fuck, fuck." The corrosion was moving inward to the center, blotting out the picture of the spread-eagled man, speckling the edges of the address itself. In desperation Elliott wrote on the screen, the pen squeaking on the glass, the address appearing in green scrawled capitals even as the original disappeared in a froth of gray.

Finally he sat back, breathing hoarsely, drenched in sweat, a pulse throbbing behind his eyes. The screen blurred; suddenly he couldn't breathe; he thought he was going to faint. Then the feeling passed and his vision cleared. The screen was steel gray, nothing else there. No words, no pictures. Over the top of it, in green marker pen, was the scrawled address.

Elliott released a long, shuddering breath. Then he gave a snort, the closest he ever came to a laugh, realizing what he could have done. He stabbed his fat fingers at the keyboard, typing in the address again. A search page appeared. Address not found. Suggestions for websites with similar addresses. Cosmetic surgery clinics; Wikipedia; song and book titles.

Scowling, Elliott tried the address again. Same result. He sat for a moment, staring at the screen. Then he thumped across to where the cordless had landed when he'd thrown it, and picked it up. He pressed the green telephone symbol and held the phone to his ear; it was still working. He thumbed in the number of the taxi firm he always used, and half an hour later was pushing open the car door, struggling from the vehicle.

His driver, a young Asian man who had been nodding his head to Bhangra music throughout the journey, hunched his shoulders to peer dubiously at the black walls rising around them.

"You sure this is the place, mate?"

"If this is the address I asked for, then yes," Elliott replied peevishly.

"But there's nothing here, though, innit?" said the driver. "It's all just warehouses and factories and that."

Elliott scowled. "How much do I owe you?"

The driver shrugged. "Eleven eighty."

Elliott paid him and the cab drove away. Elliott watched its lights bleed red as it turned the corner, and then it was gone, leaving him alone.

He looked around. This was indeed an area of factories and warehouses, most of which seemed abandoned. The walls of the silent buildings towered high on either side of him, black and scabrous. Hundreds of windows, opaque with grime, peered blindly down at him. The road was scattered with broken stone, rotting timber, and rusting machinery that looked as though it had been left out for the garbagemen and never collected. Elliott huffed out a breath that hung like a wraith in the chilly air, and stumped toward a black door that the cabdriver had pointed out to him. The door was ajar. Elliott pushed it and stepped warily into the building.

A black corridor, barely wider or higher than the door itself, stretched ahead into darkness. Elliott allowed himself a moment's doubt, and then he started down it. He could hear nothing but his own stertorous breathing and heavy footsteps. He had the impression that the corridor was sloping downward, but he couldn't be sure. Eventually he came to another black door.

This one was locked. Elliott's fleshy fist hovered in the air in front of him, and then he knocked. Almost immediately the door sighed open. Elliott stepped into blackness. The door closed behind him. There was a smell, an abattoir reek of hot blood mingled with the heady, salty tang of sex. Elliott's cock reacted to it, filling with blood. A voice beside his ear purred, "How far do you want to go?"

Elliott tried not to flinch. "All the way," he said.

The throaty chuckle of the unseen speaker seemed to echo around him. "Are you quite certain of that?"

Sweat dribbled into Elliott's eye, stinging, making him blink. "Yes," he said hoarsely.

"Well, then," said the voice, and a light came on.

It was a stark white spotlight beam, lancing down from somewhere above. Illuminated by the spotlight was a woman, naked but for a black hood and a multitude of bodily piercings. She was shaved and oiled; tattoos of battling serpents swarmed over her breasts and stomach and twined around her heavily muscled thighs. In each hand she held a secateurlike blade.

"Step into the light," instructed the voice behind him.

Elliott stumbled forward, as though led by his straining cock. He was wheezing and sweating, his heart pounding with terror and lust. As soon as the light touched him, the hooded woman stepped forward, her hands moving with lightning speed. She cut off his clothes, deliberately slicing and nicking the flesh beneath as she did so. Elliott cried out as blood welled from the neat, symmetrical wounds on his arms and shoulders and back, on his belly and thighs and buttocks.

Bleeding and gasping, Elliott's journey into darkness began. When he was naked, the hooded woman looped a chain around his neck and strode away, yanking him behind her. Elliott had to half run to keep up, and had no breath left to scream when the woman led him barefoot across a carpet of upstanding razor blades. As the slivers of metal shredded the soles of his feet, tears poured from his eyes as freely as the blood that formed a slick trail behind him.

He had never known such agony. It was already too much. He wanted it to stop—and yet a part of him craved to go further. His cock was still pointing the way, still engorged and aching. Almost fainting with pain, he stumbled behind the woman until he felt the chain slacken around his neck, whereupon he stumbled and fell to his knees. Instantly the woman strode forward and kicked him hard in the belly. As Elliott opened his mouth to whoop in air, the woman grabbed his hair and thrust her shaven vulva into his face. Instinctively Elliott stuck out his tongue and began to lap at her—and then white-hot pain exploded into his mouth and ripped through his head.

The woman had stepped back, taking half his tongue with her. Elliott heard the gristly ripping sound as the sluglike flesh parted. He tasted metal as blood flooded his mouth and spilled down his chin.

Vagina dentata. The woman plucked the clots of bloody tongue from the serrated metal teeth that lined the inside of her cunt and flicked them disdainfully away.

Elliott's head was spinning. The woman yanked on the chain, tightening it. Elliott wanted to plead for respite, for time to recover, or perhaps reconsider, but his mutilated tongue was a mass of throbbing, useless rubber in his mouth, and the cold steel around his throat was crushing his windpipe, giving him no option but to rise to his feet and stumble onward.

He passed through a series of rooms, in each of which he was forced to experience agony upon agony, humiliation upon humiliation. As he slipped to ever greater depths, he felt the essence of himself diminishing, retreating further and further into the increasingly tormented prison of his lacerated flesh. The pain was excruciating, unendurable—and yet somehow he endured. After a while his ordeal became a blur, like a series of terrible, half-remembered nightmares, a parade of photographlike images. He was fellated by the woman with the pincushion tongue; he was forced to fuck a girl who wore a girdle of metal spikes which pierced his flesh each time he thrust forward; he was strapped down while a thin, heated blade was inserted into his anus.

Finally, burned and cut, pierced and pummeled, bitten and bruised, he was dragged into a candlelit room. The floor was dominated by an intricate series of esoteric symbols enclosed within a circular frame, which was constructed of hundreds of rusty, upstanding nails. Elliott was laid atop the circle and strapped down, the nails piercing his back. He whimpered as a series of women rode his now flaccid and bloodied cock, bearing down on him with their weight, driving the nails in deeper. Eventually he was released and hauled to his feet, only to be strapped, spread-eagled, to a wall. He hung there, legs buckling, for what seemed like hours, the images on the website that had led him to this place reeling endlessly through his shattered mind. He recalled the final image, the hanging man, and hoped it was an indication that his endless night would soon be over. But what would come next? Death? Freedom? Either of those alternatives would be a blessed release.

When they finally took him down, Elliott was more dead than alive. His arms were purple and swollen where the bones and muscles, placed under too much strain, had dislocated and snapped. He crumpled onto his face, now praying for death to take him.

The women—his attendants and tormentors—refused to allow him that luxury, however. They hauled and shoved at his corpulent bulk, like abattoir workers manipulating the carcass of a bull. When they had heaved him onto his back, the hooded woman grabbed a fistful of his hair and yanked his head up. Elliott stared blearily at the section of wall to which he had been strapped, and saw that blood from his punctured back had created a messy but accurate impression of the circular construction on the floor. What appeared to be a red smoky light was rising from the bloodied symbols, co-agulating in the air in front of the wall. Elliott thought he must be hallucinating when the light seemed suddenly to harden and thicken, to form the shape of a figure.

Then there was a crack and a rush of cold air that smelled of sour milk. A flare of light made Elliott flinch, and when his vision cleared he found himself looking into the dispassionate eyes of a monster.

She—for Elliott had no doubt that the creature was female—was fully eight feet tall and had skin the color of ivory. She was naked, and endowed with six pendulous breasts, at each of which suckled a shapeless sac of thickly-veined flesh. She was heavily pregnant, but even as Elliott watched, her cunt gaped open and another "baby" was born, splatting to the floor in a muck of blood and black slime. The creature mewled piteously from a puckered aperture, but its mother ignored it. Indeed, her belly began to swell again almost immediately as another of the hideous infants gestated inside her.

The creature regarded Elliott, her expression serene, but her eyes utterly without pity. When she spoke, her voice was both gentle and terrifying.

"So," she said, "you succumbed to temptation. I knew that you would."

Elliott's lips parted. "Who . . ." he tried to say through the mangled mess of his tongue.

"I am the Matriarch," murmured the creature. "I collect children. And tonight, Elliott, I am here to collect you."

"But I'm not . . . not . . ." Elliott thought more than said.

"Not a child? Oh, but you are. Everyone is someone's child. Even you. Poor, lonely Elliott. And here are your parents to prove it."

For the first time, Elliott saw that the Matriarch was holding two thin chains in her right hand. Attached to the chains, cowering in the shadows at her heels, were creatures that were little more than mangled scraps of flesh. One was simply a few randomly linked body parts—a sliver of brain, an eye, a withered limb, a thin sac of skin containing a feebly beating heart—but the other was complete enough to identify as something that had once been human.

This second creature stared at Elliott with a combination of sorrow, rage, and regret, which seemed somehow familiar. Then he gasped. Of course. The woman in the library.

"I see you recognize them," the Matriarch said. "They visited you today. It was part of our pact. They were there to offer you temptation."

"I don't . . ." Elliott tried to say.

"Understand? Of course not. But I'm afraid that won't save you. I've already been more than generous. I've given you forty years of life." She smiled sweetly. A mother's smile. "I'm just sentimental at heart. When your parents summoned me, your mother pleaded so prettily for your life that I simply couldn't refuse her. And so I offered her a deal. I would grant you forty years of life if, at the end of it, she and your father would return to this realm to place temptation in your path. If you resisted, you would become free of my influence forever, but if not . . ." A tinkling laugh. "Your suffering, combined with their knowledge that they have become the architects of your destruction, will be so sweet, Elliott. *Sssooooo* sweet."

Squatting, she gave birth to another mewling infant. Almost instantly, her belly began to swell once again.

She came forward, dragging what was left of Elliott's parents behind her, the suckling creatures clinging to her swinging breasts. Elliott tried to scramble away as she leaned over, lowering her face toward his, but his wrecked body was a mass of unresponsive agony. She opened her mouth and he smelled the rancid sweetness of sour milk and motherly love.

"You've been such a disappointment to them, Elliott," she murmured, "but now you have all eternity to make amends." She reached out and stroked his hair, oh, so gently. "From now on we'll be one big happy family."

Sister Cilice
Barbie Wilde

F or many years, Sister Nikoletta was in the service of a higher power. She prayed nine times a day. Her life was work, prayer, a few fitful hours of sleep, then more work, more prayer. Thousands of her pious words floated up to the ether, but no answer was forthcoming; only a cruel, empty silence. When her depraved dreams became too overwhelming, mortification of the flesh was the only answer. She remembered the sainted Father Escrivá's maxim on suffering: "Loved be pain. Sanctified be pain. Glorified be pain!" . . . and so she used the whip with greater vengeance, but although she assaulted her flesh, nothing could chase the demons from her mind, those familiars that had tormented her all her life.

Throughout her childhood, entering an order was the only option available to her—the one way to cleanse her heart of the many sins her parents were convinced she had committed. "Every sin, no matter how inconsequential, is a blemish on your soul and will lead you to eternal damnation," her mother used to say. According to her parents, her every thought, word, and deed was sinful. There was no relief from the guilt. No relief from the remorseless burden of her countless transgressions. And no relief from her rage, which she hid from the world along with her dark fantasies of revenge and pain.

Sexual thoughts and acts were forbidden, of course, but that didn't mean these evils left her alone. Perhaps celibacy made it worse, although how was she to know? She'd been sent straight to the nunnery at the age of seventeen, without even kissing a boy, let alone knowing what it was like to be with a real man in the real world, flesh to flesh. And she would never know.

During her early days in the convent, in an attempt to save her rotten soul, Sister Nikoletta made the appearance of perfect devotion, to prove to the other Sisters that she had a vocation. Her every act was irreproachable, and every word she spoke was blameless. The strain of such unrelenting good behavior, of maintaining such a mask of utter innocence and sanity, was almost unbearable, but her parents—who suffered from an overdose of scrupulosity—had brainwashed her into believing that this was her only way to salvation.

Her predicament got worse when Father Xavier was appointed to celebrate Mass every morning. He was so handsome, so virile, so different from the dried-up old men that had previously seen to the nuns' spiritual needs. Sister Nikoletta was convinced that many of the other Sisters felt as she did about him. She could sense their spirits rise when Father Xavier came into the room. Feel the heat from their bodies as they knelt before him and he tenderly ministered the sacraments to them. The occasional accidental touch of Father Xavier's hand on her mouth when he gave her the Host sent little electric shocks through her body. Sister Nikoletta lived for that random physical contact, even though she knew it was meaningless to him.

Every night, after the others had gone to bed, she would mortify her bare flesh until she bled, but that didn't chase the thoughts of the good Father away; it just made her suffering more sensual. She imagined that Father Xavier was the one with the lash, beating her senseless. She'd fall to the ground exhausted, bleeding, eyes shut, body completely open and vulnerable, imagining his presence standing over her. Still with eyes clenched shut, she would use the leather handle of the whip, pretending it was him—thrusting inside of her, hurting her. His pain was loved, his pain was sanctified, his pain was glorified. She'd stuff a rag in her mouth to stifle her cries. Sister Nikoletta came for the first time like that: bloody, naked, sweat-soaked, lying on the cold, stone floor. Momentarily sated, yet for-ever unsatisfied.

After a while, she refined her technique. To heighten her plea-sure, she'd take the end of the whip and wrap it around her neck, pushing the handle deep inside her at the same time; each thrust tightening the lash and ever so slightly cutting off the oxygen to her brain to make her orgasms more intense. She would come again and again, shuddering like an old car dieseling on a frosty winter morn-ing. But the taste in her mouth was bitter, because when she opened her eyes, she was alone. Sister Nikoletta would always be alone. No man would ever come and fill the dry, empty well of her passion.

So she would get up, clean herself, wipe away the tears of anger and frustration, kneel on the cold floor and flog herself again and again for her despicable thoughts and acts.

During the day, Sister Nikoletta would wear a cilice—a small metal chain with inwardly pointing spikes—around her thigh. She would pull the cilice as tight as she could without cutting off the circulation. It was supposed to remind her of Christ's suffering, but all it did was bring back memories of her private moments with the phantom Father Xavier. Her sexual fantasies were now beginning to torment her during the day. The irony was she could not make pen-ance and cleanse her soul, because the only person she was allowed to confess to was Father Xavier. So the sins just piled up, one on top of the other, multiplying and becoming more putrefied with time.

Then a new scenario began to fester in Sister Nikoletta's mind. She *would* confess all her sins to Father Xavier. He would be horri-fied and drag her out of the confessional to the altar, rip her robes off and scourge her using a whip with metal tips, degrading her flesh until she begged him to stop. Her cast-off blood would stain the fair linen altar cloth and splatter the faces of the saints' statues. Then Father Xavier would take her, right there on the marble floor in front of the altar, underneath the enormous suspended golden crucifix. His cassock would fall away from him and reveal the wonders of his flawless body and his sex. She could only imagine what *it* would look like: ivory in color, hard, and shaped like a Knight Templar's sword perhaps. In her fantasies, Father Xavier used not only his saintly member to impale her but any other implement at hand—the holier the better—to sanctify and cleanse her polluted body and diseased mind.

Sister Nikoletta felt her sanity slipping away, fueled by her feverish, obsessive thoughts. Haunted by her desires, she continued to torment her wretched body until it was laced with scars. She asked to be assigned to the library archives in the convent's catacomblike cellar as a way of calming and cooling off her mind. There were thousands of books down there, ancient papers, letters and epistles, missives from popes and cardinals. Perhaps she could immerse herself in history to distract herself from her miserably empty present.

It was there, late one night, that Sister Nikoletta found an ancient manuscript in an old leaden box whose lock had long since rusted away. It was hidden in an alcove far from the entrance, forgotten for centuries. The box was littered with crunchy, long-dead black beetles, a few bloodred dried roses, and a dusty mummified crow; beak open and tongue lolling out as if in accusation.

The book was called the *Grimorium Enochia* and it was written in the fifteenth century by Raphael Athanasius. Sister Nikoletta spent weeks trying to translate the Latin text. For the first time in years, something was taking her mind away from the bloody world of her profane imaginings. She soon realized that she had discovered something far more engrossing than her fantasies. Athanasius was an alchemist, necromancer, and cryptographer, and was a friend of the notorious serial killer, dabbler in the black arts, and brother-in-arms to Jeanne d'Arc, Maréchal Gilles de Rais. At first glance, Athanasius's book appeared to be about his accounts of summoning forth and speaking with angels and demons. However, it soon became obvious to Sister Nikoletta that his manuscript was more than a few incantations and stories.

Athanasius's invocations were a pathway into another dimension: a place where the chthonic inhabitants might understand her needs. These beings were called Cenobites and were members of another kind of order altogether, where pain as pleasure was the norm, not a hidden vice. She was intrigued and hopeful that somehow she might be allowed access into this world, to find an answer to her torment from those who seemed to be fellow travelers.

She knew by now that she was tired of her life, disgusted by it, not because of what she did to herself, not because of her secrets and sins, but because she had always been a slave to other people's demands. She had never been in charge, never allowed to follow her cravings, subject to countless indignities of the spirit. She was soul-sick, but it wasn't her fault. She needed to get out and Athanasius offered her the way. Not back to the real world of pathetic, ordinary people, which she despised because it reminded her of her parents and all those other contemptible, hypocritical syco-phants, but into a murky, labyrinthine sanctuary of lust, pleasure, pain, sensuality, power, and blood ruled by the undivine Order of the Gash.

After several abortive attempts, Sister Nikoletta finally deciphered Athanasius's infernal recipe. Of course, the correct procedure was important, but as she delved into the text, Sister Nikoletta realized that she already possessed the most essential and vital ingredient for success: the overwhelming desire to invoke the schism that would allow the Cenobites to enter into this realm and show her their marvels.

She prepared for their entrance with care, finding an aban-doned, airless room next to the library where she equipped a make-shift altar with artifacts of torture that she thought would amuse the Cenobites. In the hospital adjacent to the convent, she found a ter-minally sick child who was too far gone to notice the pint of blood that she furtively collected from him at the fourth hour after midnight. She mixed this with some of her own menstrual blood and poured the liquid into a chalice that she appropriated from the convent's chapel. She also added her own scourge and cilice as personal decorations to her altar.

As Sister Nikoletta uttered the final cadence of Athanasius's Latin invocation, she heard the tinkle of chimes, almost too cloying and sweet to her ears, then a mournful bell tolling. The sounds weren't coming from above but from somewhere near her, down here in the dark catacombs where not long ago, dead bodies of nuns (and as rumor would have it, their illegitimate murdered offspring) were buried. The lights fluttered in time to the bell and she knew that it wasn't just an ordinary power fluctuation. Something, someone, was coming. A twinge of regret touched her heart, a touch of panic, but she pushed it away with a mental growl. She was sick to death of fear, tired of being ashamed of nothing, weary of being a weakling. She wanted strength and power and sensation for its own sake. She longed to discipline others, to make them feel as she had. She wanted to be destroyed and remade again, in the image of the Order of the Gash.

Another sound entered her mind, the sound of a metronome ticking, ticking, ticking—in time to the quickened beating of her heart. The walls of the room groaned in time to the metronome; they bulged and heaved, and between the cracks of the stones, she saw light—a yellowy, sickly white light. The walls shuddered and she stumbled back to the doorway, ready to make a hasty retreat if her courage failed her. Finally the walls parted, dust erupted in a brownish, rancid cloud. Light spilled into the room, and voices beautiful but discordant, warbled in the background, like a movie soundtrack played at the wrong speed.

A tall male Cenobite entered, followed by a few others, but she had no interest in them. She gasped, not in horror, but in admiration. The leader was stunning, a fallen angel, his princely beauty still shining through even though his face and body were mutilated and twisted by scars, lacerations, pins, wires, and nails. His black eyes were liquid with eternal suffering; eyelids stapled permanently open. His long, black leather apron was soaked with blood and speckled with bits of flesh. His naked arms were laced with multiple cilices and the razor-sharp inward spikes poked deeply into his flesh. Barbed wire was wrapped around his chest, and chains bound his legs.

He held a black leather and steel-capped cat-o'-nine-tails in his gloved hand and she knew who it was for: a special gift just for her. Sister Nikoletta sank down to her knees and opened her arms wide in a pretty, Madonnaesque pose of gratitude. He smiled, showing perfect bloodied teeth, filed into flawless little points.

A strong, warm wind scented with vanilla billowed up from behind him, knocking Sister Nikoletta down to the ground. Her robes fluttered up, exposing her secret places and momentarily blinding her. She lifted her arms above her head, and her clothes and veil ripped off and flew into the darkness, like an enormous, demented crow.

He stared at Sister Nikoletta—the naked, surrendered nun—and he was still smiling, almost puzzled by her rapt acceptance. He spoke, his voice echoing in the chamber, "Do you know what you are asking of us? Do you know what will happen to you?"

Sister Nikoletta answered, "Yes, with all my heart. Take me. Make me one of you, if you think I'm worthy. I'll give anything to you. Soul, body, mind, heart. You know they are already yours if you want them."

He laughed, joined by the others hidden back in the darkness. His merriment didn't frighten Sister Nikoletta, it just exhilarated her and made her desperate for his embraces. She longed to stand up and go to him, but her limbs refused to move. Sister Nikoletta felt something tightening at her wrists and ankles, looked and saw silvery, spiked chains pulled tight by unseen hands disappearing into the darkness—stretching her limbs out to their fullest extent, as if she were strapped to an invisible torture rack. The pain of the diamond-sharp spikes digging into her skin was excruciating, but it was nothing compared to the new sensations that were flooding her body. It was as if all her nerve endings were on fire, alert to every mote of dust that landed on her exposed flesh, every grain of dirt being ground into her back and buttocks. She felt like she was being burned at the stake; even breathing hurt—the air stung her lungs. But the pain, instead of being maddening or frightening, just sent her deeper into a bizarre ecstasy. Below her waist, the epithelial fire was flickering up her thighs, then darting inside her—burning her internally with wave after wave of searing, orgasmic thrusts. Sister Nikoletta screamed and writhed, pleasure and pain mixed in an infernal cocktail. It was what she always dreamed of, but more.

He laughed again, enjoying her delicious agony, and began working his personal magic with his scourge over her naked breasts and genitals. How was it possible to feel more pain? How was it possible to feel more ecstasy? In the shadows, the other Cenobites applauded the show. They hadn't seen anything this entertaining in ages.

The metal hooks on the leather strips of his scourge dug into Sister Nikoletta's skin and gouged out her flesh. She felt that not only her body was being flayed, but her soul. She didn't care; she desperately wanted release from her old self. She was happy to trade that tired bag of flesh for something else, something beautiful—like *him*. She wanted to *be* him: intractable, indomitable, powerful, a slave to nothing but desire. She wanted his nails, pins, wires, fingers, and teeth to bite into her, to destroy and then transmute her sad sack of sin into a blood-drenched angel of darkness—the envy of all the other demons. She sent this message to him in her shrieks of horrified delight, pleasure, and gratitude.

He finally stopped and dropped his drenched whip. He walked over and stood astride her body. The pain hadn't abated and Sister Nikoletta still cried out. He sank down slowly, a knee planted on each side of her chest, and took out a thin-bladed surgical scalpel. He leaned over, placed his hand under her chin, and gently pushed back her head. Unable to scream, feet pummeling the ground, Sister Nikoletta made muffled sounds of anguish as he slowly and artistically carved a new orifice for her. He laced thin platinum wires through her cheeks and, using these as an anchor, hooked and pulled the skin away from her gaping wound. When he had finished, he straightened up and lifted his apron to show her another present he had prepared for her.

The skin fire was nothing. Her bloody wound was nothing. The agonizing whips and chains were nothing. Whatever happened to Sister Nikoletta next would obliterate her forever, tear her apart and send her whirling down into an abyss of divine degradation, to that special place she had longed to go to for so many years.

The Cenobite entered her, using every orifice, old and new. Sister Nikoletta's choking, dreadful moans of passion gurgled from her lips, but the sounds were triumphant, and her frantically thrashing body echoed her exquisite feelings of the ultimate in sensual suffering.

Her shadowy Cenobite audience applauded yet again. What a girl! Sister Nikoletta's adoration for mutilation, sensation, and agony would be legendary, even in Hell.

For many years now, Sister Cilice has been in the service of the Subterranean Power. Hellbound to glory. She has no thoughts, no worries, no guilt, no empathy, no passion, no dreams, nothing to do but to satiate desires that can never really be quenched to the full, but hell, nothing is perfect. She assists her leader in his work; they are a perfect team. They even finish each other's threats to those who dare call upon them, and take turns flaying those unfortunates who thought they knew what they were doing when they opened the Box. The silence from above no longer greets her words, but screams for mercy. They pray to Sister Cilice now. They are her supplicants, not the other way around. The mortification of her flesh no longer gives her quite the pleasure it used to, but the delight in the pain of others is truly enriching. She is no longer concerned about the demons in her mind. She is a demon herself now and woe betide the mind that comes across her.

In a tiny corner of the shriveled, blackened brain that once belonged to someone called Sister Nikoletta, Sister Cilice hears an echo of one phrase above all others: "Loved be pain. Sanctified be pain. Glorified be pain!"

They are the only words that can still make her laugh.

Santos del Infierno
Jeffrey J. Mariotte

How does one gauge emptiness; calibrate the measure of sorrow? Or is a void defined purely by that which once occupied it? Ron Marks knew the timing of his loss, but not the degree. It took an instant, and when it ended, nothing would ever be the same.

When it ended. Later, that idea would make Ron Marks laugh, bitterly and without humor. It never ended.

When it began, when that instant came and went—that, he knew with precision. Saturday, November 10. He had gone out into the New Mexico evening at 6:50 p.m. Hayleigh had a soccer game, and Linda planned to take some of the girls out for ice cream at game's end, but they should be home by seven. In the dying of the day, Ron decided to water the lawn. Family, home stability—these things defined him.

Hose in hand, arcing water gently over patchy grass, he watched a family from the next block start across the street. He had never met them, but saw them around the neighborhood. A single mother, he believed, young, with black hair and dark eyes. She pushed an infant in a stroller, a little boy in grass-stained jeans and a flannel shirt walking beside her.

Just then, Ron heard the truck. He stepped around the corner and saw it barreling north toward the intersection: a monstrous three-quarter ton, jacked up on huge shocks and giant tires, all shiny black and chrome and pure macho aggression. It came too fast, and in the blue light of dusk, he wasn't sure its driver had seen the family stepping into the road.

Ron dropped the hose and ran into the street. At the same moment he heard a lesser engine coming from the west—Linda's Maxima. He scissored his arms over his head, trying to warn the pickup's driver to slow down. There was a stop sign at the corner, but the guy wasn't braking.

After that, it all happened suddenly. The truck swerved, missing the young family. The woman screamed and yanked her stroller so hard it tipped over in the middle of the street. The swerve put the truck in the wrong part of the intersection at the crucial moment, as Linda, presumably thinking no one would tear past the stop sign—and perhaps, Ron had to admit, distracted by the sight of her husband waving like a madman—proceeded through the intersection.

The pickup broadsided her sedan. The crunch of steel against steel, the squeal of skidding tires, and the burning stink of brakes and shredded rubber seared into Ron's brain. The car and truck, a single interlocked whole, scraped across the pavement and onto the sidewalk, coming to rest with the Maxima pinned between the truck's massive bulk and a power pole on the far corner.

Linda and Hayleigh were dead long before the authorities were able to work through bent steel and broken glass—a retrieval, one said, believing Ron couldn't hear, far too late for a rescue.

The days before the funeral were full of phone calls and e-mails and cards, flowers and food. Linda's parents and sisters came to town, as did old friends Ron hadn't seen in months or years. Then it was over and Linda and Hayleigh were in the ground and everyone went away.

And Ron fell apart. He felt as if someone had tapped his heart and broken the spigot, so all the blood and love flooded out, pooling on the floor.

Linda had been the family's main breadwinner, and her million-dollar insurance policy named Ron as sole beneficiary. The check arrived just as Ron's chronic absence cost him his government job. He couldn't bring himself to care. Work had been interfering with his drinking anyway, and he decided to apply himself to that pursuit with the dedication it deserved.

Ron became a connoisseur, not of fine liquors but of whatever concoction could speed him most rapidly into oblivion. He found that mixing his poisons worked well. He poured a fifth of the cheapest rotgut whiskey he could find into a gallon pitcher, then threw in vodka or gin, maybe some beer for flavoring. The pitcher would generally last a couple of days, because he would pass out long before he finished. If it didn't spill, he could start in again whenever he woke up.

During the hours between blackouts, he wandered the increasingly filthy house, like a ghost haunting a place in which he had once been happy. He left all three of the house's televisions on, and occasionally thought he heard Linda's voice or Hayleigh's shrill giggle. But it was always some actress or newswoman or "personality," those false friends of lost and lonely Americans living empty lives in empty houses.

When November 10 came around again, he was barely aware of the date. But his drinking took on new urgency, and although by now it took most of the pitcher to knock him out, he worked hard at spending fewer hours of each day awake and aware. The weather was unseasonably cold, with a piercing wind that whisked through the window he had broken in a blind rage that spring, then taped up instead of replacing.

Ron was on the bathroom floor when someone pounded on his front door. He came around slowly, first thinking it was the TV. Finally he realized it was a person, and that person wasn't leaving.

The pitcher was tipped on its side. Ron sniffed it, tasted the rim.

The pounding continued. He would have to mix another pitcher, but he couldn't remember if he had really run out of whiskey or only dreamed it. He couldn't remember the last time the pitcher had been washed, the last time he had showered. He ran a finger through greasy, tangled hair. His cheeks felt bristly and sharp.

The pounding would give him a headache if it kept on, especially without more whiskey. Gathering himself enough to go to the store would put a damper on his plan of spending the rest of the week unconscious, but maybe his visitor had brought a few bottles of something.

Ron pushed off the toilet, ignoring the vomit flecking its rim, and gained his feet. The pounding had settled into a steady rhythm, unchanging as he staggered toward the door. When he opened it, a man stood there, a few years younger than Ron, Latino and stocky, with black hair, big brown eyes, and a wispy goatee. He hadn't brought any bottles. Ron stared at him, waiting for an explanation.

"You don't remember me?"

"Should I?" Ron hadn't looked into a mirror in so long, he wasn't sure he'd remember himself.

"A year ago, dude. I'm the guy who was driving the truck. I killed your wife and kid."

Ron wasn't sure how to respond. The driver had been charged with manslaughter, but a sharp lawyer had managed to get him a deal: time served and community service. Now here he stood.

Ron's guts churned like someone was twisting them, and he threw a jerking, unsteady punch. Momentum tugged him off balance. His fist slid off the man's shoulder, and the man grabbed his arms and shoved him back against the wall.

"Look, I know it's weird." His breath was hot in Ron's face. "Me coming here like this. I wanted to tell you that I am so sorry. There hasn't been a single day I haven't remembered what happened and felt like shit about it, okay? I'm not saying what I've gone through is anything like your loss. But that day changed all of our lives, right? Mine too."

"How so?"

"My girlfriend left me after that, dude. Took our kids. I lost my job. Most of my friends stopped talking to me. And I know I wasn't in the system that long, but that was rough, man. Shit I seen . . ."

"Sorry for your pain," Ron said, retreating. "Now get lost." He started to close the door. The guy blocked it with his leg.

"You gotta let me in, dude. What's your name? Ronald something, right?"

"Ron Marks."

"I'm Leonardo Montoya. Lenny."

"Is there some reason I shouldn't just kick your ass, Lenny?"

Lenny laughed. "Dude, you can't fucking stand up without hanging on to the wall."

Ron had been trying to ignore that. Now that it was pointed out, he almost lost his balance and had to take a couple of backward steps. Lenny took the motion as an invitation, stepped inside, and shut the door behind him. He was right. Whatever Lenny wanted to do, Ron couldn't stop him.

It turned out that Lenny wanted to talk, to make amends somehow. He took a key, went to the store, and brought back plastic bags that made the satisfying clink of glass on glass. One had real food in it, too. Lenny made chicken tacos drizzled with lime, mixed a pitcher to Ron's specifications, and they sat in the living room. Lenny talked. Some of the time, Ron listened.

Days passed. Lenny was there a lot, cooking and cleaning and shopping. The house started to smell more like fresh air, cleaning solutions, and cooked food than rotting meat and greasy hamburger wrappers. Ron drank marginally less; with someone around to listen to, oblivion seemed minutely less important. Lenny started speaking to Ron like a friend or a spouse, discussing things they might do together, purchases they could make. Weeks went by before Ron realized that Lenny was living on Ron's insurance money.

When he called Lenny on it, Lenny laughed. "Dude, we're connected by our loss. We're brothers in pain, *compadres* of the lonely life. You have every reason on Earth to hate me, but you can't. Because I'm part of you now. We're living inside the same skin."

"I guess," Ron said, and had another drink.

A couple of weeks after that, Lenny suggested that they make the two-hour drive into El Paso. Ron hadn't been out of the house in months, except to the grocery store and gas station.

It turned out what Lenny had in mind was a strip club by the interstate. Ron didn't want to go in. Once he stopped paying the cable bill and televised porn ceased being piped in, he had mostly forgotten about sex. All those writhing bodies had been a blur to him anyway.

But the grinding, perfume-soaked attention of a voluptuous woman from across the border caused memories of that once-pleasurable activity to stir and swell, along with the usual physical manifestation of same. He could only understand every fifth word she breathed into his ear, but with pillowy breasts in his face and her devoted attention to the bulge in his pants, he decided he didn't care.

It was the first time he had truly *felt* in more than a year.

"That was nothing," Lenny said on the way home. "What I've heard, you could have a dozen virgins a day and it wouldn't compare to what you can get if you really want it."

"Where? I don't want to go to some Juárez whorehouse."

"It's more a question of *how* than *where*. In Hell, or something like that."

"I'll be there soon enough," Ron said. "When I die."

"Did I say anyone had to die?"

"You said Hell."

Lenny chuckled. "You got a lot to learn, dude. Don't worry, I'll teach you. I'll hook you up right."

The next night, Lenny built a fire and opened a couple of beers. Outside, a ferocious wind sent snowflakes flashing past the window's glow.

"Here's the thing," Lenny said. "I met this guy, while you were in this house pickling your brain. He was a drunk, too, kind who can't shut up. We're in this dive bar in Hatch, and he starts telling me about these *santos*, and—"

"Hold up," Ron said. "What's a *santo*?"

"Dude, you are one ignorant white man," Lenny said. Gold teeth gleamed in the firelight. "A *santo* is a religious art object. Sculptures, paintings, any representation of the saints. They're made by people called *santeros*. Huge deal here in New Mexico. Collectors pay thousands for good ones."

"That's fascinating," Ron said, not meaning it. "What do I care?"

"You care, because the ones this guy told me about are different from the usual kind. Most *santos* are sacred representations. But these . . . well, the guy got scared, and I had to keep buying him more drinks."

The wind died suddenly, as if eavesdropping. Lenny lowered his voice. "These ones are, like, pornographic. Guy had a different word . . . *profane*. He said they were profane, not sacred."

"Better," Ron said. "Still . . ."

"Let me finish, dude. He said these *santos* were carved by this *loco* old *santero* who lived by himself in the desert, in the early eighteen hundreds. He had a vision and he just started carving and painting. But this vision didn't come from God. God would have wanted nothing to do with this crazy bastard. His *santos* were twisted, insane. Like Saint Francis biting the head off a squirrel instead of feeding it, or Saint Hildegarde tearing open her dress and showing three huge tits, stuff like that."

Ron swallowed more beer. "Sounds like fun," he said. Fun was a concept he was just beginning to revisit. "But what's it have to do with us?"

"Here's the deal," Lenny said. "These *santos* are still around. They're indestructible. If you get seven of them, they can all be put together like a puzzle. And solving this puzzle opens the door to worlds of pleasure you can't even imagine."

"There's still something I'm missing," Ron said. "Even if it's true, what about it? It's not like we have these *santos*."

"Not *all* of them," Lenny replied.

"What does that mean?"

"I'm not done!" Lenny leaned forward. Behind him, the fire snapped and hissed. "The old guy took me home, thought I'd give him head. Instead, I made him show me his *santo* and tell me where he got it. Then I killed his ass."

Ron didn't know what to say. He couldn't believe Lenny would intentionally murder someone, or that, having done so, he would confess it, especially to him.

Lenny shrugged broadly, palms up. "The fuck, right? I already killed your wife and daughter. What's some old drunk compared to them?"

The mention of Linda and Hayleigh brought Ron unsteadily to his feet, hands grasping toward Lenny. Lenny misunderstood his sudden rage. "Pervo bastard had it coming," he said. "Dude made me sick."

"Okay, but—"

"Look, just wait here." He went into Hayleigh's room, which he had commandeered when he'd moved in, in the fullness of Ron's obliteration. He came back carrying a rolled-up cotton shirt. Unrolling it, he revealed a wooden carving fourteen inches tall, its paint chipped and aged.

There was a certain mastery to the work. Ron knelt beside it, fingered its dulled edges and smoothed patina. It was clearly old, and just as clearly *wrong*.

The woman depicted in the carving had the plump, guileless features of a farm wife. She had brown hair pulled off her face and hanging down her back. Her robes were a vivid blue, with gold trim.

Instead of standing, she crouched, her skirts bunched in her fists, pudgy thigh exposed. Her legs were spread, and from her open vagina slithered what Ron could only call a monster, black-snouted, many-toothed, with two tongues curling in different directions. He wasn't sure, but it appeared that there were the beginnings of wings on its back, the rest of them buried deep inside the woman.

"That's disgusting," Ron said. His head felt hot, his thoughts fractured. He wanted another drink. He imagined the carver slicing his hands, bleeding onto the wood.

"You ain't supposed to like it. This is Saint Pudentia. See the detail the *santero* put into her quim?"

"Nice."

"Dude, this is our ticket! Before last night I wasn't sure if you'd ever come back into the world. But I saw you smiling while that stripper humped you. You got to be in the world before you can leave it. You got to *feel* before you can know pleasure. Right?"

"I suppose . . ."

"Suppose, nothing. You got feelings again. I brought you back, but I still owe you, so I'm gonna take you to the next step."

"Which is . . . ?"

"All the pleasures of Hell, my man. Way I hear it, that crap about fire and pitchforks is bogus. Heaven sucks. Hell's where the fun people go."

"But how would we get there?"

"I know how to find the rest of the *santos*, Ron. I've been studying this while you've been drinking. All it'll take is money."

Ron still felt like his brains had been scrambled, but he was beginning to understand. This was all about Lenny wanting to spend more of his insurance money.

On the other hand, if he was right, if these *santos* really did promise some sort of ultimate pleasure, then what was the harm? He didn't have anything better to do with the money. He had been living in Hell for more than a year anyway. Maybe Lenny was right. The time had come to rejoin the living . . . even if it meant embracing the dead.

Ron let Lenny worry about finding the *santos*. He handed over the cash and stayed home, trying not to think about the journey upon which he would soon embark.

Unless Lenny's source was a liar as well as a drunk.

But soon Lenny brought home another *santo*. St. Tiberius's face looked like it was melting, the skin hanging around his shoulders in soggy strips, bones and muscles glistening underneath. Lenny's eyes were haunted, and he refused to tell Ron exactly how it had gone down. "But I got it, man," he said. "And I know where to go from here. Dude had all the four-one-one."

Ron didn't like the use of the past tense, but he let it go. "I don't see how this one connects to the other."

"Maybe it don't. There's seven of 'em, maybe these two don't connect."

Ron couldn't argue. Maybe none of them connected. Maybe the whole thing was some crazy imagining.

Lenny kept taking more money, going out, and returning with others. St. Agnes, whose spread fingers were shaped like erect phalluses. St. Nestor, a rare sitting *santo*, with a giant candle jammed up his rectum, the exposed end flaming. St. Faustina, holding her eyeballs in her hands while tears of green blood tracked down her face. St. Rogatus, his throat split down the middle; he held the wound open with his hands as bats erupted from inside him.

Lenny brought them home late at night, eyes wild, sometimes trembling with emotion. He wouldn't tell Ron what he'd been through, but it was clearly unpleasant. A couple of times, he brought back the money—but he had a *santo* anyway. Ron wondered how much blood he'd spilled for those six treasures.

Lenny came home one night wearing an excited grin, like that of a child with a secret too big to keep. "I know where it is," he said. "Number seven. We are there, dude!" He had regaled Ron with tales of what Hell would be like, once they cracked the code. He talked about the women who would service them, anticipating their every desire, however foul. They were not only free of taboos and inhibitions, but they prided themselves on being able to outdo one another in satisfying every possible perversion. Ron cared less about that than about feeling something that would convince him he was still alive.

"When can you get it?" Ron asked. As the *santos* had mounted, he had begun to believe. Anticipation, at least, was an emotion only the living knew.

"Tomorrow," Lenny replied. "But you gotta come with me. It's a long drive. And honestly, I might need some backup with this one."

They drove into New Mexico's high country under skies so gray they might have been solid pewter. The evergreen forests and grassy meadows and tiny villages could have been unchanged for the past two hundred years.

Naciemento looked like the other towns, a place the world had left behind. A scattering of adobe homes, their surrounding walls toppled, roofs caved in, windows smashed, were linked by roads paved so long ago the hardtop crumbled like dry cookie dough. A few failed businesses ranged around a central square, at one end of which a big adobe church squatted like a corpulent toad.

"You sure this is right? Place looks deserted," Ron said.

"It's supposed to be in the church."

Ron parked in the square. The car doors sounded loud in the silence. Lenny met his eye briefly, then led the way to the church doors. He pushed one open, its hinges groaning. A shaft of light from the doorway illuminated the interior. "Where?" Ron whispered.

"I don't know. We have to hunt for it."

What remained of the pews had been shoved to one side of the nave, scarring the dusty stone floor. Cobwebs big enough to snare Buicks clung to the corners. The altar had been tipped over, its legs knocked off. An ocean of trash made it an island. Wading through it, Ron's skin crawled as if someone had shaken a bowl of ants down his shirt.

He was about to suggest leaving when a door scraped open behind them. "God, fuck!" he said, startled, before realizing how inappropriate such an exclamation was. Then again, given their mission here, such considerations were doubtlessly far too late.

An ancient padre emerged from the darkness, his cassock and surplice filthy and torn. His head was oddly pudgy around nose, mouth, and cheeks, and short stalks of black hair poked from his scalp like burnt straw. "What brings you here?" he asked. His voice sounded muffled, distorted.

"The *santo*," Lenny said. "Where is it?"

"That is not meant for the likes of you," the padre said. "Leave this sanctuary."

"Not till we get it."

The priest grabbed an old candlestick from the floor and came at them surprisingly swiftly, wielding it like a baseball bat. Lenny screeched something, and Ron, heart still racing from the shock of being discovered, reacted. He snatched up a jagged chunk of the altar's broken leg and thrust it toward the advancing padre. The old man gave a strangled cry as his feet slipped on loose debris and he plunged forward onto the pointed end of Ron's weapon. The wood punched through rotting fabric and soft flesh as if he were no more substantial than a paper lantern. Blood gushed onto Ron's hands and he scrabbled backward to avoid the priest's lifeless body, toppling headlong toward him.

Ron turned to Lenny, eyes wide with horror. "That was fucking awesome!" Lenny said, grinning madly. "You just did that guy!"

"I didn't mean to!" Ron said. "He—"

"Forget it. You did what you had to, same as me. Now we just gotta find that *santo*."

"But, Lenny, I killed a priest!"

Lenny was already pawing through the refuse. "A half-dead priest with an empty church. No loss, man. Keep looking!"

They found it in a sarcophagus, deep in the church's bowels. It was pushed back into a close-fitting niche in the thick wall, and they couldn't budge it, so Ron, thinner than Lenny, had to shove aside the wooden lid and crawl inside with a penlight in his mouth. The saint clutched an enormous phallus with both hands, but the phallus was detached from his body, and veins that should have been safely sheathed were instead slithering worms with fanged mouths.

It was wedged into the deceased's rib cage, and Ron had to work it free, trying the whole time not to gag.

Ron wanted to leave town, but Lenny had brought the other *santos* and insisted on assembling them on the spot. In the empty plaza, they unwrapped the old sculptures and tried to fit them together: head to head, mouth to genitals, front to back. For all their pornographic detail, they didn't connect. Ron didn't see how they could, but when Lenny grew frustrated, Ron took over.

"I don't think it works," he said, tying Nestor upside down, facing Pudentia. "Whoever told you they did was full of shit. You spent my money and ran all over the state and now we fucking killed a priest for nothing!"

"You're not the only one killed somebody for these," Lenny reminded him. As he spoke, Ron heard a bell tolling. It might have been going for a while, just now working into his consciousness.

"The hell is that?" he asked.

"Ask not," another voice rasped. The old padre appeared at the church doors, a ragged hole in his chest. "A little joke," he said. "It tolls for thee."

"I killed you!" Ron shouted, fear and fury behind his words. "You died in there!"

The priest reached behind his own head. "Another joke," he said. "I'm full of them." He released something Ron couldn't see, and his skin—the skin he was wearing—sloughed off him like a baggy coat, dropping to the ground with a wet thump.

The being underneath it wasn't a man, but he was clearly male. He was lean, with paper-white skin stretched snugly across bulging muscles. His only clothes were dark gray pants, stitches holding them to his lower torso in lieu of a belt. A map of scars delineating rivers and mountains and roads stood in stark relief against his skin. Three thick stitches pinned his upper lip to his nose; similar needlework held lower lip to chin. Beneath his eyes, eye-shaped holes had been cut, also held open with stitches, brass buttons sewn in place as extra eyeballs. The scent of vanilla reached Ron's nostrils. The sight should have sickened him, but instead he felt a surprising stirring at his groin. What had Lenny called Hell's emissaries?

Cenobites, that was it. Lenny had tried to tell Ron all about the Order of the Gash, but Ron, only half believing and probably half drunk, had only half listened.

"You're missing one piece," the Cenobite said. He walked between Ron and Lenny and stood among the *santos*, his feet brushing two of them. "*Now* we are complete."

The bell tolled one last time, deep and resonant. The gray sky roiled and darkened to near black.

And inside a glow that seemed to come from the Cenobite himself, the *santos* moved together, their pieces swiveling and interlocking, sliding into place with satisfyingly final clicks. Pudentia linked to Agnes to Nestor to Rogatus to Faustina to Tiberius to the new one.

When they finished, the backdrop behind the hideous Cenobite had changed as well. The traditional New Mexican church was gone, and in its place was a vaguely phosphorescent passageway into infinity, with dark, indiscernible shapes darting about inside it.

"Told you we could do this," Lenny said.

Ron's mouth was so dry it clicked when he spoke. "Y-yeah, you told me. But I don't see any women, or . . ."

"Guess I didn't tell you everything, though. See, I used to live here in Naciemento. I left—we all left—when Padre Escalante summoned this Cenobite—Buttons, we call him—and got himself flayed for his trouble. But I couldn't resist coming back this one time. See, you fucked my life, dude. You running out in the road like that, distracting me—whole deal always was *your* fault. I would have missed everyone and kept on going, but *you* ruined everything. Well, it's payback time, bitch. You with your hands all over those *santos* . . . you'll get your time in Hell. But it might not be exactly what you expected."

A terrible certainty settled over Ron. Lenny had played him

from the start. If he'd been thinking clearly, he would have known the guy who killed your wife and child didn't just invite himself back into your life. His kindness had been anything but. It was too late to kick himself now. He had been stupid, and the price would be high.

"You handled the *santos*, too, Leonardo," Buttons said.

"Sure, but . . . he had 'em last!"

"But I knew *you* first."

Ron's heart lifted. Was he getting a reprieve? Did the Cenobite hold a grudge against Lenny?

"You didn't know me!"

"Do you think I wasn't aware of you? After Escalante brought me here . . . when you all ran like frightened rabbits . . . I swore none of you would escape if I could lure you back."

Lenny backed away from the Cenobite, lips quivering, a line of drool running down his chin. When Buttons fixed Lenny with a burning, four-eyed gaze, Ron caught a rank ammonia scent. A stain spread down the front of Lenny's pants.

A chain darted out—from the Cenobite? From behind him?— with a hook on the end, catching Lenny under the chin. The hook sliced up under his jaw and the barbed point thrust out his open mouth, glistening red. It reeled him in like a recalcitrant fish, Lenny stiff-legged and blubbering and weeping until he disappeared into the softly glowing blue corridor.

His screams seemed to echo for a long time.

Ron's legs felt like celery stalks days past their prime. He realized that he was ready to follow. He knew now that cruelty was as lasting as kindness, hate as powerful as love, pain was infinite and loneliness ultimately unbearable. There was nothing left for him in the world. "My turn?" he asked, his voice a pathetic whimper.

Buttons turned his full attention to Ron. His natural eyes glowed with an inner fire, and even his button eyes danced like they were alive. "Did I somehow give you that impression?" With that horrible, pinned-open mouth, he seemed to smile. "I must have been joking. One day, you'll beg to be let in." He tapped a fingernail against a button eye. "And then, we'll see."

He stepped into the blue glow and vanished, leaving Ron alone.

Another moment, another new beginning.

And once again, the emptiness he faced was beyond measure.

The Promise
Nancy Kilpatrick

You stare in disbelief at the e-mail from Ritz, unnerved by the undercurrent of what you are reading. "Goth reunion," she euphemistically calls it. The old crowd will meet at the cemetery, the usual place. The place where every August 30 for five summers of your youth you spent the night in a graveyard with your friends. Is she insane? Can't she remember what happened? But she is just keeping a promise.

If you close your eyes and don't look, maybe when you open them, this e-mail will have disappeared into the vapors. Your heart slams against your chest wall in fear; anything can happen, like last time.

You peruse the excuses flitting across your closed eyelids like the digital numbers you scan all day long. But despite wanting to run fast and far, you will be there because no one can ever move fast or far enough to escape the past. And you also made a promise.

You'll be there, as you were the last time the group picnicked like the Victorians, although it's unlikely anyone from the 1800s spent the night in a crypt. Briefly you wonder if Jeremy will be at the "reunion." But of course he will; he promised, too. You have to confess, the idea of Jeremy at the cemetery is intriguing. So many possibilities. And impossibilities . . .

It is Saturday, seven in the evening, warm, the sun has not yet set, the grass is end-of-summer green, and you admit to yourself that this close-of-day is beautiful, reminiscent of twenty years ago, the last time you set foot in this garden of the dead. Time has changed little here. Eighty seasons have passed, toppling and shattering tombstones that caretakers have cemented back together, like the lovely distressed filigreed cross for which you still feel an affinity. Other stones, victims of recent violent weather, quietly await repair. One decapitated angel, the head beside the feet, eyes turned heavenward, clearly mourns its missing hands which some collector of necroabilia has walked off with.

The climb uphill isn't as easy as it once was; two decades makes a difference. You know you're out of shape from sitting for eight-plus hours a day and microwaving frozen supermarket meals on too regular a basis. By the time you reach the first plateau, you're winded.

To the left, farther up, mostly hidden by old-growth trees and lilac bushes long past the flowering stage, is a row of enormous mausoleums belonging to wealthy families. You quickly calculate an estimate of what crypts like these would cost to build today.

The economics of crypt building leads to thoughts of death. Your own. Once so easy to digest, such musings now send a deep shudder like an earthquake in the making through your body as horror builds, and you turn away trembling, the past intersecting the present. Death has become the least of your worries. Coming here was a bad idea. A *very* bad idea. The past can't be undone. The future is set. What's the point of this? On shaky legs you turn to head back down the hill and get away from here while you still can, consequences be damned!

"Shadow!"

The sound startles you, and your bad knee locks. Jeremy has appeared out of nowhere, it seems. He was always good at that. "I call myself Karen now," you say, eyeing this Dorian Gray who, on first glance, has not aged.

Jeremy laughs, the sound as familiar as his skin and the muscles of his body once were, bringing you some calmness, although that doesn't make sense, just as it made no sense in the past.

Now that your tremors have subsided, you notice he has a cute, petite blonde attached to his arm, her cerulean eyes intelligent in a direct-marketing kind of way, her hair matching the white-gold color of his; maybe they patronize the same salon. Both are lean, healthy-looking, probably vegetarians into working out regularly. You bet they drive a BMW or Volvo and she's got some kind of high-powered, high-paying secure job with the government. The gold rings on the third fingers of their left hands speak of union in the biblical sense, and you imagine these DINKS live in a reno'ed town house featured in some glossy interior-design magazine, a property worth three times the market value of your small condo.

Suddenly you are shocked by your own cynicism. When did you become so petty? Bitter. Unhappy. You know when. And why. And who is to blame.

"This is Candy," Jeremy says, and you're startled by the name. "Karen. Once Shadow." He laughs, introducing you.

"I've heard a lot about you guys and your goth days," Candy says, as if teasing a child.

You're not sure what she knows but you're certain that Jeremy hasn't told all. How could he explain it? How could anyone?

"Yeah, well, that was quite a while ago," you mutter. "When we were young and wild and Jeremy was known as Midnight."

"You were?" Candy turns to him and laughs, a sparkling sound, full of vitality, and you wonder why she's here, in this cemetery, destined to head up the hill and greet the darkness. There can't be anything in this for her. For you, as there must be for Jeremy, there are the searing memories. And the promises made. Despite the warm air you shiver as if it is January.

You have donned a bare-bones version of a goth outfit, black tights, black minidress with an asymmetrical hem. You found a pair of Fluevog Angels you haven't worn in a while that might not be Doc Martens, but they work. An old Alchemy silver bat at your throat and seven PVC "barbed wire" bracelets you hung onto over the years around your wrist. You have nothing else left from the past. You had to get rid of everything, hoping to exorcise the memories. As if . . .

Jeremy and Candy are both clad in black designer jeans, stylish Western boots for him, Jimmy Choo ankle cuts for her, wearing complimentary black T-shirts, hers a babydoll with a picture of Elsa Lanchester as the Bride of Frankenstein silk-screened on the front, his bearing the image of Karloff as the monster. Too cute. Back in the day, when you and Jeremy were an item, before reality fractured, he would never have worn anything vaguely matching your outfit. Or anything as commercial as this shirt, which is brand-new, or so the folds suggest. Your favorite mental photograph of Jeremy is him wearing two long, studded armbands and that faded Cure T-shirt, his raven hair *à la* Robert Smith.

"So, Karen," Jeremy says casually, "are you married?"

The question you've been dreading. How can you explain that what happened here so long ago has tainted your life, left you waking from increasingly terrifying nightmares sweaty and trembling, your dream-screams ringing in your ears? You are filled with distrust of anyone and everyone. No, not relationship material anymore. Clearly, Jeremy has not been adversely affected.

"Not yet," you say, as if you are not forty-five years old and you have all the time in the world. "One day, when I meet the right industrial-music man."

Jeremy chuckles. The sound annoys you not only because he can see through you. You resent that he has continued on with his life as if nothing happened, as if four hundred and forty months ago life did not change forever? Suddenly you are angry, for his callousness, for what appears to be his easy and perfect life, for your own childish capitulation to be here, and your fantasy about grasping some sort of "closure," all the while knowing there is no such entity available to you. Fury like hot lava builds and you are about to pivot and head back down to the real world, *sans* excuses, promise broken, despite what will be the result of that.

"Oh my God!" A shriek that rings more of terror than excitement comes from Ritz. "Shadow! Midnight!"

"Vampira!" Jeremy says in a large and inclusive way. The edgy nicknames you went by back then sound banal on lips now. You could write it off to youthful folly but really, in retrospect, the names have a profound meaning.

Your little group of four, Ritz orchestrating a group hug, faces uphill. Mired in shadow, nearly obscured by trees and shrubs, not fifty meters away stands the brooding Lemarchand crypt. Suddenly you realize that it is too late to run. You are doomed.

Others come up the hill and you are surrounded by friends from the past. They all have wrinkles, gray hair, some more than others, and no one is cadaver thin anymore.

This crowd is not full of laughter and teasing. As more join the group, a somber mood descends, until the twelve—thirteen if you count Candy—have all arrived. The emotional texture is reluctance, duty being carried out, obligations being filled with a clear understanding that this is not in anyone's best interest and yet cannot be avoided.

As the sun sets you all trudge up the second shorter hill, circling around the Lemarchand crypt, and return to the spot where you used to meet, a small clearing sheltered by trees, hidden by the crypt itself, a realm disconnected from the rest of the cemetery, and the world.

You sit in a circle, by instinct. Frightened eyes lock, then look away. There is silence until Stan—who used to go by Morpheus—asks, "Anybody have that Bauhaus final tour CD?"

People nod or shake their heads. "Not the old Bauhaus, are they?" Mari Ann says.

"Nothing's like it was," Mitch adds quietly.

And then the silence takes over as you all wait for the darkness to wrap around you like a shroud.

Someone has brought a bottle of Chardonnay that is passed

around—the days of cheap red and homemade absinthe are over. After that a large bottle of Evian water appears. The ground is lumpy, and as hours grind away, your butt grows annoyed with sitting. Shadows deepen and there are moments when the silence feels like an invocation.

When there is no more light from the sky and faces have vanished in the gloom, you can still hear breathing, a bit of shifting, fruit bats flitting above, the rustling of nocturnal animals in the bushes, and the occasional snapping twig. The wait seems interminable, but wait you must, all of you, until midnight. Promises were made.

Finally, Jeremy lights a candle and gets to his feet. One by one you all stand and follow him as you did years ago to the door of the crypt.

As you approach, the coolness of the stones reaches out like tentacles to brush your bare arms, the back of your neck. It is as if this is fall air, not late summer; you notice the three steps leading to the crypt door are covered with dead leaves. A chill coils up your spine that has nothing to do with the air. You do *not* want to be here! You want to go home. You want safety. But there is none.

Jeremy finds the key in the bushes, just like before. The rusted keyhole accepts it readily.

Candy breaks the silence. "This isn't such a good idea, hon. This is private property and—"

The *thwack-thwack* of the key flipping the tumbler silences her. The door creaks as Jeremy pushes it open and leads us like lambs to the slaughter.

"I want to go home!" Ritz says, her high voice breaking. Blonde Mike puts an arm around her shoulders and Dark-haired Mike, no doubt distracted by his own terror, pats her head as if she is a rambunctious puppy. Jeremy stares blankly at her, his face aglow from the candle flame, which brings out the macabre highlights of his features.

Once everyone is inside the crypt, Stan closes the door and the sound is so final that your heart skips beats.

Jeremy sets the candle on the little stone altar of this claustrophobic chamber. Opposite the door are three white marble slabs, each three by three feet, engraved, the writing worn with time, the words indecipherable. Behind the marble are the dead. To the right of these, left of the altar, is a configuration of thirteen stones imbedded in the wall. Jeremy taps the stones in a particular order, as if this were a security system entry code. Suddenly, the stones move as one unit out of the wall and hover as a group in midair.

Someone gasps and another groans. Candy says, "What in hell . . . ?" Your heart becomes arrhythmic and you feel there is not enough oxygen in the air. Every cell in your body screams: Escape!

You watch as if time has slowed. Jeremy grasps in both hands the stones, which do not appear attached to one another yet they form one unit. He turns them around and around. There are thirteen on all sides, a strange ancient puzzle concealed here with the dead. Your memory resurrects a similar moment twenty years ago and maps it onto today. You watch as Jeremy twists the stony puzzle pieces, gaining confidence as he goes, with only one glance in your direction, until the stones glow an eerie color that you cannot put a name to.

He replaces the reconfigured puzzle of stone back into the socket in the wall, his hand still touching it as if he is charging the puzzle in some way, or vice versa.

Time pauses. The group waits quietly, passively. You are struck by the fact that there is no resistance, no bravado shown. What occurred before has eroded all of you who were so enthusiastically attuned to the dark side, who were once rebellious, defending your individuality at all costs. Back then, Jeremy insisted on spending the night here. No one protested, but the mood was different. The fervor of that evening is overwhelmed by the pensive silence of this one. It was Jeremy who found the stones. Jeremy who opened the gate. Jeremy who cut a Faustian deal, one you and your friends were grateful to get at the time.

Only Candy, an outsider not privy to the history, with no idea of the future, voices concern. "You know, it's cold in here, Jeremy. And dark. Why don't we take that outside so you can play with it?"

No one answers her because all attention is riveted on the three large marble squares. One by one they are sliding upward, revealing the darkness behind them. Candy says, "Oh . . . my . . . God . . . !"

Ritz sobs, her face pressed against Blonde Mike's chest. Everyone else stands alone. The sour sweat of fear permeates the crypt's close air. But not for long. Quickly the odor shifts to something worse, the rot of countless years, physical corruption that makes your olfactory nerves brush by everything rotten you have ever smelled, all of it balling together into the unbearable. You gag on the stink, and you are not the only one.

Dark-haired Mike and Martine bolt for the door, struggling to open it, but the door is sealed, as you knew it would be or you would have tried that yourself.

"What's happening?" Candy shrieks.

Ritz sobs loudly, the sounds of despair coming from her lips making your knees buckle and it's all you can do to stand upright and await your fate.

The rank air has a misty quality that blunts everything, which you only realize when suddenly that dissipates as if a wind has blown it away and now all is sharp-edged. Emerging from within the blackness, one by one, are three figures. Their faces, their bodies, everything about them is burned into your psyche. Now, in their presence once more, you can only hope and pray that you die, here, now, quickly, so that you will never, ever encounter them again.

The one on the left has no face. Scraps of putrid flesh cling to more breaks in bones than can be counted, shards jutting insanely in all directions. Next to him stands a woman, or so you believe. She is lean and naked, skinless, every muscle in her body sliced into precise strips that fan out from her skeleton, undulating like a demented extremophile existing in impossible conditions. The third, concentration-camp thin, is, on first glance, the least shocking. Until the eyelids flash open. These eyes are not human. Nothing like human. Within the black and red orbs you see all the torture and death people have inflicted on one another over the millennia the human race has called this planet home. Those eyes distract from the clamps and staples and safety pins and surgical sutures and barbed wire clinging to his raw, swollen flesh and make the hardware and the fact that he is over seven feet tall seem insignificant. Those eyes are all that matter. They foretell the future.

Candy is screaming. Everyone else is pressed back against the door, even you, without being aware that you moved. Only Jeremy stands facing them, like some kind of confident, demonic peer. "We came back," Jeremy says almost proudly, "as you asked."

"As you promised. As we ordained," the woman corrects him. "You could only obey."

The broken-faced one says nothing at first. His eyes flash suddenly, emitting a light that speaks of Hell, or worse. And then he mutters in a low voice, barely audible: "No, they have not obeyed."

You worry that he has directed this at you. Every part of your body feels locked into place, shackled to the cement floor beneath you. You are aware of taking shallow breaths, blood rushing through your head with the roar of a tidal wave. You listen and count the beats of your terrified heart to calm yourself. How did it come to this? What were you hoping for? Why you? "I . . . I have obeyed," you hear yourself whisper, knowing you are struggling to please, to put off the inevitable.

"Let me out! Someone let me out!" Candy has pushed between us and is clawing at the door. No one aids her. No one is willing to go against the demonic figures. All but Candy know what they are capable of.

"Look, we came," Jeremy says reasonably. "We obeyed." The implication being: What's your problem? Wasn't the last time enough?

The one with the demon eyes turns those orbs onto Jeremy, who jerks and cringes as if he has been struck.

The last time you were all here, Andrew, sweet Andrew, who loved wearing PVC and piercing his nipples, and once hung with hooks in his flesh from a tree branch, Andrew was with you. The thirteen of you gathered to drink cheap wine, laugh, listen to music, share psilocybin mushrooms, and commune with the dead. And see how many of your friends of either gender you'd end up fucking. And you had, all of you, ending up fucking each other, wildly, drunkenly, and then Jeremy found the stones. The stone puzzle that moved the marble, just like tonight. And when you and your intoxicated friends snatched the bones from the coffins and began dancing with them in a wild, ecstatic, orgiastic danse macabre, what you came to call Cenobites emerged from the land of severe darkness like religious flagellants from another time, tortured to the point of ecstasy. To the point of ultimate power. They came to tell you that when you choose death as a dance partner, death reciprocates.

They wanted Andrew. He was the sacrifice to save the rest of you and he went willingly. You watched him climb eagerly into the black hole in the wall that swallows everything. The relief you felt is shameful still.

It is his voice you hear now, calling from that darkness, not words, only sounds that crease reality and you do not know if Andrew is in pain or in pleasure. To avoid letting them touch you emotionally, you count the number of moans, thinking: he could not have lived behind the marble slabs for twenty years! And yet he has.

"You have brought another," the female Cenobite says. Her mouth opens and she sticks out her tongue, which is also sliced into strips. She stares, impassive, at Candy.

Candy is hysterical. Ritz chokes out hopelessness. Everyone else is struck dumb by their terror, the rank stink of fear-laden sweat saturating the air. You cannot believe you are living this *déjà vu*. Living your nightmares.

Jeremy says nothing and in that moment you understand. The vow you twelve made back then—to return here tonight, when the Cenobites would take another from your number—Jeremy has altered things. He has brought Candy. He wants them to take her into the darkness instead of one of your group. Instead of him.

"She is not the offering, but we accept," the one with the chilling eyes declares.

You cannot believe you are hearing this. No one can. Could salvation come to you through this vacuous woman as the new sacrifice? Has Jeremy tricked the Cenobites?

"We accept this offering, as well as one we choose."

As a unit, the three Cenobites turn toward Jeremy. Now it is clear. They will take both of them.

Jeremy steps back. The look on his face is a mixture of betrayal and pure horror. "I brought you her!" he declares. "She's the one. Not me!"

"Jeremy, what are you talking about?" Candy screams. She knows but does not want to know.

But already the Cenobites are pulling Jeremy and Candy toward them with invisible strings. The female Cenobite opens her arms toward Candy like a dancer awaiting her partner. Candy's screams become ear piercing and bone chilling; you are certain those screams will reverberate within you until your dying day.

"You said one. Not two, one! Take *her*!" Jeremy yells, all the while closing the gap between him and the broken-faced one, who does not look at Jeremy and yet Jeremy is dragged relentlessly, his body bending in supplication toward the feet of the Cenobite.

The four of them, two human, two not, flow into the openings, the blackness seeming to suck at their bodies until they are obliterated. Bodies, but not voices. Candy is still shrieking. And Jeremy has joined her, protests about unfairness giving way to cries of terror. You can still hear Andrew moaning.

Only the tall Cenobite remains. His frightening otherworldly eyes seem to take in the eleven remaining all at once. Despite the terror, you sense relief in your friends. The promise was kept, this is finally over.

"Three thousand, six hundred and fifty-two days. That is when all of you will return. This time, keep your promise. Do you agree?"

There are gasps and cries of disbelief all around. Someone mutters, "Damn Jeremy, he fucked it up!" But one by one your friends nod and whisper, "Yes," and "I agree," because they cannot do otherwise. They are traumatized. And trapped. They just want to leave here alive and will say or do anything. Like the last time.

You are the only one who has said nothing. The dangerous eyes zero in on you like lasers that burn hot, then sear cold, past your skin, through your muscles, into your bones and organs, rocking you with the excruciatingly exquisite pain of opposites. You burn and chill so rapidly your teeth begin to rattle and small sounds you did not know you were capable of making come from between your lips. The demand is that you comply.

But you have calculated the numbers, what you do best, and the Cenobite is aware of this. He blinks and whatever he has been doing to your body stops abruptly, leaving you limp and breathless, dizzy. A small movement occurs at his thin lips, not a smile exactly, and yet you cannot see it as anything but grim humor. "You're going to make us come back again and again, one less each time, half as much time, aren't you?" you gasp. "Ten years for eleven. Five years for ten. Two and a half for nine. Half as much time for eight, half again for seven. And by the end, when there is just one of us left, it will be only ninety hours before that one must return."

You do not say it, but everyone here understands: as the years pass, hope will diminish.

The Cenobite stares at you for a moment. "Your skill with counting will be . . . interesting to explore."

The being drifts backward, entering the darkness out of which still flow the haunted voices you recognize: screams, cries, shrieks. Pleadings.

The marble panels slide down and into place as though they had never moved. The crypt is filled with tense silence.

Someone pulls the handle and the crypt door crashes open. The light of day rushes in. Your friends flee, as if getting away quickly will erase the memory, stop the nightmares, block out the reality of returning, for you must all return. Each of you understands that if you do not come to them, the Cenobites will come to you.

Alone, you walk down the hill, automatically calculating the number of graves in each of the family plots you pass. You are good with numbers. You always have been. Counting rescued you as a child, and became your vocation as an adult. Numbers provide order to chaos. Comfort. And you have calculated correctly—you will be the last one standing. But that is as it should be. You are responsible for all of this, for everything that has happened and will happen. It is you who guided Jeremy's hands twenty years ago. And now you are the only one left who knows how to open the stone puzzle.

You will suffer day and night until you are old and feeble, then this suffering will end. And true agony will begin. You have no doubt that your counting skills will be sorely tested.

However ...
Gary A. Braunbeck and Lucy A. Snyder

"The great epochs of our lives come when we gain
the courage to rebaptize our evil as our best."

—Friedrich Nietzsche, "Fourth Article,"
Beyond Good and Evil

Of the three it was Penny who was finally able to get free from the manacles. So emaciated had her limbs become that she easily slipped her left hand through, but her right was still swollen at the base of the index finger and thumb where the bones were broken. She didn't make a sound, even though it was obvious to Lewis that she was in terrible pain. Pausing only long enough to pull in a deep breath, the frail nineteen-year-old gripped her right wrist and bore down with what little strength remained in her body. Her face turned red from both the agony and the effort, but still she did not cry out.

"I'm fuckin' *stuck*," she finally whispered through gritted teeth.

"Hold on," said Carl. "I got an idea. But . . ."

From his corner, Lewis said, "But *what*?"

"It's pretty gross," the cadaverous twenty-year-old replied.

"I don't care!" said Penny. "We gotta get some food or we're gonna die down here."

"Do it," said Lewis.

Carl blanched. "But—"

"Just do it, already!" Penny snapped.

Lewis watched Carl rise to his blistered feet and limp toward Penny, his chains slithering rusty trails across the concrete floor. She held out her broken, manacled hand. Carl unzipped the front of his pants and pissed over the bloodstained metal cuff. Aided now by the lubricant of Carl's urine, Penny's broken hand squeaked through the corroded manacle and she fell back against the wall, swearing under her breath as she cradled her torn, swollen, bleeding append-age. She looked ready to start crying. Carl was already tearing away part of his shirt to make a bandage, so Lewis pulled out the lace of his left tennis shoe.

Working quickly, they dried Penny's hand, wrapped it, and used the shoelace to tie the bandage in place so that the pressure was more or less even. All of this they did in less than one minute; they'd had plenty of practice. Lewis had learned first aid in a summer in-ternship at Grand Teton National Park and taught everything he knew to the others; college and his family seemed so long ago, so far away he sometimes wondered if his old life had just been a pleasant dream. His hands knew how to tie a bandage or make a sling, but if he tried to remember the first time he'd done these things, some-times he was sitting under an oak tree with the park ranger, but sometimes he was sitting here in the basement. The hope that he could get that dream back was all that kept him sane some days. He'd told the others time and again that when this day came, they would have to move fast, no matter how sick, broken, or weak all of them felt because the Cold Ones had taken to starving them for days at a time.

The Cold Ones. Carl had started calling them that because the guy was always telling the woman he was going out for "a couple of cold ones." Lewis thought the name fit. What the couple's actual names were—Smith, Jones, Cleaver, Partridge—none of them knew, and the longer they were kept down here, the longer they were used as toys, as furniture, as ashtrays, as toilets, as objects to be abused in ways none of them had ever imagined and now would never forget, and the longer this went on . . . the more power the

Cold Ones gathered to them. Lewis could feel it. The ice behind their gazes, the frost in their fingertips, the chilly echoes of their voices coming from some dark pit buried deep in the wintry chamber where a human heart should have resided, all of these things and more turned them, with every passing minute, into things beyond pain, beyond damage, beyond any Earthbound sensation that might, for a moment, stop them in their tracks.

Penny took a deep, shuddering breath and climbed to her feet. "Okay, guys. It's showtime. Wish me luck."

Lewis looked up at her. "If they come back—"

"—I drop everything and just get the box. I know." She gave the boys a quick smile, then limped toward the staircase that led up to the kitchen. She disappeared around the corner and soon Lewis heard the old wooden stairs faintly creaking under her bare feet.

Carl whispered, "What if the door's locked?"

Lewis shook his head. "He didn't lock it this morning. I listened; the door only clicked once."

They fell silent as Penny pushed open the door. Both boys stared up as her footsteps moved across the ceiling; she was in the hall heading toward the kitchen.

Lewis's stomach growled. All of them knew where the refrigerator was; they got dragged past the kitchen whenever they were taken to the upstairs living room or bedrooms. Its low hum taunted him on those nights, transforming his stomach into an angry demon. Penny was supposed to get just a few pieces of whatever was there: a couple of slices of American cheese from the fat, greasy block in the refrigerator, a couple of pieces of bread if the loaf was already started, a little bologna, a few grapes, maybe an apple if the Cold Ones had a whole bag. They'd agreed she wouldn't touch their fancy gourmet food, that she mustn't take anything obvious, nothing that would be missed. And whatever she did, she couldn't spill anything, or leave any smudges behind to let their captors know she'd escaped from the basement.

"Dude, what if they come back?" Carl was knocking his knees together like he had to pee again.

"They won't," Lewis said, making himself sound more confident than he actually felt. "It's already been more than fifteen minutes." He'd counted it down in his head: *one Mississippi, two Mississippi, three Mississippi* . . .

"But they *never* leave together, what if—"

"Carl, *chill*. They used to go out together all the time. But that was before they brought you and Penny down here. If they were gone for more than fifteen minutes, they'd be gone for *hours*. They're going to a swinger's club or something."

Lewis didn't actually know where the couple went, and told himself he didn't *want* to know, although his imagination got the better of him sometimes. Sometimes the Cold Ones videotaped what they did to him and Carl and Penny; he figured they probably sold the tapes to like-minded perverts. Or maybe *they* were the ones with the money, and today they were touring another basement in another isolated house. Lewis hoped they were selling the tapes they made, because then maybe the FBI or the sheriff would find one and figure out where they were.

However, if there weren't any tapes for the good guys to find, maybe Penny would find the black box. There wasn't any easy way for her to get help on her own—the Cold Ones had no landline phones in the house, they *never* left their cell phones behind, and the house was too damned far out in the country for Penny to try to walk to safety in her condition.

He hoped she found the box. There'd been many nights when he'd overheard the couple, mostly the man, talking about it, their voices filtering hollowly through the floorboards into the basement. From what Lewis had been able to make out, the box had some tremendous power to grant wishes. Maybe it was sort of like Aladdin's lamp with a genie inside, except it was a puzzle you had to solve instead of just rubbing on it. He'd glimpsed the box himself a couple of times, and Lewis could *feel* the power in it. Usually the Cold Ones kept it locked up in a fancy glass cabinet in the living room, but sometimes, *sometimes*, the guy forgot and left it out on the coffee table after he'd been up all night trying to figure out how it worked.

Lewis had never believed in fairies and magic and crap like that, but listening to the guy's voice . . . clearly *he* believed in the power in the box. And here, trapped in this stinking dungeon with nothing else to hope for, all his prayers to God met with utter silence, Lewis had found himself believing, too, grasping at this one thin thread of improbable hope in the face of unthinkable horror.

He had never made the best grades in school, had never been the smartest kid in any of his classes, but he knew he was damn good at solving puzzles. His uncle had given him an old Rubik's Cube one summer, and he'd been able to solve it way before any of the other kids in the neighborhood. By the end of the week, he could solve the thing within two minutes, no matter how messed up it was. In his freshman dorm, he'd gotten through the new *Resident Evil* before any of the other guys, and the week before he was kidnapped, he'd won a Sudoku contest sponsored by the math department. He was dead sure he could do better than their captors.

Penny's footsteps were moving across the ceiling again, and soon he heard the basement door open.

"I got it all, guys." Penny padded down the creaky stairs, carrying a big white picnic plate piled with odds and ends from the refrigerator and pantry. She had a big, lidded Styrofoam cup tucked in the crook of one skeletal, cigarette-burned arm, and—Lewis's heart skipped a beat—in the other was the black lacquered puzzle box.

Penny carefully set the plate of food down on the concrete floor between the young men, then the cup, and then handed the box to Lewis, her expression doubtful. "It was right there on the coffee table, just like you said it would be."

"Outstanding!" Lewis ran his fingers over the surface of the box, mesmerized, his hunger forgotten. This was the first time he'd been close enough to see that each side of the box was shaped like a face of some sort, but not a human face . . . or maybe they were faces of things that had once been human but weren't anymore. Oh, whoever had made this was some kind of genius. Lewis envied anyone who was that smart, that clever. Just looking at it—even looking at it up close—he couldn't find one seam, one indentation, one pressure point that even *hinted* at how you went about opening it.

The horrible pressure of the situation suddenly made his hands shake and his heart pound. If he couldn't open it, or if he did open it and nothing happened, oh, God . . .

Pretend it's that stupid Rubik's Cube, he told himself, trying to calm himself down. *Pretend that you're doing this on a dare. Pretend that it's something fun.* This was the best way to go, to think of it as a fun game . . . because, holding it in his hands now, feeling as if the six faces were laughing at him, Lewis realized that there was no going back. He *had* to solve it, to open it before the Cold Ones came back. If he didn't, if he was still messing with it when the couple got home, they would probably gut him like a fish—or gut Penny or Carl. And make him watch.

Fun, he reminded himself. *Think of this as a game, nothing more.*

And there it was—the seam. He probed its edges, its surface, the contours of the face in which it was hidden; clockwise, counterclockwise, side to side, up and down, and then—

—click!

The sound was so quiet, so soft, so subtle, that none of them should have been able to hear it, but hear it they did, and for a moment all stared in wonder as a section of the box slid out, revealing an interior that was so shiny Lewis could actually see part of his face reflected.

"Is that some kind of a music box?" asked Penny.

It took a moment, but then Lewis heard it, as well; a soft, tinkling melody like a bird's song at morning.

Lewis lost all track of time after that; for him, the world was the box, its faces, his eight fingers and two thumbs, and the fervent hope that he was still the best puzzle-solver anybody had ever seen.

His fingers danced over the surface of the box, finding more seams that opened to reveal hidden indentations that in turn offered up more clicks. Lewis hunched over the box, possessed by it, enamored of it, his concentration total, his control the strongest it had ever been when confronted with a riddle, brainteaser, or puzzle. As with the toy cube in a life that seemed so long ago and no longer part of him, he eventually fell into a rhythm, found his heart beating in time with his breathing while his fingers pressed down in countertime, on the upbeat. He didn't know how or why but his whole body—his entire *being*, within and without—seemed now to be part of an orchestra, every digit a note, every movement a new instrument joining in the music, every breath a change of key, every *click!* the sound of the conductor's baton tapping against the podium as the next section of the symphony began. Part of him knew the music was coming from the ever-opening box, but he would not allow himself to think about that because to do so would invite wonder, and wonder would invite hesitation, and under no circumstances could he hesitate now. The box was offering its secrets up to him, almost as if it were telling him where next to press, to tap, to push, caress, and pull.

It's letting *me open it*, he thought to himself. *It wants me to succeed.*

His fingers danced a glissando over the six sides once more, and when the final clicks revealed the mirrorlike interior of the last six sections, the box came alive in his hands, rose from his palms as if it were a bubble, a leaf in the wind.

And it began to spin. There was no way to tell if it was spinning slow or fast because the interior sections caught the light from the single bulb overhead and turned it into a prism, the colors shooting out and slicing over the surface of the basement walls, the music from within nearly deafening as now the sound of a great pealing bell overpowered all others. Lewis· could feel his heart slamming against his rib cage in time with the bell. He looked over and saw that Penny now sat close to Carl, the two of them holding each other, staring at the miraculous thing happening in front of their eyes.

The whirling colors slowed as the dancing box began to spin downward, and with each turn the light in the basement flickered in, then out, until, at the last, everything was cast into a darkness so complete that for an instant Lewis thought he might have just died and discovered that there truly was no God, after all. Not even a *hint* of a God. Only *nothing* . . . except, however, suffering and loneliness.

A moment later the single bulb came back on, only now it seemed to glow much brighter than before. Looking around, it seemed to Lewis that the structure of the basement had changed; there were corners where none had been before, and areas once easily seen were now in cavernous shadows. The place even *smelled* different; the overlaying stink that had been their constant companion was gone, replaced by something damp and heavy with rot. Were things like this supposed to happen when you released a genie?

He began to say something to Carl and Penny but the first word came out as a broken whisper and fell to the ground, writhing there for a moment before it crumbled to dust.

Lewis was aware of every aspect of his physical self in so complete a way that he would not have been surprised to hear his very cells talking to one another. Even the house seemed to be breathing. Lewis froze in place, his eyes wide, and that's when the genie that had been hiding in one of the newly shadowed corners began moving into the light.

It is *magic!* Lewis sang within himself, barely able to contain his joy. The box was magic and there was a genie and he knew exactly, *precisely* what his first wish was going to be . . . but then he pulled in a deep breath and nearly gagged on the damp, heavy stink of putrefaction that assaulted him.

"Who summons us?" said the genie.

Lewis's mouth hung open, lips and tongue dumb meat, made mute by a single word: *us. Who summons* us?

Sounds of movement from other corners, deeper shadows, crept and slithered forward. Lewis looked around once, quickly, and then closed his eyes as he tried to rid his mind of what he'd glimpsed; unable to do that, he willed these sights to break apart, to fragment, to become the disconnected pieces of a picture puzzle that by themselves were still horrible, but so much easier to confront than the whole. This was an old trick he'd taught himself long ago, when the searing ugliness of things he'd seen, things he'd been forced to do, to watch, to imagine, threatened to consume him: take the memory, the image, the lingering sensation and all thoughts connected with it, snap them apart, and scatter them to the wind.

And so he scattered:

> impressions of things turned inside out;
> flayed skin that billowed out like a dress caught in an updraft;
> fresh, sick-making scars that covered entire bodies;
> eyes burned closed;
> noses split down the center and peeled backward;
> hooks and nails and staples mangling genitals;
> shiny black liquid dribbling from torn lips;
> bowels on the outside, stretched into tubes that fed a
> creature's own filth back into its mouth . . .
> . . . break and scatter . . . break and scatter . . .
> . . . *there.*

Facing the first genie—which surely wasn't a genie at all—he steeled himself and opened his eyes.

"I asked a question," said the creature. "Who summons the Order of the Gash?"

"I did," Lewis managed to get out, finally. He shot a quick glance toward Carl and Penny; the two were now wrapped tightly in each other's arms, faces buried in each other's shoulders as they shuddered and whimpered.

Good, he thought. *Stay that way. Don't move, don't speak, and keep your eyes closed.*

The creature moved farther into the light. "And what do you want of us, worm?"

"*Tasty worm . . .*" said another creature somewhere behind Lewis, its voice a mockery, clogged with something thick roiling from a throat equal parts metal and muscle.

The creature that had spoken first stopped moving, looked at

Lewis, and then turned its jaundiced eyes toward Carl and Penny. "Ah," it said. And smiled. Its mouth was filled with too many small yellow, jagged teeth, all of them shaped like tiny backward hooks. "Sweet, tender flesh."

"Sweet meat . . ."

"Such a treat . . ."

"Juicy to eat . . ."

Hook-Mouth held up one of its hands, silencing the others. "You summoned us. What do you want?"

Lewis looked once more at Penny and Carl. This had been a terrible, horrible mistake, he knew that now, but maybe he could still save them.

"I called you," he said to Hook-Mouth. "They had nothing to do with this."

"Answer me. What do you want of us?"

"Help us get out of here."

Hook-Mouth burst out laughing. *"Help* you? You have no idea what you've done." It began moving closer and closer to Lewis as it spoke. "We help no one but the Order of the Gash. We are not in the business of saving bodies or souls. We are more interested in *feeding* on them. Slowly, with a dark delight you cannot even begin to imagine."

"Then take *me*. Help them get out of here safe, and take me."

"You still don't understand. There is no bargaining here, no deals to be made, no compromises to be reached. *All* of you are coming with us. And knowing as I do how much grief you will feel over the fates of your friends—because their fates *will* be your fault—that only makes consuming you more enchanting, and the taste of your suffering even more delectable."

It was so close now that Lewis could feel its diseased breath on his face.

"Ah," said Hook-Mouth. "Behold, my brethren—the tears of defeat."

"Defeat . . ."

"Sweet . . ."

"Juicy meat . . ."

Hook-Mouth lifted a hand, reaching for Lewis's throat. "You and your friends are going to know such glorious agony. The things we have in store for you are such excruciating pleasures that a useless pile of walking offal like you can never *begin* to—" As soon as Hook-Mouth's hand gripped Lewis's neck, the creature froze.

Lewis felt as if the live end of a power cable had just been jammed into the top of his skull. Everything went white and became anguish—but why should this be any different than the life he and the others had been forced to live for a seeming eternity?

Hook-Mouth pushed Lewis away, slamming him back into the wall. His breath and strength hammered from his body, Lewis sank to the floor. Carl and Penny gripped each other even more tightly as their shuddering and whimpering intensified.

Hook-Mouth seemed to have lost its balance. It stepped back, its legs—or, rather, the things that had once been legs—shaking. When it pulled in its next breath, it was a ragged, thick, wet sound. It looked past Lewis to its companions in the shadows and began shouting in a language Lewis had never heard before, but he didn't need to understand it to know the intention behind the words; the inflections were more than enough.

Hook-Mouth was angry, yes, but more than that, it was shaken and confused. After screaming for a few seconds more, it closed its mouth and eyes, regaining its composure.

Lewis struggled back to his feet, making a terrible decision. "Do whatever you need to do. Just . . . do it fast."

Hook-Mouth, still a bit dazed-looking, shook its head. "We've always known humans like you existed, but I never imagined that we'd . . ." It closed its eyes again, for just a moment, and slowly shook its head.

"No," it said, nailing Lewis to the wall with its sickening yellow gaze. "Here you were, and here you'll stay." It moved quickly, placing its hands on Carl's and Penny's heads. The pair shrieked and Hook-Mouth laughed—but this time it was not a laugh of mockery, no; this was the sound of a terminal cancer patient chuckling at a tumor joke.

"We will go now," it said, and began turning to walk away.

"You can't just leave us here!" screamed Lewis, regretting the words as soon as they were out of his mouth.

Hook-Mouth whirled back to face him. "Oh, yes we can, and that is precisely what we are going to do."

"Why?"

"Because there is nothing we can do to you that hasn't already been done, or that you haven't already imagined! You have *nothing* to offer us. You have wasted our time."

"But—"

"Enough!" Hook-Mouth stared at Lewis for a moment. "I do have to thank you, though. For a moment there, as I shared your pain and your thoughts and memories, I nearly . . . envied your remaining here. That will disturb me for a long time to come. It may even pain me. Oh, how I hope it does just that."

"Then if you really want to thank me, get us out of here!" Lewis was only vaguely aware of hearing the back door open upstairs, followed by the sounds of the Cold Ones stomping back inside.

"If you want to thank me, then get us—"

Hook-Mouth only grinned and shook its head once again. "You have nothing to offer us, nothing we want, nothing with which to bargain."

From upstairs there came a loud crash, followed by more stomping, and then a male voice screaming, "If you hadn't gunned the goddamn engine, she wouldn't've run away from me like that! I almost *had her*, you stupid fuckin' cow! She was a pretty little thing, too!"

Hook-Mouth, seemingly intrigued, looked up at the ceiling, listening, following the stomping and sounds of fists hitting flesh with his eyes.

"The box!" shouted the woman. *"Where's the fuckin' box?"*

Lewis bent down and picked up the black box, staring at Hook-Mouth.

Upstairs, the Cold Ones continued to snarl accusations and strike each other.

Lewis held up the box and began to push the pieces back into place. "Well, if we don't have anything you want . . ."

"*You* don't," said Hook-Mouth, gazing at the ceiling.

And then, looking at Lewis, grinning broadly: *"However . . ."*

'Tis Pity He's Ashore
Chaz Brenchley

Sailor Martin. You should not be here."

The voice came from the tangle of shadows in the back of the shop. It was salt-abraded, familiar, unchanging. Live long enough, go far enough, you will find those things that never change: the places, the people, the truths.

Not many of them, and not all are welcoming or welcome, but still: they stand like islands in the sea, islands in the storm.

Johnnie was, is, always will be, one of those. Johnnie calls himself a chandler, and that's as dishonest as he's ever been. Johnnie sells much that came from the sea, but nothing that's useful to a sailor, nothing that any boat should ever want or need.

Johnnie and I, we've got history. He likes to say I'm his best customer. Sometimes I think I'm his *only* customer. The shop is a collection, more a museum than a place of exchange. The only trade is inward. Johnnie loves to buy, if a thing is rare or dark or strange enough; he hates to sell. Except perhaps to me.

"You should be afloat," he said. "Stood well off, in deep water. Bad weather coming."

I knew it, I could feel it: a tension all through the city from harbor to high-rise, a breathless unease, a readiness. Not only for the typhoon in the offing, though that was the reason I'd put in. Any other trouble I preferred to meet at sea, but delivering a billionaire's new yacht to KL, I thought I'd best not turn her up storm-toss'd.

"What do you hear, Johnnie?"

"I hear everything. You know this."

Of course I knew. The true question was *What do you believe?*—which of course he would never tell me, and I could never believe him if he did.

This was how we dealt with each other, in hints and doubts and rumors; it was how he dealt with everybody. Even his name was not Johnnie. That was a joke, perhaps, or several jokes. Surabaya Johnnie for obvious reasons; Rubber Johnnie because he always bounced back; Johnnie-come-lately because he had been here on this waterfront, in this store, forever. I could attest to that.

For a man his age he was still robust, still unrepentant, and some of his teeth were still his own. The cracked and ancient ivories, those few. The gold ones, mostly not: he mortgaged them at need. A man needs negotiable wealth, and his stock-in-trade won't serve if he will never agree to sell it. I held lien over one of those teeth myself, from the last time I'd touched port.

"Go back to sea," he said, "sailor."

I shook my head. "Not until the storm blows over." That, or something other.

"Well, then. Come here. I have a thing for you."

Johnnie's storefront was neon-lit, as gaudy as any of his neighbors'; his window that season held a shabby stuffed bird of paradise, some unconvincing scrimshaw work at unlikely prices, an uninteresting kedge. This was the stuff he might actually be willing to sell to strangers, except that nothing there would ever entice a stranger through the door.

Farther back, where the goods were more curious and you might actually want to look at them, the light was correspondingly fugitive and unforthcoming: a few dim bulbs half hidden behind stacks of tea chests and sea chests that might open up to disclose a seventeenth-century mariner's journal or a shrunken head from

Java shore or a knotted mess of hooks and lines that was once a patented system for catching mermaids.

Take them out, carry them forward into a better light, and perhaps you'd see that the mariner's maps depicted no known coastline; that the shrunken head was actually a monkey's, dribbling cold sand from an opening seam; that the fishing tackle was no more than a standard Whitby mackerel rig, somehow strayed half a century, half a world, out of its proper time and place.

Where Johnnie sat, there was no light at all, unless he chose. He lurked in the crevices between the heaped and hidden stock like a wary spider watching his things, his occasional customers, me. To us, he was invisible; to him we were brightly lit, exposed. Untrusted, of course. Even me.

Especially me, perhaps. How could he trust the man most likely to leave here with something that used to be his own?

Nevertheless, he called me back into his absolute domain, the little cubby where he kept his utter treasures, utterly in the dark. I had to grope my way past the rough iron touch of ancient spars, the salt-sour harshness of coiled cable, cold, smooth-polished wood that might have been anything. Then he lit a storm lantern, and I laughed at him.

"Hush," he said, all wrinkles and wind-ruined skin, wizened but not wise, "storm is coming. Ready or not, Sailor Martin."

There was a kitten asleep on an upturned barrel. He scooped it up with stubby misshapen fingers, sailor's hands; slipped it into a silken pocket in his sleeve. If it woke, it didn't stir or peep.

The lantern hung from a hook above, showing walls of furniture all around us, secret ways of access that might shift like channels in sand between one tide and the next.

"Now," Johnnie said, reaching into darkness and drawing out a wooden box, laying that on the barrelhead, opening its lid. "I had this out of a condemned whaling junk in Kowloon. The binnacle I sold to a copper millionaire, to make a bar for his apartment; but I took this out under his eye, and he didn't know what he was looking at."

No more did I, except the obvious. It came from a binnacle, it had a needle under glass, above a card. "It's a compass," I said.

"Sailor. It's a *right* compass. This would find you your way through Hell."

One thing for sure, it would be small use to anyone at sea. The master of that whaling junk must have kept another needle to find his way from point to point, from port to port, to know his course across the wasteful ocean. A right whaler knows his fish from their spout, from how they blow; he can tell a sperm from a minke from a bowhead, a right whale from a rorqual.

Any sailor knows one thing about a compass. Never mind what the card says, in whatever language; what matters is the way the needle points.

This compass, this *right* compass of Johnnie's, it wasn't pointing north.

I lifted the box in my hands, felt the solid weight of brass and wood—dark and old and salt-worn, but not rotten—and saw how that needle shifted not one second from its line, however I turned or tilted it. It knew where it meant me to go, or what it was trying to tell me. The ignorance here was my own.

Held closer to the light, it was still reluctant to enlighten me. The card beneath the needle was no printed rose; it had been hand-written, and long ago.

And in Chinese, which would have been no trouble in a regular compass. Besides, I can read Mandarin a little. Enough to tell my northings from my eastings, *bei* from *dong*, that at least.

The thing about Chinese characters, though: they don't work like an alphabet, where you can spell out an unfamiliar word and have an idea at least of what it sounds like, what other words it might have come from, the general drift of its meaning. You know a character or you don't, and if you don't you cannot work it out.

Whatever this needle was inspired to point toward, I couldn't understand it. Johnnie might, but I couldn't quite understand Johnnie either, not tonight.

He said, "I owe you money," which was no way to start a negotiation. Direct is one thing, open surrender is something else.

"You do, Johnnie." A gold tooth's worth of money: more than the value of the tooth, in honesty—the mortgage was a token, an insistence, a gesture of honor—but not as much as this compass was worth, in its brassbound box with all the heft of its age and mystery and scientific question. Not by a distance.

Still, he said, "Take this, keep it, use it; we're all square."

"I don't know how . . ."

"Be smart, sailor. You will need it."

Any other night, Johnnie would have found me a bed; or more likely given me his own, upstairs among the aromatic shadows of his stock, the smells of joss and camphor wood and dust from a thousand holds and homes and marketplaces, a thousand separate journeys from there to here. He'd sleep in the shop, or else shift himself to some back-alley doss-house for a night or a weekor however long I stayed, stranded between one voyage and the next.

Tonight, though, he was boarding up the storefront and moving out himself, heading for higher ground. And so I came from Johnnie's back to this: a room that I could almost call a suite, thanks to the way it bent around the hotel's corner to give me two walls of glass and two distinct spaces, one for bed and bathroom and one for sofa, TV, desk. Properly meant for business, no doubt, but I had done all mine: I could use it simply for typhoon-watching, until the storm passed through and I could away to sea again.

I set the compass on the desk, still in its box. It could wait, and so could the typhoon. I wanted to sleep first, in a broad deep bed that didn't rock me, before I woke to wind and wuthering.

Before that a shower, hot and hard. Then I meant to call down for food, to sit at my high windows here and watch the lights of the city and the dark of the sea until I was thoroughly ready for bed; but I was still drying my hair when there was a knock on the door and a voice called, "Room service!"

I pulled on a robe and opened the door, although I hadn't ordered yet. I'm like that. Besides, I knew where I was.

There was a boy, a young man, in the corridor with a tiffin box in his hand, a stack of stainless steel containers that glistened with condensed steam.

"Hullo," he said. "I'm called Shen."

I quirked an eyebrow, and asked the obvious question. "Did Johnnie send you?"

"Of course." A swing of narrow hips and he slid past me as though he was oiled. Went to set his burden on the desk, found it occupied already by the compass in its box; pursed his lips, drew out a coffee table and spread mats to protect its gleaming surface before he disengaged the various containers from their handle. Lids were marked with scribbled characters; lifted off, inverted, they turned into bowls. Chopsticks were supplied. As he laid out my dinner, Shen glanced from me to the room's minibar and back, so emphatically that I was almost apologizing as I went to fetch beer. Beers.

Generous to a fault, Johnnie is, once business is put out of the way. To several faults, and some of them my own. Shen was hospitality, no more: a gift, that competitive generosity that encompasses, seems sometimes to define a relationship in the east.

To Johnnie, that is, Shen would be an expression of hospitality. Also a message: *Stay where you like, I can always find you, always trouble you with gifts.*

To me, Shen was very obviously trouble: that kind I leap to welcome, to embrace. A man should seek his sorrow where he can, seize it when the chance arises.

He was one of those slender, short Chinese men who look almost too young, although they are not; almost too pretty, though not that either. He looked seventeen, so he was probably twenty-five. He looked as smooth as a girl, as though he barely troubled shaving; that was probably true.

His smile was as solemn, as self-possessed as his hands were neat and swift among the dishes: the lustrous gleam of oyster omelettes, the powerful aniseed smell of chicken in basil. And rice, of course, and yard-long beans coiled in a sesame sauce, and thousand-year eggs with their gray yolks and translucent black albumen, that could only be there to frighten the foreigner. Except that he would never be so crude or so ill-informed, and I would not be frightened. So they were there for my pleasure, as it all was.

As he was himself, of course. Well dressed, well briefed, well ready.

He ate a little—half an egg, some of the beans, rice—to keep me company, and sipped at a beer for the same reason. Likely he was that kind of person who has an uneasy relationship with alcohol, except that nothing in his life would be uneasy; if he could not drink in comfort, he would not drink at all except like this, for manners.

His chopsticks were busier on my behalf than his, selecting choice pieces of chicken, a stray oyster, a slice of tofu, and laying them encouragingly in my bowl. To oblige him, I ate more than I might have done, though not—never!—as much as there was to eat. That would have been a mortal insult, to him first and so to Johnnie.

Questions are impolite, so he asked none. We talked lightly, inconsequentially, of the sea and the city, nothing personal. Time passed, food disappeared, the sky darkened and the wind built. I fetched another beer for myself but not for him, who did not want it. While I was still picking, filling up the corners, he drifted across the room in search of music; and found the compass instead. Opened the lid and looked, touched curiously, glanced at me, his face alive with questions.

There was one question I could legitimately ask him, a privilege I could lay before his feet: "Can you read the characters?"

"Of course." And was delighted, his sudden smile declared, to do it; delighted that I had asked.

He held his hand out, and I went to him.

His grip was soft, enticing; his voice the same. Between them, they held me entirely. "This here, at south, this is the character for sorrow, for lamentation."

Oh, my prophetic soul: I had called him, privately, my sorrow.

I could kiss him now. I did kiss him now. He tasted of tea and smoke, and no surprise.

"This at the west, this is pleasure. At east it is pain, or extremity. At the north, though"—where the needle pointed, because I had set the box that way: straight out of the window, across the bay, southwesterly and directly toward the coming typhoon—"this is a character I do not know. I do not think it is a true character," though it famously took a lifetime to learn them all. "See, it has the radical from sorrow, and from pleasure, and from pain: it is a construction, a configuration of all three. I do not think that there is such a word."

He didn't say it like a confessional, *I cannot read this after all*, in shame at breaking a promise. Rather it was an excitement, as though the very strangeness of it were something achieved.

We talked about it a little more, we searched a Mandarin dictionary on the Internet until the connection went down, we disassembled the compass to see if there was anything written on the back of the card. There was not. I magnificently failed to explain how I had come by it, he magnificently failed to ask; we were both, I think, rather pleased with ourselves.

At last I took his hand in my turn and drew him from the table, from the box; drew his distracted gaze from the window, the line of the needle's pointing, the dark of the building storm; led him around the glassy corner to the bed.

Now he did surprise me. He stood quite still and allowed me to undress him. Not from shyness, never that. Not from shame either, though another man might have thought it, when he saw what lay beneath the fresh black shirt and jeans.

Shen stood in the shaded light of a single lamp on the nightstand, and that only made his scars stand out the heavier, as the sun's angle shows the moon's craters more clearly at the half than at the full.

The smooth, supple body I had been feeling for was . . . disfigured, disrupted by a regular pattern of deep scarring, a checkerboard effect all up his arms and across his chest, down his thighs and calves, wherever he could see and reach. If those scars weren't self-inflicted, they were surely administered by consent. It might have been a mark of passage, a ritual achievement, if he had belonged to another kind of people. As it was—no. I thought he had done this himself.

Here are the characters for pleasure, and pain, and sorrow. Here is another character, the roots of all three intermingled.

I thought perhaps that compass should be pointed directly at him; it seemed to encompass him. That must be why his eyes had gleamed above it, why he had seemed to yearn, or else to sigh in satisfaction; it had spoken to him, sung to him, far louder than it did to me. I was intrigued by the thing; Shen, I thought, was hungry for it.

Even now his eyes were moving in that direction, even while he stood with his body, his privacies exposed to my eyes, to my fingers, to my questions . . .

It's not polite to ask questions. I took him to bed, and never mind what strange artifice his yearning called him to; with me he would find cleaner, simpler pleasures. At least, I had hopes that they would please him. For certain, he did me.

One thing about being so high above the city: you might feel disconnected, but you don't have to draw the blinds.

One thing about that night, that kind of night: neither of us was in any hurry. There was no rush to sleep, no rush to wake or fuck or be away. My time was my own, and so was his; the room was paid for, and so was he.

Through the darkness, then, there were times when we were only lying in bed, talking idly, playing idly, and listening to the storm in its own hurry. There was a physical sense of rushing, of increasing solidity and urgency to the air, even before the rain struck, and the lightning.

■　　■　　■

Smoke and fire and hush in here, in the glass by my bed, in the Lagavulin that I sipped; smoke and fire and noise out there, beyond the windows, in the storm, like a battle fought at sea. God's man-of-war, the typhoon.

I may have said that aloud.

That, and other things equally foolish. The night was long, and short on sleep; he was interestingly delightful, even besides his unmentionable markings, and the storm brought an unexpected focus into the room and the moment. Every one of the moments, as though every single needlepoint jab of a tattoo mattered equally. Or, I suppose, every slice of a razor.

I said, "I'm sorry, did I hurt you?"

He said, "Don't be sorry."

I said, "Roll over, then."

Dawn must have come in some higher place above the clouds, sunlight trapped in the ridges of the whirl, sucked into the funnel of the eye. Even below, it did grow lighter.

Shen got out of bed, went to the bathroom; claimed to be surprised, a little, that we still had electricity. Half the city had gone dark, district by district, as the storm turned the lights out.

Then he went to stand naked by the window-wall, gazing out at the typhoon where it still thundered and rushed, young transient flesh and ancient eternal weather separated only by a fixity of purpose, glass as statement, *Here I stand and there you are, and this is the gulf between us.*

Lightning made the patterns of his scarring stand out, stark and brutal.

Then I thought I saw another figure, stood beyond the glass.

In midair, that would be, on the solidity of wind, twenty-three stories above the city streets.

It was naked, too, that shadow-shape; and of course it was only a reflection, window turned to mirror, so that Shen was looking at himself and so was I.

Except that the storm must have distorted the reflection somehow, because the figure it held was none so straight as Shen and none so clean, it seemed twisted somehow and its scars were differently organized; I thought they cut a diagonal cross into its chest, from shoulder to hip both ways, as though it might unfold like origami. And then it moved; it lifted its hand to the glass, seeming as though it stood on the other side of a doorway, someplace still and bewildering, hints of a labyrinth behind, where a man might need another kind of compass to navigate . . .

And then I put the lights on, one bedside switch to brighten the whole room. I wanted to see quite clearly how wrong this all was, what a nonsense, no figure at all out there once the light fell onto it.

And there was the figure in full light, and there was Shen staring at him, lifting his own hand in the irony of a slavish reflection, and I saw that he had the compass between his feet there, box and all.

And then the window blew in.

Blew out.

Blew away.

Was gone, all that glass in a sudden shatter, all noise. Like a blast without wind, or a wind without direction.

The glass was gone, that separation was gone between one state and another, and Shen was gone, too. Just—gone. He had been standing in arm's reach of the window when it ruptured, and now that place was empty.

I hadn't been looking, not properly. I'd been flinching in anticipation of flying glass that never came, that never reached me. Even so, I had two contrary impressions in my head: one, that he'd been snatched away, that the figure outside had reached in and taken him; the other, that he had reached out. Stepped forward. Gone willingly.

Both were nonsense, of course. There had been no figure, stationary in a typhoon, two hundred feet above the city. There was no such Hell, to be glimpsed in storm and reached *in extremis*. Only a reflection distorted and a mundane tragedy, a window imploding under pressure and a young man seized by dreadful wind, carried off to a dreadful death.

That same wind was in the room with me now, something living, appalling. It pulled the duvet from the bed and dragged it out into the sky; it took what furniture was closest, the TV on its stand and never mind the weight of it, that lifted too before I saw it fall. The standard lamp was seized and thrown, hurled across the room to break a mirror in the other wall.

For a little moment, perhaps my body wanted to hurtle over to that missing window, in a desperate lunge after the vanished Shen. I know my voice snatched after him, I know my arm flew up in echo, instinct over intellect. And met that wall of wind, felt it against my fingers, and—well, no.

If a sailor knows one thing, it would be the wind. If he knows another, too, it would be a lost cause, when not to reach for what is gone already. I have seen men washed overboard, lovers walk away. The trick is to survive them, not to chase.

I didn't shift a willing foot toward the window.

North Sea gale or Gulf hurricane or roar down in the Forties, your first massive wind will blow all pride, all shame out of you. I crawled from the bed to the door, crawled naked on my belly except to snatch my money belt from the nightstand as I passed. I dug my hands deep into the thick, heavy carpet and dragged myself along, didn't try to stand, even at the door. I reached up from the floor to work the handle, hauled it open and slithered through, let it slam behind me and felt my ears pop at the change of pressure.

Stood up cautiously into no wind at all, the still air of a hotel corridor and the faint distant buzz of voices, someone having a room party, entirely safe behind their window-walls; and made it only halfway to the lift before a member of staff appeared, calm and utterly unsurprised. Perhaps she had seen me on the CCTV and come to intercept; perhaps it was purely routine to discover naked men astray outside their rooms, in times of storm or otherwise.

She took me into a linen cupboard, found me a robe while I was telling her about the window gone, my friend gone with it. Her shock was swift and professional, impersonal, efficient; my own was climbing me like a monkey in the rigging, I could feel the tremor of it in my fingers, knew what it was, could do nothing about it.

Then there were police, the hotel doctor, a large whiskey and a little pill, another bed in a room without a window. I had tried to say, I had said—time and again, I think I said it—that I was used to this, I had seen men die this way; but to the hotel of course it was terrible and they were determined that it should be terrible to me, too.

The pill gave me a deeper, perhaps a better, sleep than I could ever have achieved on my own account; my body doesn't like to sleep in storms. I woke to the hush and ruin of what follows on land, and longed to be at sea where all the damage is swept away or left behind. When I called to ask for food, I got the manager instead, still horrified by the morning's news. A window gone and a life lost—a guest's friend, subtly and discreetly to be distinguished from a guest—such a thing might be common news in the typhoon, might almost be commonplace at other establishments but had never happened, should never have happened, here. Should not have been possible. The glass was guaranteed, promised to be proof against the strongest wind. There must have been a fault in that one sheet, that triple-sheet, or perhaps an unregarded twist in the frame, damage from the last quake, though the whole hotel was promised to be earthquake-proof also. There would be an investigation, of course. And in the meantime, of course, I was a guest of the management for so long as I cared to stay; and if my, ah, friend had any family living locally, the hotel would do everything in its power to ease their transition through this difficult period . . .

Did Shen have family? I couldn't say; I found it hard to care. Johnnie would know, perhaps. I put him on to Johnnie.

The police, too, I sent them round to Johnnie with their questions and my apologies. It's no kind thing to bring the attention of the law down on a waterfront trader, who may lack import licenses and invoices, whose contacts might well prefer their anonymity; but I couldn't be kind that day. I answered what questions I could, not many, and most of those with "Best ask Johnnie."

I asked one question of my own: What of the yacht I'd left in the marina, had she survived the storm and the tidal surge? The management there had claimed their covered berths in their isolated dock to be typhoon-proof, but then, so did the management here . . .

They promised to let me know, as soon as practical. They implied that they had more urgent matters to attend to first, the recovery of bodies, Shen's among them, and how could I be asking about a boat?

I didn't say it, but I doubted they would ever find Shen's body.

I didn't say much of anything, indeed. I gently let them infer that I was still in the grip of shock or tranquilizers, both; I said I wanted to go back to my room, and they obliged me. Offered an escort, indeed, which I declined.

For good reason, because I had let them assume I meant the new room, the windowless, the safe.

I still had my original keycard in my money belt, and they hadn't thought to recode the door; why would I go back there, why would I *want* to go back?

There was no watch in the corridor, for much the same reason. The police had been, had seen, had taken what evidence, what photographs, they needed; why should they want to go back? Or to keep guard? It wasn't a crime scene, after all. Officialdom was done with this place. A minor tragedy, after all, in a city overtaken by them . . .

I let myself in and found that the absent window had been replaced with deadlights, boarded up. Otherwise, the room had been left largely untouched except by storm. The police would have wanted it preserved, of course, at least for their cursory inspection; the management would see no hurry in it now, when they had live guests to attend to.

My things: someone might have been sent to fetch out my things, but they had not. Not yet. They might still come, of course, at any moment. I didn't overly care. If they caught me here, they caught nothing but a disturbed guest among his own possessions.

Among what was left of his possessions. Anything that had been lying loose in the room was gone, scoured away by too much wind, *tai feng*, and its attendant water. But I'm a sailor, long trained to neatness and alert to storm; I had unpacked, of course, and put most of my things away.

The nightstand was gone, with its drawers. With my watch, my phone, my cash purse and medications. No matter.

The wardrobe was extant, built-in. The sliding doors were off their tracks, but only wedged more firmly in place; it took ocean muscles and a degree of ocean experience to shift them. Behind, everything was sodden that could be soaked: which meant my better clothes, but there were few enough of those. All my practical wear is waterproof by necessity, by definition. As is my bag, and the useful stuff it carries; and . . .

And I was here for none of that. Of course. I was only displacing the moment.

Close by the boarded window stood the compass box, not quite where Shen had left it: set aside, I supposed, by the men who came to seal up that appalling breach.

I thought Shen had meant to take it with him, and had not been given the chance.

Left behind, it was closed up tight against the weather. Locked up tight, apparently, when I tried the lid; although there had only been one key and that was with me, in my money belt.

When I tried it, the brass lock moved as sweetly as if it sat in an oil bath; when I lifted the lid and looked inside, so did the compass needle.

It pivoted and spun, reacted to any movement of the box, paid no heed to any outside force or inclination: nothing to point at, nowhere to go.

Wherever Shen had been taken, you couldn't get there from here. Not anymore.

Next day, I carried the box back to Johnnie's place. On foot, necessarily, through streets still full of ruin, busy with people, no wheeled traffic at all.

I found him dealing with the aftermath of his own broken window, sweeping up glass in the street.

I put the compass down and helped haul out ruined stock—all those things that no one had ever wanted; anyone could have them now, if they would only take them away—and said, "I thought you were safely boarded up before the typhoon hit?"

"I was," he grunted. "Someone came, ripped down the boards, broke the window to get in."

"Christ. What did they steal?"

"Nothing. Nothing's gone."

How he could tell, I was not clear; everything was overturned, broken open, torn apart. He was entirely certain, though. And oddly phlegmatic, I thought. If he was angry that morning, it was with me. "Sending the police to me—to me!—over some whore-boy I do not know . . ."

"Wait, what? You didn't send . . . ?"

"I did not. I am not your pimp."

That was a blatant lie; he had pimped for me for longer than either of us would credit, but I let it by.

And went on fetching and carrying, until there was as much sodden trash outside as in; and then, remembering, I glanced aside for the compass where I had set it down just by the step there.

No one had come, but it was gone, and I was somehow not surprised at all.

Afterword
Doug Bradley

Hello. Welcome to the other end. Did everyone make it out okay? I do hope so, we can't go back in for the bodies, you know.

For some reason, I seem to be getting the last word here. If this was a film, I'd be the credits. Half of you are already grabbing your coats, stuffing your empty popcorn buckets under your seats, and heading for the neon EXIT signs. "Sorry! Excuse me! Sorry!" While the other half—the cinephiles or cineastes: it always sounds faintly wrong, don't you think?—are determinedly watching, convinced it's going to somehow do you good, but really wanting to get the hell out. Or in this case, perhaps get the hell out of Hell.

Anyway, bear with me. I promise I'll try to be brief. . . .

Great labyrinths, it seems, from little puzzle boxes grow. The thread that Clive began to unwind somewhere in Crouch End, North London (sometime in the early eighties), and unraveled somewhat farther among the weeping willows and duck ponds of Cricklewood (a handful of years later), shows no sign of reaching the end of its skein: it has raveled on cinematically through Carolina and Holly, through Captain George Vancouver's place to the Paris of the east where, at the time of writing at least, it seems to have ground to a halt.

It is twenty years and more since Clive plucked the Lemarchand Configuration and its attendant intrigues and custodians from the recesses of his restless mind and placed it in our midst, yet its fascination shows no sign of waning. Quite the opposite, in fact. It appears to have reached every corner of the globe (a delightful geometric impossibility that, isn't it?) and still be traveling.

Around the world in eighty perversions, perhaps.

Some ten to fifteen years ago, I was asked to undertake a similar exercise to this in writing an introduction for a collection of *Hellraiser*-inspired comic strips. I commented then on how exciting it was to see a group of writers and artists take a basic idea from one writer/artist/director and run off with it in myriad different directions, with nothing but their imaginations as a compass. Here we are again, and exactly the same thoughts are coming to mind.

I suppose I'm here as some kind of Keeper of the Flame. And it is clearly true that I have been the one consistent link through the series of films. True also that it was Pinhead who very quickly became the figurehead for the series: the face and the image that everyone now associates with the *Hellraiser* films, so much so that I even hear the character being sometimes referred to as "Hellraiser" rather than Pinhead (which is of course not the character's name at all; for me he really has no name and if you ever called him Pinhead, he'd ignore you). I've been in lots of situations where people have said they don't know the *Hellraiser* films and don't watch horror films. And yet they all know the image of "the guy with the nails in his head." "Oh *him*! That's *you*? That's amazing . . ."

It has been his face on all the DVD boxes, the *Hellraiser* films always being sold on the promise of more and more Pinhead even when, in some cases, he was barely to be seen in the film contained within.

And yet you'll have searched in vain for Pinhead featuring among these pages. There are other Cenobites, yes, newly sprung from the imaginations of the contributing authors here, and at least one very familiar to fans of the original films. But no Pinhead, at least not in the strictest sense. Does that bother me? Not one jot. Quite the opposite, in fact. Consistently, though not uniformly, the writers have gone straight to the real heart of the *Hellraiser* "mythology," if such a thing exists. To the Lemarchand Configuration, the ever innocent puzzle box: and beyond that to what Lemarchand's plaything represents and points toward. The labyrinth, the puzzle, internal and external, the riddles and enigmas.

And is there, I was just wondering, any precedent for this? Oh, novelizations aplenty. But a horror franchise throwing out original off-shoot stories like this where the central character—the "monster"—is conspicuous by his absence? And surely not a precedent for not one but two cast members from the films to contribute their own original pieces of fiction. Take a bow and some plaudits, Mr. Vince and Ms. Wilde, for boldly venturing where this thespian has never trod.

And we've been on quite a journey, haven't we? From London's South Bank to Constantinople, from the fifteenth to the twenty-first centuries, from convents to cemeteries, puzzle boxes in computers and labyrinths in strange gardens and more. It would be invidious of me to list everything—and slightly pointless as well, perhaps. It is to be assumed you've just read them. Or, if you're one of those people who likes to flip to the back of a book first, you're just about to.

And once again, these gathered words, whether you've read them yet or not, are vivid testimony to the power and the glory that is the imagination of my friend Clive Barker. It would be an exercise in stating the blindingly obvious to say that without him none of this would have been possible, but it's also to me an exercise in stating a wonderful truth: that the last twenty years (for me personally, obviously, but I make a broader point), particularly in the world of horror, would have been a much poorer place without *Hellraiser*. Yet again, my thanks to him.

And final plaudits here to Paul and Marie. For being mad enough to take this project on board and patient enough (in my own case at least, above and beyond the call of duty) to see it through to the finish.

So there you are. Thank you for coming. Please take a moment before you leave to look around and make sure you have all your personal belongings with you. Like your souls, perhaps. . . .

Doug Bradley
London
February 2009

About the Authors

CLIVE BARKER was born in Liverpool, England, where he began his creative career writing, directing, and acting for the stage. Since then, he has gone on to pen such bestsellers as *The Books of Blood*, *Weaveworld*, *Imajica*, *The Great and Secret Show*, *The Thief of Always*, *Everville*, *Sacrament*, *Galilee*, *Coldheart Canyon*, and the highly acclaimed fantasy series *Abarat*. As a screenwriter, director, and film producer, he is credited with the *Hellraiser* and *Candyman* pictures, as well as *Nightbreed*, *Lord of Illusions*, *Gods and Monsters*, and *The Midnight Meat Train*. He lives in Los Angeles, California.

STEPHEN JONES lives in London, England. He is the winner of three World Fantasy Awards, four Horror Writers Association Bram Stoker Awards, and three International Horror Guild Awards, as well as being an eighteen-time recipient of the British Fantasy Award and a Hugo Award nominee. A former television producer/director and genre movie publicist and consultant (the first three *Hellraiser* movies, *Night Life*, *Nightbreed*, *Split Second*, *Mind Ripper*, *Last Gasp*, etc.), as an editor and writer he has had around one hundred books published, including *Creepshows: The Illustrated Stephen King Movie Guide*, *The Essential Monster Movie Guide*, *The Illustrated Vampire Movie Guide*, *Clive Barker's A–Z of Horror*, *Clive Barker's Shadows in Eden*, *Clive Barker's The Nightbreed Chronicles*, and *The Hellraiser Chronicles*.

PETER ATKINS is the author of the novels *Morningstar* and *Big Thunder* and the screenplays for *Hellraiser II*, *Hellraiser III*, *Hellraiser IV*, and *Wishmaster*. With Glen Hirshberg and Dennis Etchison, he cofounded the Rolling Darkness Revue, which tours the west coast each October, bringing original ghost stories, live music, and theatrical effects to bookstores and libraries. His short fiction has appeared in several award-winning anthologies, and he has also written for the stage and television. His latest novel, *Moontown*, was published last year, and a new collection of his short fiction is forthcoming.

CONRAD WILLIAMS is the author of the novels *Head Injuries*, *London Revenant*, *The Unblemished*, and *One*. His novellas include *Nearly People*, *The Scalding Rooms*, *Rain*, and *Game*. Some of his short fiction was collected in *Use Once then Destroy*. As Conrad A. Williams, he wrote *Decay Inevitable*. He is a past recipient of the British Fantasy Award and the International Horror Guild Award. He lives in Manchester with his wife and three sons. At a convention in the 1990s he picked up, from a display table, one of the actual models of Lemarchand's Box used in the *Hellraiser* films. He apologized profusely when its guardian had a conniption fit and is happy to report that, to date, he has not suffered any kind of Cenobitic visitation, punitive or otherwise.

SARAH PINBOROUGH is the author of five horror novels—including *The Hidden*, *The Reckoning*, *The Taken*, and *Tower Hill*—and various short stories. She has been short-listed twice for the British Fantasy Award for Best Novel and lives in Milton Keynes, England, with her cats, Peter and Mr. Fing. Her next horror novel, *Feeding Ground* (Leisure Books)—a sequel to her popular book *Breeding Ground*—will be out in all good bookshops in the United States in October 2009. Her first thriller, *A Matter of Blood* (Gollancz), will be out in the UK in 2010. Sarah is also a member of the MUSE writing collective with fellow authors Sarah Langan and Alexandra Sokoloff. To find out more about her, visit www.sarahpinborough.com.

MICK GARRIS is an award-winning filmmaker who began writing fiction at the age of twelve. By the time he was in high school, he was already writing music and film journalism for various local and national publications. Garris hosted and produced *The Fantasy Film Festival* on Los Angeles television for nearly three years, and later began work in film publicity at Avco Embassy and Universal Pictures. It was there that he created "Making of . . ." documentaries for various feature films. Steven Spielberg hired Garris as story editor on *Amazing Stories* for NBC, where he wrote or cowrote ten of the forty-four episodes. Since then he has written or coauthored several feature films (including *The Fly II* and *Riding the Bullet*) and teleplays (such as *Quicksilver Highway* and *Nightmares & Dreamscapes*), as well as directed and produced in many media: cable (including *Psycho IV: The Beginning*), features (like *Sleepwalkers*), television films (such as *Desperation*), series pilots (*The Others*), and network miniseries (*The Stand, The Shining*). He created and executive produced the *Masters of Horror* anthology series of one-hour horror films written and directed by names like John Carpenter and George Romero. He also created the NBC series, *Fear Itself*. *A Life in the Cinema*, his first book, is a collection of short stories, and his short fiction has been published in numerous books and magazines. *Development Hell* is his first novel. Garris lives in Studio City, California, with his wife, Cynthia.

CHRISTOPHER GOLDEN is the author of such novels as *The Myth Hunters, Wildwood Road, The Boys are Back in Town, The Ferryman, Strangewood, Of Saints and Shadows*, and (with Tim Lebbon) *The Map of Moments*. Golden cowrote the lavishly illustrated novel *Baltimore, or, The Steadfast Tin Soldier and the Vampire* with Mike Mignola. He has also written books for teens and young adults, including *Poison Ink, Soulless*, and the thriller series *Body of Evidence*. Upcoming teen novels include a new fantasy series coauthored with Tim Lebbon and entitled *The Secret Journeys of Jack London*. Golden was born and raised in Massachusetts, where he still lives with his family. His original novels have been published in more than fourteen languages in countries around the world. Please visit him at www.christopher golden.com.

MIKE MIGNOLA is best known as the award-winning creator/writer/ artist of *Hellboy*. He was also visual consultant to director Guillermo del Toro on both *Hellboy* and *Hellboy II:The Golden Army*. Most recently he was coauthor (with Christopher Golden) of the novel *Baltimore, or, The Steadfast Tin Soldier and the Vampire*. Mignola lives in Southern California with his wife, daughter, and cat.

TIM LEBBON's many novels include *The Island, Bar None*, the *30 Days of Night* movie novelization, *Hellboy: The Fire Wolves*, and *The Map of Moments* (with Christopher Golden). He's published on both sides of the Atlantic, and has won the British Fantasy Award (three times), the Bram Stoker Award, and a Scribe Award, among others. Several of his novels and novellas are currently in development as movies.

KELLEY ARMSTRONG is the author of the *Women of the Otherworld* paranormal suspense series—which includes *Bitten, Stolen, Dime Store Magic, Industrial Magic, Haunted, Broken, No Humans Involved, Personal Demon*, and *Living with the Dead*—the *Darkest Powers* YA urban fantasy trilogy, and the Nadia Stafford crime series. She grew up in Ontario, Canada, where she still lives with her family. A former computer programmer, she's now escaped her corporate cubicle and hopes never to return. Her website is www.KelleyArm strong.com.

RICHARD CHRISTIAN MATHESON is an acclaimed novelist, short story writer, and screenwriter/producer. He has written and cowritten feature film and television projects for Richard Donner, Ivan Reitman, Steven Spielberg, Bryan Singer, and many others. For TNT's *Nightmares & Dreamscapes* miniseries, he wrote the critically hailed adaptation of Stephen King's short story "Battleground," starring William Hurt and directed by Brian Henson. As a prose writer, his critically lauded fiction has been published in major, award-winning anthologies, including multiple times in *Best New Horror*, *Year's Best Fantasy and Horror* and *Year's Best Fantasy*. Matheson's stories are collected in *Scars and Other Distinguishing Marks* and *Dystopia*. His critically acclaimed debut novel, *Created By*, was Bantam's hardcover lead, a Bram Stoker Award nominee for best first novel and a Book-of-the-Month Club lead selection. It has been translated into several languages. Matheson is considered an expert on the occult and worked with the UCLA's parapsychology labs, investigating haunted houses and paranormal phenomenon. He also plays drums with Smash-Cut, a blues/rock/jazz band, which recently recorded a live album, *Live at the Mint*.

NANCY HOLDER has received four Bram Stokers from the Horror Writers Association and has been nominated for two more. She co-edited *Outsiders* with Nancy Kilpatrick, and is the coauthor of the popular YA dark fantasy series *Wicked*. She wrote the YA horror novel *Pretty Little Devils* and many novels in the *Buffy the Vampire Slayer*, *Angel*, *Highlander*, and *Smallville* universes. A former HWA trustee, she is on the Clarion Foundation board for the Clarion program at the University of California, San Diego. She also teaches writing at UCSD and in the Stonecoast MFA program at the University of Southern Maine. She lives in San Diego with her daughter, Belle; their cats, David and Kitten Snow Vampire; and Panda Monium Holder, their Cardigan Welsh corgi.

SIMON CLARK, at the age of five, narrowly avoided drowning when he fell through ice on a lake. That brush with eternity might have colored his view of life ever since. Certainly, his award-winning fiction is brushed with darkness. He lives in Doncaster, England, with his family—well away from deep water. His books include *Blood Crazy*, *Darkness Demands*, *She Loves Monsters*, and the award-winning *The Night of the Triffids*, which continues the adventures of Wyndham's classic *The Day of the Triffids*. Simon's latest novel is *Ghost Monster*, a ghoulish feast of the horrors that befall a community when they are possessed by the spirits of sadistic outlaws.

NEIL GAIMAN has written highly acclaimed books for both adults and children and has won many major awards, including the Hugo, Nebula, and Newbery. His novels include *Neverwhere, Stardust, American Gods, Coraline, Anansi Boys*, and most recently, *The Graveyard Book*. His collections include *Smoke and Mirrors* and *Fragile Things*. *Neverwhere* was turned into a BBC TV series, while both *Stardust* and *Coraline* have been adapted to the big screen. His multimillion-selling series for Vertigo/DC Comics, *The Sandman*, was described as "the greatest epic in the history of comic books" by the *Los Angeles Times*.

DAVE McKEAN is an acclaimed illustrator, graphic designer, and filmmaker. He is a long-term collaborator of Neil Gaiman and has worked with him on many titles, including *Mr. Punch, Signal to Noise, The Wolves in the Walls*, and *The Graveyard Book*. He both wrote and drew the acclaimed *Cages* and has won many awards for his illustration, including a World Fantasy Award for *The Sandman* comic series. His short films include *The Week Before* and *Neon*, and he made his feature directorial debut with *MirrorMask* for the Jim Henson Company.

STEVE NILES is one of the writers responsible for bringing horror comics back to prominence. The success of his *30 Days of Night* comic series led to a number one box-office smash with *Spider-Man*'s Sam Raimi producing, David Slade directing, and Niles cowriting the screenplay. He is currently working for the top American comic publishers—IDW, DC, Marvel, Image, and Dark Horse—and recent projects include *Simon Dark* with artist Scott Hampton and *Batman: Gotham After Midnight* with artist Kelley Jones. Niles has been nominated for multiple Eisner Comic Industry Awards and was the recipient of two Spike TV Scream Awards for Best Horror comic and Best Comic Adaptation. He (and coauthor Jeff Mariotte) also won a 2007 Scribe Award for the novel *30 Days of Night: Rumors of the Undead*. At present he is writing a screenplay for legendary director John Carpenter and Dimension based on the comic *The Upturned*

Stone, and his graphic novel *Freaks of the Heartland* is being developed for film by David Gordon Green. He resides in Los Angeles.

SARAH LANGAN's first novel, *The Keeper* (HarperCollins, 2006), was a *New York Times* Editor's Pick. Her second novel, *The Missing* (Harper-Collins, 2007), won the Bram Stoker Award for outstanding novel, was a *Publishers Weekly* favorite book of the year, and an IHG outstanding novel nominee. *The New York Times Book Review* recently compared her to Mary Shelley, extolling Langan's "mournful end-of-the-world narrative," and her "vision of a society perishing from within, exhausted by its own excesses." She has published a dozen short stories, several essays, and her third novel, *Audrey's Door*, about a woman who moves into a haunted apartment building on the Upper West Side, is due out from HarperCollins in October 2009. Her website is www.sarahlangan.com.

NICHOLAS VINCE was born in Germany in 1958 and lives in South London. He met Clive Barker while he was at Mountview Academy of Theatre Arts and was later cast as the Chattering Cenobite in the first two *Hellraiser* movies, and Kinksi in *Nightbreed*. For Marvel he wrote stories for the *Hellraiser* and *Nightbreed* comics plus the series *Warheads* and *Mortigan Goth*. He modeled for the art of John Bolton and for Dave McKean in *Cages*. He served as chairman of the Comics Creators Guild. His interview series "The Luggage in the Crypt" appeared in the magazine *Skeleton Crew* and his short stories in *Fear*. Most of the details of his biography on www.wikipedia.org are fantasy created by his nephew. His first name is definitely not Sean.

YVONNE NAVARRO lives in southern Arizona, where by day she works as an operations officer on historic Fort Huachuca. By night she chops her time into little pieces, dividing it among her huge adopted Great Danes, Goblin and the Ghost; her husband, author Weston Ochse; her dad; her writing; and two people-loving parakeets, Edwina Allan Poe and BirdZilla. She's written seven solo novels and a number of film tie-ins, including the novelization of *Ultraviolet, Elektra, Hellboy*, and seven novels in the *Buffy the Vampire Slayer* universe. Her work has won the HWA's Bram Stoker, plus a number of other writing awards. She's currently hammering on a novel called *Highborn*. Visit her at www.yvonnenavarro.com or http://yvonnenavarro.livejournal.com/.

MARK MORRIS became a full-time writer in 1988 on the Enterprise Allowance Scheme, and a year later saw the release of his first novel, *Toady*. He has since published a further fifteen novels, among which are *Stitch, The Immaculate, The Secret of Anatomy, Fiddleback, The Deluge*, four books in the popular *Doctor Who* range and one for the spin-off *Torchwood*, a novel entitled *Bay of the Dead*. His short stories, novellas, articles, and reviews have appeared in a wide variety of anthologies and magazines, and he is editor of the highly acclaimed *Cinema Macabre*, a book of fifty horror-movie essays by genre luminaries, for which he won the 2007 British Fantasy Award. Forthcoming work includes a novella entitled *It Sustains* for Earthling Publications and a new short story collection, *Long Shadows, Nightmare Light*.

BARBIE WILDE is best known for her portrayal of the Female Cenobite in Clive Barker's classic horror movie *Hellbound: Hellraiser II*. She has also performed cabaret in Bangkok; appeared as a robotic dancer in the Bollywood blockbuster *Janbazz*, and was a vicious mugger in *Death Wish 3*. In the early 1980s, Barbie performed at the top venues of New York, London, and Amsterdam with the mime/dance/music group, SHOCK; supporting such artists as Gary Numan, Ultravox, Depeche Mode, and Adam & the Ants. As a television presenter/writer, Barbie hosted *The American Hot 100* for Skytrax TV; *The Morning Show* and *Supersonic* for Music Box; *The Small Screen* for ITV; *Hold Tight* for Granada; *The Gig* for LWT; and *Sprockets* for Sky. After completing her first novel, *The Venus Complex*, about the making of a serial killer, Barbie is currently working on an erotic vampire novel called *Valeska*.

JEFFREY J. MARIOTTE is the award-winning author of more than thirty novels, including the border horror trilogy *Missing White Girl*, *River Runs Red*, and *Cold Black Hearts*, *The Slab*, the *Witch Season* teen horror quartet, and others. He also writes comic books and graphic novels. Some of his work includes the graphic novel *Zombie Cop* and the bestselling comic book *Presidential Material: Barack Obama*. His long-running horror/Western series *Desperadoes* was named the Best Western Comic Book of 2007 by *True West* magazine. He's a co-owner of specialty bookstore Mysterious Galaxy in San Diego, and lives in southeastern Arizona on the Flying M Ranch. For more information, please visit www.jeffmariotte.com.

NANCY KILPATRICK is an award-winning author who has published seventeen novels, around two hundred short stories, one nonfiction book and has edited nine anthologies. She writes mainly horror, dark fantasy, mystery, and erotica and has been working on two new novels over the last year. Her most recent short fiction has appeared in *Blood Lite* (Pocket Books); *Bits of the Dead* (Coscom Entertainment); *The Living Dead* (Night Shade Books); and *Traps* (Dark-Hart Press). Look for upcoming stories in *Darkness on the Edge* (PS Publishing); *The Moonstone Book of Zombies*; *The Moonstone Book of Vampires*; *Monsters Noir*; and *Don Juan*. She has just finished coediting with David Morrell *Tesseracts 13*, an all horror/dark fantasy anthology. She is about to edit her tenth anthology, this one all-vampire and as yet untitled. You can check out Nancy's latest at her website: www.nancykilpatrick.com.

GARY A. BRAUNBECK is the author of the acclaimed Cedar Hill cycle, which includes the novels *In Silent Graves*, *Keepers*, *Mr. Hands*, *Prodigal Blues*, *Coffin County*, and the forthcoming *Far Dark Fields*. A majority of the Cedar Hill short stories have been collected in *Graveyard People*, *Home Before Dark*, and the forthcoming *The Carnival Within*, all from Earthling Publications, as well as *Destinations Unknown* and *Things Left Behind*. His work has received five Bram Stoker Awards, three Shocklines "Shocker" Awards, an International Horror Guild

Award, a *Dark Scribe Magazine* Black Quill Award, and a World Fantasy Award nomination. He lives in fear of his five lovable cats, who will not hesitate to draw blood if he fails to feed them on schedule. For more information about Gary and his work, please visit his website: www.garybraunbeck.com.

LUCY A. SNYDER is the author of *Sparks and Shadows*, *Installing Linux on a Dead Badger*, and the upcoming Del Rey novel *Spellbent*. Her writing has appeared in *Strange Horizons*, *Farthing*, *Masques V*, *Doctor Who Short Trips: Destination Prague*, *Chiaroscuro*, *GUD*, and *Lady Churchill's Rosebud Wristlet*. You can also find her interview with Clive Barker in *Writers' Workshop of Horror* from Woodland Press. She currently lives in Worthington, Ohio, with her husband and occasional coauthor Gary A. Braunbeck. Learn more about her and her books at www.lucysnyder.com.

CHAZ BRENCHLEY has been making a living as a writer since he was eighteen. He is the author of nine thrillers, most recently *Shelter*, and two major fantasy series: *The Books of Outremer*, based on the world of the Crusades, and *Selling Water by the River*, set in an alternate Ottoman Istanbul. A winner of the British Fantasy Award, he has also published three books for children and more than five hundred short stories in various genres. His time as Crimewriter-in-Residence at the St Peter's Riverside Sculpture Project in Sunderland resulted in the collection *Blood Waters*. He is a prizewinning ex-poet and has recently been writer in residence at the University of Northumbria, as well as tutoring their MA in Creative Writing. Several of his books have attracted movie and TV interest. He was Northern Writer of the Year 2000, and lives in Newcastle upon Tyne with two squabbling cats and a famous teddy bear.

DOUG BRADLEY is probably most famous for his role as *Hellraiser*'s Pinhead. As well as the *Hellraiser* series, Doug has starred in Clive Barker's *Nightbreed*, alongside his friend Robert Englund (Freddy from *A Nightmare on Elm Street*) in *The Killer Tongue*, and in two award-winning short horror films *On Edge* and *Red Lines*. Other film and TV appearances include *Inspector Morse* and the movies *The Prophecy: Uprising* and *Pumpkinhead: Ashes to Ashes*. Doug's theater work includes his one-man show *An Evening With Death*. He also showed us his literary skills in the insightful and entertaining book *Behind the Mask of the Horror Actor*. Doug is currently a member of Renegade Arts, which has launched the *Doug Bradley's Spine Chillers* series: he performed and directed the award-winning audio/visual presentation of H. P. Lovecraft's *The Outsider* in 2008 and is currently working on a similar adaptation of Poe's *The Tell-Tale Heart*, as well as a series of horror audiobooks.

About the Editors

PAUL KANE has been writing professionally for twelve years. His genre journalism has appeared in such magazines as *The Dark Side*, *Fangoria*, *SFX*, and *Rue Morgue*, and his first nonfiction book was the critically acclaimed *The Hellraiser Films and Their Legacy*. His short stories have appeared in many magazines and anthologies on both sides of the Atlantic (as well as being broadcast on BBC Radio 2), and have been collected in *Alone (In the Dark)*, *Touching the Flame*, *FunnyBones*, and *Peripheral Visions*. His novella *Signs of Life* reached the shortlist of the British Fantasy Awards 2006 and his others include *The Lazarus Condition* and *RED*. His first mass-market novel was *Arrowhead*, a post-apocalyptic reworking of the Robin Hood myth published by Abaddon, and a sequel has recently been released called *Broken Arrow*. In his capacity as Special Publications Editor of the British Fantasy Society he worked with authors like Brian Aldiss, Ramsey Campbell, Robert Silverberg and many more. In 2008 his zombie story "Dead Time" was turned into an episode of the Lionsgate/NBC TV series *Fear Itself*, adapted by Steve Niles and directed by Darren Lynn Bousman (*SAW* II–IV). Paul's website can be found at www.shadow-writer.co.uk. He currently lives in Derbyshire, UK, with his wife—the author Marie O'Regan—his family, and a black cat called Mina.

MARIE O'REGAN is a British Fantasy Award–nominated writer of horror and dark fantasy, based in the Midlands, UK, where she lives with her husband—author Paul Kane—her children, and the creature of the night known as Mina, the family cat. Her fiction has been published in the UK, United States, Germany, and Italy, and she has had reviews, interviews, and articles published in many magazines both in the UK, United States, and Canada—her essay on *The Changeling* was published in the award-winning *Cinema Macabre* from PS Publishing. Her first collection, *Mirror Mere*, was released in 2006 by Rainfall Books in the UK, and she served as chairperson of the British Fantasy Society for four years (2004–2008), during which time she co-edited several publications, including *British Fantasy Society: A Celebration*, as well as a number of FantasyCon convention souvenir booklets. She has also edited the BFS flagship magazine, *Dark Horizons*, and their newsletter *Prism*. In 2008 Marie co-chaired what is widely regarded as one of the most successful FantasyCons in recent years. To find out more, visit www.marieoregan.net.

Wordsworth.

Short story by Neil Gaiman, for Dave McKean

'Words are but pictures, true or false designed,
To draw the lines and features of the mind.'

BUTLER—<u>Upon the Abuse of Human Learning.</u>

(OK: THE TEXT ON THIS PAGE I IMAGINE AS BEING LAID OVER AN AL-
MOST ARBITRARY PANEL GRID. IN THE PANELS ARE REALLY NASTY THINGS.
REALLLLLLY NASTY THINGS MADE OF PLASTICENE AND HOOKS AND K.Y.
GEL TO MAKE IT GLISTEN AND DRIPPY WAX BITS AND RUSTY METAL SLIVERS
STICKING OUT AND LEATHERY BITS AND STUFF YOU'D FREAK OUT IF YOU
TOUCHED IT WHEN YOU WEREN'T EXPECTING TO . . . POSSIBLY A GLASS EYE
COVERED IN A THICK TRANSLUCENT MEMBRANE . . . THAT KIND OF STUFF.
DO IT IN 3D – JUST GIVING ENOUGH ILLUSION OF PANEL BORDERS TO GIVE
THE IMPRESSION THAT WE'RE SEEING LOTS OF STUFF, THAT THIS STUFF
GOES ON FOREVER, THAT IT COULD BE BITS OF THE PEOPLE, OR IT COULD
BE A WALL, AN INFINITE WALL . . .)

Examine please the writhing tapestries of choice violence implicit in every scratching and syllable. Smell the beast-blood trickling into each wound, spelling out new ways to violate sweet innocence.

Hooks rend. New blasphemies configurate upon the inside of my eyelids: tales worked in blood and bone and flesh and semen, traced in spittle; a dash of bile here, a slice of kidney there.

Gather round damned children, and together we shall lament and celebrate the configuration that made us what we are, today and forever.

So: do you writhe and shiver in the pangs of darling agonies undreamable, wriggling and gasping and giggling, anticipating the tumescent thrill of another's damnation?

Good.

Then I'll begin . . .

PAGE 2

OK – FORMAL STORYTELLING FOR THE NEXT FEW PAGES. (INCIDENTALLY, I HAVEN'T BOTHERED TO SET TIME OR PLACE ON THIS, BUT I ASSUME IT'S LONDON, PROBABLY 1950S, ALTHOUGH IT COULD BE SET TODAY AS EASILY.)

WE'RE IN A SECOND CLASS CARRIAGE, A SMALL, SMOKE-FILLED COMPARTMENT, ON A SUNNY MORNING. THE SUN COMING THROUGH THE WINDOWS BECOMES SOMETHING MUGGY AND UNHEALTHY. CLAUSTROPHOBIC. A LITTLE MAN, WORDSWORTH, DRIED-UP AND GRAY AND SHRIVELED SITS ON THE LEFT. A HUGE GUY SITS ON THE OPPOSITE SEAT, READING A MAGAZINE. THE HUGE GUY HAS NO FACE, JUST STARING, PIGGY LITTLE RED EYES STARING OUT OF THE SHADOWS. WORDSWORTH IS DOING A CROSSWORD.

His name is Wordsworth.

The final clue, 12 down: <u>You imply no blazing fronds grow in the abyss?</u> <u>(7)</u>.

<u>Inferno.</u>

He writes it down and sighs dustily.

(WORDSWORTH PUTS HIS PAPER DOWN ON THE EMPTY SEAT NEXT TO HIM.)

Then, crossword completed (6 minutes, 12 seconds), <u>Daily Telegraph</u> abandoned, Wordsworth stares out of the carriage window at a parade of allotments, at the ugly backs of houses.

Unsatisfying.

The train shudders into the city center and a fly makes languorous love to the grimy window. Wordsworth lights his cigarette, and reads, unconsciously, the name of the brand that circles the base.

Half an hour to go before he arrives at the library.

Half an hour to kill.

(WHEN THE STRANGER OPPOSITE TALKS, I LIKE THE IDEA OF COLORING HIS WORD BALLOONS GENTLY, JUST AROUND THE EDGES, SO THEY LOOK LIKE THEY'RE WRITTEN ON OLD PARCHMENT.)

Man Opposite: You finish puzzle.

Wordsworth: Sorry?

Oh, the crossword.

I see.

Yes, yes I'm afraid so.

(THE MAN OPPOSITE SMILES; HIS FACE IS IN SHADOWS. POSSIBLY HE HAS NO FACE, JUST A SMILE, WITH A HINT OF SOMETHING SHARP AROUND THE CANINES. HE SAYS:)

Man: Words.

Wordsworth: Er . . . Yes.

(THE MAN STANDS UP, RIPS A PAGE OUT OF HIS MAGAZINE, HANDS IT TO WORDSWORTH.)

Man: You need good puzzle. Here.

(WORDSWORTH SITS, HUDDLED IN HIS SEAT, NERVOUSLY CLUTCHING THE BIT OF PAPER.)

Wordsworth: Oh. I see. Right. Well, uh . . . thank you.

(SILENT PANEL/S: THE FACELESS STRANGER, HIS SMILE NOW GOES FROM EAR TO EAR — AND I MEAN THAT QUITE LITERALLY, A SMILE FAR WIDER THAN ANYTHING HUMAN. HE'S GETTING OFF THE TRAIN. WORDSWORTH SITS ON THE TRAIN, LOOKING OUT OF THE WINDOW TOWARDS THE STRANGER.)

OVER THE PAGE TO PAGE 4:

WE ARE LOOKING FROM WORDSWORTH'S VIEWPOINT AT THE PUZZLE. NOW, ONE POSSIBILITY MIGHT BE TO MAKE IT THIS KIND OF SHAPE:

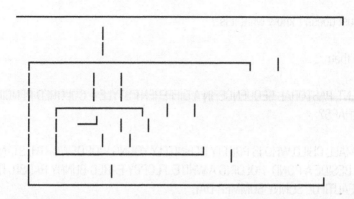

—A SQUARED-OFF SPIRAL OF LITTLE SQUARES, LIKE CROSSWORD SQUARES. DOWN THE SIDE A NUMBER OF CLUES ARE PRINTED, BUT WE CAN'T READ WHAT THEY SAY. EVERY NOW AND THEN ONE OF THE LITTLE BOXES SHOULD HAVE A NUMBER IN IT. FAILING THAT YOU MIGHT JUST WANT TO CUT OUT A BLANK CROSSWORD PUZZLE FROM THE TIMES OR GUARDIAN OR WHAT-EVER, WORK INTO IT A LITTLE, PERHAPS. IF YOU DO THAT THEN ADD (DOWN) AND (ACROSS) TO THE CLUES GIVEN HERE – OR JUST GIVE THEM TO ME TO RENUMBER.

Wordsworth gazes at the paper [in dismay. No true crossword here[1]]. He scans the first clue, expects nothing of substance.

1. What you did to the rabbit. (7)

(SLIM PANEL OF A RABBIT'S FACE LOOKING AT US.)

Wordsworth ponders. An anagram, perhaps? He combines permutations of 'you', and 'U', with both 'Rabbit' and 'hare', and, as an afterthought, 'lapin.'

It isn't coming.

But deep in his dry soul something flutters. He knows he knows the answer . . .

(RABBIT PICTURE AGAIN)

---

[1] Lose this section in square brackets if you make it in a proper crossword.

He just doesn't know what it is.

And then . . .

SILENT, PASTORAL SEQUENCE, IN A DIFFERENT STYLE – COLORED PENCILS, PERHAPS?

A SMALL CHILD WHO IS PRETTY DEFINITELY YOUNG WORDSWORTH, STANDING BESIDE A POND, HOLDING A WHITE, FLOPPY-EARED BUNNY RABBIT. IT'S A BEAUTIFUL SUNNY SUMMER DAY.

(Wordsworth was seven.)

(His rabbit was called Flopsy.)

THE BOY, WHO IS ABOUT SEVEN, KISSES THE RABBIT.

THEN, HOLDING IT BY THE EARS, HE PUSHES THE STRUGGLING BUNNY INTO THE POND.

IT THRASHES FOR A BIT, THEN GOES LIMP IN THE WATER.

THEN WE'RE BACK IN THE HERE AND NOW LOOKING AT WORDSWORTH, WHO IS WRITING SOMETHING.

. . . he knew.

AND WE CAN SEE THE FINAL PANEL ON THE PAGE, WITH THE BEGINNING OF THE PUZZLE ON IT. IN THE FIRST SEVEN SQUARES IS THE WORD <u>DROWNED</u>, HANDWRITTEN IN INK, IN BLOCK CAPITALS.

OVER THE PAGE TO PAGE 6.

A HUGE MUSEUM LIBRARY. STACKS OF BOOKS AND PAPERS EVERYWHERE. IT'S DUSTY AND DRY AND OLD. A SYMPHONY OF DUSTY BROWNS – THE

ONLY COLORS WE CAN SEE ARE SPLASHES OF BRIGHT CLOTHES AND LIP-STICK WORN BY THREE YOUNG, ATTRACTIVE FEMALE LIBRARIANS. WORDS-WORTH IS ENTERING, HOLDING A BRIEFCASE. THERE'S A BALCONY, A MEZZANINE FLOOR, AROUND THE SIDE OF THE BUILDING, WHERE THE FIRST FLOOR OUGHT TO BE. WE COULD BE PANNING AROUND, LOOKING AT THE BOOKS, THE WOMEN, WORDSWORTH HIMSELF.

Wordsworth worked in the museum library, in the stacks of books, organizing and classifying.

There were over 200,000 books and manuscripts in the museum. They were friends, albeit friends composed of words and stories.

True friends, unlike his workmates — creatures so incomprehensible to him as to be almost alien: Miss Watson; Miss Priddow; Mrs Kelly.

The second clue was this:

2.) Miss Watson's cry of book-borne pain. (5, 7, 4).

WORDSWORTH IS UP ON THE BALCONY BY NOW. HE'S HOLDING A LARGE BOOK. LOOKING DOWN AT THE WOMEN BELOW HIM.

HE LETS THE BOOK FALL.

Cry from below: Jesus sodding wept! Owwwww!

WORDSWORTH, LEANING DOWN, TALKING TO THE PROSTRATE GIRL. HE LOOKS CONCERNED.

Wordsworth: I, I beg your pardon, Miss Watson. I'm afraid my elbow knocked The Albigensian Crusade off the mezzanine ledge.

Are you all right?

UP TO YOU HERE – YOU MIGHT EITHER SHOW THE GIRL ON THE FLOOR WITH THE OTHER GIRLS AROUND HER. OR YOU MIGHT JUST WANT TO SHOW WORDSWORTH UP ON THE BOOK-COVERED BALCONY, WITH THE GIRL'S WORD BALLOONS COMING FROM THE BOTTOM OF THE PANEL. SO WE NEVER SEE HER – JUST HIM.

Girl: 'Course I'm not all right, you stupid old tit-mouse! I think my shoulder's broken!'

WORDSWORTH IS SMILING.

WE SEE THE NEXT SECTION OF THE PUZZLE FILLED IN IN WORDSWORTH'S NEAT CAPITALS. JESUS [.] SODDING [.] WEPT.

OK – FROM HERE OUT WE'RE ABANDONING LINEAR STORYTELLING. GO FOR COLLAGE, OR FOR FLEETING IMAGES, SO THAT WE CAN PORTRAY WORDS-WORTH'S DESCENT IN OCCASIONAL IMAGES: POSSIBLY LAY THE OVERALL DESIGN (BLOWN UP) OF THE CROSSWORD OVER THE PAGES?

Wordsworth doesn't know where the puzzle comes from, nor does he care. The puzzle is all. The words are everything.

3. The gift of the Scavenger's Daughter? (5)

He finds out, and fills in the answer on the puzzle in his precise, neat hand-writing.

IT'S BLOOD, BY THE WAY. I'LL LEAVE IT TO ANYONE READING TO DISCOVER WHY, ASSUMING YOU'RE INTERESTED. A SCAVENGER'S DAUGHTER IS AN AR-CHAIC INSTRUMENT OF TORTURE.

Answers.

Wordsworth discovers there is a specialized vocabulary in the more uncom-promising realms of bondage and flagellation.

From that province he takes away a scarred back and expertly pierced genitalia; and, more importantly, he fills another nine squares on the puzzle.

Wordsworth attends a meal, at which noble and affluent coprophiliacs[2] dine for twelve courses on forty kinds of human shit.

He's there for the last word on the menu: it turns out to be <u>coffee</u>. Someone has a sense of humor . . .

The delights of reluctant perversion chill him, although each new experience has a specific end in view.

Words.

For a word he cuts a dog apart and casts its entrails upon his kitchen floor, seeking sense in the loops and whorls of its intestines.

(WE SEE A WORD – <u>LUNAR</u>, POSSIBLY, OR ANY FAIRLY LOOPY AND CURLY WORD – SPELT OUT IN INTESTINES AND BLOOD, IN A LOOPY HANDWRITING.)

For a word he violates a small child.
There are some clues he could guess. <u>9) The taste of Janet Priddow's flesh (4).</u>

He could guess. But he had to <u>know</u>.

(WE SEE THE PUZZLE FILLED IN, AND THE WORD IS <u>PORK</u>.)

All his life he had loved words; now he found his love to be a demanding, meticulous mistress.

His job was abandoned, following the fire that destroyed the museum and almost claimed his life.

NEWSPAPER HEADLINES POSSIBLY; <u>90 DIE IN MUSEUM FIRE</u>.

---

[2] Actually the technical term should be coprophages—dung eaters—rather than coprophiliacs—dung lovers. But I think we can assume this bunch tended to do more than just eat the stuff.

He no longer ate. His actions were solely defined by the puzzle . . .

And, in the end, there were only four spaces to fill in. One word. One clue.

50) The doorway (4).

And the thing that had once been Harrison Wordsworth grinned through messy, suppurating lips, and wrote:

(WE SEE THE LAST PLACE ON THE PUZZLE FILLED IN. THE INK IS REDDISH-BROWN. BLOOD COLOR. THE WORD IS: HELL)

NEXT PAGE:

THE PUZZLE, COMPLETED, BUT THE MIDDLE OF IT IS IN FLAMES, AND THROUGH THE CENTRE OF THE BURNING PUZZLE WE CAN SEE AN INFINITE CORRIDOR, LINED WITH BURNING, TWISTING PEOPLE, BLEEDING AND CHEWING AT THEIR OWN FLESH.

THEN A HUMAN BEING, WORDSWORTH, NAKED, IN ABSTRACT, BEING RIPPED APART.

Ohhh the sweetling pulsing joy, the coming through the pain, Wordsworth feels the probe slide down the throat, pierce the wrecked anus, puncture the skull . . .

The plasma ceases to pump through the arteries, the liver no longer secretes bile, the urine dries to salt in the bladder, but the blood washes over us all . . .

In the night of hell, that glows with its own black light, I remember the burning spasms and freezing pangs that beset me when our lord took me and terribly refashioned me according to his will.

Will it ever, can it ever, be that good again?

Ripped to shreds and patched together, I knew then consummately what I was. What I am. What I always will be . . .

OK. NEW PAGE HERE. EXTREME CLOSE UP ON A BLURRED, DISTORTED WORDSWORTH, HIS HANDS COVERING HIS FACE.

THEN HE TAKES HIS HANDS DOWN AND OPENS HIS EYES. ONE EYE HAS A WORD – STORY – TYPED ON THE EYEBALL. THE OTHER HAS A WORD LIKE LOVE OR DESIRE OR KISS CARVED OR SCRATCHED ONTO THE WHITE OF THE EYEBALL.

THEN WE PULL BACK SLOWLY. HIS SKIN – FACE AND FLESH – IS A MASS OF WORDS. SOME CREATED FROM HOOKS, SOME FROM SCARS, SOME IN BRUISES OR TATTOOS. SOME IN BIRO, SOME HACKED AND CARVED WITH KNIVES, SOME IN BARBED WIRE, SOME UNDOUBTEDLY IN COLLAGE.

UP TO YOU WHETHER YOU WANT TO GO BACK INTO WORD BALLOONS HERE, OR WHETHER YOU STAY IN CAPTIONS, OR A MIXTURE OF THE TWO.

See me.

Love me.

Look at my words. (Examine the writhing tapestries of choice delight implicit in each scratching and each syllable.)

I guard the words.

I keep them tenderly, express them with my tangled flesh and tattered tongue.

Words that form stories, or tales, or patterns.

Words that can but hint at the delights of damnation, of the ultimate pleasures that wait for them all on the beyondside of pain.

NOW HE'S STARING STRAIGHT AT US AS WE PULL AWAY FROM HIM. WE CAN SEE THAT OTHER THINGS ARE CLUSTERED AROUND HIM, LISTENING, AS ONE DOES TO A VILLAGE STORYTELLER. WE CAN'T MAKE OUT ANY DETAILS, JUST THAT THEY'RE MONSTROUS, DISTORTED, DELIGHTFULLY SHATTERED AND REBUILT. ICONS OF THE PERVERSE. SLOWLY WE START TO PAN IN ON THEM AND WE'RE BACK ON A SIMILAR SEQUENCE OF FINAL PANELS TO THE OPENING PAGE, ALL HOOKS AND LEATHER.

(COULD WE SNEAK IN THAT IMAGE FROM <u>APOCALYPSE CULTURE</u>, OF THE HOOK THROUGH THE FOOT?)

Stay with me, my shattered children. Stay and listen and stare and learn. Was that tale good?

I'll show you another.

I've got thousands of them. I hold the stories. I guard the words.

Love me.

ENDS.